DEATH of a DRUG

DEATH of a DRUG

By: Christine Schmidt

Reginald Russell Press
Blue Bell, Pennsylvania USA

Death of a Drug

This is a work of fiction. Names, characters, places, and incidents are the products of the author's imagination or are used fictitiously. Any resemblance to actual events, locales, or persons, living or dead, is entirely coincidental.

Published by

Reginald Russell Press
Blue Bell, Pennsylvania
USA

For information, contact:

reggieschmidt@verizon.net

ISBN: 9780615370170

First Edition: October 2010

Front Cover photograph: Helen R. Carson

Back Cover painting: Deb Hartmann

Print-Ready Cover and Text Preparation:
John A. Oberteuffer

DEDICATION

To my father, my brothers, and all those who know what it's
like to travel the long, lonely road of sales
. . . and the smile never fades.

PART I

A Walk in her Shoes

Chapter 1: Debbie Kaminski

Wednesday evening, March 9, 1996

DEBBIE TURNED TOWARD the backseat of Mark's pickup truck and admired Harry's profile as he gazed out the window. Her long arm easily reached Harry's back and she ran her hand over his smooth coat. Immediately he turned away from the window and, with one swoop of his tongue, licked her face from chin to forehead. Debbie squinted and then giggled, which Harry understood as encouragement to continue. She stroked his head and curled her fingers around his velvety ears, and finally said, "Harry, stop. That's enough sweetie."

Mark could see Harry in the rearview mirror and without turning around, he said, "Hey what's up Buddy? Huh?" Harry's tail wagged his entire body in waves of excitement until Mark said, "OK. OK. Settle down now."

Harry returned to his original post at the window. Debbie didn't have children, so her dog was a sort of surrogate. He received excessive attention and affection. The way Debbie saw it, after a divorce and relationships that sparked and later fizzled, Harry was her one true companion.

As Mark approached the traffic light, Debbie saw the Acme market in the shopping center on the left. She said, "Mark, let's stop at the Acme and I'll run in and get some steaks for dinner."

"Sounds good to me." Mark made a quick turn into the parking lot.

Mark said, "We'll wait here. Right, Harry?"

Harry yelped, as Debbie got out of the truck.

"I'll be right back." She wasn't surprised that Mark, as usual, made no offer to pay for the food. She felt a little embarrassed at these moments. After all, she was raised with the conventions of a generation of women who did not pay for dates or groceries. The man was supposed to bear the financial burdens of their courtship. But for the past few months, Debbie had been paying for everything and she told Mark she wasn't comfortable with it.

"Why am I expected to continue paying for everything?" Mark had said.

From a logical perspective, Debbie could see his point but instead she said, "It's just how I was raised." Sometimes she worried that Mark was using her for her money. But Mark assured her it wouldn't last forever. He just needed her to help out and pay for stuff until he got his business back on its feet.

Debbie looked at the customers milling around the produce aisles of the Acme store in Elkton, Maryland. For the most part, they had the faces of heavy smokers and hard drinkers. They were missing teeth and lacking education. A smaller percentage of shoppers were well groomed, good looking and financially comfortable. They had long ago adapted to the diversity of Maryland — a state whose residents, for the most part, loved either being on a horse or being on the water. The houses on the waterfront varied from town to town and, in some places, from property to property. It was contingent upon the body of water. Oceanfront properties had a homogenous population of well-to-do residents, whereas the Chesapeake Bay and its rivers drew the haves and the have-nots in equal proportion. The grand estates on acres and acres of horse country thrived on old money and transient caretakers. And small towns like Elkton were filled with growing families whose children were destined for a college education or the county jail.

Debbie grabbed a head of lettuce, tomatoes, and cucumbers for a salad and then picked out a couple of steaks to cook on the grill. When she got to the bakery section, there were no brightly lit cases of delicate pastries and tortes; just metal shelving that had been stripped of its limited selection of pre-packaged, highly processed cakes and donuts. Debbie wasn't there for dessert. She was looking for some freshly baked bread and found none.

She walked toward the front of the store. With a sweeping glance, she determined which lane had the shortest line. She picked the one with a cart pushed by a woman who looked like she was in a hurry to get out the door for her next cigarette. Debbie was looking at the point-of-purchase displays when she spotted a wooden stand just a few feet away with an array of freshly baked breads. She was pleasantly surprised as she reached for a loaf of multi-grain bread and inhaled the aroma of warm dough.

While she waited for room on the conveyor belt to place her items for check-out, she looked at the groceries scattered there by the woman in front of her. She thought to herself, "Now here's a woman who is overweight by an easy seventy pounds and yet she's buying cookies, ice cream, potato chips, and a cake. She probably hasn't exercised for the last twenty years."

Debbie had little tolerance for women who let themselves go. In her opinion, most of them just weren't capable of the self-discipline and hard work it takes to exercise and eat right. She knew this firsthand because she herself had run the gamut from being extremely thin to overweight, until she did the right things to arrive at and maintain a healthy weight.

Debbie was 5 feet 11 inches tall and extremely thin during her teenage years. But at age 15, she decided she had heard enough rude comments like "Oh my God, you're so skinny!" or "I guess your body weight hasn't caught up with your height." And of course the dreaded question with an intonation that implied she was a freak, "How tall *are* you?"

She couldn't change her height but she was determined to gain weight, so she designed an eating regimen that was sure to add pounds to her thin frame. She had a breakfast of cereal, juice and toast. Then she packed a lunch for school, which consisted of three peanut butter sandwiches, which she would swallow down with a couple of cartons of milk purchased from the school cafeteria. She discovered that lunchmeat sandwiches didn't work for her because it took too long to eat them. They required too much chewing. A peanut butter sandwich was mushy and could be eaten very quickly. This was important to Debbie because she was finished eating at the same time as her friends. That way she could join them when they went outside into the school courtyard to hang out after lunch.

For dinner Debbie ate whatever her mother prepared, but always added a slice of bread. Around 9:00 at night she would sneak into the kitchen and take a few slices of bread from the bread box over the refrigerator. She had to be very quiet because her mother was in the next room watching television. If her mother heard Debbie in the kitchen getting a snack, she would yell out, "What are you doing in the kitchen? You just ate dinner!" (even though a couple of hours had gone by since dinner). At that point, Debbie would lie and say she was just getting a drink of water. She knew all hell would break loose if her mother came stomping into the kitchen to see what was really going on. So she learned to be as quiet as a mouse. She would take the bread upstairs and shut the bathroom door. She sat on the side of the tub and ate it quickly. She filled the palm of her hand with water from the sink to wash down the bread.

Gradually, over the course of a year and by age 16, Debbie had gained enough weight to fill out her frame. When she returned to high school for her senior year, she had "meat on her bones," as her older relatives would say, and she was happy. She had a new confidence because she knew she looked good. But she refused to be friendly to the boys who would not so much as say hello to her during the previous years. She remembered her sophomore year when she had asked Luke Altschuler to the Sadie Hawkins dance. She had a crush on him and had nervously approached his locker the week before the dance. As she neared him, Luke turned toward her and she blurted out "Hi, Luke. Are you going to the Sadie Hawkins Dance?"

Luke replied, "Not with you!" Then he slammed his locker shut and walked off in the opposite direction.

During her senior year, Debbie continued with the same eating regimen just to see if her boobs would grow bigger. Unfortunately, the size of her boobs had maxed-out and, instead, she started to gain weight in the wrong places. Her dad and brothers started to tease her about the extra weight that was creeping around her midsection. Her father said she was shaped like a pear and then added, "Seriously, you better start cutting back on the calories."

Then one day a classmate told her that a rumor had been going around that Debbie was pregnant. Debbie was oddly complimented by this. She had thought a rumor like that meant her classmates must think she was cool and wild. Only the cool and wild girls were having sex at that age. Debbie had never done anything more than kiss a boy.

She still couldn't grasp the concept that she had to lose weight until one night, after a bath, she snuck into her mother's room to look at her naked body in the full length mirror. She thought she looked good when she observed herself facing forward. But when she turned to see her profile, her slender legs looked odd with a little belly on top. She had to agree that she looked a little bit like a pear--on a popsicle stick.

Gradually, she cut back on the number of sandwiches she ate for lunch until she was down to one sandwich. She also stopped eating bread in the bathroom at night. By the time she started to attend Montgomery County Community College in the fall, she had lost close to ten pounds. She felt good about herself again. And now that she was free from the cliques and labels of high school, she saw herself differently. She was friendly and outgoing, and she was surprised by how natural it felt. The years of junior and senior high school had actually inhibited her from being who she truly was. She learned that if you're not one of the popular kids in school, no one will bother you as long as you "know your place" and keep quiet on the sidelines of life.

In 1970 when Debbie's family moved to the suburbs of Philadelphia, it was a real step up in social status. Debbie remembered waiting in the car with her sister and two brothers while their mother went inside to register them at their new schools. Her brothers were laughing and joking; her sister was lost in her own thoughts; and Debbie was busy fantasizing about her new classmates. She visualized a classroom filled with the laughter of children. They were laughing because Debbie had just said something so funny that even the teacher, who had tried to suppress a laugh in order to maintain order, finally gave in and joined the fun. After a few minutes, her new teacher would say, "Oh, Debbie, you're so funny. But let's get back to our subject." And then class would resume.

Unfortunately, Debbie's fantasies of popularity were not to be realized. She and her sister attended the same junior high school. Debbie was in seventh grade and her sister was in eighth. Within the first few weeks of school, they became two more victims of the school's worst bully — a girl named Melanie. Melanie and her friend were not physically violent, just emotionally destructive. They made fun of anyone who was different, and that included Debbie and her sister because they were tall and thin. Every time Debbie saw Melanie coming down the hallway, she was anxious with anticipation. Debbie knew that Melanie would embarrass her and yell out "stringbean, toothpick or beanstalk."

The scariest moments were when Debbie ran into Melanie and her friend in the restroom, where they were completely relentless because there were no teachers around. Debbie would quickly dart into the stall and lock the door. But that didn't stop Melanie. She would bang on the door and say "Hey, stringbean, is that you in there?" When Debbie came out and tried to walk over to the sink to wash her hands, Melanie blocked her path. She would say things like, "I think you're really a boy. Look at you. You don't have any tits. Hey, I'm going to get Miss Nash and tell her there's a boy in the ladies room." The other girls in line to use the bathroom stalls would laugh uncomfortably. Debbie was embarrassed and self-conscious and she hated Melanie. But, she also hated herself and her tall and skinny body. So often, Debbie would hope that Melanie's friend would intervene and tell her to stop it, or maybe a teacher would step in and confront her. But it never happened.

Debbie and her sister finally confided in each other about Melanie's abuse. That was even difficult to do because neither one of them wanted to talk about it. It was as if the whole thing wasn't really happening as long as they didn't talk about it. Finally, Debbie and her sister decided to tell their mother. But they didn't confide every detail, and they even managed to make it sound less horrible than it really was. Their mother was concerned and loving and gave them advice for the best way to handle people like that. Debbie remembered her mother saying, "Just act like it doesn't bother you. Just smile when you see her and say hello and continue going about your business." Debbie remembered that she felt a tender sadness about her mother's naiveté. Of course this wouldn't work. But Debbie did as her mother suggested. Oddly enough, it did seem to diminish the painful effects of the taunting. Debbie somehow felt as if her mother was with her in those moments and smiling proudly as she said hello to Melanie, or when she grinned even after Melanie ridiculed her.

Fortunately, Melanie's family moved by the time senior high school started. The torture had ended, but Debbie was careful to go quietly about her business in high school. She had friends, but she knew that the fun and wild times, the joyful shouting in the hallways, and the attention of other kids was only for the popular boys and girls — the cheerleaders and the jocks, or the bad girls, and the reckless boys.

It was the year 1976 when Debbie began to attend the community college. Running was becoming a popular sport for men and even women. City parks and suburban roadsides were cluttered with men and women jogging. Debbie started to date a guy who practiced karate. He invited her to watch some of his matches at the college gym. Debbie was more impressed with his good looks than with his sport. But it was this guy, Michael, who first told Debbie that she had an athletic body. Debbie was happy, yet suspicious. She never played a team sport and she didn't have any athletic hobbies. Those old feelings came back to her from junior high school. "Is he just making fun of me?" Debbie worried, "or is it true?" She had wanted to shed some more pounds before the spring and the start of bathing suit season. She decided to believe what Michael had said and thought, "Maybe I can be athletic. After all, my Dad and my brothers are great at sports. Maybe it runs in the family."

She started jogging around the streets of her neighborhood three nights a week, then four and sometimes five nights in one week. Even on dark and freezing cold winter nights, she was out there puffing frosty air and pushing herself to go a little further than the night before.

By springtime, she had lost another ten pounds and was finally satisfied with how she looked at 135 pounds.

That was twenty-six years ago. Debbie had continued to exercise and eat right. She was sensible about food, money, her job, everything . . . well, everything except men.

"Do you have your Acme savings card ma'am?" the cashier asked.

Debbie's thoughts returned to her groceries and she said, "Ah, yeah. Just a minute," as she fingered through the discounts cards in her wallet. "Here you go."

The cashier said, "Thanks ma'am." Debbie gave her a patronizing grin. She hated being called "ma'am." It was a reminder that, at least in the cashier's eyes, her age was showing. She no longer fit into the "thank you miss" category. Debbie paid the cashier and picked up her plastic bag of groceries. When she got outside, she started to jog toward Mark's truck.

Chapter 2: Following Her Footsteps

A few hours later on Wednesday night

THE NIGHT AIR was still, until Dr. Friedman's car stirred up the stones on one of the back roads. He rolled to a stop and opened his car door. He placed the running shoes on the ground. He had bought a pair exactly like Lee's shoes. He swung his torso around and wedged the balls of his feet into the size 5 ½ shoes. Then he leaned over to tie the laces tightly. He stood up on his tiptoes and, using the car door for leverage, lowered his size 10 feet so they could overhang the back end of the shoes.

He shut the car door and began to walk.

"Ooww!! Shit!" The rigid padding on the heels of the shoes arched into triangles that dug into his feet.

"Goddamnit!" His feet reflexed into an arch and he leaned on the hood of the car as he winced in pain. He reminded himself that he couldn't make a move without the shoes. He would have to endure the discomfort. He straightened his posture and shuffled toward the trunk on the balls of his feet. He popped the trunk open and stopped to survey the darkness around him. He listened for cars in the distance. Reassured by the quiet, he bent down and easily lifted her body out of the trunk. She was still very lightweight because rigor mortis would not set in for a couple of hours.

He walked into the field as grass and weeds crackled beneath his feet. He was careful to make some deliberate steps before he lowered her body to the ground. He didn't use too much pressure because the footprints had to appear as if they were caused by *her* body weight. A heart attack would have caused faltering steps as she staggered to a fall. He took off one of her shoes and rubbed it against the ground just enough to pull up a couple of weeds to further indicate a stagger. Then he put the shoe back on her foot and tied the laces.

He picked Lee up again, under her arms, and let her knees rest on the ground. He found the next part distasteful but it had to be done. He grabbed the back of her running shirt with one hand and crouched down in back of her. With his other hand, he jammed against the bend of her knees in order to scrape them against the hard, cold ground. He let go of her shirt and her body fell over. He took a flashlight out of his jacket and observed her kneecaps. They were braised with dirt and it was still early enough after her death, that she bled a little.

"Perfect," he thought.

Then he lifted her once more so the right side of her upper torso was facing the ground. This was to simulate a twist at the waist as she turned left toward the road to look for help. She would have dropped to the ground on her right side, as she was seized by overwhelming chest pain.

Finally, he lifted her head with gloved hands and dropped it against the ground with a scrape. He applied enough force as he deemed consistent with the impact of her fall. Again, he turned on the flashlight and carefully observed her face. He flushed with obscene pleasure when he saw a few droplets of blood, and smudges of dirt on her cheek. It was a good bruise. He put her head back into position. Her right arm was outstretched, as would have happened if she grappled in desperation before losing consciousness.

There was no need to conceal the body. He wanted it just far enough from the road so she wouldn't be found for a couple of days. This would buy him time to portray himself as the frantic husband, beside himself with worry about his missing wife.

Dr. Friedman stood upright and began to walk toward his car. He felt his heart racing and he breathed heavily. He was never athletic, except for the sporadic tennis he had played over the years. But that changed after he'd met her back in 1992.

It was at the Marvin Hamlisch concert at The Playhouse in the Hotel Dupont. It was a benefit for the Dupont Hospital for Children. After the performance, the audience proceeded to The Green Room of the hotel for a late buffet and silent auction. As he waited at one of the open bars for his chardonnay, he saw her approaching. He felt that momentary surge of panic that had plagued him since puberty whenever a good looking woman came near him. He knew he wasn't the best looking guy around, so he always felt nervous the first time he met a beautiful woman. He had been married, divorced, and had two teenaged sons who lived with their mother. His daughter was away at college. He was the Chief Partner in one of the most lucrative and flourishing family practice groups in the entire state of Delaware. His real estate investments included an office building and two condominiums in downtown Wilmington. He collected monthly rent on these properties and his stocks were heavily concentrated in the pharmaceutical industry.

When he had married his first wife some 22 years ago, he was the first Jewish doctor to buy an 11,000 square foot mansion in the bucolic town of Greenville, Delaware. This was *the* old money zip code which, until his arrival, had been populated with a pedigree of White Anglo-Saxon Protestants, including a few generations of the Dupont clan. Dr. Friedman correctly assumed that they thought of him as their nouveau riche Jewish neighbor. But it was his self-conscious anxiety that motivated him to compete for more of everything, including material possessions he liked to think of as toys.

Dr. Friedman reached to take his wine from the bartender. Lee Young was now standing beside him. He felt nervous and intimidated. He wanted to talk to her. He reassured himself with an attitude toward women that he had fashioned into a personal mantra, "All women want from a man is money. Looks don't matter." He was suddenly awash with confidence and it was time to make his move.

Lee Young had a ready smile when he turned to her.

"Hi, I'm Dr. Friedman," he smiled coyly and added, "Excuse me, *Donald* Friedman, and I know you're Lee Young."

Lee offered a practiced wink, as she placed her tiny, feminine hand in his and said, "It's nice to meet you Donald." Then she smiled flirtatiously and asked, "Now, how did you know my name?"

"I see your ads in the Real Estate Section all the time. . . 'Lee Young: The Number One Real Estate Agent in New Castle County.'"

Lee smiled and Donald added, "That's the only section of *The News Journal* I read."

"Yeah, me too; well, that and the restaurant reviews."

Donald asked, "Would you like a glass of wine?"

"Yes. I would love a glass of chardonnay."

It was now about 30 degrees outside, as he walked away from Lee's body. Cold air smoked from his lips and dried the saliva at the corners of his mouth. The road was just a few paces ahead of him. If anyone saw him walking toward his car and stopped to offer help, he would say he was alright. He just had to take a piss and couldn't wait any longer. He would make some joke about getting older and say his prostate problems left him with no choice--when he had to go, he had to go.

If the inevitable police investigation led to someone who claimed to have spotted his car in the area that night, he had an excuse for that too. He would say he was on his way to visit his elderly parents in Margate, New Jersey. They had just returned from wintering in Florida. Dr. Friedman hadn't seen them in months.

In fact, he had called his mother the day before to tell her he would stop by to see them the following night. The visit provided him with an alibi. It didn't matter what time he arrived at his parents' home. In fact, they would expect him to arrive late in the evening because of his office hours. Most likely, they would not pay attention to the time of his arrival. Even if they did, and were later questioned by the police, they would concur with whatever time Donald said he had arrived there. It was typical for him to take the back roads through Salem County to get to their beach house in Margate.

Suddenly, Dr. Friedman's feet began to wobble. He had gotten lost in his thoughts and was no longer self-consciously tip-toeing in the running shoes. The toes of each foot were now jammed against the shoe tips and he couldn't stop the momentum — he was headed for a fall. He swung his arms up into the air and tried to catch his balance, but the clumsy motion only hastened his fall to the ground.

It felt like all of his weight landed on his right arm.

"Ah shit!" He rolled onto his back and sat up slowly. He made a cursory assessment and thought, "Good. Nothing's broken." His vision had adjusted to the darkness and he looked at his feet. The running shoe from his right foot lay on the ground next to it, and his left shoe hung by the laces on his toes. He stretched out his arms and surprised himself with a loud, painful groan. The pain subsided instantly as adrenalin coursed through his body. "I've gotta get out of here."

He looked around to reassure himself that he was still alone. His face was twisted in a grimace as he felt his right arm again. "Shit! I must have sprained it," he said out loud. His heart was pumping wildly as he leaned forward. He was careful to limit his movements to avoid any more imprints of his body in the grass. He grasped the lip of each shoe and slipped his feet in halfway. Once the balls of his feet rested in the middle of the shoes, he tied the laces. He lifted himself to a crouched position and then swiveled around and stretched out his left arm. He began to brush over the grassy weeds that had been flattened by his body weight. Then he slowly stood upright.

He looked back in the direction of Lee. He knew it was crazy, but suddenly he felt the need to make sure she was dead before he left. He made his way back to her body. Spit sputtered from his quivering lips. He crouched down next to her and touched the side of her neck to check for a pulse. There was none. Then he thought of something else. Lee's hair was in a tight ponytail. She always pulled her hair back when she ran. But it was too tight. It didn't look natural. He loosened the band and pulled out a few wisps of her fine, black hair to rest on her cheek. He made a self-satisfied grin and stood up again.

He felt angry when he looked at her engagement and wedding rings still adorning her left hand. He thought, "I have to leave them on. It would arouse suspicion if she wasn't wearing them. Even if somebody comes along and steals them, the Medical Examiner will see the impression of the rings on her left hand."

He gently shuffled his feet around Lee's body and this time he walked slowly toward his car. He had parked almost in the middle of the gravel road, rather than on the side of it. That way there were no tire tracks in the dirt. It was a back road off Route 29, and it led to a campground that was empty this time of year. Donald had checked it out in advance. He knew the area would be desolate at night, unless a couple of teenagers decided to cruise up the road for a private party.

Fortunately, there were no passersby during his brief stay. He chose this night in March for a few reasons. Lee only jogged across the Delaware Memorial Bridge on Monday, Wednesday, and Friday. It was one of the new routes she created for her latest round of marathon training. Friday nights were just too risky because there was more traffic in the area. A Wednesday night was a more logical choice for his alibi. Even his parents would think it was odd if he visited them after a busy Monday at the office.

He opened the car door and turned to lower himself onto the seat so he could take off the running shoes. As he leaned over, his right arm suddenly surged with pain.

"Shit!" He slumped against the car seat until the pain subsided. Then he leaned over again and undid the laces with his left hand. He let the shoes sit in the street for a moment while he swung his feet onto the floor of his car. Then he reached over to the passenger seat for the trash bag. He turned back and, with his left hand, he thrust the bag open over the street. He carefully placed the running shoes into the bag and let them slide to the bottom. He pulled up the drawstrings of the bag and dropped it onto the passenger side floor. He grabbed his brown shoes and put them on again. All of this took longer than planned because he tried to minimize the use of his right arm. Fortunately it wasn't broken but it was a bad sprain.

He started the engine and slowly cruised down the road in first gear. As he approached the intersection of Route 29, he glanced to the left and then to the right. There were no headlights in sight in either direction. He made a left onto Route 29 and shifted to second, then third gear. He was careful to stay in third gear and maintain a speed of 35 miles per hour.

The car warmed up as the miles passed. After a while, he looked at the clock in his car. It was 8:30, and he was now a half hour beyond Pennsville. He twisted his mouth and then let out a disgusted sigh. "Shit. I have to call her cell phone." The macabre nature of this chore wasn't lost on him, but he had to leave a few messages during the course of the night so it appeared he was becoming progressively more worried about Lee.

He forced himself to breathe slowly as he called her cell phone. The first call would have to sound nonchalant. Fortunately, it was a computerized voice that asked him to leave a message. "Hey Lee. I'm on my way to mom and dad's. Just thought I'd give you a call. I won't stay long because I'm really beat. I'll give you a call again later."

He ended the call and thought, "That wasn't bad. Not too emotional. Not too cute. It sounded . . . like me."

Then unexpectedly, for a brief moment, he felt remorseful. "No. She deserved it," he quickly reminded himself. He inhaled deeply and then exhaled a sigh that managed to wipe away his guilt. He felt vindicated. He thought to himself, "You can't embarrass me anymore Lee."

Chapter 3: The First Day in August

Seven months earlier, August 1, 1995

LARRY BERMAN, A lawyer and Chief Partner of one of the preeminent law firms in Wilmington, Delaware, was not a friend to corporations. His firm was perceived as a consumer watchdog, as it took on cases ranging from violations of environmental law to false claims regarding pharmaceutical therapies. This mission proved to be very lucrative. Larry prided himself on being one of the first firms in the tri-state area to fill the niche to fight for environmental zealots. And he had enough physician friends to be convinced that pharmaceuticals were the backbone of their practices. Every patient visit ended with a prescription. And as Larry himself was taking four different medications for his high blood pressure, ulcers and occasional migraine headaches, he saw the potential for errors in judgment. He had learned enough to know that he could spin a story to convince a jury that it was ultimately the pharmaceutical company at fault for the misuse of a drug.

But on this Tuesday afternoon, Larry was concerned about a different issue. He sat at his desk, bending a paper clip for a moment, until he decided it was time to tell his friend, Donald Friedman, the bad news. He reached over and tapped in the numbers for Donald's cell phone.

After three rings, Donald answered, sounding breathless and impatient, "Hello?"

"Donald, how about dinner tonight?"

"Are you buying?"

"Yeah, I'm buying you spoiled son of a bitch." They both laughed. Larry said, "Hey maybe you can bring along one of your drug reps so she can pay for our dinner."

Donald laughed and said, "OK, I will."

"No, no. Don't do that. I need to talk to you privately," Larry said.

"Uh oh, sounds serious."

Larry was silent for a moment. This worried Donald but he didn't show it. Instead he said, "I don't know what time I'll finish with my patients today. It's been crazy."

"No problem bubby. I'm here. Call me when you're done and we'll go to Harry's Grille."

"OK, I'll call you later."

By 8:00 that night, they were seated at a corner table. They made small talk until their drinks arrived and the waitress left after taking their order. Then Larry got right to the point, "Donald, Lee was in to see Joanna Foster today."

Donald felt his stomach flip. Joanna Foster was a divorce attorney and her firm was located on the floor below Larry's, in the same building. Donald knew Larry for too many years to feel the need for a charade of calm. Instead, he was visibly shaken. He said, "You don't mean. . . Lee talked about divorce?"

Larry said, "You didn't hear it from me, but Joanna came up to my office after Lee left. She said Lee wants out."

Donald was speechless. Then he asked in disbelief, "Are you serious?"

"I'm afraid so."

Now Donald felt a rush of anger well up inside of him. "That bitch! Well, she's not getting anything from me. I should have known she would do this."

Larry asked, "What do you mean?"

This time Dr. Friedman was almost too embarrassed to elaborate. But then he said, "For over a year now she's been semi-retired from her real estate work and having 'back problems.'"

Larry shook his head in disgust. He knew that "back problems" was code for "we're not having sex."

"Larry, thanks for the heads-up. I'll have to start hiding my assets."

"Don't tell me you didn't have a pre-nup."

"Of course I did, but it provides Lee with a stipend of one million dollars if we break up."

"What! Are you crazy?"

"Well, yeah. I am now. And from what I hear about Joanna Foster, she'll try to squeeze more out of me."

"Look . . . take a minute. Relax. I'll be right back." Larry walked toward the men's room.

Donald had wanted to impress Lee by including a stipend in the pre-nup. Lee was beautiful, charismatic and, at least before their marriage, she was really hot in bed. He wanted her to be his wife and worried that a pre-nuptial agreement would not be acceptable to her. He remembered thinking, "She might not marry me if I suggest a pre-nup." The solution was to offer an amount that would entice her to marry him, but not so much that it could motivate her to leave him. Without telling Lee exactly what he was worth, he made sure she knew that several million dollars in liquid assets were easily available to him. He knew it was the bait that would reel her in. But Donald had worked hard for every dollar he'd made and he didn't want to lose a penny of it.

He drank a gulp of his martini and watched a tall blonde walk past his table. She had a plunging neckline that revealed her ample cleavage. He took another gulp and it warmed him down to his groin. He thought about the first time he had slept with Lee. It was their third date. After drinks and dinner and lots of conversation that included discreet and obvious references to his wealth, he knew Lee was warming up to him. She was wearing a grey silk dress that hugged her shapely figure. Her silver necklace rested against large breasts. From what he could surmise, her breasts were too perfect to be natural, and it was not typical for petite Asian women to have large bosoms. He assumed they were implants, but he knew from past experience that implants felt just as good as the real thing.

Lee had been flirting with him all evening. By the time their dessert arrived, their lust was palpable. Donald looked at the dish of strawberries and crème fresh in front of Lee and he asked, "Do you really want that, or should we go back to my place?"

She looked at him with her dark eyes and sensuous red lips and said, "Let's go."

When the valet brought his car around, Donald held the car door open for her. She teased him by sliding her dress up her thighs as she sat down. He went around to the driver's side and got in. Before putting the car in gear, he looked at her. The streetlights streamed in through the shadows and rested on her protruding nipples. She shivered and said she was cold as she gently reached for his hand and then squeezed it against her breast. He sensed that she wanted to play rough so he slid his hand up her thigh, as he shoved his tongue into her eager mouth. He was panting when he finally turned to put the car in gear. It was an awkward drive back to his house. They were forcing idle conversation the way couples do when they're trying to suppress their animal instincts. Donald began to worry that Lee would change her mind during those twenty minutes.

When they reached the top of his driveway, Lee said, "Oh Donald, your house is gorgeous!" She pretended she hadn't seen it before, when in fact, she had already checked it out after their first date.

As soon as they entered the house, Donald offered her a drink. If her lusty mood had dissipated, a Remy would stem the tide. He tried to sound nonchalant, "Would you like a Remy to warm you up?"

"That would be great."

He took her coat and slipped it over the arm of a chair as he headed toward the bar in the great room. Lee made herself comfortable on the couch and slipped off her shoes. Donald turned on the gas fireplace with the remote control. He was so wired with nervous excitement that he discreetly drank a shot of tequila to calm his nerves. He felt the warmth radiate inside of him, and he was ready. He poured Remy into two brandy glasses and walked over to Lee and handed her a glass.

Lee said, "Perfect." Her confidence gave Donald the impression that she was comfortable with him. She touched his fingers as she took the glass from him. "Thanks."

Donald sat down on the couch next to her. Lee gave him a demure look and held his gaze as she brought the glass to her lips and drank. He watched her swallow. She licked her lips. His mouth was open as he moved toward her in animal heat. She turned to put her glass on the side table and her dress stretched over her breasts and up her thighs. Donald put his glass down and reached for her . . .

Larry interrupted the memory when he returned to the table. It was like a cold shower. If he was honest with himself, Donald was never in love with her. In the beginning, he was addicted to her beauty and their sex. But even after her back problems started and the sex waned, he still wanted her. Donald knew that other men were impressed that Lee Young was his wife. Now, he felt humiliated and it was just too much to bear.

He finished his martini and said, "So Larry, do you know if Lee is having an affair?"

Larry had just caught the attention of the waitress and they each ordered a second drink. Then he said, "Rumor has it, she's been seeing Edgar Schaeffer."

Donald gasped, "Edgar Schaeffer?" He shook his head in disgust. Then he let out a mocking laugh and said, "That German bastard! It figures."

Larry leaned into the table and lowered his voice, "Look, I know Edgar. I've done some work for him. And I also know he's a player. If he's having an affair with Lee, I'm sure she means nothing to him." Larry put his hand on Donald's arm and said, "Let me talk to him."

Donald drew his arm away and protested, "What? No. Don't do that!"

Larry said, "Look, if it *is* true, I'll tell him you already know."

"And then what?"

"He'll probably ask how long you've known."

"So what's your point?"

Larry said, "If I tell Edgar you've known for a while, it'll blow his mind. He'll start to second guess himself about Lee."

"What do you mean?"

"Look, if a guy is fucking somebody else's wife, part of the thrill is thinking that he's getting away with something for nothing. Right now, Edgar's got it made because they're each married to somebody else, so Lee can't hassle him by pushing for a commitment."

Donald asked, "So wouldn't it be better to tell Edgar that Lee and I are getting divorced?"

"No, we'll let Lee do that — that is, if she hasn't already."

Donald shook his head and said, "What a goddamn mess."

Larry quickly added, "Look, let's not jump to conclusions. Let's assume that Lee hasn't said anything to him. My guess is that she has a master plan and she thinks nobody's on to her."

Donald look confused.

Larry continued, "I think a better approach when you're dealing with an egomaniac like Edgar is to hit him where it hurts. If I tell Edgar that you know about the affair but you're still *with* Lee, Edgar will start to wonder why you're not doing anything about it. He'll start to get paranoid and think that Lee might be some kind of psycho bitch and you're letting her run around so she latches onto someone else."

Donald made a knowing grin.

Larry was happy they were finally on the same wavelength. He said, "I won't tell Edgar that we know Lee is filing for divorce. And we'll let *her* break that bit of news to him."

Donald laughed at the irony and said, "Yeah, Lee's stock will drop in a big way when she tells Edgar she's leaving me for him."

Larry said, "And then Edgar will start to back away from Lee because he'll realize she's planning to set up house with him." Larry paused for a minute and then added, "The bad news is that you'll probably lose a million dollars because of the stipend agreement. Joanna Foster knows how to play hard ball. But at least you'll have the satisfaction of knowing that we managed to cut Lee off from Edgar Schaeffer."

Donald looked grim and said, "Lee will end up with no 'sugar daddy' at all. And the way she spends money, she'll have to come out of retirement and go back to real estate."

Larry patted Donald on the back and said, "You're better off without her bubby."

Donald was silent for a moment. Then he said, "Edgar Schaeffer. I don't even know him but he's one of those guys I just had an immediate dislike for, without a legitimate reason. What does Lee see in him? He's much older than her and he's . . ."

Larry interrupted and said sternly, "Look Donald, she sees his money. Edgar has been an Orthopedic Surgeon for about 25 years now. He's probably pissing money at this point."

Donald felt a surge of jealousy and hatred. It was bad enough that Lee had lied to him, withheld sex from him, and then cheated on him but, for Donald, the worst blow was the thought of losing one million dollars!

He gave Larry a blank stare, and then shifted his gaze to his glass. He was suddenly awash in an eerie calm. Something snapped inside of him. He made a break from morality and logic. He had no idea how he would go about it, but he knew what the end result would be. After a moment, he shifted in his seat uneasily, as if Larry could read his mind. Instinctively, he took the opposite tack and heard himself say, "There's always a possibility that, if I confront Lee, she'll end the affair with Edgar."

Larry was incredulous. "And then what?"

Donald shrugged his shoulders and said, "Alright. Alright. So even if Lee doesn't end the affair, maybe a worse fate for her is for me to refuse to give her a divorce." It was a diversionary tactic. He had no intention of carrying it out, but it was important that Larry believed it.

Larry asked, "What's in it for you?"

"She'll never get the money."

Larry waved his hand and admonished him. "It's only money Donald. True — a lot of money. But what about your life? Forget it! Give her the divorce and find yourself a nice Jewish girl."

Donald smiled and said, "Yeah, I should have done that starting with wife number one." Donald agreed with Larry on one point. He didn't want Lee hanging around even if she ended the affair with Edgar Schaeffer. If she had one affair, she would have more, all while living off of his money.

After a moment, Larry gave Donald a quizzical look and said, "Wait a minute. Don't tell me you're still hooked on her?"

Donald feigned embarrassment and said, "Alright. So I won't tell you."

Just then the waitress approached and asked, "Can I get you anything else tonight?"

Larry gave her a patronizing grin and said, "Bring us the check when you get a chance hon."

Donald looked at his watch and said, "It's late. Let's get out of here."

Once they were outside, Larry gripped Donald's shoulder and said, "Look bubby, you know I only want what's best for you. But let me say something to Edgar. I guarantee he'll go screaming into the night. So what've you got to lose? If you decide to stay with her, for whatever reason, at least he'll be out of the picture."

Donald turned toward Larry and shrugged. "Alright. Let me know what he says."

They parted and started to walk toward their cars when Larry shouted out, "Donald, I'll call you tomorrow."

Donald waved and said, "Thanks Larry."

As he drove away from the restaurant, Donald thought about the many times he had been suspicious about Lee's ability to prepare for marathons by running an average of sixty miles a week and yet her back was suddenly in tremendous pain whenever he wanted to have sex.

By the time he arrived home that night, he was furious. He entered the quiet house at 11:30 p.m. He knew Lee was already upstairs in bed. He poured himself a Remy, flipped the switch for the gas fireplace, and dropped into a chair. He thought, "Two years. We've been married almost two years and we haven't had sex in about six months because of her back pain. And, for the most part, I believed it."

He rubbed his upper lip with his finger before taking another gulp of brandy. He thought, "But some of it had to be real because I saw her take the pain meds right in front of me. I guess it was worth it to her, as part of her act." Then he imagined Lee with Edgar Schaeffer. He saw them naked and clawing at each other with rough, passionate sex. Then he thought about Lee's meeting with Joanna Foster and their conversation about divorce!

Suddenly he pounded the arm of the chair with his fist and sprung up. He thought, "How could I be so naïve?" He started to pace back and forth, energized by his anger. He thought, "She's not getting away with this. She can humiliate me with the affair, but she's not getting my money!"

His thoughts turned dark and vicious again, and he looked into the fire with a sneering grin. "I'll get rid of her for good." He imagined himself snapping her neck before he shoved her against the railing. "No," he thought, "I have to be much more discreet than that."

Chapter 4: Betrayal

July 1994

DONALD AND LEE had dated for six months before he asked her to marry him. After a six-month engagement, they were married in November of 1993. Lee was happy because she managed to marry a rich doctor, and she started to cut back on her hours at work. Donald was pleased with his trophy wife and satisfied to have sex three or four times a week; the same frequency as when they were dating. Lee's attraction to Donald's money and power had a titillating effect on her libido. But even so, after about five months of marriage, her desire for Donald began to wane as she found herself bored by his predictable routine. She knew lots of women who avoided sex with their husbands by claiming to have back pain, migraine headaches, or some other illness. Lee chose back pain as her excuse. But she didn't cut Donald off completely because she wanted to keep him and, more importantly, her lifestyle.

Then she met Dr. Edgar Schaeffer in July, 1994 when he joined his wife, Emma, for a house tour. Lee had been working with Emma for two months, to help her find a new house. Edgar and Emma had been living in the same house they bought when Edgar started his surgical residency. An 8,000 square foot house in Greenville would not have been affordable for a medical resident were it not for the money that Emma's family gave them. Her father was on the Board of the Dupont Company and her mother was a descendant of the Dupont family. Emma was their only child and they wanted her to continue to live in the manner she was accustomed to — not in some rented apartment.

Emma and Edgar had a son in college studying pre-med and a 15-year-old daughter in high school. They were looking for a larger house to accommodate Emma's latest passion--her orchids. Emma was a good friend of Dr. Joe DiStefano and his wife, also avid orchid enthusiasts. Dr. DiStefano, a wealthy Cardiologist, had just built a greenhouse for his orchids and the carefully controlled environment was producing the most fantastic orchids Emma had ever seen. She wanted to find a house that would allow the skillful hand of an architect to design a greenhouse by renovating a portion of the existing structure. Emma would have nothing to do with new construction. She was only interested in sturdy historical homes, with walls of heavy stone masonry that surrounded generations of Delawareans.

Emma was immediately charmed by Lee. She was excited when Lee told her she found the perfect home for the Schaeffer family and, of course, Emma's potential greenhouse. Lee was right. Emma fell in love with the house the first time she walked through it.

Emma introduced Edgar to Lee when the three of them met at the house. Emma wanted to get Edgar's approval, even though she knew the decision was hers. Edgar gave Lee a firm handshake and a lingering look. "Lee, it's nice to meet you. Emma has really enjoyed house hunting with you."

Lee said, "I've enjoyed helping Emma. We have similar taste." Suddenly she flushed with a self-conscious awareness of the irony of her comment. She felt an immediate attraction to Dr. Schaeffer. He was more than six feet tall with blonde hair and blue eyes. She presumed he was a good fifteen years her senior, but the lines that formed around his eyes and his mouth when he smiled gave him a virile and rugged look. He wore a tweed jacket over a polo shirt with jeans, and Lee could see that he was athletically built. He had a deep intonation to his German accented voice.

Lee found herself focusing on his full, sensual lips when he spoke. Her intuition was that Edgar was a player. He exuded confidence and sexuality. Lee almost felt guilty because she liked Emma. She quickly added in a more formal tone, "Well Dr. Schaeffer, let's take a look around and see if you agree with Emma."

His manner was relaxed and he was boldly flirtatious. He smiled and said, "Call me Edgar."

Emma paid no attention to them because she was already walking toward the kitchen. Lee turned to follow Emma and spoke in a loud voice, "I'm sure you know my husband, Donald Friedman."

Edgar said, "Oh, sure." And then he corrected himself, "Well, I know him to see but we've never met."

Lee wasn't surprised. She knew that Donald had a ridiculous aversion to everyone and everything German. He had told Lee that it was ingrained in him since childhood that World War II had made it impossible for his parents, or any Jew, to move beyond an unforgiving prejudice. Donald confided in her, when they were dating, that he could not even bring himself to buy a German car. He had joked, "That's why I drive a Lexus--the Jewish Mercedes."

Dr. Schaeffer even had a German accent, so she knew Donald would have steered clear of him. She asked Edgar, "How long have you lived in the States?"

Edgar said, "Oh, so long now I forget."

Lee didn't pursue the topic any further. Dr. Schaeffer, like many foreign born citizens, and particularly those of his socioeconomic class, wanted to be perceived as fully integrated into the neighborhoods and country clubs of their choosing.

Lee and Edgar joined Emma in the kitchen. Emma asked, "Well, Edgar, do you agree with me now, that we should buy this place?"

Edgar said, "Let's do it."

Lee said, "Great. I knew you'd love it. I think it's perfect for you."

Emma asked, "When can we go to settlement?"

Lee said, "I'll contact the seller tonight with your offer, and then I'll call you. Will you be home tonight?"

Emma said excitedly, "Yes. Call me."

Six weeks later, on the day before the property settlement, Lee scheduled a "walk-through." Emma and Edgar were supposed to meet her at the house at 4:00 p.m. Emma called Lee in a panic at 2:00 p.m.

"Lee, I'm so glad I caught you." Emma's tone was anxious.

"Is everything alright?"

Emma said, "I have to rush over to Amanda's school. The nurse called and said that Amanda is feeling nauseous and wants to come home."

"Oh, I hope it's nothing serious." Lee feigned concern about Emma's daughter. Her real worry, at that moment, was how to get the walk-through done.

As if Emma read her mind, she said, "I've already called Edgar. His assistant said that he's still in surgery, but she'll have him call me as soon as he gets back to the office. He's expected there any time now."

Lee was relieved and asked, "Do you think Edgar can do the walk-through?"

"Yes. I don't think there will be a problem as long as his surgery is finished soon." Just then, Emma said, "Oh, hold on. I have another call coming through."

"OK."

Within seconds, Emma was back on the line. "That was Edgar. He finished his surgery a little early. He said he can meet you at the house for the walk-through as planned at 4:00."

"Oh, great. I'll meet him there at 4:00," and then she added, "I hope Amanda feels better soon."

"Thanks Lee. You've really been so helpful through all of this. I'll definitely recommend you to all of my friends."

"Thanks, Emma. You've been a pleasure to work with too."

Shortly after 4:00 p.m., Lee heard a car pull up the driveway. She walked to the front door, which she had purposely left open. She felt a little excited and even nervous, as she watched Edgar walk toward the house.

Edgar smiled as he approached and said, "Lee, it's good to see you again."

Lee smiled and reached out her hand to shake his. "It's good to see you too." This time she felt a strong, mutual attraction. She asked, "How's Amanda?"

Edgar said, "She's fine. Emma always overreacts." There was a brief silence as Lee mulled over the negative tone in Edgar's voice when he mentioned Emma.

Then Lee said, "Well, let's get started."

As Edgar followed her upstairs, she felt self-conscious in the silence. She tried to make conversation. She asked, "What type of surgeon are you?" She knew he was an Orthopedic Surgeon but she figured that would get him talking.

"I'm an Orthopedic Surgeon."

Lee said, "Oh, that's interesting."

Edgar said, "Well, it's really just like being an auto mechanic. It was a natural fit for me because I've always loved tinkering with machines and tools. Fixing bones and joints gives me a chance to play with hammers and saws. I love it."

Lee said, "I'm sure it's a lot more complicated than you say."

By now, they were standing by a window in the bedroom. The sunlight warmed the vacant room. For a moment, Edgar looked distracted and impatient as Lee made idle conversation. He moved close to her and looked into her eyes and, for a moment, Lee was intimidated by him. She thought, "His eyes look so blue and those lips. . ." Suddenly, Edgar boldly slipped his arm around her waist and pulled her toward him. Lee gasped and said, "Edgar, we . . ." With his other hand he gently touched her face. Lee swallowed hard and felt the heat of desire swell in her. It had been a long time since she felt this way. Edgar gently kissed her on the mouth. As he pulled back from her, they looked into each other's eyes. Then his hand moved around her neck and gripped her hair with a tug. This time, their mouths opened with breathless heat and they kissed passionately. He reached around and unzipped her dress. Then he stood back from her as if he was teasing her. Lee stood motionless while she watched him remove his shirt. Then he reached toward her and cupped her face in his hands. He kissed her so deeply that she tilted back and he caught her in his arms. He slid his hand down her back and her dress puddled around her ankles.

Lee and Edgar were sweaty and breathless when they drew away from each other. A moment later, they turned toward one another again.

Edgar said, "I wanted you from the moment I met you."

"Really?" Lee smiled coyly.

Edgar reached over and kissed her gently on the mouth.

"Oh, Edgar, I feel so bad."

"Why?"

"Because Emma is so sweet and kind."

"We're not hurting Emma."

Lee protested, "But she . . ." Edgar silenced her with a kiss.

It was just after 5:00 p.m. when Lee looked at the only thing she was still wearing--her watch. She was relieved because she had anticipated it would be later. She thought to herself, "I can't believe all of this happened in an hour."

Just then Edgar said, "Lee, I have to go." He smoothed her hair with his hand and got to his feet and dressed quickly.

Lee felt a twinge of humiliation as she was still dressing and Edgar had already left the room. Just then, Edgar called to her from downstairs. "Lee, the house is perfect."

Lee walked to the top of the stairs and Edgar looked up at her. He said, "Tell Emma that everything went fine and we're on for settlement tomorrow."

Lee didn't know if she was relieved or disturbed by his nonchalance. When she reached the bottom of the stairs, Edgar walked over to her and rubbed her back. "Lee, let's see each other again soon. I can't be at the settlement tomorrow because I'll be in surgery, but I'll call you." He started toward the door.

Now Lee was put off by his casual presumption. She said, "Edgar, I am married and so are you."

Edgar reached out and took her hand in his. He said, "So does that mean we can't enjoy each other?" He kissed her and then stepped back to look at her more fully. Lee's eyes were full of longing. And Edgar knew he had her. He kissed her once more and said, "I have to go. I'll call you later."

Chapter 5: Back Problems

February 1995

LONG BEFORE LARRY Berman told him about Lee's affair, Dr. Friedman began to have suspicions when he couldn't remember the last time they had sex. Lee had been complaining about painful back spasms and yet she continued to do her running. If Donald started to touch her in bed, Lee had a pat response, "Oh Donald, you know how much I want you, but I'm afraid I might throw my back out again. Maybe if we wait a couple of days I'll feel better and . . ."

Donald would inevitably interrupt her and say, "It's OK." He wanted to believe her. But his thoughts inevitably turned to what his friends revealed to him about their marriages. It was an odd coincidence that some of their wives had also developed back pain shortly after the honeymoon.

His friend Barry had said, "She used me to get my money. If I divorce her, she gets at least half of what I've worked for. So, what's a guy to do? I'm stuck. But at least I get to screw some cute, young nurses on the side. And those drug reps . . . even better."

Donald was too proud to admit he shared at least some of their problems. And then he decided to do something about it. He started bringing home samples of every non-narcotic pain reliever they had at the office. He asked Lee to try them. He was frustrated when nothing seemed to work. He became obsessed with alleviating her pain--not just for her benefit but for his. It wasn't simply that he missed the sex. He was terribly afraid that Lee was making a fool out of him.

When all else failed, he even tried to convince Lee to try some of the narcotics he prescribed for his patients, but she refused and said they made her sick to her stomach.

Then in February, 1995 Inhaber-Taft, one of the top five international pharmaceutical companies, launched the first in a new class of drugs called Cox-II Inhibitors. They were classified as NSAID's (non-steroidal anti-inflammatory drugs), but instead of inhibiting only Cox-I, as traditional NSAID's did, they also inhibited Cox-II. This difference in the mechanism of action provided greater pain relief and dramatically less incidence of gastrointestinal side effects.

Dr. Friedman had been to many a dinner, sponsored by Inhaber-Taft, that promoted the superior pain relief of this new drug called MELAVOX. Each dinner included a presentation by a specialty physician, who touted the drug's benefits and tolerability. Dr. Friedman listened to Gastroenterologists, Rheumatologists and Orthopedic Surgeons, who provided anecdotes about patients who had suffered from intractable pain for years. They tried everything for pain relief, but with limited success.

Traditional NSAID's worked initially but the pain always returned and rendered the drug ineffective. Then the patient tried MELAVOX, and within a half hour to forty-five minutes, they felt pain relief and an increased range of motion they hadn't experienced in years.

MELAVOX was indicated for long term treatment of osteoarthritis and short term treatment of acute pain. Again and again, the specialists reassured the family practice physicians that, "You won't see troubling side effects like stomach perforations and ulcers. And scoping of patients' GI tracts consistently revealed a smooth and healthy pink lining."

This was all the evidence Dr. Friedman needed to convince him to try MELAVOX for Lee and to prescribe it for his patients. But, as was his habit, he gave the pharmaceutical sales reps a hard time when they asked him to prescribe it.

Dr. Friedman knew exactly how to play it with the pharmaceutical companies. He knew that their market research provided two important pieces of information about him: 1) He was an early adopter and, as such, he was always one of the first physicians to write scripts (prescriptions) for new products. He was categorized as a thought leader and highly influential. 2) Dr. Friedman was a "big writer," as the reps called it. However, the official marketing terminology was a "high potential/high volume prescriber."

Simply put, Dr. Friedman wrote a lot of prescriptions for Inhaber-Taft's products. His family practice group, Better Health Physicians, treated a huge number of patients. New Castle County is the most heavily populated county in Delaware. Better Health Physicians had just one office in Wilmington, but as real estate development spread further south in the county, his practice opened an additional office in Newark. It was one of the most profitable family practice groups in the entire state of Delaware. There were nine physicians in the group and Dr. Friedman, alone, saw an average of 35 patients a day. His potential to write scripts for pharmaceuticals weakened the knees of sales managers.

Each office location of Better Health Physicians designated a large room for drug samples, and it was here that pharmaceutical sales reps were instructed to wait in order to talk to the physicians. Dr. Friedman and the other physicians would charge into the sample room in between patients to retrieve samples of drugs to give to their patients.

The original intent of drug samples was to alleviate some of the cost for patients with little or no insurance coverage. But that practice had long since been abandoned and, for years, doctors had been showering all of their patients with samples. Both the doctors and the pharmaceutical companies knew it was the best way to entice the patient to go to the pharmacy to have their prescription filled. The patients were happy to get a free bottle of tablets (usually enough for the first week of therapy), even if they had insurance coverage to pay for the prescription. It made the patient feel good about the doctor, the drug, and incidentally the drug managed to treat their disease in the process.

Dr. Friedman would challenge the sales reps by presenting hypothetical scenarios designed to site obstacles to their assurances of the product's efficacy. The new sales reps would nervously address his obstacles with pat answers from their sales training classes. The more experienced reps knew they could joke around with Dr. Friedman, but they had to hold their ground with solid facts about the product. And they knew the best way to close the sale was to offer Dr. Friedman a trip or money. The money was more delicately referred to as "fees for consulting" or "fees for post-marketing clinical trials."

Unlike the legitimate clinical trials conducted before a drug is approved by the FDA, the "post-marketing clinical trials" sounded good and even looked good on paper but, they were nothing more than a doctor prescribing a drug and then delegating the required paperwork to a file clerk.

The perks varied among pharmaceutical companies. Inhaber-Taft was historically much more conservative than other big pharmaceutical giants. The companies with the best perks were those with headquarters based outside of the United States. They didn't have to play by the same rules as nationally based companies. Although guidelines existed, in 1996 there were no laws governing the sales and marketing practices of pharmaceutical companies. For those with headquarters based in the United States, the companies tended to comply with generally accepted business practices that are loosely set forth by a consortium of drug manufacturers, and the American Medical Association (AMA).

The only monitoring body for the industry is the Food and Drug Administration (the FDA). And the FDA can only monitor sales and marketing materials to be certain that they comply with their approved indications and usage of the product. It is an industry with varying degrees of ethical and unethical promotional strategies.

Each of the big players in the industry has its particular reputation, or corporate culture. Physicians know the differences among companies. Dr. Friedman knew the most he would get out of Inhaber-Taft was free lunches/dinners and consultant fees. On the other hand, he knew that Prescott-Williams would offer much more when they launched their own version of MELAVOX, a "me-too" drug (second drug on the market in the same therapeutic class) within the next six months.

Prescott-Williams, headquartered in the United Kingdom, was the darling of most physicians. Not only did Prescott-Williams provide tremendous dividends on its stock, which always managed to trend upward, but they provided limitless and lavish perks, as long as the physicians were writing scripts for their products.

The Prescott-Williams reps were already telling Dr. Friedman they would send him to Marco Island, Florida, when their COX II Inhibitor (TENAVOX) was launched. The trip would include the mandatory two or three hours that he would have to attend lectures relevant to the product. Other than that, all expenses were paid and he was free to enjoy a variety of leisure activities with his wife for an entire week.

On this Wednesday in February 1995, Debbie Kaminski and Molly Proctor, Inhaber-Taft pharmaceutical sales reps, had each been to the Wilmington office of Better Health Physicians. There was a total of nine Inhaber-Taft sales reps in each territory. They tried to coordinate their routing so there weren't two or three of them calling on the same physician's office on the same day. They already had to compete with all of the other pharmaceutical companies' sales reps for a physician's time and attention. But once in a while, the Inhaber-Taft sales reps bumped into their territory counterparts as they made their rounds in the same medical building or zip code.

Debbie had called on Better Health Physicians in the morning and Molly, in the afternoon. They each detailed the new product, MELAVOX. Oddly enough, their timing could not have been better.

Dr. Friedman thought to himself, "MELAVOX. That's it. I'll try the MELAVOX. If Lee's pain is real, MELAVOX will relieve it. It's the best way to find out if she's being truthful about her pain." He took some samples of MELAVOX 75 mg home with him.

The next morning, as Lee started to stir with wakefulness, Donald lightly brushed her cheek with the back of his hand. Lee was initially startled by his presence when she woke up. She had expected to be alone in bed. When their eyes met, Donald saw the all-too-familiar expression in her eyes. She glared at him with disdain for just a second until she caught herself. Then she grinned and said, "Good morning Donald." She started to stretch and then stopped suddenly and furrowed her brow, "My back . . . " She wanted to avert any attempt he might make for sex. She sighed and said, "I wish I could do something about this. I need to make an appointment with a chiropractor or a surgeon. Maybe I should stop all this running." But they both knew she would never do that. Then she gave Donald one of her ingenuine apologies, "I'm sorry Donald. Maybe tonight."

This time he was undaunted. He said, "I think I may have found the drug to alleviate your pain."

"Really?" Lee sounded interested, but she was actually very annoyed.

"Remember the dinner we went to last week at The Striped Bass in Philadelphia?"

"Donald, you know I can't keep all these dinners straight."

"Do you remember the one where Dave Beckett talked about MELAVOX?"

Lee gave him a blank stare.

Donald said, "Remember you had the pan seared sea bass that you raved about?"

Lee smiled. "Umm. Now I remember. It was the dinner with the Inhaber-Taft reps and Michael Poong."

Donald said, "Yeah. That's the one." His thoughts were distracted for a moment by the mention of Michael Poong. He assumed Lee bonded with him because they were both Asian. Michael was Vietnamese and Lee was Korean. Donald was aware of their mutual admiration and he even felt a little jealous, that is, until he reminded himself of what Lee wanted for her lifestyle. He knew Michael was probably making a good living as a sales manager for a pharmaceutical company, but his income was hardly comparable to a physician's. Donald was secure in the knowledge that Michael could never provide Lee with what she wanted.

Lee interrupted his thoughts and asked, "Donald, what about this new drug?"

"Dave Beckett raved about how well his patients with osteoarthritis were doing with MELAVOX."

Lee said, "But, I don't have osteoarthritis."

"I know Lee, but MELAVOX is also indicated for acute pain."

Lee was silent for a minute.

"You've tried so many different meds."

Lee frowned and said, "Yeah. Tell me about it."

Donald got out of bed and continued to talk as he walked toward the bathroom. Lee could hear him opening a drawer and then the crackle of plastic. He shut the drawer with a bang. "Here," he said as he walked over to the bed and handed her a tablet. "Why don't you try MELAVOX?"

"OK, why not?" She propped herself up against the headboard of the bed in a slow, deliberate motion. "Can you get me a glass of water?"

"Oh sure. Sorry about that." Donald did an about-face and went back into the bathroom to retrieve a glass of water.

Lee raised her voice so that Donald could hear her. "Now I remember. This is the new wonder drug for pain."

Donald returned to her bedside. She took the glass of water from him. He watched her place the tablet on her tongue and swallow it with a gulp of water. He was happy that she was willing to try it. He went on to explain, "It's a new class of drugs called Cox II Inhibitors. They don't cause the ulcers or stomach irritation that traditional NSAID's do."

Lee smiled and said, "You sound like a pharmaceutical sales rep." She knew this because she had been to countless dinners with Donald, at the best restaurants in Wilmington and Philadelphia, all on the tab of the pharmaceutical sales reps.

Donald smiled and said in a sarcastic tone, "The only possible adverse effects are cardiovascular events like heart attack or stroke."

Lee laughed a little. She had always liked his sense of humor. "Great. Thanks a lot Donald."

He sat down on the edge of the bed next to her. "Come on Lee. With your marathon running and athletic prowess, you obviously don't have to worry about having a heart attack. Besides, the cardiac events occurred in less than 1% of patients in clinical trials."

Lee grinned at him and got out of bed. "Alright Donald. Let's see how this works."

He stood close to her and gave her a quick kiss. It was a nice moment for both of them.

Chapter 6: Pain Relief

July 1995

ONCE AGAIN LEE found herself standing in the doorway to the garage of another anonymous mansion she was trying to sell. She smiled and waved goodbye to Edgar.

"I'll call you." Edgar yelled out to her before he got into his car. Then she pressed the button to open the garage door for him.

She and Edgar met at these places whenever his surgery schedule allowed him some free time. For Lee, lust had turned into love for Edgar. She wondered if he felt the same way. She locked up the house and drove home quickly to change for her daily run. She arrived home in minutes because the house where she had been with Edgar that day was also located in Greenville.

She changed into her running gear and then sat on the floor to pull on her socks and running shoes. When she stretched forward to tie her shoes, her left flank contracted with a sharp pain. She sat there for a minute, contorted by the pain.

Lee *was* experiencing muscle soreness and knee pain. She also had a propensity for migraine headaches, usually in conjunction with her menstrual cycle. She had recently begun her training program to prepare for another marathon. This time it was for the New York City marathon the following spring. Initially, she would substantially increase her daily mileage – ten-mile runs, five days per week, and a long fifteen-mile run on Saturdays. The following week, she would decrease her mileage and concentrate on quickening her pace. She would alternate this regimen for the first few months of her training.

Lee was 42 years old and her body was beginning to fatigue more easily. Although she hadn't been diagnosed with it, she was developing osteoarthritis, which is the wearing away of cartilage that cushions the joints. Osteoarthritis is a normal process in the biology of aging. However, it is ironically exacerbated by high impact exercise in middle-aged adults.

Lee thought, "I better take a MELAVOX before I leave just to be on the safe side. I forgot to take one this morning." She had initially resented that Donald pushed her to take pain meds. She knew he missed the sex and she correctly assumed that was his real motivation to help her. She didn't want to take narcotics for pain because they made her feel sluggish and, even worse, constipated. Some of the other meds gave her headaches. But when Donald suggested MELAVOX, she wanted to try it because she had also been impressed by what the specialists said about its remarkable efficacy and tolerability.

She thought cynically, "Knowing Donald, he's counting me as one of his patients enrolled in a post-marketing clinical trial for Inhaber-Taft. That way he'll get paid for writing the script or, what do they call it — assessing my clinical outcome."

Lee had been pleasantly surprised when she felt relief of her aches and pains within about 30 minutes of taking her first tablet. Most days, she remembered to take a MELAVOX tablet because it alleviated the pain in her knees and stiffness in her muscles. She took an additional tablet whenever she felt the signs and symptoms of an impending migraine headache. She discovered it was also effective in relieving the discomfort of menstrual cramps.

Lee was among a growing number of patients who thought MELAVOX was a wonder drug. She never had any stomach or intestinal discomfort and she never worried about long-term side effects.

She walked into the bathroom and opened the second drawer of the bathroom vanity. It was usually filled to the brim with blister packs of MELAVOX samples. But her supply was getting low. She kept reminding herself to ask Donald to bring home more samples, but she was usually asleep when he left in the morning. Now there were only about half a dozen samples left.

She pressed her thumb against the clear plastic package and forced the tablet to pop through the foil on the other side. She swallowed the tablet with some water and then pulled her hair back into a ponytail, as she used the toilet.

When she returned to the bedroom, she grabbed her keys and her cell phone from her dresser. She dropped the keys into her fanny pack next to a small packet of tissues. She thought, "I'm going to remind him right now before I forget again." She keyed in the number for Donald's office.

Joyce, the receptionist at the Wilmington office, answered the phone. The physicians' direct phone lines were automatically transferred to Joyce if their line was busy.

"Better Health Physicians, can you hold?" Joyce blurted out.

"No, I. . ." Lee had not even finished her sentence when Joyce immediately placed her on hold.

"Why do they do that? They don't even give you a chance to answer the question. They just automatically put you on hold! I have to talk to Donald about this. I'm sure it drives everyone crazy." Lee was exasperated. "Why didn't I just call his cell phone?" She fidgeted with nervous energy. She thought, "This is ridiculous, I can't even. . ."

Joyce said, "Hello, thanks for waiting. How can I help you today?"

Lee's voice was loud and angry. "Joyce, this is Lee Young-Friedman. How can you just put me on hold? I mean you barely answered the. . ."

Joyce interrupted her with an anxious tone, "Oh, Lee! I'm so sorry I put you on hold . . . I . . . I mean. . . it's been so busy here today that I . . ."

Lee heard the anguish in Joyce's voice, but she continued her rant. "It is completely unprofessional to put people on hold the very second you pick up their call. Not to mention the fact that it is unnerving and irritating. Suppose a very sick patient called in and you did that? It would have to make them feel even worse, after being so abruptly interrupted."

Joyce answered meekly, "I'm terribly sorry Lee. I won't let it happen again." By now Joyce's thoughts were racing, "Oh my God. This is all I need — to get fired for upsetting Dr. Friedman's bimbo wife!"

She continued her apologies for fear of losing her job. "Please forgive me Lee. I'm just a little overwhelmed today because my daughter is sick and I had to run home at lunch time to check on her." None of this was true but Joyce thought, "I can probably soften her up if I tell her something about my pathetic life." But she was wrong.

Lee continued as if she hadn't even heard the part about Joyce's daughter being sick. She said, "Well, if you are overwhelmed by your job, then maybe it's time for the practice to hire someone younger."

Joyce was shocked. Her mouth dropped open and she didn't know what to say. Suddenly, Dr. Margotitis dropped a stack of charts on her desk. It was as if she didn't notice, or didn't care, that Joyce was on the phone. Joyce looked up at her with such a pained expression that Dr. Margotitis asked, "Are you OK, Joyce?"

Joyce sat up straight and thought to herself, "I need this job. I have three kids and no husband." She answered, "I'm fine thanks," and forced a little smile.

By now Lee was thinking, "Someone younger? How stupid! She could file an age discrimination lawsuit!"

Suddenly, Joyce was aware of Lee's voice again on the phone. "Well Joyce, I guess we're both having a bad day." Then Lee tried the sympathy tactic herself. She said, "I'm actually calling to ask Donald to bring home some MELAVOX samples because my back is in severe pain right now."

Joyce felt a softening in Lee's voice and she was relieved. She said, "Of course Lee. I'll tell Dr. Friedman to bring home more samples of MELAVOX. Are you OK?" Joyce was hopeful that a show of concern would put her back in Lee's good graces. She was right.

Lee said, "I'll be fine. Thanks, Joyce. Just remind Donald when you have a chance."

"I'm writing a big note right now and I'll tell Dr. Friedman as soon as I see him."

"Great. Thanks Joyce. Oh, and make sure you tell him 75 mg of MELAVOX. If he brings home 25 mg tablets, I'll have to take three of them."

Joyce said, "OK, 75 mg. There, I just wrote it on the same note. You're all set."

"Thanks Joyce. And I hope your daughter gets better soon. Is it anything serious?" Lee pretended to be concerned.

"It's just some kind of 24 hour virus. She'll be fine. But thanks for asking."

"Sure. Have a good day,
 Joyce."

Lee pressed the "end" button on her cell phone as Joyce's voice trailed off saying, "You too."

Lee thought, "Now I know why I hesitate to call Donald at the office." She put the phone in her fanny pack and zipped it up, as she walked out of her room. She ran down the stairs and slammed the front door shut behind her. She glanced at her watch to check the time. When she reached the end of the driveway, she began to run at a brisk pace.

Her thoughts turned to Edgar and she felt rejuvenated and happy. She visualized his handsome face and muscular body. She felt a warm, pulsating sensation in her groin when she thought about their hot sex earlier that day. "I better think about this later if I want to get a good run in." She straightened her back a little and felt the strength of her muscles lifting her through the air. For a while, she thought about nothing and simply relaxed and enjoyed the freedom of the open road.

Almost one and a half hours later, Lee turned the key of her front door. She had run ten miles at an average pace of eight minutes per mile. She walked the last 10 minutes to cool down her muscles. After a long hot shower, Lee studied her body in the mirror. She was proud of it because she worked hard to stay in shape. She admired her long, black hair. She liked the way it fell against her lower back. She smoothed moisturizing lotion over her calf muscles and then up over her thighs.

She decided to stretch a bit before she got dressed. She knelt down and slid her hands forward as she humped her back into a cat stretch. Then she bent her back the opposite way and felt her muscles relax. After several repetitions, she lowered her body onto the rug. She turned her head to the side and lay still.

About twenty minutes later she woke up with her mouth open in a sloppy drool. Out of nowhere came a sudden, sobering thought, "I hope Emma doesn't find out about our affair until after Edgar divorces her."

Lee was certain Edgar would eventually leave his wife for her. But she worried that if Emma found out about the affair during the divorce process, she would be vindictive and take half of his money away. She thought, "Of course Edgar will have to give her a portion of his wealth, but certainly not half, not if he has a good lawyer."

As she got to her feet, she wondered how she could subtly move things along with Edgar. "If I want Edgar to take me seriously, I have to take the first step and file for divorce from Donald. How can I expect him to leave Emma, if I haven't left Donald." She slipped on her panties and then fastened her bra as she headed toward her walk-in closet. She chose a pair of beige pants and a white polo shirt. She thought, "At the very least, I'll get one million dollars from Donald." She stopped to admire herself in the mirror again and thought, "But I'm sure I can get more than that with the right divorce lawyer."

She had learned from some of her real estate clients, who were in the process of divorcing their husbands, that it was quite possible to get more money than the amount agreed upon in a pre-nuptial agreement. Lee thought, "A financial safety net is a good idea, just in case Edgar stalls on marriage."

At this point in her life, Lee was quite comfortable in her luxurious surroundings. She had long ago lost the feeling of being an outsider, as she ascended through the social stratosphere. She was happy that she had chosen a career in real estate sales. It provided the visibility and contact with wealthy clients that she wanted. Before she could really afford it, she bought a Mercedes C36 AMG. She spent fortunes to buy clothes and beauty treatments at all the right boutiques and salons. It was good bait for the men she wanted to meet. The men she dated provided her with the jewelry and travel that she enjoyed.

Lee's first husband was a successful realtor. His financial success was a credit to his selling skills, as well as his many investments in real estate. But Dr. Friedman's wealth was much more significant.

Now Lee hoped to win over Dr. Schaeffer. His wealth, as an Orthopedic Surgeon, daunted that of a family practice doctor. Although Edgar was born in Germany, he had married into an old money family in the States. He and Emma had been married long enough that Edgar was now perceived as part of that insulated social circle. And just as significant, Edgar saw himself that way. Lee figured her biggest challenge with Edgar was that people with old money always married within their social strata--an unwritten rule among the upper class. But there were exceptions. Lee had learned, over the years, that there were two types of men who married below their class. The first type was a man who had old money but was a maverick. He lived outside of social mores and picked a different sort of woman by design or by accident. If he did so by accident, it was because he had fallen in love. If he did so by design, it was for lust or simply to piss off his stodgy family. The second type of man was a nouveau riche guy who just wanted to kick back with a down-to-earth woman. In some cases, he saw himself as a diamond in the rough and wanted the challenge of re-shaping a similar woman. He enjoyed a woman whom he could impress with experiences and possessions she had never known. Of course Donald was the later, and Lee knew Edgar was a maverick. She was certain he would eventually marry her for love.

Lee smirked and thought, "Even with Donald's substantial wealth, Edgar is worth much more . . . and why should I feel guilty? Donald just wanted a trophy wife." She remembered a party she attended with Donald the previous summer. As they stood in the grand entrance hall of Joe DiStefano's house, Donald had said to her, "We drove here in my convertible and now I'm sipping a martini next to a beautiful woman. I feel like James Bond."

Lee started down the stairs. Donald wouldn't be home for at least another hour and they weren't scheduled to attend a drug rep dinner. She decided to make herself a salad. When she reached the foyer, she pushed a wisp of hair from her cheek and thought, "It's so ironic that marrying Donald was *my* achievement. I wanted his money and status and the mansion in Greenville, and I got it all. I just have to figure out a way to keep as much of it as possible."

She walked into the kitchen and poured herself a glass of wine. She took a sip as she looked out the window. She was pleased with her choice of flowers this year and the layout she had designed with their landscape architect. She caught herself in a self-satisfied grin and thought, "Maybe I should pay a visit to Joanna Foster. Everybody says she's cool about giving you advice on how to get as many of your husband's assets as possible. It's those important first steps that make a difference, before you file for divorce."

As she finished her salad, she heard Donald's car pulling into the garage. She looked at the clock. It was 7:45. She thought, "I'll call Joanna's office tomorrow for an appointment. I have to plan my exit strategy."

Chapter 7: The Seeds of Doubt

mid-August 1995

DR. FRIEDMAN HAD heard various interpretations of the results of the METAPO drug study. But it wasn't until he finally *listened* to the nuances of the study that his plan to get rid of Lee unfolded.

It had been two weeks since he had dinner with Larry Berman. The media was abuzz with news of a drug study conducted by Inhaber-Taft.

The Food and Drug Administration requires pharmaceutical companies to continue to monitor the safety and efficacy of drugs, even after the drug is approved for marketing and sales.

The METAPO study was initiated by Inhaber-Taft to alleviate concerns about the incidence of thromboembolic events (heart attack or stroke) that occurred in less than one percent of patients, taking MELAVOX 75 mg, during clinical trials.

It had been six months since MELAVOX was launched and sales were exceeding initial objectives, as a result of physicians writing so many prescriptions for it. But now the competition was suggesting to physicians that MELAVOX may not be safe in patients with even borderline hypertension. Pharmaceutical sales reps, and some physicians, were reporting back to the home office of Inhaber-Taft, that this tactic had picked up momentum. The competition was stealing their thunder because the sales reps were spending their precious few minutes in front of physicians handling their obstacles about safety, instead of presenting their slick, glossy detail pieces that provided evidence of the profound efficacy of this new drug.

Inhaber-Taft's research and marketing divisions had hoped the METAPO study would provide results that would arm their sales reps with additional information about treatment outcomes that further assured the efficacy and safety of MELAVOX.

Pharmaceutical companies entitle studies with words that form catchy acronyms. This enables physicians and sales reps to refer to the study using the acronym rather than the literal, verbose language in the title. Thus, the "MELAVOX Efficacy and Safety in the Treatment of Acute Pain and Osteoarthritis" study was referred to as METAPO.

The study had two arms and involved a total of 25 patients who volunteered to participate in the study, knowing the potential benefits and risks.

One arm of the study assessed pain relief in 5 patients who had recently undergone joint replacement surgery. They suffered from acute pain and did not have a history of cardiovascular disease. Each of these patients received the study drug--MELAVOX. None of them received placebo because it is unethical to treat post-surgical patients with a placebo for acute pain. Each patient was treated with MELAVOX 75 mg once daily for 14 days. Then the dose was titrated down to 25 mg of MELAVOX once daily for the next 2 weeks. If they had breakthrough acute pain during those 2 weeks, they were given a MELAVOX 75 mg tablet for one day and then returned to the lower dose regimen. At the end of each two week period, the patients were titrated up to 75 mg of MELAVOX once daily, if needed, for a maximum of fourteen days. Then the cycle was repeated.

The second arm of the study involved 20 patients. Ten of the 20 patients had pre-existing heart disease, which was broken down as follows: 6 patients had mild hypertension and 4 patients had moderate hypertension.

The other 10 patients had no evidence of, or propensity for, heart disease based on physical examination and assessment of family history.

All of the patients in the second arm of the study suffered from osteoarthritis. These 20 patients were randomly selected to receive either the study medication (MELAVOX) or placebo.

The distribution was 10 patients treated with one tablet of MELAVOX 25 mg once daily, and the other 10 patients were treated with a placebo tablet once daily.

The second arm of the study was a double blind study, which means that neither the patients, nor the physicians knew which patients were receiving MELAVOX or which ones were receiving a placebo.

In both study arms, patients took no other medications for the duration of the study, which was planned to be 6 months long. However, the study was stopped at 3 months after 4 out of the 20 patients, in the second arm, experienced a thromboembolic event. Three patients suffered a myocardial infarction (heart attack) and one patient suffered a mild stroke.

20% of the patient population (or 4 out of 20), in the second arm of the study, who experienced cardiovascular events were those patients who had pre-existing heart disease and, most notably, they were not taking their blood pressure medication during the study.

The 3 patients who suffered a heart attack had pre-existing moderate hypertension.

The 1 patient who suffered a stroke also had moderate hypertension.

Inhaber-Taft would have their sales reps point out to physicians that "20%" sounds like a large number, but it was a small patient population of only 20 patients. The 20% was an incidence of only 4 out of 20 patients.

The sales reps quickly turned physicians' attention to the results of the first arm of the study (the patients who were recovering from joint replacement surgery). Each of these 5 patients experienced fast and effective pain relief within 30 minutes of taking MELAVOX 75 mg. After 14 days, they were still relatively pain free during the two-week intervals of the MELAVOX 25 mg dose. Occasional breakthrough pain was effectively treated with MELAVOX 75 mg. Study medication, along with physical therapy, resulted in a gradual return to full range of motion for these post-surgical patients.

The final selling point was that none of the 25 patients enrolled in the study experienced any gastrointestinal (GI) side effects. Endoscopy revealed no ulcers or perforations, and the integrity of the gastrointestinal tract was intact.

The FDA reviewed the study results. They concluded that the benefits of MELAVOX outweighed the risks. The FDA noted that thromboembolic events occurred in patients with pre-existing heart disease who had agreed to stop their blood pressure medication while enrolled in the study.

The FDA reiterated the approved dosage and administration for MELAVOX:

For the chronic (long term) treatment of osteoarthritis, the approved dose is MELAVOX 25 mg once daily.

For short term treatment of acute pain, the approved dose is MELAVOX 75 mg once daily for 14 days.

Inhaber-Taft informed the FDA that it would promote MELAVOX 75 mg once daily for the short term treatment of acute pain for a more conservative duration of 5 to 10 days (versus the 14 days that the FDA would have allowed).

The competition was quick to seize the opportunity to spread the word to physicians that traditional NSAID's (non-steroidal anti-inflammatory drugs) were safer. They made bold generalizations like, "COX II inhibitors antagonize (or block) prostaglandins. (Prostaglandins are involved in the regulation of blood pressure). In certain patients, the obvious result would be heart attack or stroke."

Prescott-Williams' sales reps were careful not to denigrate the new therapeutic class because they were about to launch TENAVOX, a new drug in the same class. Instead, they used a carefully crafted message to physicians: "MELAVOX is about two hundred times more potent in its inhibition of COX II than our new drug. It is this greater inhibition of COX II that causes heart attack and stroke. The Prescott-Williams' COX II inhibitor has an improved chemical structure which makes it safe for your patients."

All of the morning news shows sensationalized the results of the study and, in the days and weeks that followed, virtually every news outlet ran a different version of the story. Inhaber-Taft's stock dropped ten points per share in the first week and continued to linger at the devalued cost per share for weeks.

A flurry of phone calls inundated doctors' offices across the nation. Patients wanted to know if they should stop taking MELAVOX.

Meanwhile, each of the nine Inhaber-Taft sales reps, who co-promoted MELAVOX, called on all of their physicians' offices to earnestly review Inhaber-Taft's spin on the results of their post-marketing study.

The truth was, physicians were not alarmed by the METAPO study results because it was clear to them that the patients who experienced thromboembolic events were only those who had pre-existing moderate hypertension and had stopped taking their blood pressure meds. Physicians were well aware of the media hype that blew such studies out of proportion to keep viewers watching television. And they knew, they would be bombarded by the MELAVOX sales reps and all of their competitors, each with their particular company's spin on the study.

It was obvious to Dr. Friedman, and other physicians, that Inhaber-Taft had coached their reps with a standard blurb. On this particular Friday in August 1995, Dr. Friedman rushed into the sample room to grab some sample bottles. As usual, a pharma sales rep had been waiting for him to dash into the room in between patients. This time it was Debbie Kaminski.

"Hey Deb," Dr. Friedman was then lost in his thoughts until he decided to listen for a minute as Debbie rambled on ". . . and secondly, MELAVOX 75 mg should only be used for short term treatment of acute pain. The FDA approved 14 days' of treatment at the max dose, but Inhaber-Taft is recommending a more conservative five to ten days."

Dr. Friedman said, "I thought it was a good drug until I heard about the METAPO study."

Debbie grinned coyly. She knew he was playing devil's advocate. "Dr. Friedman, the 4 patients who experienced adverse effects had a history of heart disease and . . ."

He interrupted and said, "Well, Inhaber-Taft designed the study, so they must have expected different results."

Debbie said, "As a matter of fact Dr. Friedman, there were very positive clinical outcomes included in this study. MELAVOX relieved the extreme, acute pain suffered by patients after joint replacement surgery. And MELAVOX was . . ."

"Alright, alright," Dr. Friedman interrupted again. He smiled and said, "You convinced me. I'll still write for MELAVOX."

He waved his pen in the air and asked, "Do you need me to sign for samples?"

"Yes." She held out the form for him to sign. As he scribbled his signature, Debbie added, "Don't forget the appropriate dosing . . ."

Dr. Friedman smiled and said, "OK. Thanks." He raced out of the room and grabbed a chart from the plastic holder on the exam room door. He glanced down at it for about ten seconds and then knocked on the door and entered.

The next day, another Inhaber-Taft sales rep, Ken Welder and his manager, Michael Poong, called on Dr. Friedman. Ken and Michael had a different strategy to win Dr. Friedman over.

They purposely arrived at the Wilmington office just after 5:00 in the afternoon. They invited Dr. Friedman to join them for drinks and dinner that night, after he finished office hours. He agreed because the other pharma dinner he had planned to attend that night didn't start until 6:30 and he felt like finishing up early. There were enough doctors in the office to see the remainder of patients. Besides, Lee was not planning to go to the dinner with him because she had said she was showing some houses to a client.

Most of the sales managers for Inhaber-Taft followed the direction of their executive management and coached their reps to promote drugs in accordance with FDA approved indications and use. But conveniently for Dr. Friedman's purposes, Inhaber-Taft, like all other pharmaceutical companies, had its less ethical sales managers and sales reps.

During their first round of drinks, Ken and Michael reiterated that the METAPO study had been misinterpreted. Michael Poong said it was just another opportunity for their competitors to perpetrate misinformation about the drug.

Michael said, "The Prescott-Williams reps, in particular, are using a verbatim to imply that the use of MELAVOX for the treatment of acute pain is not safe. Now it's obvious they're just laying the groundwork for the launch of their inferior COX II Inhibitor. When they submitted an NDA (New Drug Application) to the FDA, they hoped to get two indications for the treatment of acute pain and osteoarthritis. But the FDA did not approve an indication for the treatment of acute pain because their drug does not inhibit COX II to the level that is necessary to block severe pain." Michael laughed smugly and added, "The only way they can hope to compete with us is to say their drug is safer because it has weaker inhibition of COX II. It's just ludicrous. The truth is, MELAVOX *is* safe and much more effective."

Michael talked fast and his slight Vietnamese accent meant that his listeners needed a moment to catch up with him. All three of them were silent for a moment. Dr. Friedman finished his drink as the waitress approached the table. They ordered a second round of drinks. Dr. Friedman and Michael each ordered another gin and tonic. Ken asked for a second martini. They nibbled on some complimentary appetizers, sent over by the restaurant manager in appreciation for their regular patronage.

Michael leaned into the table and lowered his voice with a sense of drama. He said, "Dr. Friedman, in my opinion, Inhaber-Taft has understated the dramatic efficacy of MELAVOX 75 mg. It's the only non-narcotic drug on the market that can provide such fast and effective pain relief."

But the pivotal moment for Dr. Friedman was this:
Michael said, "Dr. Friedman, you know that many drugs are used outside of the FDA approved indications, based on a physician's experience with the drug and the patient's diagnosis. Off the record, Inhaber-Taft is very conservative in its approach to product promotion. They undersell the merits of their drugs."

Michael looked at Ken and then back to Dr. Friedman. He made a conspiratorial grin and said, "Dr. Friedman, we want you to feel comfortable writing for MELAVOX 75 mg for the treatment of pain *for as long as your patients need it.* All this paranoia over how many days the max dose of 75 mg can be used is just silly. Look at all the drugs that once required a prescription and now patients can walk into a pharmacy and buy them over the counter."

Dr. Friedman's eyes lit up and he straightened his posture. He thought to himself, "MELAVOX … and she's already taking it. But I can't count on it to *cause* a heart attack. I'll have to add something … something undetectable."

Michael and Ken took his momentary silence as an indication that Dr. Friedman was buying into Michael's sales pitch for a much more liberal use of MELAVOX. In a way, they were right, because Dr. Friedman was thinking, "How ironic that a pharmaceutical company would provide me with a two-fold plan."

Michael knew it was time for the sales close. He said, "This is off the record, but Inhaber-Taft has finally leveled the playing field. I happen to know that our marketing department is developing a post-marketing clinical trial program. It will only be offered to our top writing physicians, and it will probably be rolled out in the fourth quarter of this year, or at the very latest, the first quarter of next year."

Dr. Friedman smiled and said, "Well, it's finally happened. Inhaber-Taft has jumped on the bandwagon."

Michael and Ken laughed.

Ken said, "Well, ya gotta do what ya gotta do."

Michael said, "You know the drill Dr. Friedman. We have to wait until we have sales numbers for the first few rolling quarters after product launch; that way our market research department can determine which physicians are writing the most scripts for MELAVOX. And, as I said, those physicians will be paid to conduct a post-marketing clinical trial."

It was obvious to Dr. Friedman that Michael was providing him with an incentive to write a lot of MELAVOX scripts. But it was actually against company policy to discuss sales reports with physicians. Of course, physicians know that pharma companies pay market research firms to compile sales data. They know the market research firms, in turn, pay pharmacies for information about the number of prescriptions written for each product by each physician. The data is provided over a rolling 60-day period, so results are about two months old by the time the field sales group receives their sales reports.

The sales reports are organized by zip code so management can drill down to the individual territory level and see the sales results achieved by a particular sales rep. Each rep calls on approximately 300 physicians. The number of zip codes varies depending upon the size of a territory geography; i.e., rural versus urban.

Michael said, "All you have to do is sign the paperwork that indicates you're a post-marketing consultant for MELAVOX. And as you know, the clinical trial is basically reporting how your patients respond to treatment with MELAVOX. You can have one of your file clerks fill out the paperwork. And you'll receive $50 for each patient who gets a MELAVOX script for the duration of the trial."

Dr. Friedman smiled and said, "OK Michael. Fair enough. I think it's a good drug and I'm impressed with it so far."

Michael and Ken were very pleased with themselves. They knew they could hook Dr. Friedman once the Consultant fees became available later in the year, but they didn't think they could get him on board so quickly. Little did they know *why* Dr. Friedman would become intimately connected to Inhaber-Taft.

After Ken took care of the check, they walked out of the restaurant and shook hands with each other in the parking lot.

Dr. Friedman said, "OK. MELAVOX 75 mg once daily for pain, and *for as long as my patients need it.*"

Michael smiled and said, "That's the spirit. Leave all the squeamish worries to the idiots at the FDA who can't get a better day job."

They all laughed.

Dr. Friedman said, "Thanks for dinner guys. Goodnight."

Ken said, "Take her easy Dr. Friedman." The three of them giggled at the innuendo.

Dr. Friedman said, "You too Ken."

Ken and Michael turned in the direction of their cars on the other side of the parking lot. They walked side by side and Michael said quietly, "I think we've converted Dr. Friedman to our side."

Ken smiled and said, "Yeah. You did a good job selling it Michael but let's face it, once we dangled the money carrot, we closed the sale."

Michael said nothing. He just grinned.

On his way home, Dr. Friedman felt his pockets to see if he might have slipped in one of his prescriptions pads. Apparently not. "Shit," he said out loud, and then thought, "So what's one more day. I'll just do it at the office tomorrow."

The next day was Saturday. Lee was sleeping soundly when Donald woke up at 5:37 a.m. He knew the exact time because his eyes opened to the red glare of the digital clock on the bedside table. He turned off the alarm, which was set to go off at 6:45. He was too anxious to get much sleep. After lying in bed for about ten minutes, he went downstairs and made coffee. He toasted a bagel, poured a cup of coffee, and opened the French doors onto his deck. At this hour, the warm summer air felt soothing. He was happy to leave the air conditioning inside. He sat in a lounge chair and sipped his hot coffee when, suddenly, he felt a wave of melancholy.

He thought, "How did things turn out this way? It's not what I wanted."

He thought of his ex-wife Ellen. She was a beautiful blonde, whose WASP parents were adamantly against her marriage to a Jew. It didn't matter that he was a doctor. They knew Ellen could take her pick of successful young men, who were the sons of friends from their exclusive country club. For a young woman of her class, conforming to social mores was expected. But Ellen met Donald during the rebellious fervor of the 1960s. She wouldn't dream of experimenting with free love or drugs. The extent of her defiance was to date a Jewish boy, and marrying him would send her parents reeling.

After another sip of coffee, Dr. Friedman's mind wandered to memories of old girlfriends. There was Maria--a nice, pretty Italian girl. They had a lot of laughs together and she truly cared for him, but she could never marry him and disappoint her parents. They expected her husband to be Italian and Catholic.

"Myra Goldenberg!" he said out loud. He dated her during medical school--a sexy, beautiful Jewish woman. Myra planned to specialize in cardiology and they planned to marry once they completed their residency programs. But Myra met someone during her cardiology training and she broke off her engagement to Donald.

"Debbie Kaminski. Now she's a nice woman." In fact, he had liked her from their first meeting. There was just something about her that made her stand out from the other reps. She was tall and attractive and closer to his age. But it wasn't that. She had a sense of humor and she just *got it* when he joked around with her. She wasn't a precious young thing like most of the other reps who tried to charm and chat with him at the office day after day. And there was an appealing naiveté and earnestness about her that was lacking in the others. She took her job very seriously. He remembered her telling him that she truly believed in the mission of Inhaber-Taft . . . "to improve patients' quality of life."

That was seven years ago, when Dr. Friedman decided to ask Debbie out. They were both single at the time, and he invited her to attend the wedding of another physician. Debbie liked Dr. Friedman and felt comfortable with him, but she wasn't the least bit attracted to him.

As it turned out, they both had a great time, but it didn't change the way she felt about him. Dr. Friedman asked her out a few more times but she only agreed when they were going out with a group of people. At times, Debbie wished she had a romantic interest in him, but the chemistry wasn't there. She thought it was just as well because there was an unwritten rule that sale reps were not supposed to date physicians. But, in reality, lots of pharma sales reps were bold enough to have torrid affairs with the mostly married physicians in their territories. Or they discretely dated the handful of single physicians. As long as it didn't adversely affect sales, nobody really cared. In fact, it was quite the opposite, depending on the sales manager. Some managers were all for it because they knew, as long as a hot affair was going on between a rep and a physician, the physician would write lots of scripts for the products the rep was selling.

Dr. Friedman was gracious when Debbie said "No" the last time he asked her out. She told him she had met someone else and he seemed to take it all in stride. But now, remembering those days, he thought, "Too bad she never felt the same way about me. I don't think she would have cheated on me."

As he wallowed in self-pity, he replayed Larry's words, when he told him that Lee was having an affair. Suddenly, he became angry. "What a despicable, phony whore! . . . I'll be free of her soon enough."

With tongue in cheek, he mused, ". . . and I owe a debt of gratitude to Michael Poong and the makers of MELAVOX." He knew that once a study like METAPO is published, the seeds of doubt about a product's safety have been planted.

The chirping birds were getting progressively louder in the tall trees surrounding his property. "I wonder what time it is." He always worked on Saturdays. He went back inside and checked the clock in the kitchen. It was almost 7:00 a.m. He walked over to the kitchen cabinets and opened the small cabinet next to the refrigerator. There were bowls and pans for baking, so the cabinet was rarely opened. He thought, "This is the perfect spot to hide the small bottles of MELAVOX 25 mg, in the back of the cabinet."

Originally, he was going to wait for six months from the day he started picking up MELAVOX 25 mg (for Lee) at the pharmacy. Then he realized that in six months, it would only be February. There might be snow on the ground, which would show his footprints in the field where he planned to dump her body. He decided to wait until March.

He closed the cabinet and went upstairs to get ready for work. Thirty minutes later, he grabbed his keys from the kitchen counter, and left for the office, while Lee slept soundly upstairs.

Joan, his office manager, caught up with him before he started seeing patients. She said, "You look happy today Dr. Friedman. Did ya get lucky last night?"

He hesitated for a moment and then said, "Ah yeah. As a matter of fact I did get lucky last night."

"Good for you."

He slipped into his office and flopped into his chair. He took the prescription pad out of the upper right pocket of his lab coat. He scribbled, "Lee Young" at the top and then, "MELAVOX 25 mg once daily." Underneath that he wrote, "bottle of 30." He signed the bottom of the script and then reached over to his telephone and called Joyce at the reception desk.

"Better Health Physicians, can you hold?" Joyce said.

Dr. Friedman blurted out, "No. Joyce, it's me."

She made an embarrassed giggle. "I'm sorry Dr. Friedman. I didn't see that it was an inside call. What can I do for you?"

"Call Wilmington Pharmacy and tell them I need a script filled for MELAVOX 25 mg — a bottle of 30. It's for Lee."

"Oh really? But doesn't Lee take the 75 mg dose?" Joyce remembered her nerve wracking conversation with Lee when she called to remind Dr. Friedman to bring home some free samples. Lee had specified the 75 mg dose. She had said, ". . . otherwise I'll have to take 3 tablets."

At first, Dr. Friedman was dismayed that Joyce had apparently made a mental note that Lee was taking the max dose of MELAVOX. But he realized he could turn it around to his advantage. He said nonchalantly, "Oh sure, Lee sometimes take the 75 mg dose of MELAVOX for acute pain but I make sure she takes the lowest dose on a regular basis."

Joyce sighed and said, "Maybe someday I'll meet a prince like you."

Dr. Friedman laughed and added, "Tell the pharmacy I'll stop by tonight to pick it up and then fax them the script. I'll leave it on my desk."

"Consider it done Dr. Friedman."

Dr. Friedman planned to write a prescription each month for Lee. It would be for a bottle of 30 tablets of MELAVOX 25 mg. Wilmington Pharmacy maintains patient files in their computer. The file for Lee Young would indicate that he prescribed MELAVOX 25 mg (the lowest dose) once daily for Lee's osteoarthritis. Although Lee was never diagnosed with osteoarthritis, she would never know that her chart indicated otherwise. Dr. Friedman knew from experience that, given Lee's age and marathon running, she was certainly developing this insidious condition.

Then each month, Dr. Friedman would pick up the prescription at the pharmacy and store the bottle in the kitchen cabinet overnight. The next day, the bottle would end up in the hazardous waste bag at the office.

In the meantime, he would continue to bring home samples of the highest dose of MELAVOX 75 mg--the dose that had the potential to cause a heart attack or stroke if taken continuously. The sales reps left mountains of samples at his offices and he just grabbed a bunch to take home each week. Lee would never know about her prescription for MELAVOX 25 mg. If she ever found out about it, Donald would tell her the pharmacy made a mistake. He knew Lee wouldn't bother to give it much thought.

Donald hoped that Lee would take the max dose of MELAVOX on a regular basis. Judging from the ever-diminishing supply in their bathroom drawer, Lee was definitely taking it, but he couldn't be certain that she would take a tablet every single day. He thought of a way around that too.

It came as a surprise to Lee when Donald suggested that they spend more time together.

"Why don't we plan to have dinner together more often?"

Lee immediately became paranoid. Her affair with Edgar Schaeffer had been going on for just over a year. She worried, "Does Donald suspect something or, worse, does he *know* something? Is it possible I've gotten careless?"

Before she could answer Donald added, "I mean, not just the drug rep dinners — but the nights when we're at home too."

Lee composed herself and tried to sound casual, "That would be nice, but you don't get home until 8:00 most nights."

Donald walked over to Lee and put his hands on her shoulders. He looked directly into her eyes and grimaced apologetically. He said, "I know. I know. But I'll adjust my schedule and tell the girls not to schedule anyone after 6:30. That way I'll be out of there by 7-ish and we can have dinner by 8:00." Then in practiced fashion, as if it was an afterthought he said, "And I'll do the cooking."

Lee tried to look happy. She tilted her head upwards and pursed her lips for a kiss. Donald dutifully kissed her, as she thought to herself, "Maybe he knows about Edgar and he's simply trying to hold on to me." But suddenly she felt a surge of panic when she recalled her meeting with Joanna Foster, the divorce attorney. She thought, "Maybe I better put Joanna off for a little while because if Donald has proof of an affair, he might be able to cheat me out of the stipend we agreed on."

She heard Donald asking, "Lee, is anything wrong?"

She realized her anguish must have shown on her face. She quickly changed her expression and smiled. "No. Are you kidding? You know I love your cooking. It sounds like a great plan."

Donald smiled.

Lee said, "You can make some of your pasta dishes and even add bread because I'm starting to eat more carbs. I want to run a marathon in the spring."

Donald said, "Good. It's always more fun to cook for us when you're not watching every calorie. Do you want to go with me to the Italian Market in Philly on Saturday? We can pick up some meat and fish to go with my pasta dishes."

"I'm sorry Donald, but I can't make it this Saturday because I have a property settlement." Lee did have a property settlement, but that was in the morning. In the afternoon, she planned to meet Edgar.

Donald was chagrined. He knew Lee was lying. He walked over to the kitchen sink and poured himself a glass of water. He comforted himself with the thought, "It doesn't matter now. I've made up my mind. It's just a matter of putting the plan in motion."

He said, "No problem. I'll go to the market by myself and I'll catch up with you on Saturday night."

Lee walked over to him and rubbed his back for a moment. He turned and kissed her on her forehead. Lee knew something was up, but she figured it was in her best interest to maintain the façade for now. She said, "I think we *should* spend more time together."

Dr. Friedman planned to cook dinner at least twice a week so he could crush a MELVOX 75 mg tablet into her meal. The half-life of the drug was 24 hours, which meant that at least some of the active ingredient would remain in her system for two days. He wanted to get enough MELAVOX into her system, over a seven-month period, so it could potentially cause damage to her heart. But, most importantly, the Medical Examiner's toxicology report would find MELAVOX in her system.

Chapter 8: Deception

Wednesday afternoon, March 9, 1996

LEE CAUGHT A glimpse of herself in the rearview mirror. Her eyes were happy and she rose slightly in her seat until she could see her whole face. She had a broad grin, as she sat back in her seat and sighed. Earlier, Edgar met her for what he called "sex and a sandwich." Sometimes he would ask one of the residents to wrap up a couple of sandwiches that a sales rep brought to the surgical residents' lounge. Edgar would bring them with him to wherever he was meeting Lee. Today he had walked into the house to find Lee straddling a chair in the kitchen, wearing nothing but black lace stockings with a garter belt and spiked heels.

On days like this one, Lee felt certain that it was only a matter of time before Edgar would tell her he was leaving Emma. Several months before, she had told Edgar about Donald's suggestion that they spend more time together. Edgar was nonplussed. His natural reaction to anything — good or bad — was cool and cavalier. He snickered and said, "You always know you're in trouble when you hear 'we need to spend more time together.'"

Lee was irritated by Edgar's nonchalance. It made her edgy and she had blurted out, "Edgar, where are we going with this?" He walked over to her and held her face in his hands and kissed her softly. Then his beeper went off. After glancing at it, he said, "I have to go. It's the OR calling." Edgar knew Lee wanted reassurance. He said, "Don't worry about it. Just go along with whatever Donald's suggesting." He held her tightly and whispered in her ear, "You've got the poor guy twisted in knots." He grabbed her butt and then pressed himself into her groin, as she backed up against the wall behind her. She could feel him getting hard again. But, for the first time, she wasn't in the mood. She took advantage of his intense desire and looked into his eyes and said, "Edgar, I'm going to divorce Donald."

Suddenly Edgar's beeper went off again. He stepped back and said, "It sounds like they need me. I have to go Lee." He started toward the door and said, "Let's talk about this later."

Lee sounded desperate when she asked, "When?"

Edgar said, "Let's see. Tomorrow is Sunday. Is Monday afternoon OK?"

Lee was silent. She had fantasized that Edgar would sweep her up into his arms and say he thought about leaving Emma a thousand times and now he would. Soon they would finally be together.

Edgar reached for the door and asked again, "Monday then?"

Lee knew in her gut that she shouldn't make it so easy for him. But her desperation won out and she walked over to him. "Sure. Uh, I don't know what time. I . . ."

Edgar gave her a quick kiss on the cheek, "don't worry. I'll call you."

Neither one of them had brought the topic up again.

Lee's Mercedes purred up the driveway and slowed to a stop as she pressed the remote control to open the garage door. Her cell phone rang. She thought it might be Edgar.

She was smiling when she said, "Hello?" in a soft voice.

"Mom, hi. It's Grant."

"Oh, hello darling. How's the job going?" Lee always made a point to ask Grant about his job. She reminded him either literally or subliminally, each time they talked, that she expected him to hold on to his job with Inhaber-Taft.

She had used every opportunity at the pharmaceutical company dinners to tell the sales managers about her son Grant.

"He's so intelligent and he really knows how to communicate with people effectively because he majored in psychology," she would say, and then quickly add, "but he's also very business minded and he's developed a keen interest in sales and marketing. I think he's going to pursue an MBA."

Lee knew all of the right things to say to make Grant sound like a good fit for the job of a pharmaceutical sales rep. She knew that sooner or later one of the sales managers would be savvy enough to realize that, if they hired *her* son, it would mean payback from Dr. Friedman in terms of prescriptions written for their products.

Michael Poong proved to be the sales manager Lee was waiting for. He was immediately responsive. "How can I get in touch with Grant to schedule an interview?" was Michael's immediate reaction.

Lee knew the truth about Grant. He was spoiled and lazy. He was 25 years old and bounced from job to job after graduating from the University of Delaware. After working at a job for two to three months, he always complained to Lee that he was bored. She knew the boredom was a result of Grant's mindset that it was pointless for him to work. As an only child, he would most likely inherit all of his father's money, unless his father remarried and had more children.

Grant's father, Lee's first husband, had managed to get his life back on track after going to Alcoholics Anonymous.

Grant also stood the chance of benefiting financially from his mother's marriage to Dr. Friedman. Although Donald had three children to support from his first marriage, Grant was certain his mother would manage to convince Donald to carve out a small portion of his wealth for her son. Donald, like everyone else, knew that Grant was "part of the package" with Lee.

Grant said, "Everything's great Mom. I'm just checking in to see how you're doing."

"I'm fine darling. In fact, I just got home. I'm going to start my run a little early today."

"How's your training going for your next marathon? I hope you're not overdoing it."

Lee could hear the concern in Grant's voice. "I'm not getting any younger, but I know I've got a couple more marathons in me."

"I just worry about you getting hurt or hit by a car or something."

"Honey, you know I'm careful."

"Yeah, but you run along busy roads sometimes and that's dangerous."

"Well, as a matter of fact I just started a new route that puts me on the back roads of New Jersey, of all places."

"What? What are you talking about?"

Lee anticipated Grant's admonitions. She hated the whole role reversal thing and for some reason, Grant was becoming more fatherly with her lately, which made her feel old. She sounded like a defiant teenager as she said, "I know you won't approve of it, but I run across the Delaware Memorial Bridge. I can't believe I didn't think of this before. It's absolutely exhilarating!"

"The Delaware Memorial Bridge? Isn't that dangerous? Aren't you afraid?"

"Now Grant, you should know from all of my skiing adventures that I'm not afraid of heights."

"But how do you get to the bridge? I mean, there's so much traffic and ."

"I start out running from Greenville into Wilmington and cut over to New Castle along Route 141. That takes me to the footpath that extends the entire length of the bridge."

"And then what? Then you're on Route 295 — another highway!"

"Just for about 3 minutes and then I run along the exit road that turns onto Route 29."

"Jesus mom. That's unbelievable! How many miles is that?"

"Oh it's a long one — 16 miles."

"What? 16 miles?"

"Darling, I don't run that route everyday. In fact, I was only doing the sixteen miles on Saturdays until a few weeks ago, when I increased the frequency to three days a week."

"So I guess today is a long run?"

"You got it."

"Well, the weather's awesome, so it should be a good one." Grant knew there was no chance of changing his mother's mind about running another marathon or, for that matter, which route she should take.

"Hey, what about you? Are you still on territory?" Lee asked.

Grant had been home since noon. He had become fast friends with Ken Welder, who made it his business to mentor the new sales reps about how to work the job his way. Only Grant pushed the envelope even further. Sometimes he only worked two days a week. But he lied to his mother and said, "Yeah, I'm still on territory. It's going really great. A lot of docs are using my products — so it's all good."

Lee worried about whether or not Grant was telling her the truth. She loved him dearly but she knew his shortcomings.

"How's 'the Donald'?" Grant asked. He knew his mother liked rich men and he knew that's why she married Dr. Friedman. Over the years, Grant began to believe what his father told him about his mother's flaws, but he loved her anyway.

His father, Mason Preston, had made a fortune in real estate — and that's when Lee entered his life. Unfortunately, he picked up a nasty drinking habit along the way. His fortunes fizzled down to a moderate income by the time he finally managed to get help through AA meetings. But it all happened too late for his mother's taste, according to his father. He said that when she saw his empire crumbling, it was a convenient time for her to leave and blame it on his drinking.

After Lee and Mason divorced, he was still very generous with Grant, even though he couldn't really afford to be. When Grant graduated from college, his father bought him a BMW convertible. Grant accepted the gift, but with some trepidation. He knew that his father was embarrassed by his diminished social status. But at that point in Mason's life, the car was a way to reassure Grant and himself that AA was beginning to put him back on the right track.

Lee said, "'The Donald' is doing great as usual. Haven't you been to his office lately?" Lee was concerned because she knew that Donald's practice was part of Grant's sales territory.

Grant was offended by the insinuation. But he took a deep breath and said, "Don't worry Mom. I'm doing my job. In fact I was just at his Newark office yesterday, but he was at the Wilmington location."

Lee sensed that Grant was offended. She thought, "Who am I to judge him? I just met my lover this afternoon, and I'm trying to figure out when I should re-initiate divorce proceedings." Suddenly she felt edgy and nervous, as if Grant could read her mind. She quickly added, "I'm sorry Grant. I didn't mean to imply that you're not doing your job. It's always nice of you to ask about Donald."

"Mom, is everything OK?"

"Of course it is. Why do you ask?"

"You just seem a little agitated, that's all."

"I'm sorry darling. I'm just worried about getting one of my listings sold. It's been on the market for three months now." Lee knew that Grant would believe her if she blamed it on work pressures.

"Mom, you know that if anyone can sell it, you can. Don't worry about it. Which house is it anyway?" Grant asked.

Without hesitation, Lee answered, "It's that gorgeous place on Bethel Road in Greenville. Do you know Dr. Burton, a cardiothoracic surgeon?"

"I've heard the name, but I don't know him."

"Well, Dr. Burton is going to retire at the end of July and he and his wife are moving to Florida."

Now Lee *was* becoming agitated, but not because of a house that lingered on the market. Donald was making dinner at home tonight and she wanted to get a long run in before that. She said, "Well, I just parked the car so . . ."

Grant cut her off and said, "Alright Mom. Have a good run and I'll catch up with you later."

"Thanks darling. And tell Jillian I said hello. Are you two still seeing a lot of each other?"

"Yeah, I'm taking her out to dinner tonight in fact. Yeah, Jilly is doing great. I'll tell her you were asking for her."

"Alright, bye Grant."

"Bye Mom." Grant ended the call and stretched out in his comfortable leather chair in the living room. He picked up the remote control and turned on the television. He felt relaxed. He had no worries. His counterparts at Inhaber-Taft were impressed that his mother was married to Dr. Friedman. And Dr. Friedman always referred to Grant as "his son" because he knew the other reps for Inhaber-Taft and, for that matter any of their competitors, would treat Grant with kid gloves. Donald knew if Grant was happy and successful in his career, then Lee would be happy. Whether or not Grant was any good at his job, he was untouchable because everyone knew his mother was married to one of the biggest prescription writers in Delaware.

Once in a while a sales rep would tentatively approach Grant and ask in a whisper if it was true that Dr. Friedman had adopted him. Grant would always laugh a little and then say coyly, "Sure. Of course he adopted me." He figured they didn't need to know that his real father was still very much alive. But it did get him to thinking about his potential to be included in Donald's will. Grant thought, "He doesn't have to adopt me to include me in his will. I just have to play my cards right and stay on his good side."

Chapter 9: Lee Went Missing

Thursday morning, March 10, 1996

DR. FRIEDMAN DROVE to his Wilmington office. He knew the other physicians in his practice would not be surprised that he showed up for work, even after they heard the terrible news. After all, everybody knew he was a workaholic.

Dr. Althea Margotitis was already in the office when he arrived at 8:00 a.m. He asked his office manager, Joan, to join him in Althea's office. When Dr. Margotitis looked up from her desk, she knew immediately something was wrong by the look on his face. She asked, "Donald, are you alright?"

With slumped posture, he proceeded to one of the two chairs positioned in front of her desk. Joan walked into the office right behind him and shut the door. As soon as Joan saw his face she asked, "Dr. Friedman, what's going on?"

In his usual terse style, Dr. Friedman just blurted out, "Lee is missing."

In unison, Joan and Dr. Margotitis gasped. Dr. Margotitis operated at a baseline of high anxiety. This news made her voice crack, as she fired questions at Dr. Friedman. "Donald, what do you mean? For how long? Did you call the police?"

Dr. Friedman began to tell, for the first time, *his* version of what happened the previous night. He said, "I called the police last night when she hadn't arrived home by 11:30. I told them I had talked to her briefly in the late afternoon before she went for a run. I reminded her that I was going to visit my parents in Margate, after office hours. Lee wasn't scheduled to go anywhere last night, but I thought she might have gotten a call from a client and decided on an impromptu dinner meeting. I . . . I called . . ." He stopped and pretended to need a moment to collect himself. Joan immediately jumped out of her chair and rubbed his back in a maternal fashion. Dr. Friedman rubbed his forehead and then looked up at Joan and said, "I'm alright Joan."

Joan sat down again, as Dr. Friedman looked at Dr. Margotitis and continued, "I called her cell phone and left a message around 8:30. And I called several times after that, but I still haven't heard from her."

Joan asked, "Does she have any family in the area?"

Dr. Friedman said, "Her parents live in Pennsylvania but she rarely ever talks to them."

Dr. Margotitis asked, "Is there anything we can do to help Donald?"

"No Althea. I just wanted you to know what's going on, in case I seem a little distracted today."

Joan asked, "Are you sure you want to stay? Dr. Bichotti and Dr. Bergman are due in at 10:00. I could call Dr. Bichotti and ask him to come in early and then . . ."

Dr. Friedman shook his head, "No, no. I need to be here or I'll go crazy worrying."

Dr. Margotitis said, "Well, I know you Donald, so I know I can't change your mind about that."

Just then there was a knock on the door and Joan jumped up to answer it. It was Patty interrupting with a patient calling for Dr. Friedman. Joan and Dr. Margotitis looked at him to assess his reaction. He inhaled deeply and said, "It's time to go to work." And with that, he put both hands on the arms of the chair and began to hoist himself to his feet. Suddenly, he fell back in the chair with a shriek of pain. He panicked because he realized he had put too much weight on his right arm, which he had fallen on the night before--in the field where he left Lee's body.

Dr. Margotitis sprang from her chair and shouted, "Donald!"

Joan grabbed his right arm and asked, "Are you alright?"

Dr. Friedman waved Joan away with his left hand and said, "I'm fine. I just felt a little faint for a minute." He was relieved when Joan backed away.

He had to suppress his reaction to the additional discomfort she had caused by grabbing his arm.

Dr. Margotitis stood in front of him and said in a comforting tone, "Donald, let me check your pupils." She stood with her penlight at the ready.

He thought to himself, "Perfect. I'll just play along that I'm more physically and emotionally distraught than I realized." Again he said, "I'm OK. I just felt a little dizzy, that's all." Dr. Margotitis touched his hand as she flashed her penlight into each of his eyes. His pupils constricted when the light hit them. She said, "Well, you look fine now," and she straightened up and leaned against the front of her desk.

Joan asked, "Dr. Friedman, why don't I see if I can reschedule some of your patients today?"

"No, Joan, I'm fine, really." This time he moved himself to the edge of the chair and leaned on his left arm to get up. He couldn't let them find out that his right arm had been injured.

Dr. Margotitis said, "Donald, just say the word when you need to get out of here today." And she added sternly, "I mean it."

"OK Althea. I promise I will."

With that, Joan and Dr. Friedman left her office and headed toward the exam rooms, which were already filled with patients. Joan stopped outside of Exam Room 2 and was about to hand Dr. Friedman the patient's chart, when he said, "Give me a minute Joan. I have to make a phone call."

"No problem," Joan said.

Dr. Friedman shut his office door. He thought it would look good if he called the police again.

Detective Patrick Healy had already been assigned to the case. It was unusual for the average missing person case to have a detective assigned to it so soon, but this case was different. The Chief of Police knew how to play politics. He knew that it was important to keep the wealthy taxpayers happy.

Dr. Friedman was transferred to Detective Healy after he said he was calling about Lee Young. "Detective Healy speaking."

"Good morning Detective. I'm Dr. Friedman."

"Oh, yes, of course Dr. Friedman. Have you heard from your wife yet?"

Dr. Friedman felt awkward for just a second before responding, "No. I haven't. That's why I'm calling. Have you made any progress?"

"No, Dr. Friedman. Not yet. I'm sorry because I know how difficult this is for you."

Dr. Friedman uttered glumly, "You have no idea."

Detective Healy took his work very seriously, but he was also acutely aware of the unfortunate politics of police work. If Lee Young was the wife of a *Mr.* Friedman, from the west side of Wilmington, she would not have been classified as "missing" at this early stage. And the report would not have ended up at the top of the paperwork stack on his desk.

Detective Healy asked, "Can I stop by your house tonight to ask you some questions?"

Dr. Friedman felt a surge of panic, but he said, "Sure. I'm scheduled to see patients until about 6:00, so maybe. . ."

Detective Healy interrupted, "Why don't we say 7:30? That'll give you time to have some dinner and, believe it or not, my wife and kids like to see me for dinner now and then too."

Dr. Friedman resented the detective's pretense of friendliness, even as he scheduled the interrogation. But he thought, "I better get used to it because I'll have to suffer fools like him for a while until this whole thing blows over." He said to the detective, "7:30 is perfect. I assume you have my address."

"Yeah, we do. In fact, I was already out there to poke around outside the house a little bit."

There was a moment of silence. Dr. Friedman wondered if he was being set up. He worried, "Did they find something already? Did I leave anything lying around?" He knew he had to say something. Finally he said, "Oh good. Did you find anything suspicious?"

"No. Nothing turned up, but I'm sure it will eventually."

Dr. Friedman felt a pang of anxiety. He said, "Thanks Detective. I'll see you tonight then." He stood there for a moment and became aware of the throbbing pain in his right arm. He reached into his desk for some MELAVOX. He popped two 75 mg tablets into his mouth and suddenly stopped himself from swallowing. For a second he almost gagged as he looked at the sample packet. "How ironic," he thought. He held the tablets between his tongue and the roof of his mouth and left his office. He went into the kitchen to get some water.

His arm was in so much pain now he could hardly hold the glass in his right hand, and then suddenly, it slipped. He dropped the water glass into the sink with a thud, against the stainless steel. He grabbed for it with his left hand and felt relieved that no one else was in the kitchen at the time. Just then, one of the file clerks, Susan, walked into the kitchen. He refilled the glass with water and swallowed.

Susan said, "Dr. Friedman, I'm so sorry to hear about your wife." She noticed that Dr. Friedman looked pale. She asked, "Are you OK?"

Dr. Friedman said, "Oh, yeah, I'm fine. I'm sure everything will be fine." Then he started opening and closing cabinets and finally, he asked, "Hey, Susan, do you know where we keep the ACE bandages? I need one for a patient."

Susan said, "As a matter of fact, I do." She walked to the overhead cabinets on the other side of the kitchen. She said, "I had to find them for Dr. Goldman the other day."

Dr. Friedman walked over to Susan and took the box from her. He said, "Thanks" and then rushed out of the room. He went into his office and closed the door. He grabbed the buttons of his white coat and opened each one quickly. He thought it was a good idea to wrap his arm with an ACE bandage to prevent further strain. As he bent his arms and slipped his white coat over his shoulders, he felt a sharp pain in his arm. He stopped for a moment until the pain subsided. Then he slowly removed the coat completely and tried to avoid spilling the pens, script pad, and notes in his top right pocket. He unbuttoned his shirt with his left hand and slipped it over his shoulders. This time he was careful to move his right arm very gingerly. He began to wrap the ACE bandage tightly around his arm, starting just below his armpit. Suddenly his office door flung open and Joan walked in.

She gasped when she saw Dr. Friedman struggling with the ACE bandage. She asked, "Dr. Friedman, are you alright?" She put the patient charts down on one of the chairs and rushed over to him.

Dr. Friedman gave her a startled look. He was angry that he hadn't thought to lock his door. He said sternly, "Joan, shut the door please."

Joan did an about-face and quickly grabbed for the office door and pushed it shut.

Dr. Friedman heard the anger in his voice. He lowered his voice and said calmly, "It's just my tennis elbow acting up again. I played for a couple of hours last week and my arm has been sore ever since."

Joan was already taking the roll of ACE bandage from his hand. She said, "Let me help you with that."

Dr. Friedman gave in. He let Joan finish wrapping the ACE bandage tightly around his arm. He handed her the metal clips and she pinned the cloth at the top and the bottom.

"There you go. You're all set."

"Thanks Joan." He slipped his shirt on and tried to change the subject. "What's up Joan?"

"It's David Borrick again. He's at the front desk insisting that you see him right away. He said he had to work some OT after the third shift ended, and he's already late to pick up his daughter from his ex-wife and . . ."

Dr. Friedman asked, "What's wrong with him now--another STD?"

Joan said, "Yeah, that's what the symptoms sound like. He said he's got blood in his urine and he's in pain when he takes a piss."

Dr. Friedman laughed ironically and said, "Jesus, these people know how to fuck up their lives!"

Joan said, "You got that right."

Dr. Friedman laughed again and said, "Tell him he just needs to keep it in his pants."

Joan laughed and said, "We both know that'll never happen. Just give me a script for Dextracycline and we'll count it as a visit and get him out of here."

"Sounds good." He scribbled on his prescription pad and tore off the top sheet and handed it to Joan.

"Thanks Doc."

As the day progressed, the news about Lee had spread throughout the office — to his staff and even to some patients. And Dr. Friedman was right-- no one was surprised that he came into the office to work. He had just finished using the staff bathroom, when he saw Joan walk out of the kitchen.

Dr. Friedman asked, "Who's next?"

Joan answered, "Mrs. Rudiman is in Room 3. She's got chest pains again."

"Mrs. Rudiman again? Wasn't she just here?"

"Yeah, and this is a free one if you see her. Her insurance won't cover this visit since she was just here."

Dr. Friedman asked, "Are we near our managed care patient cap for the day already?"

"We're getting close," and she looked at her watch as she said this. It was Joan's responsibility to monitor the number of managed care patients seen each day and balance them with Medicare and Medicaid patients. Ultimately, she had to be sure the practice had the potential to be paid for each patient seen. The managed care plans would only reimburse the practice for a finite number of patient visits each day. If they exceeded that "ceiling" they would not be paid for any more visits or services rendered that day, regardless of the costs incurred. In 1996, all physicians' practices accepted Medicare because, at that time, Medicare paid them 100% of the cost of the office visit. (It wasn't until a few years later that Medicare dramatically cut back on coverage and patients had to supplement Medicare coverage with an insurance plan.) But the Better Health Physicians' practice was ahead of its time. They operated the practice like a business with the mission of making money. They accepted every managed care (insurance) plan and every state and federally funded health services coverage, including Medicaid.

The typical suburban practice did not encompass the lower socioeconomic class that included Medicaid patients. In the towns and cities that *did* draw Medicaid patients, not all physician practices accepted them because they didn't want to treat those patients. They were typically much more complicated and time consuming because of unhealthy lifestyles. But some physicians were simply snobbish and they didn't want to tarnish the image of their practice with Medicaid patients. Additionally, by the mid-90s, AIDS was spreading its tentacles among socioeconomic classes, but it was most prevalent among Medicaid patients. Most general practice physicians were not comfortable treating the many complications of the disease. And, like other healthcare workers, some physicians and their staff, feared contact with bodily fluids so an AIDS patient sneezing and coughing with a cold, or requiring a urine sample for a urinary tract infection, was immediately referred to an Infectious Disease specialist. (Among doctors and nurses, this was known as "dumping" the patient). There were also many patients with no health insurance coverage at all — usually those who chose to live under the radar. They didn't vote and they didn't pay taxes. Some were illegal aliens. Whatever the reason, they wanted to remain anonymous. These patients could only be treated in a hospital emergency room or a clinic that received federal grants for their care.

Medicaid patients fell into the hands of either caring physicians with a true mission of treating the sick or, more often, greedy physicians who resentfully took Medicaid patients to make more money. Whereas managed care companies put a limit on reimbursement, there were no limits to physician payment for Medicare and Medicaid patients in 1996. It was actually to their advantage to accept it because once they exceeded their managed care reimbursement census for the day, the only patients they could still make money on were Medicare and Medicaid patients.

Dr. Friedman and his group worked long hours, Monday through Saturday, and processed patients through their offices like cattle. They ran their practice like a clinic. They took all comers, so it was a diverse patient population. They could have had a revolving door at the entrances to their offices in Wilmington and Newark, in order to accommodate the high volume of patients seen each day.

Joan had followed Dr. Friedman into his office. He picked up some pink message slips on his desk. "Nothing from Detective Healy yet. I can call the rest later." He pretended to have an afterthought, "Hey Joan, don't mention my tennis injury to anybody. I don't like to remind people that I'm getting too old for this stuff."

Joan laughed and said, "Your secret is safe with me."

Dr. Friedman smiled but he was disturbed when Joan uttered the word "secret." He knew this wasn't a good time for anyone to think he was being secretive.

In fact, Joan paused for a moment. She thought Dr. Friedman was being uncharacteristically self-conscious. He was very open about his life and his opinions. Everyone knew his hobbies, his politics, and much more. The grapevine of the local medical community was always rife with rumors and intimate details about the lives of doctors and nurses. Pharmaceutical sales reps were included in the buzz of the grapevine because they traveled in the same circles.

As they headed out of his office, Joan lowered her voice and asked, "Dr. Friedman, do you want to get out of here?"

Dr. Friedman said, "Oh no, no. I'm fine."

Joan said, "But you must be sick over this whole thing with Lee."

"I am, but what can I do? I'm just hoping to get a call from her and then this nightmare will be over."

Joan said quietly, "Just get out of here whenever you need to."

It was almost 5:00 when Dr. Friedman had grown tired of the staff whispering about his predicament. He was already weary from his self-conscious effort to play the role of a worried husband. "And this is only the first day," he thought. He went into his office and took another MELAVOX 75 mg tablet. This time he didn't bother to go to the kitchen to get a glass of water. He just brought up some saliva and threw back his head, as he swallowed the tablet. He thought to himself, "I hope I don't have a heart attack from the MELAVOX. That would be a cruel joke." He glanced at his watch and thought, "Only a little more than two hours before Detective Healy shows up at my door. I better get home to make sure there aren't any loose ends around the house." He didn't think there were. He just needed to be home and claim his space before it was further invaded by the police. He planned to take a hot bath in his jacuzzi, to soak his arm and relax with a drink before Detective Healy arrived.

Dr. Margotitis had left the office for the day around 3:30, so Dr. Friedman popped his head into Dr. Bichotti's office before he left.

"I've got to get out of here Paul."

Dr. Bichotti looked up from his desk and squinted behind his glasses. He was always squirrely and nervous. He swallowed hard before he spoke, "Donald, I'm sorry to hear about Lee. Have you gotten any news?"

Dr. Friedman knew that Dr. Bichotti was intimidated by him. He was shy and quiet and not quite sure how to take Dr. Friedman's bold manner and sarcastic wit. He shook his head and said, "It's so terrible Paul. You have no idea. There's no news yet, but I've already gotten a detective from the Wilmington police department involved. I don't know what to think. I just keep hoping my cell phone will ring and I'll hear Lee's voice."

Dr. Bichotti grinned. He was concerned that too many questions might upset Dr. Friedman. He tried to put his mind at ease and said, "I'm sure there's a simple explanation. She'll probably turn up tonight." Dr. Bichotti cringed after he heard those last words come out of his mouth. He realized it sounded trite. He was trying to think of something more appropriate to say when Dr. Friedman said, "I'm meeting with the detective tonight. I expect him to make this investigation a priority." He made it sound as if it was his idea to meet with Detective Healy. He wanted to give the impression that he was in charge of the situation and demanding results. He added, "I'll just keep pushing for some answers."

Dr. Bichotti didn't know what else to say, so he just grinned with an empathetic look of frustration.

"Goodnight Paul. Thanks for covering for me so I can get out of here."

"Sure Don. No problem."

As he walked down the hall, Dr. Friedman saw Joan in the sample room. He stood in the doorway and said, "Thanks for your help today. Paul and Ira should be able to cover for me."

Joan walked over to Dr. Friedman. Her face was prematurely aged from years of smoking, heavy drinking, and domestic disputes. By this time of the day, she always had a far away look in her eyes like someone who's only seventy percent there but trying hard to compensate for the other thirty percent. Her breath was a mix of cigarettes, alcohol and peppermint gum. She said, "Everything's under control. Go home and take it easy Dr. Friedman. I can't even imagine what you're going through. Everyone knows how much you love Lee. You must be so upset."

Dr. Friedman said, "I have to admit I'm surprised I haven't heard from Lee yet. Now I'm really worried."

Joan gripped his left arm and gave a firm squeeze to reassure him. "Don't worry Dr. Friedman. I'm sure she's fine and there's a reasonable explanation for all this."

Dr. Friedman was grateful that Joan was standing on his left side and didn't grab his right arm for consolation.

She continued, "There must be some kind of mix-up. Maybe you forgot that she had plans with friends or something."

"Yeah, you're probably right."

Joan finally loosened her grip and stepped aside.

Dr. Friedman was solemn for a moment and then he grinned and said, "She'll probably walk in the door tonight and we'll all laugh about this tomorrow."

Joan said, "Yeah, right." She turned away from Dr. Friedman, toward the drug sample bins, and then added, "Have a good night." She barely got the rote expression out of her mouth when she realized how ridiculous it sounded, given the circumstances.

Dr. Friedman didn't respond. He was already out the back door of the office.

Chapter 10: The Interrogation

Thursday night, March 10

WHILE DRIVING HOME that evening, Dr. Friedman was stricken with panic. He worried, "Is it possible Detective Healy has suspicions about me?" He felt his pulse quicken, "I wonder if anyone found Lee's body yet." He started to feel hot and queasy, ". . . and who will find her?" Lee had no identification on her, just a house key and her cell phone in a fanny pack around her waist. The police could identify her from her cell phone number.

Donald worried, "Is it possible that someone could figure out what really happened? And if they did . . . then what?" He thought of the recent case of the politically connected lawyer, in Delaware, who was found guilty of killing his mistress. His picture was on the front page of *The News Journal*, wearing an orange jumpsuit, with his hands cuffed behind his back. He thought, "Even if I was found innocent, my reputation would be ruined by the publicity and the rumors."

In spite of the car's warmth, he felt cold. Then he realized that he was shivering. He hadn't vomited in years, so he hardly recognized the warning signs. Fortunately, he pulled over to the side of the road just in time to lunge out of the car as he began to vomit profusely. He had hoped to make it to the passenger side so no passersby would notice him. But it came on too quickly. He groped the car's body as he tried to steady himself. He retched a couple of times and then straightened his posture. The shivering stopped. He felt calm. He thought, "I better get back in the car before someone sees me."

As he reached for his car door, a gust of wind from a passing car made him shiver again. His shirt was clinging to him because it was wet with sweat. As he got into the car he looked down and discovered that he had vomited on his jacket and pants. He was careful not to move too much so the vomit stayed where it was and didn't make more of a mess. "I'll clean it up at home," he thought. He started the engine, put the car in gear and slid back onto the road.

He pulled into the garage and sat back with a sigh of relief as the garage door closed behind him. When he got inside, he pulled a bunch of paper towels from the rack under the kitchen cabinet. He ran the water until it was lukewarm and then wiped the vomit from his pants and jacket. For a moment he was concerned about whether the dry cleaner would be able to remove the water stain from his pants. He looked at the clock. It was 6:27 p.m. He made himself a gin and tonic and drank it down. He made himself another, but added a slice of lime. This time he sipped the drink and inhaled the fresh lime scent as the carbonation fizzed around the tip of his nose. He hung his jacket in the laundry room to air it out. Then he climbed the stairs to his bedroom suite.

First he turned on the water for the Jacuzzi and, as he began to undress, he mentally ran through a virtual tour of his house. He thought, "There isn't anything in the house for the detective to find. There was no struggle. There was no blood. I got rid of the needle and vial in the hazmat trash container at the office."

A moment later, he was slowly descending the steps into the Jacuzzi. He grabbed the safety bar with his left hand and then submerged his body into the hot, bubbling water. He uttered a moan of relief when the water jets pulsed against his right arm. After he settled into the water, he thought about the drive home. "Maybe it was the MELAVOX tablets that made me so nauseous." He propped his head on the spongy bath pillow and turned slightly to check the clock on the wall. It was almost 6:45. He had about 45 minutes before Detective Healy would arrive. He thought about the likely turn of events in the coming weeks. There would be questions, speculation, and suspicion on the part of the police, his peers, his staff, his friends, and even his children. "It'll be a media circus too," he thought and for an instant, he began to feel sick again. Suddenly, there was a shrill sound of the phone ringing in the cavernous bathroom. His heart skipped a beat. "I have to answer it. It might be the detective." He struggled to his feet and reached for the phone on the bathroom wall.

"Hello?"

"Donald, I just heard about Lee. I'm so sorry." It was Larry Berman.

The sound of Larry's voice made him feel vulnerable, as if Larry could see through him. He said, "Yeah, thanks. I'm really shaken up about it."

"Of course Donald. I know you were really trying to work things out with Lee." Actually Larry knew nothing of the sort but he made the assumption, since they hadn't divorced. And it was a show of support.

Donald felt awkward, but he said, "You know me Larry. I'm hounding the police to find Lee as soon as possible. In fact, I'm meeting with a detective tonight."

Larry asked, "How long has she been missing? Is it just since last night?"

"Yeah. I talked to her yesterday afternoon as a matter of fact . . ." He went on to tell Larry the same thing he told Dr. Margotitis and Joan.

Larry asked, "When was the last time you saw her?"

Now Donald felt a little defensive. But he reminded himself, "I have to keep my cool. I'll probably feel the same way when Detective Healy asks questions. This is good practice."

He said, "I saw Lee yesterday morning before I left for work. Of course, she was still sleeping at the time." Now he just wanted to get Larry off the phone.

Larry said, "Well, if there's anything . . ."

"I know. I know Larry. Thanks."

"Alright. Stay in touch Donald."

"I will." He thought about Larry. He was a good friend, almost paternalistic, and maybe that's why he couldn't bring himself to tell Larry the truth. Not only did Larry tell him about Lee's affair but, as he promised, Larry had also talked to Edgar Schaeffer back in August. To their surprise, Edgar proved to be even more of a narcissist than either of them had imagined. Apparently he considered himself invincible. In fact, when Larry told Edgar, "Donald Friedman knows about you and his wife Lee," Edgar didn't flinch.

He didn't even change his expression. He stood there for a moment as if to say, "Is there anything else?" When he finally spoke, he said arrogantly, "I guess I have his blessing then." Edgar was unmoved. He just didn't care. Naturally, Donald was furious, "Fucking German bastard. He was probably fucking Lee just to piss me off. The Jew-hating bastard!"

Donald grabbed a towel and began to dry off. In minutes he was downstairs mixing another drink. He never thought of himself as a drinker. Not when he witnessed his colleagues consume copious amounts of alcohol at drug rep dinners and still have the ability to function well the next day. When he and Lee dined at a restaurant, which was almost always on the tab of a pharmaceutical company, he had a cocktail before dinner and a glass of wine with his meal. But lately, his drinking had increased. He quickly tossed together his third gin and tonic and left the bottle on the counter because he intended to offer the detective a drink. He figured it would be appropriate for him to *appear* shaken and out-of-sorts, but he did not want to *feel* that way.

He looked at the clock and said out loud, "7:20, only ten more minutes before he arrives." He headed toward the dining room and nervously paced around the table, until he finally walked over to a chair and sat down.

He jumped out of the chair when the doorbell rang at exactly 7:30. His heart was pounding as he started toward the foyer. He stopped in his tracks and coached himself, "Relax Donald." But then he thought, "No. . . no, this is good. My obviously nervous disposition will be perceived as desperation about Lee." He quickened his pace and took a couple of long strides to the front door.

He wore a resolute grin as he reached out to shake the detective's hand. "Detective Healy, thanks for coming."

The detective stepped into the foyer and said, "Dr. Friedman, it's nice to meet you. Again, I'm sorry about your wife."

"Thank you Detective." He motioned in the direction of the next room. "Let's go have a seat."

"Thanks." Detective Healy walked into the room ahead of Dr. Friedman.

"Would you care for a glass of wine or a drink?" Dr. Friedman's demeanor was urbane. He wanted to disarm the detective because he assumed that he might be intimidated by the elevated social class of a physician.

"No thanks Dr. Friedman."

"Call me Donald."

The detective grinned but said nothing. He liked Dr. Friedman's down-to-earth manner but he wasn't comfortable with the idea of calling a physician by his first name. Besides, he had already spent enough time thinking about him as Dr. Friedman.

As soon as they sat down, Detective Healy proceeded with all of the questions that Donald had anticipated. There were questions about where and when they had last seen each other; where Lee worked and who her friends were. And finally, the gentle prodding about the nature of their relationship-- was there marriage "in good stead?"

Dr. Friedman responded with a pat answer, "We've had our problems, like most married couples, but we work at it." He diverted his glance for a moment and pretended to be embarrassed by the intimate revelation he was about to tell the detective. After a pregnant pause, he leaned forward in his chair and made direct eye contact with the detective. He said, "We love each other Detective Healy." And then in a deliberate tone of yearning he added, "Lee is the best thing that ever happened to me." Then he turned his eyes downward to simulate despair. Dr. Friedman was careful to use the present tense when he discussed Lee and their relationship. He was starting to feel confident that he had won over the detective with his display of emotion.

Within a little more than twenty minutes, Detective Healy got up from his chair and reached out to shake Dr. Friedman's hand. "Don't worry Dr. Friedman. We'll find her. The information about your wife's marathon training routes is very helpful. I'll contact the Pennsville and Carneys Point, New Jersey police departments immediately."

"Thanks Detective." He was uneasy that the detective called him Dr. Friedman, instead of Donald. He sized up the detective as a man of integrity, but it bothered him that he was also apparently a rigid, "by the book" type of guy. He said, "Where are my manners? . . . what is your first name Detective?"

"Pat . . . well Patrick . . . my friends call me Pat."

Dr. Friedman grinned. He got the message that the detective preferred an air of formality.

They walked toward the front door and Detective Healy added, "Be sure to call us immediately if you hear from her."

Dr. Friedman said, "I will, and please call me with any information you may find."

"Certainly." And with that, he left.

Dr. Friedman shut the door and grinned smugly as he thought, "He doesn't suspect a thing." He leaned against the door on his right side and suddenly recoiled. His right arm throbbed and he winced in pain. It must have been the rush of adrenalin during his meeting with the detective that managed to numb the pain.

After a moment, he looked at his watch. It was only 7:55. He decided to drive to Wilmington Pharmacy to buy some ACE bandages. He knew there were more at the office, but he didn't want his staff to find the supply dwindling. "They might not think twice about it but, then again, if questioned, it could be a detail someone would remember," he thought . . . "of course, there is the problem of Joan." He pictured Joan bursting into his office just as he was wrapping his arm with the bandage. But he reassured himself, "What am I worried about? She believed it was my tennis elbow acting up. I just have to calm down."

He grabbed his keys from the credenza and walked through the kitchen to the laundry room. He felt his jacket. It was dry. He sniffed it. All he smelled was leather — no scent of vomit. He opened the door from the kitchen into the garage. He looked at his car for a moment and felt anxious. "Shit! I better vacuum out my trunk! There could be hairs or cloth fibers in there from Lee. Just because Detective Healy believed me tonight, it doesn't mean he won't have a change of heart later. He could come back with a warrant to search the house and my car. But what if he's lurking around outside the house? All I need is for him to hear a vacuum machine running. I'll just take care of it later tonight."

Chapter 11: A Chance Encounter

Same day/night

MARK LOOKED UP from his computer screen when a slight breeze beckoned him to the window. Even on the coldest days of winter, he kept the window open just enough to let some fresh air into the room. It was a third floor apartment that he had converted into office space for his software development company. The building was located on the main street of the University of Delaware campus. Down the hall, there lived a visiting professor from India who made a habit of cooking spicy Indian food at various and unpredictable times. On dank gray days, the pungent odor of curry and garlic sometimes sickened Mark, as it wafted through the air and down the corridor to his office.

As he stood at the window, he looked down at the sidewalk where he could see college students striding casually between classes. The trendy clothing stores, eateries, bars and coffee shops tempted them away from their studies. For Mark, it was the tease of unseasonably warm weather that distracted him from his work. He thought, "It's going to take me a couple of days to straighten out this software program. What's the difference if I take a few hours off? This weather is too good to pass up."

He decided to head over to Riverside Airport where he rented a hangar for his biggest project — rebuilding a seaplane. He shut down his computer and thought, "I can work on this program tonight at the cabin. I'll get some work done before Debbie arrives." The plan seemed sensible enough and within minutes, Mark locked up the office and ran down the stairs to the parking lot in the back of the building.

Riverside was a small airport in Maryland, where Mark and other recreational pilots housed their single and twin engine planes. Mark was a packrat who collected and renovated almost anything with an engine. On Saturdays, Debbie met up with Mark at the airport. Mark did all of the mechanical work and Debbie was his tireless assistant, while Harry napped in the grass just outside the hangar. Mark was a frugal perfectionist. He asked Debbie to do things like clean out the groves of old screws with a wire brush, so they could be reused. He thought it was wasteful to throw them away. Debbie also made the lunch run to the local deli, and then she and Mark would take a break and eat with the pilots who were hanging around the airport.

On weekends, the pilots were day-trippers. Some of them had been, or still were, commercial pilots. Some had served in the military, or were simply car enthusiasts who now had enough money for bigger toys. The pilots were all men, except for Missie, the office manager. Missie was still as feisty as ever, even at 71 years young. She was a retired nurse, a writer for the local newspaper and county magazine, and an occasional pilot. Missie was not computer friendly so she used an electric typewriter for her office work. She only made coffee in the morning. After that, it was the duty of anyone who felt like drinking it. She talked with the pilots who radioed in their flight plans, and she collected money for aviation gas and flying lessons.

The small town airport lunch conversation was much the same as the talk around a corner bar, or even a locker room. If the men were not talking about women, cars or airplanes, they were telling drinking stories. The women in the room were snuffed out by all of the testosterone. To these men, the purpose of the women present at the table was to be their audience. It was a foregone conclusion that the presence of a woman in this environment was to shut up and listen and give the men the floor. The larger the pack of men present, the more intimidating they were. Debbie and the other girlfriends, mistresses, or occasional wife, felt victorious whenever they managed to gain the attention of the men. This was rarely accomplished with conversation. However, it was easily accomplished with a pair of short shorts or a tight blouse that managed to curve in all the right places.

Mark had worked on his seaplane for most of the day, when he decided it was time to head home. He pulled into his driveway minutes before Debbie's car rolled down the hill. Harry saw Mark in the distance from his perch on the backseat. He pushed his head further out of the window and barked with anticipation. Mark looked around toward the car and quickly snapped his cell phone shut. Debbie felt a pang of anxiety in the pit of her stomach as he approached the car. She worried, "Was he on the phone with Gretchen?" Mark opened the back door to let Harry out. "Hey buddy!" he shouted.

Debbie got out of the car smiling. She told herself not to say it, but the next minute she blurted out, "So who were you talking to just then?" She could never suppress her distrust of men. She could never play it cool or manage to be subtle.

Mark got defensive and responded sarcastically, "Oh it was Gretchen. We were just making plans for later tonight."

In a futile attempt to hide her emotions, Debbie twisted her mouth into a grin. "I'm sorry Mark." She was almost certain that Mark was kidding, but they both knew she had her suspicions about Mark's ongoing friendship with his ex-girlfriend, Gretchen. Debbie tried to be trusting. And she wanted to believe that Mark and Gretchen only saw each other when he drove up to her home in Philadelphia to fix her computer. She reminded herself that all of the young people she worked with went out with male and female friends all the time. Some of them were even engaged or married, and yet they trusted each other enough to go out and party with friends of the opposite sex.

"I brought chicken for the grill. I marinated it overnight so it should be nice and tender. And of course I brought wine too," Debbie said.

"Alright! Sounds good Deb. I'm hungry." Mark helped her with the grocery bag and they walked toward the cabin. He said, "I cut out early today and went over to Riverside to work on the plane."

"Oh, well . . . it must be nice." Debbie smiled coyly at Mark.

Mark got a little defensive because Debbie often insinuated that he had an easy job. When they argued about money, she would say things like, "Well maybe if you actually worked everyday, you wouldn't have money problems."

Mark said, "Deb, you know if I cut out of the office during the day, it only means that I have to catch up on my work at night."

"Then it looks like we both have our work cut out for us tonight. I have to head home early because I have to start getting my stuff together for the district meeting next week, and we have a cluster meeting tomorrow morning."

The group of sales reps who shared the same territory was referred to as a cluster. Inhaber-Taft required them to meet once a month to develop their routing schedules for the next month and to discuss business. They typically met more often to coordinate new sales campaigns and other marketing initiatives.

Mark looked disappointed and he said, "I thought you were going to stay tonight and leave for work in the morning from here."

Debbie hugged Mark and said, "Well, if we both get some work done tonight, then we won't have as much work to do this weekend."

"That's true. Even better, let's try to finish all of it tonight, and then we can just play all weekend."

"That's a great idea. Hey, why don't you fire up the grill so we can get this chicken going soon."

"Sure. In fact, I'll light the charcoal right now." Mark didn't have a gas grill. He liked a charbroiled taste to his food. He was back a minute later and walked up behind Debbie and put his arms around her waist. Debbie sighed and leaned into him.

"I'm sorry about teasing you earlier," Mark whispered in her ear.

She knew he was referring to his comment about Gretchen. "It's OK."

"No, it's not because I know you have a difficult time with trust and I shouldn't make it more difficult for you by teasing you."

Debbie turned around to face him. "I love you Mark."

"I know. I love you too." They kissed deeply until Harry interrupted them with a whimper, as if he was jealous. Mark laughed and said, "OK Harry. I love you too. Come on. Let's go outside."

Thirty minutes later, Debbie and Mark were about to sit down at the kitchen table to eat dinner. Instead of turning on the harsh overhead light, Mark lit his antique oil lamps and placed one on the kitchen table. He put the other one on the mantle of the fireplace. Debbie poured the wine. She was happy Mark didn't overindulge in drinking. One glass of wine or beer and he stopped. Her ex-husband Bernard was an alcoholic, or as Bernard phrased it, he "liked to drink." Bernard had gotten violent more than once, when Debbie accused him of being an alcoholic. Ironically, he was drunk on those occasions.

Mark cut the last two bites of his chicken and said, "Alright Harry. Here's your portion." Harry had been sitting at the tableside waiting patiently for this moment. Mark said it was "good bonding" to let Harry have a taste of the meal when they were finished.

Debbie began to fill the dishpan with hot water and soap. Mark came up behind her and whispered through her hair, "Great meal, Deb."

She loved the warm feeling of his breath in her hair. She turned toward him and kissed him. "I wish I didn't have to go home to do paperwork."

"Yeah, I wish you were staying Deb." He held her close to him and said, "Maybe we can take a little nap before you leave." He kissed her and his lips surrounded her mouth and she was turned on by the warm wetness of his touch. They both knew that "taking a nap" would happen only after they made love.

She slowly pulled back from him and looked into his eyes. "Oh Mark, I wish we could. But I'm already tired and I have to drive almost an hour to get home and then . . ."

Mark interrupted her, "I know Deb. It's OK. We'll have plenty of naps this weekend."

Debbie smiled and Mark asked, "Why don't you let me wash the dishes?"

"No. I don't mind. It'll just take a couple of minutes."

"Are you sure?"

"Yeah. It's no problem."

Mark went outside again with Harry and Debbie quickly finished up. Then she went out to her car and retrieved a duffle bag, which was packed for the weekend. It would be one less item to bring along with her when she returned to the cabin on Friday night. She was careful to place the duffle bag on a corner chair. Mark wasn't a great housekeeper so the wood floor was dusty, and Debbie never knew when she might come across an exotic bug that crept into the cabin from the heavily wooded surroundings. Occasionally a mouse found its way inside but Harry's scent managed to deter their regular visits. Debbie cleaned the kitchen and the bathroom on occasion. If she complained about it being dirty, Mark would say, "So clean it." But Debbie was at least assertive about that. She kept her own townhouse clean and told Mark she would clean up the rest of his place if and when they got married, otherwise, it was his job.

Debbie opened the passenger side of her Ford Taurus and put her pocketbook and briefcase on the seat. She always brought her computer with her in case she had a few minutes to check email or to do some work. She walked around to the front of the cabin, which faced the river. Mark and Harry were sitting on the fishing pier. Debbie walked swiftly to the top of the stairs leading down to the pier. She held the loose railing, as she carefully descended the shaky, wooden steps.

She called out to them, "OK, guys. It's time to go." Harry jumped up and ran over to her with his tail wagging. She rubbed his ears and kissed him on the snout. "I know you don't want to leave, but we have to go buddy." Debbie somehow felt homesick whenever she left Mark and his cabin in the woods. She was beginning to feel like she belonged there with him.

Mark ran his hand through Debbie's hair and their eyes met. They loved each other deeply, but Debbie was still not certain that Mark felt the same way about her. She had suffered through a failed marriage to Bernard and a six-month relationship after her divorce that ended because she found out the guy was cheating on her.

Harry saw a squirrel and bounded up the stairs. The whole pier shook from his weight. "I'll see you tomorrow night," Mark said softly.

Debbie said flirtatiously, "We can 'tap a nap' after dinner." Mark smiled.

When they reached the top of the stairs, Debbie called out, "Come on Harry. Let's go." Harry came running out of the woods. He had a tennis ball in his mouth and Mark tried to free it from the grip of his teeth. "Come on Harry. Let me throw it." He finally loosened his hold and Mark grabbed the ball. Harry jumped back a couple of feet in anticipation and watched Mark wind up the pitch. He followed the direction of the ball as it sailed through the air and landed on the hill of the driveway. He ran and pounced on the spot where the ball landed, but he had to make a quick turn to his right to chase the ball as it bobbed down the stony driveway.

Mark and Debbie walked over to her car. Harry ran up behind them and dropped the ball at Mark's feet.

"No Harry. That's enough. We have to get going." Debbie opened the door to the back seat and Harry jumped in. He was already pacing in the back seat when Debbie got into the driver's side and shut the door. She pulled her seatbelt around her and began to drive up the steep grade of the driveway. Through the sound of crunching stones beneath her wheels and Harry yelping, she heard Mark shout, "Call me when you get home."

She yelled out of the car window, "I will."

From Route 40, Debbie made a right onto the exit for I-95 North. Suddenly she said out loud, "Oh shoot, I have to stop at Wilmington Pharmacy for my prescription."

On the drive home, Debbie started to think about what her friends had said when she told them Mark was frequently driving up to his old girlfriend's house to fix her computer. The consensus among her friends was that she better be careful. Their comments varied from, "Sounds like he's not over her" to "Don't be naïve Deb. He's not going up there to fix her computer."

About forty-five minutes later, Debbie passed Wilmington Pharmacy. "Oh no!" She said out loud when she realized she had passed it. She pulled into a nearby parking lot and turned her car around.

As she headed toward the pharmacy in the back of the store, she stopped to peruse the jewelry case. It was a U-shaped, deli-style glass case. It was filled with necklaces of only slightly better quality than the fake strands of pearls that hung from flimsy cardboard on racks that dotted the countertop. Debbie always gave a cursory glance at the selection, just in case she spotted something that looked decent enough to wear.

Unlike most pharmaceutical reps, Debbie didn't buy jewelry, clothes or watches according to the "in" label or store. She often bought jewelry from consignment shops or the hospital gift shops that were run by the ladies' auxiliaries. Whenever she called on physicians in the medical buildings of hospitals, she made her rounds to the hospital coffee shop, the restroom, and finally the gift shop. She was always pleasantly surprised when she discovered something that looked classy but cost only a few dollars. She got a kick out of it when one of the reps complimented a necklace or a pair of earrings that she bought there. She was always prepared for their next question, "Where did you get it?" Debbie knew they would be appalled to learn the truth, so she lied and said, "Oh, my aunt gave it to me." But if she was in a cocky mood, she would touch the necklace or an earring and say, "Oh, it's from an old boyfriend." The reps always liked that answer better and usually gave her a knowing smile and a wink.

During her first year in pharmaceutical sales, Debbie became aware of the intense peer pressure to "keep up with the Joneses." All of the reps--male and female--bragged about shopping at the right stores, buying the right brands, and living in the right neighborhoods. The women wore the latest Yurman and Tiffany necklaces, rings and bracelets. The watches were Tag Heuer. Debbie wore a Swiss Army watch that Mark bought her for her birthday.

She credited her mother with raising daughters who were not material girls. Her mother taught them that good taste did not necessarily correlate to the amount of money spent. However there were wardrobe staples, like a winter coat or a suit, that were worth spending a fair amount of money on.

When Debbie was still a secretary at Inhaber-Taft, she went to night school to get her Bachelors Degree because she wanted to go into pharmaceutical sales. She read an article in a business magazine that suggested that if a woman wanted to move up the corporate ladder, she should dress for the job she wants — not for the job she has. She decided to follow the advice so she took some money out of her savings and went on a shopping spree. At that time, Joseph A. Banks was one of *the* stores where corporate women shopped. Debbie felt a little intimidated when she entered the store. After all, she was still a secretary who wore skirts and blouses to work everyday.

In the 1980s and early 1990s, women in pharmaceutical sales and marketing wore conservative traditional clothing. They wore navy blue or gray suits in the winter and beige or khaki suits in the summer. Once a week they would switch it up with a classically plain, or subtle print dress. A woman's suit consisted of a skirt and jacket — pants were not in style then. Debbie bought half a dozen suits, two dresses, and a navy blue gabardine raincoat. She thought of it as an investment in her potential career.

During her tenure in sales, the work attire for corporate women progressed to bright colors with feminine flourishes. Professional women decided they didn't have to wear the same colors as their male counterparts.

Eventually the attire regressed to the pre-feminist era. By 1996, skirts were replaced by tight pants and jackets with low cut blouses. Debbie continued to wear her skirts and jackets. She had a nice figure but she refused to flaunt it. She had been a secretary during the years when men got away with sexual harassment. She wanted to be a successful sales rep because of her brains and personality — not because she gave the doctors an eyeful of cleavage.

Debbie didn't spot anything of interest at the jewelry counter, so she continued on to the pharmacy. She looked at the signs over the windows at the pharmacy in the back of the store: "Drop Off," "Pick Up" and "Consultation." She grinned and thought cynically, "Oh yeah, the *consultation*. Is that the one they advertise on television where the well-groomed, caring, female pharmacist talks quietly and listens intently to the customer? She then earnestly describes how the medicine works and informs the customer about possible side effects."

In the real world, the scene Debbie saw over and over again when she called on pharmacies was an overweight male pharmacist in his 50's, with greasy clumps of hair thrust across an oily forehead. He stood in front of his computer screen and plucked away at the keyboard. He angrily answered the pharmacy tech, when she informed him that a customer wanted to talk to him, "Tell her I don't have time. I've got about twenty prescriptions to fill. Just find out what she wants." Then the pharmacy tech returned to the *consultation* window and said, "The Pharmacist is really busy now." At that point, the customer sheepishly responded, "Oh, OK, never mind then. I'll just call my doctor's office tomorrow." Then the pharmacy tech asked, "Ma'am, can you sign here to indicate that we addressed your concerns?" And the customer signed the form.

Debbie walked over to the "Pick Up" window. There was a man waiting in line in front of her. She looked at the back of his head. He was balding, with a wiry patch of hair that circled around his head. He was about six feet tall and wore a leather flight jacket. By now, Debbie was enjoying her sarcastic mood. She thought, "There's two types of guys who wear flight jackets — pilots like Mark, and guys who like the way the bulky leather hides their fat stomachs. This one is the later." She noticed he tapped his leg impatiently with the box in his hand. She tried to see what was in the box.

"Condoms?" she mused. Just then he moved one of his fingers and she could read "ACE bandages" written on the side.

She looked up after he sighed with frustration when the pharmacy tech left the "Pick Up" window and walked over to the pharmacist. They seemed to be conferring on something, as the pharmacist stared into the computer screen. When they finished, the tech walked back to the window. The man in front of Debbie placed the box of ACE bandages on the counter. In the meantime, the pharmacist looked up and did a double-take.

"Hi Dr. Friedman."

The man in front of Debbie said, "Hi John. How are you?"

"Good. Hey, as long as you're here Dr. Friedman, my records show that your wife is due for a refill on her MELAVOX prescription. Do you want that now?"

Dr. Friedman was growing increasingly irritable because his arm was in pain. Without thinking he responded, "No, no, I don't need that *now*." He cringed as soon as he heard the phrase come out of his mouth and his stomach flipped. But he recovered quickly and said, "I mean, sure, yeah. I might as well pick it up for her while I'm here."

The Pharmacist asked, "That's the 25 mg strength of MELAVOX?

"Yes. MELAVOX 25 mg."

"OK then, just give me a minute to fill that."

Dr. Friedman was startled when he heard, "MELAVOX . . . that's nice to hear." He knew the voice was familiar and he turned around.

"Hi Dr. Friedman." Debbie had a big smile on her face.

"Oh, Hi Debbie. How are you?"

"Good, I'm happy to hear that you're picking up MELAVOX."

Dr. Friedman did his best to appear nonchalant. He said, "Yeah, Lee's been taking MELAVOX for her osteoarthritis."

"That's great! I mean, I'm sorry that she has osteoarthritis, but I'm happy that MELAVOX is helping."

The pharmacy tech interrupted, "Dr. Friedman. . ."

Dr. Friedman turned and reached up with his right arm to take the little white bag from her hand. He stopped short when pain gripped his arm and he let out a sound like a whimper.

"Are you alright?" Debbie and the Pharmacy Tech asked simultaneously.

His face flushed to a crimson shade. Debbie could see that he was flustered and it made her uncomfortable. She had never seen him like this. She didn't even think he was capable of being embarrassed because of his tremendous ego.

Dr. Friedman thought he'd better make light of it. He said "Sure, I'm fine. It's just my tennis elbow acting up again. I must be getting too old for tennis."

"That must be it," Debbie teased.

Dr. Friedman was one of those doctors the pharmaceutical sales reps referred to as "rep friendly." He challenged them about their products, but he also joked around with them. And sales reps generally liked any doctor who took the time to talk with them. Some physicians didn't want to be bothered with salespeople. They resented the interruptions of so many pharma sales reps streaming through their offices everyday. But they usually endured them as a necessary evil in order to get free samples of drugs for their patients.

The "rep friendly" physicians typically engaged in conversation on a more personal level. It was a welcome break from their sick and complaining patients. Everyone knew that Dr. Friedman played tennis, so his explanation of the pain in his arm was perfectly viable.

Debbie said, "I guess the ACE bandage helps, but you should take a MELAVOX 75 mg for the acute pain."

Dr. Friedman said, "The bandage helps to stabilize the elbow, and you're right about the MELAVOX." Suddenly, he thought about the meeting he just had with Detective Healy. Nothing had come up about which drugs Lee was taking, but he knew the detective would address that eventually. Dr. Friedman decided to add something just in case Debbie was ever questioned about this conversation. He said, "You know, Michael Poong and the other Inhaber reps continue to assure me that I can prescribe MELAVOX 75 mg for chronic therapy."

"Well, I disagree with them." She was never a shrinking violet when she knew she was right. And she knew Dr. Friedman was probably just trying to rattle her. He enjoyed controversy.

Debbie smiled and said demurely, "Dr. Friedman, I've reminded you many times that the prescribing information for MELAVOX states that only the 25 mg dose can be taken as long term therapy. The 75 mg dose is only for .

. ." She stopped suddenly because she was momentarily embarrassed by her formal, scripted response. After all, this was just a chance encounter not a sales call.

Fortunately, Dr. Friedman broke the silence. "Well, you guys need to get your story straight," he said sternly and then smiled.

Debbie grinned and thought, "Now he sounds like himself — sarcastic and slightly antagonistic." She let him have the last word.

Dr. Friedman reached up again to take the bag from the pharmacy tech. This time he used his left arm. He turned back to Debbie and said, "I have to go. Have a nice night."

"You too, Dr. Friedman."

He was already walking away when Debbie added, "Tell Lee I said hello."

He turned around and grinned and said, "I will."

Debbie stepped up to the counter.

The tech asked, "Can I help you?"

Debbie waited a moment to respond. She was afraid that Dr. Friedman might still be within earshot. Then she thought, "I don't have to say the name of the drug." She said, "I called in a prescription."

"What's the last name?"

"Kaminski."

The pharmacy tech walked over to the shelves behind the counter and rifled through the white bags in the "K" section.

"Kaminski. Here it is." She returned to the cash register where she slipped a paper in front of Debbie and said, "Sign here please."

Debbie signed off on the agreement that she had received a complete consultation about the product, which wasn't at all true, but it saved everyone a lot of time. The tech handed her the little white bag and said, "Your insurance covers 100% of your prescription."

Debbie took the bag and said, "Thanks." She turned and walked slowly to the front of the store and thought, "I hope Dr. Friedman is gone." If she bumped into him again, she knew he would be bold enough to ask what her prescription was for. She really didn't want to tell him that she had to take FLAGIT for a urinary tract infection. Debbie was relieved when she saw no sign of him. "Oh, good" she thought, "He's gone."

Out in the parking lot, Dr. Friedman slammed his car door shut and thought, "Debbie Kaminski." He shook his head and said out loud, "I don't believe it. Of all the people to run into . . . a goddamn sales rep. And a MELAVOX rep at that!" It hadn't even crossed his mind that he might run into someone he knew.

He thought, ". . . and when she said, 'Tell Lee I said hi,' what else could I have said? I think it was perfectly natural that I didn't launch into any details about how Lee is missing." He shook his head and snickered when he realized he had even managed to convince himself that Lee was missing. He thought, "Thank God I used the present tense when I talked about Lee. I have to be really careful about that."

Then he wondered how Debbie would remember their conversation tonight, once she found out Lee was missing. He worried because she had seen him wince in pain because of his arm. He thought, "And she saw the ACE bandages. Will she wonder why I didn't tell her that Lee was missing?"

He shifted his car into reverse and backed out of the parking space. He started to drive out of the parking lot when suddenly he hit the brakes. He said out loud, "Oh shit!" He remembered when the Pharmacist asked him if he wanted the MELAVOX script for Lee, he said, 'No. I don't need that *now*.'" It was bad enough that the pharmacist and the tech heard him; but they might not give it another thought. He shook his head in despair, "Unfortunately, Debbie is the type who would remember something like that if she's questioned by the police. How could I be so careless?"

The person in the car in back of him beeped the horn. The sudden noise made his heart skip a beat. He looked in his rearview mirror and waved apologetically.

By the time he got home from the pharmacy, Dr. Friedman was worrying obsessively, "What am I saying . . . *if* she's questioned by the police about running into me at the pharmacy tonight. . . it's more like *when*. Goddamn it! I know she'll remember the details of what I said." He sank down into a chair and rubbed his mouth and chin. He was physically and mentally drained. "Maybe I'm being too paranoid. I need a drink." He stood up and thought, "I just hope they find Lee's body soon. At least that will put everything in motion. The anticipation is killing me."

He knew that once she was found, the missing person investigation would be converted into a criminal investigation. But he was confident that it would end quickly; as soon as the Medical Examiner did an autopsy and found that Lee died from a MELAVOX-induced heart attack. He thought, "Then I'll have the evidence I need to file a lawsuit against Inhaber-Taft. And it will all be over after that."

PART II

Working Smart versus Working Hard

Chapter 12: The 80/20 Rule

Friday morning, March 11

BLAIRE SHIMMIED OUT of her satin pajamas and shivered with cold as she fastened the straps of her running bra. She pulled a turtleneck over her head and stepped into her microfiber pants. She sat on the edge of the bed to pull on her socks and shoes. When she bent over to tie the laces, her husband Steven said, "Good morning Blaire," as he got out of bed to initiate similar preparations for himself.

It was 5:15 a.m. and in ten minutes they would start their morning run. Their dog, a black Lab named Parker, stretched across the still-warm sheets and yawned. Blaire and Steven giggled at him as they were about to pass each other at the end of the bed. They stopped short and gave each other a quick kiss.

In minutes, all three of them were struggling for space as they negotiated the stairs to the foyer. Steven took the house keys and Parker's retractable leash. It was 5:25 when Blaire caught up with Steven and Parker at the end of the driveway. They started out at a comfortable warm-up pace and gradually increased their speed as Blaire moved to the front of the pack.

Narberth was a quiet neighborhood adorned with large Victorian houses, most of which had long ago been subdivided into twin homes. The single homes, constructed in either classic Dutch or colonial American architecture, were hidden behind neatly trimmed hedges. The residents consisted of either 30-something professionals or mixed income, middle-aged couples. Blaire's neighbors in the twin next door were Carol, a social worker at a Presbyterian Hospital in Philadelphia, and her husband George, a tenured history professor at Villanova University.

When Blaire met Steven, she was working as a physical therapist for the University of Pennsylvania Health Care System. She told him, "I love my job. My patients mean everything to me. Maybe someday I'll get married and have children, but I'll always want to have my career."

Blaire and her friends knew this was what every young, professional guy wanted to hear. They didn't want a woman who had marriage and family at the top of her list of priorities. They wanted a woman who was dedicated to her career and didn't complain about work. They wanted marriage and kids, and wives who continued to work and bring home good salaries. It lifted some of the financial burden from them. These young men were liberated from the need to be the sole provider for the sake of their egos. They wanted a comfortable lifestyle as much as the women did. It was a cultural shift that embraced dual careers and day care.

But Blaire, like some of her closest friends, planned to stay home and provide the childcare herself — not because of altruistic, maternal instincts, but because it was the path to follow to transition into early retirement. And her husband would be the last to know.

By the time Blaire and Steven were married, a couple of her friends from college were working as pharmaceutical sales reps. After learning about their salaries and bonuses, Blaire decided to apply to some of the top pharmaceutical companies. She thought, "Why not? I've always been interested in science and healthcare, so it's a natural fit. I can maintain my PT license working part time on the weekend."

About six months later, Blaire finally got the call. A woman from the Human Resources Department of Inhaber-Taft asked Blaire to call the next day so she could schedule an interview.

Blaire was interviewed at a time when there was no regional or national expansion of the sales force going on and that made the interview process quite different. The first set of interviews was conducted at the main office of Inhaber-Taft. Blaire was interviewed first by a district manager, next by a sales trainer, and finally by an executive professional representative. She successively advanced after that series, so she was scheduled for a "day in the field" with a professional representative. This allowed her to observe first-hand all of the responsibilities of a sales rep during a typical day. Later, the sales trainer questioned the rep, whom Blaire spent the day with, to get her feedback about Blaire's comfort level and whether or not she seemed to be a good fit for the job.

Finally, Blaire was interviewed by Michael Poong, because he was the district manager with a job opening.

Blaire had said in her interviews that she could not relocate. She lied and said her husband was a junior partner at his law firm in Delaware County, Pennsylvania. They couldn't relocate because of his career. In truth, he was doing well with the firm, but he had not yet reached a junior partner level.

Michael Poong liked Blaire immediately and thought she had the intelligence, personality, and good looks to be a successful pharmaceutical sales representative. As a physical therapist in the Penn Health System, Blaire had a large network of relationships with Orthopedic Surgeons (Orthopods) who practiced in Philadelphia. However, Michael's district did not include Philadelphia and, even if it did, Blaire could not be assigned a Philadelphia territory because she did not have an MBA.

Philadelphia and the surrounding counties were in close proximity to the main office of Inhaber-Taft. These territories were reserved for MBA's, who were assigned sales territories that were considered prime real estate — close to the main office in Delaware County and therefore, Inhaber-Taft's influential network.

The 1980s and 90s were the decades of the MBA and the term YUPPIE had seeded itself into corporate culture. In the pharmaceutical industry, an MBA no longer just referred to the degree, it labeled a person as being on the fast track of a career that meant one promotion after another — barring any egregious behavior. And, importantly, the degree could not be from just any school. Industry leaders like Inhaber-Taft selected candidates from the top ten graduate schools in the country. Likewise, an MBA considered only the top 50 companies on the Fortune 500 list, as potential employers. They were elitists who were bred for each other. After several grueling interviews, only the "cream of the crop" were chosen. Impressive transcripts, a poised manner, articulate speech, and an air of confidence were a must. Once assured of each other's good breeding, the company and the candidate hired each other.

The MBA was revered by corporate America, and they knew it. Whereas employees of more humble beginnings had great expectations of themselves, the MBA had great expectations of their employer. And Inhaber-Taft was one of the players who consistently rewarded their performance by advancing their careers and increasing their salaries. They were placed into field sales for a "tour of duty." The length of the "tour" was six to ten months in the field. That was considered enough time for an MBA to get to know what makes physicians tick and how they can be sold on a product.

After they were promoted "inside" to a position within the Marketing Department, the pattern continued. Every six to ten months, they were promoted again . . . and again, hence the term "fast trackers." By the time they reached their late 30's, some had moved on for a better offer at another pharmaceutical company, or they had advanced through the pyramid of the corporate hierarchy. At that point, they assessed whether or not they were "tapped out" at the company. The competition stiffened as the pyramid narrowed into marketing and sales executive management, but the number of players swelled. If a Vice President position was not perceived as a near term option, most of them jumped ship and spent the rest of their careers bouncing from one pharmaceutical company to another, usually within the same stratosphere. A few stayed and either advanced to the precious few positions at the top, or they took an early and comfortable retirement. After that, they became consultants.

Michael Poong explained to Blaire why she was not eligible for a Philadelphia territory. He convinced her that she could easily manage the twenty-minute commute from Delaware County, Pennsylvania to New Castle County, Delaware. However, the territory encompassed the entire state of Delaware, and she would have to drive almost two hours to the southern end of the state. But, he assured her, she only had to do this a couple of times each month. Michael promised Blaire that once she achieved consistently outstanding sales performance, he would see to it that she was transferred to the Philadelphia territory. Blaire accepted the job offer. In truth, Michael knew that Blaire would never get a Philadelphia territory, but he had sized her up as a "short-timer" in field sales. Besides, in another year or so, Michael planned to be back inside — promoted to a Marketing position.

During her first month on the job, Blaire was ready to quit every other day. She hated it. She was constantly getting lost while trying to find the best route to the physicians' offices in her territory. The year was 1995, and consumer-friendly global positioning systems were not standard issue in company cars. Most days she encountered one or two near-miss accidents because she had to slow the car down to a crawl as she scanned addresses on houses and office buildings. She forgot about the drivers behind her, until they beeped loudly and made obscene hand gestures.

She was bogged down with so much paperwork and computer work that she could only manage to work a couple of hours every other Saturday — just enough to maintain her PT license. But Blaire formed an unlikely alliance with Ken Welder and Frank Panini, two of the few remaining dinosaurs — both over 55 years old — in field sales. (In the mid-90s, pharmaceutical companies were quietly selecting only young, good-looking salespeople — most of whom were women and recent college graduates. This allowed companies to fulfill their corporate Affirmative Action quotas within the sales division. And it was the perfect fit since most doctors were males, who were more likely to spend a few minutes talking to a beautiful, young woman. Of course a small percentage of token white men were hired. But if a person was overweight or over 35, he or she would not get past the first in-person screening interview.

In the era when Ken, Frank and their peers started, the job entailed very little paperwork. There were no cell phones, no laptop computers, and only one sales rep covering a large territory. The end result was no accountability on the part of the reps for how they spent their time. Back in the day, being a pharmaceutical sales rep was the sweetest job an educated salesman could hope for. They were called pharmaceutical detail men--not salesmen. The products basically sold themselves based on the pristine reputations of the stodgy companies who manufactured them. The detail men simply provided physicians with information — or details — about the products.

Until the late 1970s, the industry had a male only, good-ole-boy sales force. They were expected to wear a nice suit and a smile, tell a good joke — preferably a dirty one — and spend a few minutes flirting with the nurses and the gals at the front desk.

But no matter how dramatically times changed, some people stayed the same. Ken Welder, Frank Panini, and others sought out new reps that they deemed to be like-minded. They wanted to teach them how to play the game, their way. This provided some assurance that the new reps could not threaten their positions by over-achieving and out-performing them. It was thrilling for reps like Ken to divulge their secrets of how to beat the system.

But over the years, Ken got careless and started telling everybody his tricks. It brought him the attention and shocked reactions that he hoped for. One of Ken's catch phrases was "FIDO," which was an acronym for: "Fuck it, drive on." This meant if you drive to an office and you can't find a parking space, or if the office is in a bad neighborhood and you're just not in the mood to deal with it, then you should just say to yourself, "Fuck it" and drive on. The surprising part was that Ken would still record it as a sales call. After all, the way he saw it, he *was* at the office.

Ken had informed Blaire that she really only had to work 3 days a week. He told her, "Look, once you know your territory and your docs, you can meet your daily sales quota by noon on most days, or by 2:00 if you have to bring lunch to an office. So just work until 5:00 or 5:30 a couple of days a week so you can double up on the calls you make."

Blaire was inclined to distrust Ken. In her opinion, he was a tacky, old-school salesman. But she was curious, so she had to ask, "How can I possibly talk to 15 or 16 physicians in one day?"

Ken had seen Blaire's type a hundred times before — the attractive young woman, worldly beyond her years, trying to appear naïve. But, ever the charmer, Ken played along and said, "You'll learn very quickly the only part of sales training you need to remember is the science behind your products. You can toss out all the other horseshit about call planning, physician categories, and market analysis."

Blaire gave him a genuine smile. She began to feel relieved and saw a light at the end of the tunnel.

Ken continued, "In reality, the docs are too busy to talk to all the reps that hound their offices everyday. Once you've called on them for a while, they really don't want to see you more than once a month. Any more than that and you'll just piss them off by taking up their time. Now of course your manager and those ivory tower folks in marketing preach a lot of bullshit about call frequency and they just keep upping the ante. Now they want us to see our top writers every two weeks! But trust me, once you've established yourself, the docs only want to see you if you have a new product or if you get a new indication — something like that. If you don't bother them all the time, then they're happy to see you. When I run in to see the docs every 4 to 5 weeks, they're happy to bullshit for a couple of minutes in between patients."

Blaire couldn't believe what she was hearing; but considering the source, she wasn't shocked that Ken would handle the job this way. But still, something wasn't adding up. Blaire thought to herself, "If he's only calling on physicians every 4 to 5 weeks, he may not even be working 3 days a week. He may only be working a couple days a month!" She wasn't sure if she wanted to know more. She spoke hesitantly when she asked, "You said something about working 3 days a week by calling on 16 or so physicians in a day — to double up on calls. But are you really *talking* to those physicians?"

Ken gave her a devious grin and said in a quiet voice, "What do you think?"

Blaire asked, "But what about samples? How do you keep samples well stocked if you're only going in every 4 to 5 weeks?"

Ken said, "Well that's one advantage of Inhaber having 9 goddamn reps in a territory. Chances are there's always a rep re-stocking samples in any given doc's office every week. And hell, the offices call us if they run out of samples."

Blaire smiled and shook her head in frustration ". . . ah . . . I . . don't know Ken."

Ken said, "Look, since you brought up samples, the advantage of hauling all these goddamn samples around is that they provide you with a paper trail. You have to create a paper trail to cover your ass. So for your call reporting, you can easily make up some bullshit about what you and the doc talked about. As far as samples, you have to get the doc to sign your paperwork for samples. But you can always hand the signature form to a nurse or a receptionist and ask them to grab the doc for a signature in between patients. Now, not every office will need samples everyday, so you just have to collect about 3 or 4 signature forms per day, on average. Put the actual date on half of the sample signature forms, and the next day's date on the other half. That way, you just "worked" two days instead of one. Take it easy the next day and make enough sales calls for one day. Again, be sure to adjust the date on the sample sheets, because by now you're up to Day 3 on paper. Finally, on the third day, you make two days' worth of sample drops and . . ."

Blaire smiled and interrupted him, ". . . and be sure to adjust the dates."

Ken sat back in his chair and sighed. "You got it Blaire. Then, boom, you're done for the week and you get a four day weekend — not bad huh?"

Blaire laughed and said, "Kenny, you're a trip." She didn't confirm or deny that she would give it a try. She took it with a grain of salt and figured she would talk to some of the other reps she had become friendly with, to find out if Ken suggested the same thing to them. She didn't think Ken was trying to sabotage her career, but she wanted to find out from the friends she could trust, if they would dare to do what Ken suggested.

In a cautionary tone, Ken said, "Now naturally when you're first starting, you have to call on every doc a few times, until they get used to seeing you and they can connect you with your products — or at least one of your products. So, in your case, with your experience as a Physical Therapist, they'll easily connect you with MELAVOX. And make sure you tell them you're a PT because that'll give you more credibility."

Blaire smiled. Ken continued, "And when a good looking woman like yourself calls on a doc for the first time, he'll definitely talk to you."

Blaire took the compliment graciously, but it annoyed her that good ole boys like Ken always had to diminish a woman by assessing her value based on her looks.

Ken continued, "When the docs first meet you, they want to size you up and find out a little bit about you. They'll even listen to your spiel the first couple of times to find out if you really know your shit about your products and your competition. And you'll always have docs like Friedman who like to bust your balls and tell you how lousy your drug is. But, if they like you, and your company gives them enough perks, they'll write for your drug. Hell, even if they hate you and they get enough money and travel from your company, they'll write for your drug." Ken laughed. He was apparently enjoying listening to himself.

Blaire had a partronizing grin on her face. She wasn't sure if she hated Ken and his antiquated macho attitude and, for that matter, the whole idea of being a sales rep. She tried to hide her emotions as she asked, "If what you're saying is true, it sounds like it doesn't even matter if a drug is any good."

Ken said, "Look, Inhaber-Taft is a great company with great products. But all these companies have good drugs. How else can they afford to have so many sales reps running around? All this stuff they tell you in sales training about market research that shows the docs write based on efficacy and tolerability of the drug and the features and benefits . . . that's true to a point. I mean a doc isn't going to risk a lawsuit or his reputation and write for a crappy drug. But there really aren't any crappy drugs out there. Well, except for the generics that are starting to pop up. Anyway, my point is, you have nothing to worry about because Inhaber-Taft now has the latest breakthrough, blockbuster drug on the market and that's MELAVOX. All the docs are going to write for it, left and right. Forget about early adopters and the usual MBA bullshit about product life cycle. I'm telling you *all* the docs are going to write for it because the specialists have backed it up and managed to make even the family docs comfortable with writing for it. And let's face it, your MELAVOX numbers will go through the roof because, as I said, the docs will give you more credibility once they find out you're a PT, selling a drug for osteoarthritis."

Blaire smiled, even though she was puzzled by the way Ken contradicted himself. It almost made her head spin; and then she thought to herself, "Maybe that's what makes him a good salesman."

For his part, Ken could see he was winning her over and he grinned as he shook Blaire's hand, as if welcoming her into a secret society.

Then, there was Frank Panini's advice. Frank worked a territory in Baltimore, which was included in the same district as Blaire's territory. They both reported to Michael Poong and attended his district meetings at the end of each quarter. After the first day of her first district meeting, Frank Panini sat down with Blaire in the lobby of the hotel where the meeting was being held.

Frank asked Blaire, "What's your background? Did you study marketing in college?"

Blaire said, "No. I'm a licensed physical therapist."

Frank was taken aback. He straightened his posture and raised his eyebrows. For a second, Blaire wasn't sure if he thought this was good or bad. Then Frank smiled and said, "Well, that's great. So you're familiar with medical terminology and you probably had an easy time with the science included in sales training."

Blaire smiled, "Yeah. I already knew a lot of the stuff. I mean, the anatomy and physiology. But most of the diseases were new to me because my background is concentrated in sports injuries and trauma."

Frank nodded pensively. Blaire had the feeling that he was making an assessment of her potential for success.

Finally he said, "Well I'm sure you'll do a great job selling MELAVOX."

Blaire said, "I hope so. It shouldn't be too difficult based on what Kenny Welder told me."

Frank knew immediately that she was of the same ilk. "She'll do alright," he thought. He didn't even have to ask what Ken had said. But he couldn't let Ken have the last word. He looked at his watch and then said, "If you have a couple of minutes, I'll give you some quick and dirty pointers about the marketing piece."

Blaire looked at her watch. They had about forty-five minutes before they had to meet in the lobby to go out to dinner with the rest of their district team. Blaire said, "Sure. We have plenty of time before dinner."

Frank leaned forward in his chair and rested his elbows on his knees and then slowly interlocked his fingers. He tried to look casual, but there was a current of palpable excitement surrounding him, like someone who was about to share salacious gossip. Blaire had a sense of déjà vu. It was because Ken Welder had behaved exactly the same way, when he was about to tell her the scoop about how the job *really* gets done.

Blaire mimicked Frank's body language and listened eagerly.

Frank said, "You can work hard or you can work smart. You're going to have a lot of demands on your time, from meeting your daily quota to scheduling lunches and dinners — not to mention all the goddamn paperwork. So, you have to learn how to work smart."

Blaire shook her head in demure agreement and uttered, "OK."

Frank continued, "Now first of all, you have to practice the 80/20 rule. Twenty percent of your docs will account for eighty percent of your business. So you have to spend your time on the twenty percent. You'll get to know the offices that are worth going to because the doc is a 'big writer,' which means he writes a lot of scripts for your products. Just look at the sales reports you receive from the main office. Take the time to study them and find out which docs are using which products — and not just Inhaber-Taft products but your competitors too. And for a new drug like MELAVOX, look at the names of the docs who are classified as 'early adopter' physicians. They're smart, enthusiastic, and usually young docs. And they're well liked by their patients too."

Frank straightened up for a minute in a dramatic, pregnant pause. Then he continued, "Now, most docs are motivated by the Hippocratic Oath to 'first, do no harm.' But there are other motivations."

Blaire sensed where he was headed with this and she didn't want Frank to think she was naive. She said, "Frank, I've worked with physicians for a while now as a physical therapist, so I know there are good ones and bad ones, and some who are even pretty sleazy."

Frank smiled. He was relieved that Blaire wasn't as "green" as a lot of the new reps. He said, "Alright, so you know most docs are driven by ego and money. They prescribe the newest drugs for their patients because they want to be the first to use them *and* because they get paid for it."

Blaire said, "I always wondered if that was really going on. The nurses in the hospital were always spreading rumors about that."

Frank said, "Just like the docs, there are lots of pharmaceutical companies that walk a thin line between ethical and unethical practices. Companies like Prescott-Williams, for example, get away with paying docs to write scripts — at least for a little while."

Blaire asked, "Isn't that illegal?"

"It is on the face of it, so they change the face of it."

"What do you mean?"

Frank said, "Years ago, Prescott-Williams figured out how to pay docs to write scripts for their products, and get away with it. They just call it a post-marketing clinical trial. On paper, it's structured like a legitimate clinical trial because it requires the doc to chart a patient's baseline status at the start of therapy. They have to monitor the patient's progress and clinical outcome."

So far, Blaire didn't see the problem. She said, "It sounds legitimate to me."

Frank said, "But the catch is that in reality, there is no formal post-marketing clinical trial being conducted. The doc just writes a script as he normally would and makes notes in the patient's chart, as he always does. Then he tells his file clerk to fill out the pharma company paperwork. The clerk just scribbles the patient's stats for blood pressure, cholesterol, and other labs. Then she updates the paperwork each time a dose is adjusted or some new lab results come in."

Blaire grimaced and shook her head, "Wow, so it's really the file clerk who should be paid for participating in the clinical trial."

"Sure. But the good news is, these post-marketing clinical trials don't last forever. They all seem to run for about two months after the drug is launched. That's enough time for the drug to catch on because the docs see the results of treatment and are comfortable writing for it. And once their patients feel better after taking it, they're going to ask the doc for the drug.

The bad news is that Prescott-Williams created a monster because they set a precedent by paying docs to participate in these so called clinical trials. The docs used to write for new drugs for free. Now, most of them won't write a script for a new product unless the company pays them to do it. And of course it's disguised as a clinical trial."

Blaire had seen a lot of unethical behavior among physicians in the hospitals, but the world of pharmaceuticals was new to her. She asked, "Does the FDA know about this?"

"The FDA knows about the payments to docs but as long as there's a paper trail providing evidence of a legitimate study, there's nothing they can do about it. Besides, the FDA is not a governing body so they can't legislate the sales practices used by the pharmaceutical industry."

Blaire look confused. "I thought they could make . . ."

Frank interrupted, "Ahh, see, there's an important distinction. The FDA has the authority to approve a drug so it can be brought to the marketplace. Then the FDA approves a product's labeling for specific indications. And finally, it reviews the sales and marketing materials to ensure they coincide with approved usage. But after that, there's nobody standing in that sample closet or the doctor's office but you and him — or her, when you're trying to sell them on your product."

Blaire gave Frank a knowing grin.

Frank said, "Basically the FDA is responsible for oversight once a drug hits the market. In other words, they monitor the efficacy and tolerability of drugs through truly legitimate studies and also reports of side effects that the docs are required to submit to them. The FDA can't tell a doc not to accept payment or not to accept a dinner, or a trip or anything else for that matter."

Blaire was beginning to understand. She said, "And now, there are so many companies doing it, it's become a standard of doing business. But . . . does Inhaber-Taft pay physicians to write prescriptions?"

Frank frowned and sounded disappointed, "For so many years, Inhaber-Taft never played in the mud. They always had the highest standards of ethics and integrity. But I guess some marketing genius asked the question — if you were a physician, would you write for an Inhaber-Taft drug for free, when you know you could write a script for a Prescott-Williams' drug and get paid for it?"

Blaire looked inquisitive.

Frank said, "The answer to your question is, yes. Inhaber-Taft has decided to jump on the bandwagon. I've heard a rumor that we have such a huge sales goal for MELAVOX this year that they're going to start having us promote post-marketing clinical trials by the end of the year or the beginning of next. Even though MELAVOX will have been on the market for almost a year by the time we roll out the clinical trials, it'll give us a real boost in market share. Don't forget, with a pain med, we'll easily hook the patients as much as the docs."

"Wow," Blaire said glumly. She sat motionless and thought, "What did I get myself into?"

Frank said, "The upside is that Inhaber-Taft is trying to level the playing field. Unfortunately for us, the docs already *love* companies like Prescott-Williams because, quite honestly, they also make great drugs and they've been paying the docs for years, either directly or indirectly. Wait till the docs start telling you about the lavish trips and entertainment some of these companies provide. They tell you because they want you to do the same things. Some will insinuate it, but other docs will come right out and tell you that you just can't compete."

Frank was pleased with himself. He found a bit of sadistic pleasure in hitting the new sales reps with the cold, harsh realities of pharmaceutical sales. He was fifty-six years old and planned to retire at sixty. He had been a sales rep for Inhaber-Taft for thirty-one years. He had been well compensated with regular salary increases, bonuses, stock dividends and stock options. He would surely retire a millionaire.

Frank saw new reps come and go. Most of them lasted only a couple of years in the job. The dramatic increase in the attrition rate was due to greater demands on the reps to meet and exceed their sales goals. And now there were all sorts of methods to measure performance and monitor accountability.

Some of the older reps stayed in field sales because they loved it. But others did so because they had no choice but to stay. After a certain age, they would never be considered for a promotion. They would never be hired by another pharmaceutical company. Age discrimination was pervasive in the industry but also impossible to prove.

Blaire shifted in her seat in a moment of uncomfortable silence. She thought, "I better say something or Frank will know I'm completely bummed out about the job . . . and the whole industry for that matter." She decided to change the subject. She asked, "What about all of the other physicians that are on my list — the ones who aren't in that twenty percent that you talked about? Don't I have to call on them too?"

Frank said, "It's really not worth the time to call on docs who have a small patient population because you won't get much sales volume out of their practice. And that translates into zero change in your market share. And as far as the 'late adopters,' they won't try a new product until it's been on the market for a year. So there's no point in beating them over the head with details about MELAVOX, until a year has gone by. I mean sure, there are reps who are out there every day of the week, working hard from 8:00 to 5:00 and calling on every goddamn doc on the list of 300 in the territory. But I guarantee you that for all the extra hours and effort, they're only achieving an extra 5% max in sales."

Blaire remembered what Ken Welder had said about working three days a week. Now she could see how it was possible. Still, she wasn't convinced that it was so easy to get away with it.

Frank continued, "And don't waste your time calling on docs who have written for competitive products for years. They write for the same drugs year after year until the patent expires. In those cases, you can't change their prescription writing habits. Once the patent expires, they have no choice but to try something new. Once the 'me too' drugs come out, the early adopter physicians will typically select two or three products in the same therapeutic class. These physicians are savvy about pharmaceutical company perks, so they fluctuate their writing of products according to which company has 'done something for me lately.'"

Blaire could tell Frank was getting a little bit tired of her questions. He didn't have the same energy and enthusiasm that he showed when they started talking. She looked at her watch and said, "Thanks for the scoop Frank. It's good to learn the ropes from somebody who's been around and knows the reality of the job."

Frank smiled and said, "Yeah, things were a lot different when I started. It's gotten a lot more complicated over the years. There's so much paperwork now, or should I say computer work. And competitive-man, it's a dog eat dog business now. Reps trying to stab each other in the back and . . ." He stopped himself. Suddenly, he felt a little guilty when he heard how negative he sounded. He quickly added, "But, don't get me wrong. It's a fun job and you impress me as someone who didn't just fall off the turnip truck, so I think you'll do just fine."

Like most reps, Blaire found a middle ground — a way to do the job that she could live with. One thing Frank had said, that really made sense to her, was learning how to work smart instead of working hard. By her fifth month on the job, she was able to increase her hours on the weekends, working as a physical therapist in the hospital.

After six months on the job, Blaire still worked every day, but she found out Ken Welder was right. If she made her first sales call by 8:30, and fudged her paperwork a bit, she met her daily quota by noon. Most days, though, she had to bring lunch to an office. But, even then, she finished up by 2:00. The exceptions were the days when she had to drive to Kent and Sussex Counties. Blaire had anticipated that none of those southern Delaware physicians would fit into the "80/20" rule, but as luck would have it, there were half a dozen physicians in those counties who were among her top writers. She had no choice but to drive down there every four weeks. On those days the driving time or, as the reps called it, "windshield time", was at least four hours in one day.

The rest of the month, Blaire started to sneak in a few hours during the week for her PT job. It was becoming more common for physical therapists to work per diem (per day) but healthcare workers were in such short supply that they were even hired to work by the hour. This meant that Blaire could work whatever schedule she wanted to, as a PT, and get paid by the hour. She was hired by a home care company called New Day Home Care. She worked three hours, three days a week for them.

Blaire worked at the hospitals on weekends only, because it was too risky during the week. Pharmaceutical sales reps called on hospitals and it wouldn't take long before someone spotted her there during the week. It wasn't worth the risk.

After ten months, Blaire was becoming brazen. It seemed the more she got away with, the more she "pushed the envelope." She began to squeeze her Inhaber-Taft job into three days per week. The other two days she worked full time as a PT.

On her morning runs with Steven and Parker, Blaire checked out the landscaping and the front porches of her neighbors' houses, as she sprinted past them. She didn't plan to live in Narberth for more than a couple of years. Her short term plan was to get pregnant during her second year with Inhaber-Taft. She figured it would take about that long before Steven made junior partner at his law firm. Then he would get a substantial salary increase, and with the money they had both saved by then, they could buy a small, single home in the heart of the Main Line, one of the wealthiest areas in the Delaware Valley. Blaire already knew what she planned to say to Steven when she told him she wanted to resign. "My priorities have changed, and I think the most important thing I can accomplish right now is to raise our children." She knew that Steven would be impressed by her noble shift in priorities. He would miss the contribution of her income, but with his new position, they were financially secure. Besides, Blaire would need to devote her time to the social obligations of their elevated status. She would help Steven to expand his professional network by entertaining and mingling with the right people. Blaire thought she was well suited for her eventual role as a Main Line matron.

Blaire grinned and thought, "I love Steven, but there are just some plans that a woman has to keep to herself."

Chapter 13: The Cluster Meeting

AT 8:22 A.M. ON Friday morning, Blaire was speeding along Route 1 at close to 80 miles per hour. She was on her way to meet with her counterparts for a cluster meeting. It was scheduled to begin at 8:30.

With a flick of her wrist on the steering wheel, she checked the time on her watch. She said out loud, "Why the hell do we have to meet so often? And why the hell are we meeting all the way down in Middletown?"

She shook her head in disgust as she thought, "That goddamn Grant Young better be on time for once. If his mother wasn't married to Dr. Friedman, he never would have gotten a job with Inhaber-Taft. He is such an asshole! He'll probably show up for the meeting and then go home and go back to bed."

Blaire's thoughts were interrupted when her cell phone rang. She grabbed it out of the cup holder and impatiently snapped, "Hello!"

Her mood changed instantly when she heard Molly's voice. She responded, "Oh, it was great," referring to her usual morning run with Steven and Parker. "I love this brisk weather in the morning. It's so much nicer than freezing my ass off like I do in January and February. Steven and I ran eight miles and . . ."

Molly interrupted, "Eight miles?"

"Yeah. I wanted to do more, but I knew I had to rush around to get to this cluster meeting."

Molly asked, "Did you come up with a list of physicians to target for our 'MELAVOX Blitz'?"

Blaire answered with the gentle admonition of a sorority sister, "Didn't you read the four page email from Michael Poong?"

Molly responded coyly, "No, I met up with Todd for dinner last night and we went back to his place."

Blaire didn't hide her frustration. She made a disgusted sigh and said, "Molly, I give up. When are you going to learn?"

Molly was silent with guilt.

Blaire continued, "You know Todd is still sleeping with Lyndsey! And besides, don't you think it's a bad career move to sleep with the region's specialty sales manager?"

Molly's heart sank for a minute. But then she said bravely, "He told me last night that he broke up with Lyndsey for good. He's really sick of her bullshit. And as far as my career, did you ever consider the fact that sleeping with one of the sales managers might be *good* for my career?" Now that she said it, Molly was a little worried about Blaire's reaction.

"Molly, I think you've read too many trashy novels. Real life works differently." Just then Blaire saw the exit for Middletown and slowed down a little to turn. She said, "Let's talk about it later. I'm almost there."

Molly felt a little wounded by Blaire's reaction, and she desperately wanted to win her over again. After all, Blaire was well liked by Michael Poong and the other managers. She was a good friend to have. She quickly added, "When I got home this morning I synchronized my database while I was in the shower." She looked at her laptop screen and said, "Let me just open up my emails."

Blaire asked, "Are you already there?"

"Yeah, I just ordered a bagel. Are you close yet?"

Blaire pulled into the huge parking lot of the shopping center and turned left toward Bob's Big Boy. "Yeah, I'm here and guess who just pulled up next to my car?"

"Let me guess, Grant?"

"Yeah, I guess Michael is going to work with him today. Otherwise he'd be late as usual."

Molly heard Blaire talking to Grant as she was apparently getting out of her car.

Molly spoke loudly into her cell phone, "Blaire, I'll see 'ya in a sec."

"OK," and they both ended the call.

In quick succession, three more sales reps steered their Ford Taurus company cars into the parking lot of Bob's Big Boy.

Blaire gave Grant a friendly smile and asked, "Are you working with Michael today?"

Grant shook his head and said, "No. Not today. Why?"

"Oh, I was just wondering."

By 8:43 a.m., the waitress, with the help of her manager, had moved two tables together to accommodate a total of nine people who would eventually be in their group. Two more reps arrived at 8:45.

Debbie Kaminski had been there since 8:15. She knew that a few of the reps would be on time, but most would be late as usual, so she busied herself by reading the MELAVOX target list again. When Molly arrived, they talked for a couple of minutes and then Molly sat down at the opposite end of the table.

Harrison pulled out the chair next to Debbie.

"Hey Deb, how are you today?"

"Good thanks. How about you?"

"Great. It's Friday, so how can I complain."

Debbie smiled and then waved to Rose Heinrich, who was walking toward them. Rose was one of the *first* female pharmaceutical sales reps. She worked for Prescott-Williams for six years before she joined Inhaber-Taft. This year she would celebrate twenty years of service with Inhaber-Taft, and a total of twenty-six years in sales. Rose weaved through the group and squeezed a chair in place next to Debbie.

"Hey winner! What's up?" Rose said to Debbie in her raspy, smoker's voice.

Debbie got a kick out of Rose. She was 58 years old and had back problems, kidney problems, hormonal troubles, and walked with a limp. But she was as perky, sharp, and energetic as the rest of the group. Rose had been an ICU nurse at Johns Hopkins University Medical Center for eleven years. She had injured her back seriously at least seven times during those years, while trying to maneuver patients. By the age of thirty-one, she suffered from chronic back pain and decided to listen to the suggestions of the pharmaceutical sales reps who told her she should pursue their line of work. Rose knew that the pharma sales guys were more motivated by her influence on the physicians than by actually wanting to work with her. When the residents and/or attending surgeons visited their patients in the ICU before surgery, she suggested a prophylactic antibiotic based on patient history and the other meds they were taking. And if a patient had a difficult surgical recovery and was sent back up to the ICU, it was usually Rose who suggested the appropriate meds. The doctors trusted her judgment because she never made a mistake.

The reps needed to have Rose in their corner. She was the gate keeper who allowed the sales reps she liked to schedule breakfasts, lunches, and dinners in the surgery lounge. She knew the residents were overwrought, exhausted, and under-nourished, so food always proved to be mutually beneficial. When the reps showed up with food, the residents swarmed into the surgical lounge and stuffed themselves with pizza, pasta, or sandwiches, while the sales rep told them about "X" study in "Y" journal. Through ravenous chewing, sidebar conversations and beeping pagers, the sales rep always pressed on with enthusiasm about their product. The conclusion of the rep's talk was always the same--their product was superior to the competition and the benefits outweighed the risks.

One of the residents was designated to slip out of the doctors' lounge to tell the surgical teams when the sales rep had stopped talking. Then the anesthesiologists, attending surgeons and senior residents swaggered into the lounge with their caps still tied at the nape of the neck. They were stripped down to their sweaty, blue scrubs. They were distinguished from the rest of the group by two things: a pair of surgical booties that had not yet been removed, and an air of confidence like an athlete who had just won a game and was chosen as the MVP.

They stuffed their plates with food and mumbled to each other, as the sales rep closed by asking for the business, "Will you use product 'A' as your first choice, prophylactic antibiotic in your next abdominal surgery case?" In that group setting, most physicians didn't bother to answer. But there was usually someone designated to "cover the grenade," which meant that resident had been selected to talk to the sales reps. He or she was obliged to say, "Sure,

I'll give it a try." And then ask a question that was 2 parts feigned interest and 1 part genuine, such as, "What was the dosing on that again?"

Debbie smiled at Rose and moved over to make room for her at the table.

Rose giggled and said, "Oh great, another cluster meeting, huh winner?" Everybody knew that Rose's choice of "pet" names for her counterparts was derived from her canine vernacular. Rose and her husband bred Jack Russell Terriers on the rolling green acres of their property nestled in the horse country of Maryland. Rose inherited the land, the house, and half a dozen horses from her father.

Rose's husband trained a few of their dogs to compete in agility contests. These competitions are included in the opening events of a steeplechase — a horse race with a course through rolling countryside instead of a race track. The way Rose saw it, Jack Russell Terriers were a good breed to compete in agility contests because they're smart, tough, and fast. It was typical to find the breed on horse farms because of their less glamorous ability to kill mice and other such critters in the barn.

As a fellow dog lover, Debbie actually took it as a compliment that Rose called her "winner." She knew it was the name of one of Rose's champion Jacks.

Debbie looked at her watch. It was almost 9:00. And, it was Friday. Most sales reps, no matter what industry they're in, finish their "field work" by noon on Friday. The rest of the day was spent running errands or going directly home to finish up their paperwork. Some reps already had their bags packed to get out of town, while others got a jump on happy hour. Of course, there were always those with integrity and maturity, who worked to meet their daily quota of sales calls — even on Friday. Reps like Debbie and Rose.

The sales reps ordered from the menus and chatted about everything from movies to the upcoming district meeting. Debbie spoke loud enough to rise above the chatter and said, "Hey guys, why don't we get started?"

Most of the group ignored her plea, but Blaire looked up from her tête-à-tête with Molly. They had been alternately focused on Molly's laptop screen or Blaire's.

Debbie straightened up in her chair and looked in Blaire's direction. She caught Blaire's eye and mouthed "Hi Blaire," and gave her an eager half smile.

Blaire looked at Debbie and gave her a superficial grin that dissolved into disinterest seconds later.

Debbie flushed for a moment when she saw Blaire's facial expressions, and their emptiness. She had tried many times to befriend Blaire and some of the other young, female reps. But they weren't interested in her. They just wrote her off. In their eyes, she was too old to have anything in common with them. She wasn't on the career fast track and hell, she wasn't even married with kids. The truth was, they weren't interested in anyone who wasn't exactly like them. But Debbie's insecurity made her feel awkward at those moments. She took it personally and she often felt like a misfit. And she *was* a misfit because she was forty-three years old.

She was twenty-nine years old when she changed her career at Inhaber-Taft. She had been hired as a secretary when she was twenty years old. At that point, she had an Associates Degree. Eventually, she began taking night classes at a local college, while continuing to work full time. She graduated magna cum laude with a Bachelors Degree in Business Administration and Marketing. She had applied for the position of professional representative (sales rep) for Inhaber-Taft and accepted interviews in various states around the country. She was told that her chances of getting the job were greater if she was willing to relocate. But the rejection letters soon followed. And, even worse, they were not even personalized letters but *form* letters because the first sentence was always, "Thank you for your interest in working for Inhaber-Taft." They didn't even take the time to learn that she was already an employee of the company.

One Human Resources manager advised her to pursue another direction for her career because she did not have a science degree. But by the late 1980s, pharmaceutical companies started to change the selection process, as the industry became more and more competitive. As the top companies continued to bring blockbuster drugs to the market every couple of years, the Sales division started to seek out candidates with potentially good selling skills. There were legend stories about sales interviews, where the managers would toss a pencil toward the candidate on the other side of the desk and say, "Sell me this pencil."

Debbie decided she could increase her chances of getting hired as a pharma sales rep if she had sales experience. She thought it was best if the job was somehow related to healthcare. She was hired for a part-time sales position at a local Nutri-System weight loss center. She worked two nights a week and Saturday's, and continued to work full time as a secretary for Inhaber-Taft. After about six months, she resigned from her part-time job just in time for a nationwide expansion of Inhaber-Taft's sales force.

Debbie had to compete with candidates who were, for the most part, new college graduates. The average age was twenty-three and the range was twenty-two to twenty-five, depending upon whether or not they had already attained a Masters Degree. Typically, those who were hired attended the country's top universities, where they joined sororities and fraternities. They came from wealthy families — a mostly "silver-spoon" crowd.

But there were other candidates like Debbie, who attended small town colleges and came from middle class families. There was a time when, their only hope of being hired was by someone who liked the underdog. Fortunately, Affirmative Action opened the door for women and other minorities, including those who were pushing 30 years old, like Debbie. Her willingness to relocate; graduation from night school with honors; her initiative to get a part-time job in sales; and her continued pursuit of the sales job in spite of rejection, proved she had tenacity and enthusiasm. She was hired for a territory in Delaware, so she had to relocate only about an hour and twenty minutes from her home in Pennsylvania.

By the mid-1990s, the face of the pharmaceutical sales force had changed, and white males were the new minority. Most of the reps were sophisticated, petite, blonde and beautiful women. But all of them were smart and well-mannered. They were women who seemed to have it all and definitely wanted more.

Debbie thought to herself, "Maybe they wouldn't write me off as 'old' if I didn't act like a mother hen."

Just then, Blaire raised her voice and said, "OK, let's talk about the purpose of this cluster meeting — the MELAVOX Blitz."

Some of the reps groaned, others sat up to listen, and still others just zoned out.

Blaire continued, "Molly and I were just reviewing the physician target list that Michael sent us. It looks like . . ."

Rose interrupted Blaire and said, "Hey Blaire, my computer died last night!" Rose laughed and so did Debbie and a few of the others. Rose continued, "Does anybody have an extra printout of the list that Michael sent?"

Brad said, "Yeah, I have a couple of copies," and he started to stand up.

"Ah, leave it to my Brad," Rose said. She didn't sound patronizing. Rose may have been perceived as a tough, old broad by some, but Debbie saw through the rough exterior. When Rose didn't like someone, she kept quiet instead of making derogatory comments or gossiping about them. If Rose liked someone, she lit up with charm and usually crowned them with a dog's name.

Brad walked to Rose's end of the table and said, "Here you go Rose." He was proud of his preparedness. He gave Rose a genuine smile. He wanted her to like him. He wanted everyone to like him.

Rose knew this and said with exaggerated enthusiasm, "Hey, thanks speedy! I knew I could count on ya."

Brad smiled again and winked at Rose before turning to go back to his seat.

Blaire took advantage of the momentary lull and jumped in to say, "There are sixty physicians on the list that Michael sent to us from Marketing. These physicians are targeted for the MELAVOX Blitz, which essentially requires us to increase the number of calls and the number of lunches with these physicians. Basically, we will have to call on them twice a week. So we have to make some changes to our zip code routing."

Grant made a frustrated sigh, but he tried not to sound negative when he said, "But we already know who is scheduled for which zip codes each week of the month."

Before Blaire could comment, Molly, Debbie and Brad started to answer in unison, "Yeah, but we have to . . ." One by one they trailed off when they realized they were all speaking at once.

Blaire looked at Grant and said, "You're right. We have an established routing for each rep in our cluster, but we have to adjust it for the

MELAVOX Blitz. So first we'll look at our weekly routing and then drill down to daily routing."

Grant shook his head in disgust, as did Harrison and Meredith. Grant lowered his voice and mumbled, "Man, this sucks!" He dropped his pen on the Franklin Planner in front of him and then folded his arms and leaned back in his chair.

Molly felt the same way, but she wore a façade of cheerfulness and a positive attitude. It was the only way to get promoted — say "yes" and smile about the assignment, no matter what your true feelings are.

The MELAVOX Blitz was yet another "fire drill" assignment, devised by the marketing team to help the sales force meet their barely achievable sales goals. It created a lot of extra work and none of the reps were ever convinced of the merits of these ad hoc sales campaigns, although Marketing always provided stats that proved otherwise. The reps took these with a grain of salt because rumor had it that the product marketing teams inflated the stats to justify their own existence. The truth was somewhere in the middle. And in the end, there was an increase in sales, but often only temporary.

Molly said, "Look, guys, it's not so bad." She seemed to capture the attention of the group, as they were eager to hear an easy solution. That's what sales reps did. They took a complicated and convoluted assignment and analyzed it a bit. There was always at least one person in the group who was clever enough to figure out an easy way to accomplish the task. But nobody stood in front of the group and announced the quick and easy solution. Instead, each rep found out through the grapevine of his or her trusted friends.

If the solution was related to pounding the pavement, the experienced reps were the first to figure it out. But more and more, the solution was found in computer data and it was a matter of querying reports and analyzing trends. The young reps were computer savvy so they could quickly figure out a short cut to complete an assignment and then tell their cliques.

The older reps had done the job successfully for many years before the introduction of computers to the field sales force in 1992. But there was a larger problem. It wasn't just Debbie's imagination. The older reps *were* mostly ignored by the younger reps. Their attitude was shaped by the corporate culture of the 1980s and 1990s. Any sales person over thirty years old was destined to be a "lifer" in field sales because promotions along the career fast track were expected to begin by the age of 25. Any sales rep over forty had no chance of influencing anyone's promotion; so it wasn't necessary to socialize with them. The young reps saw them as completely washed up. In some cases, they were right. In most cases, they were wrong.

In reality, the older reps were no different from the younger reps. Some were conscientious about their job. They diligently completed their assignments and met or exceeded their daily call quotas and sales goals. Others spent a great deal of time figuring out a short cut for every assignment and a way to falsify information so the results "on paper" reflected the desired outcome.

Harrison asked Blaire sheepishly, "What is the MELAVOX Blitz about anyway?" It was one of those questions that most of the cluster group had on their minds, but everyone was afraid to ask. They were afraid to ask because they assumed it was probably clearly explained in an email they didn't bother to read. And no one was going to admit it.

Blaire shot a glance at Brad. He had already been promoted to the position of specialty representative for MELAVOX, and he planned his next career move to be a promotion "inside" to Inhaber-Taft's market research department. In order for this to happen, he had to walk the line between his sales rep peers and management. It was important not to piss anyone off. This meant he had to keep his cool and always have an air of confidence and dedication.

Blaire had an intuition that she and Brad were thinking the same thing. They could see that the group was getting frustrated and bored.

Brad thought, "I've got to be the leader here. If I can motivate them, we'll all benefit." He knew his sales numbers would be affected by how much effort they put into the MELAVOX Blitz, so he was determined to sell them on the idea. "Look, it's easy. Just look at the list of physician targets for the MELAVOX Blitz. As a group, we have to call on each of them every day instead of twice a week."

Rose said, "Oh my God! What? Everyday?" She giggled and said, "Jesus, they'll kick us out of the office!" and she giggled some more.

A few people said, "Yeah really."

As a company man, Brad got a little defensive, but he maintained his pleasant demeanor. He said, "Come on Rose," and he gave her a charming half smile. Now he was afraid of becoming the victim of the cluster's "kill the messenger" sentiment. He quickly added, "Hey guys, come on. Blaire just explained the same thing two minutes ago. The MELAVOX Blitz is just for one month and. . ."

He was interrupted by Debbie, who said, "Yeah, one month or until the sixty targeted physicians are sick of us and say, 'No more Inhaber-Taft reps in the office!'"

Meredith looked up. She had been preoccupied with assessing her manicure. She said half-heartedly, "The MELAVOX top writers are already sick of us being there *twice* a week, but every day?"

Grant spoke just loud enough for one side of the table to hear. He said, "Look, all it takes is a few extra taps on your keyboard and you've made the extra sales calls."

Everyone within earshot gave a guarded laugh.

Each rep has an office set up in their home. Some reps are on the road by 8:00 a.m., others by 10:00 a.m. Some reps steer their car toward home by 2:00 p.m., others by 5:00 p.m. Ultimately, it is management's responsibility to use the grueling interview process and annual performance reviews to evaluate an individual's integrity and motivation as best they can. Sales managers spend at least one day a month with each sales rep to assess their progress and selling skills. However, it is much easier to evaluate tangible skills than it is to assess an individual's character.

Inhaber-Taft constantly reminds its employees, through overt and subliminal messages, that the competition for their jobs is intense. In sales training, the reps are told day after day, how many applicants there were for their jobs. The industry is cutthroat and competitive all the way up the food chain. Each individual knows that there is always someone breathing down their neck waiting . . . just waiting . . . for them to get promoted, or fired, or to leave the company.

Salespeople are motivated by money, recognition, and awards. But nothing motivates them more than competition--competition with their peers and competition with themselves. Successful sales reps are like athletes who face themselves in the mirror each morning and rally their spirits to do better today than yesterday. This is what gets them out of their warm, cozy beds in the morning. This is what keeps them driving to the next physician's office after being rudely rejected at the one they just left. This is what makes them stay up until 2:00 a.m. to get their "ducks in order" before they work with their sales manager the next day.

But, there are always exceptions. Bad apples are hired and somehow manage to stay under the radar. These are the sales reps who tarnish the image of their profession and the industry. They party every night and sleep until noon. Some days they never get out of their pajamas. But they sit down at their computers at night and complete their daily call report to make it look like they made their quota of eight to ten physician sales calls.

Of course, there is a lot of paranoia among sales reps that "Big Brother" is watching. But this doesn't stop some of them from falsifying their records. It just means they are very careful about how to go about doing it so they don't get caught. If a rep is more of a risk-taker, they will record the calls during the day, but only after they change the time on their computer. Their laptop computers are company property. They have to "call in" with their computer hooked up to the phone line, and a synchronization process takes place each night. This process downloads all the information the rep inputs into their laptop and synchronizes the information with the other reps who share the same territory. So, on Thursday, Harrison can look up a physician in his territory and find out who called on him or her the previous day and what they talked about. If a rep is not really working on a particular day (or days), it is not difficult to make up a conversation. As Grant said, "It just takes a few taps on the keyboard."

By now, everyone was immersed in sidebar conversations. Suddenly, everyone looked up from the table at the sound of a man's voice.

"Mornin' everybody." It was Ken Welder.

About half the group said hello. Some grinned and continued to talk. Others shifted their eyes back to their laptops.

Blaire rolled her eyes at Rose, but Rose did not return the sentiment. Instead she said, "Hey Kenny! What's up?" as Ken began to walk to her side of the table.

Debbie could smell Old Spice cologne on his hands when he began to massage her shoulders as soon as he reached her. She thought, "Oh God, I can't stand this. He's such a dirty old man." But instead she turned around with a smile and said sarcastically, "Nice of you to show up Ken."

Ken removed his hands from Debbie's shoulders and said, "Yeah, well I figured I'd grace you guys with my presence for a little while."

Rose gave a half laugh and said, "Well, Kenny, we're glad ya decided to do that."

Ken took a couple of strides past Rose and grabbed a chair from another table. There was no way they could fit one more person on either side of the table, now that everyone had their paperwork strewn about. So Ken pulled the chair around to the table's end and plopped down in the chair with a sigh. He rubbed his upper lip with the side of his hand and said, "Man, it's hot in here." He fidgeted in the chair and turned his body to face the table. He looked over at Grant on his left and said, "What's going on? What do we have to do for Michael now?"

Grant smiled. Then he pushed his laptop toward Ken and said in lackluster fashion, "We have to coordinate our routing for the MELAVOX Blitz."

"Oh Jesus!" Ken shook his head and then added, "We already coordinate our routing, so what's this bullshit about?"

Grant laughed and said, "Well, you heard the message from Dean Wallace, didn't you?"

"No, what did our brilliant Vice President of Sales have to say?" Ken never checked his voicemail as often as they were required to do.

Rose overheard them. She giggled and said, "Boy, I'll tell you Kenny. You are walkin' to a different drummer."

And he was. If Rose was one of the "last of the Mohicans," Ken was the father of the "last of the Mohicans." Ken Welder was a "lifer" and proud of it. He had been a pharmaceutical sales rep for 39 years. Despite his bending and breaking of the rules, he appeared to be untouchable. He dressed like an urban cowboy. He wore polyester leisure suits with western rodeo ribbing and, of course, cowboy boots. He had a receding hairline with long gray sideburns and curly gray hair that touched his collar. He rarely dusted off the dandruff that was always visible on his dark colored suits. Ken was divorced several times and an unabashed womanizer. And he was full of contradictions. He loved martinis and easily drank three at a sitting, but he had a MADD (Mothers Against Drunk Driving) bumper sticker. He bragged about breaking all the rules, but he was the first one on the scene for every early morning, medical conference exhibit. He'd brag about his newest love interest and then flirt with the waitress at the restaurant. Ken managed to endear himself to young female reps by telling them he knew all the tricks that men played with women. This would naturally arouse their curiosity, and he got their attention. The male reps liked him because they enjoyed hearing about his sexual escapades. And all of the sales reps quietly committed to memory every trick he taught them about how to beat the system. Some would tuck the information away and never actually use it. It was the kind of thing a rep could pull out of their hat on a bad day when it was fun just to fantasize about doing it. It was really only the slackers; or quite the opposite — reps with another job on the side--who actually used Ken's devious tactics.

Blaire overheard Grant and Ken. She looked over at Ken and smiled and said, "Hey Kenny. How are you?"

Ken smiled and said, "I'm good darlin'. How bout you?"

Blaire said, "I'm doing fine," and she gave Ken a coy smile. Then she said loudly, "OK. Good news. I just finished a routing grid for the Blitz, and I'll send it to each of you in an email. Now remember, each person will have to increase their daily calls to 11.5 instead of the typical 8 to 10 calls per day."

Rose started to speak between gasps of laughter, "What? Oh, this is rich! How do we call on a .5 physician?"

Harrison giggled and said, ".5 of a physician . . . that's interesting." He laughed a little and then shook his head and said, "Typical, typical." He was referring to the often absurdly literal, analytical style of the market research department.

Even Blaire and Brad couldn't resist feeling exasperated by another assignment that, on the surface, appeared to be a good idea. However, the practical implementation once again proved to be an arduous task. It was the classic struggle between marketing and sales.

Ken leaned so far back on his chair that it was propped up on just two legs. His body language announced his disinterest. But his frown turned to a smile when he saw the waitress approach with a giant tray of plates.

Another waitress carried a second tray to the opposite end of the table. Everyone breathed in the aroma of bacon and sausage as the plates were passed around.

"Bacon, scrambled eggs, and hash browns?" asked the waitress as she reached over Harrison and lowered the plate in front of him.

Harrison said, "Yeah, that's me."

By the time the waitress returned to the table, Ken had already cleared his plate. He wiped his mouth with a paper napkin and tossed it onto the plate as the waitress removed it. Ken said, "Thanks hon." Then he leaned forward and rested his forearms on his legs and pushed his shoulders into the table edge. He looked past Grant to Meredith and asked, "How are ya sweet pea?"

Meredith gave Ken a smile and said, "I'm fine Kenny. How are you?"

"Excellent. I'm excellent." Meredith heard the insinuation in his tone. She knew Ken well enough to know that he was referring to his sexual prowess — not his general health.

Ken got away with everything from double entendres to hugs and shoulder massages. His behavior was classic sexual harassment but management looked the other way because the doctors loved Ken. They admired his charisma that made women descend to the level of schoolgirls for his attention. If the doctors were faithful to their wives, they saw Ken as the guy who was out there doing what they could only fantasize about--sleeping around. If the doctors cheated on their wives, then Ken was the kind of guy they could ask to cover for them. They would tell their wives they were going golfing, fishing, or hunting with Ken Welder.

Brad said, "There's one final point to this campaign. You will have to cancel any other lunches that you may have scheduled during the month of the MELAVOX Blitz."

"What? This is crazy!" shouted Ken.

Debbie had been flipping through her calendar. She said, "Wait a minute, I have a lunch scheduled with Dr. Danvers the week after next and it took me about 3 months to get the appointment!"

Now the entire group was complaining and talking amongst themselves.

Brad said, "Alright. Debbie has a good point. Michael Poong said the only exceptions are those lunches that took 3 or 4 months to get. So to answer your question Deb, you don't have to cancel your lunch with Dr. Danvers. But, we do have to cancel all other lunches."

Everyone quieted down again. It was a combination of too much food and information overload.

Brad took advantage of their vulnerability and said, "OK, as the specialty rep for MELAVOX, my territory overlaps with a total of 3 clusters (territories). I have to support the needs of the docs and the reps in each of these clusters. But, for the Blitz campaign, the specialty reps were told we also have to call on the top 10 primary care physicians (PCPs), who are ranked as "high potential."

Physician ranking is calculated by the market research department. A physician was labeled as "high potential" for two reasons: 1) if they treat patients with the disease that the product is indicated for, and 2) if the physician writes a lot of prescriptions for drugs in the therapeutic class (in this case, the class is COX II Inhibitors and MELAVOX was the only COX II Inhibitor on the market at that point).

Brad continued, "So I can help you with calls on the top 10 PCPs."

Meredith said, "Oh, OK. I was wondering who you were going to call on for this assignment."

Rose said loudly, "Oh, that's great speedy. I knew I could count on ya!"

Debbie leaned over to Rose and whispered sarcastically, "Yeah, I'm sure we'll be seeing a lot of him."

Rose laughed and said, "Ah, winner you're something else."

Debbie whispered again, "I know Brad works, but let's face it, with the size of his geography, *we're* the ones who will have to run around like nuts doing the MELAVOX Blitz and trying to get to our other physicians."

Rose said in a low voice, "Yeah, I'm gonna have to cancel a couple of lunches and appointments so I have time to call on all of these MELAVOX targets."

Harrison said, "Yeah I have a lunch with Dr. DiStefano next Thursday that I'll have to cancel."

Debbie said, "Oh well, at least with him, you can still see him without lunch."

Harrison said, "Yeah, well, that's true. He's a piece of work, isn't he?" He laughed a little and continued, "He has reps bringing lunch to his office everyday. But then he'll leave the rep sitting there in the kitchen, after he jumps up to go see a patient or he'll stop by the sample room and talk to another rep, all while the rep who brought lunch is wondering if he's going to return to the kitchen. I swear that guy has some kind of hyperactivity disorder."

Debbie laughed and said, "I know! He can't even stand still while he talks to you. He's always in motion. And his office manager told me once that everybody loves his energy but when you work with him it's a different story because he's so disorganized. She said he has too much on his plate and he forgets about meetings; or his wife calls and asks her to remind him about things like vacation." They both laughed.

Harrison said, "Yeah, he's a trip. And I don't know how he does it all — I mean — a solo practice with 3 office locations and he does his own hospital procedures."

Debbie said, "Well I heard recently from the Prescott-Williams rep that he's going to hire a Physician Assistant."

"That makes sense, but I wonder why he doesn't just hire another Cardiologist."

Debbie said, "He'll have to eventually or he'll just burn himself out. Right now I think he's young enough to handle it and it's also an ego thing. He wants to prove he can do it all."

"You got that right."

Debbie asked, "Is he an in-your-face talker with guys too?"

"Not that I've noticed."

Debbie said, "Oh, believe me, you'd notice! All the female reps I talk to say he does the same thing to them. He shuts the door to the sample room and it's just you and him in this big room, which by the way is much bigger than most sample closets . . ."

Harrison interrupted, "I know. You wonder if he messes around with some of the reps or somebody on his staff in there. I mean, why is the room so big?"

Debbie's expression changed to a sly grin. She looked directly at Harrison and said, "I guess you haven't been here long enough to know about DiStefano and one of the Inhaber-Taft reps who used to call on him."

Harrison didn't know about the affair. His eyes widened and he said, "Get outta here!"

"Oh it's true. In fact, he practically came out and admitted it to me."

"What'd he say?"

"Well you know I've worked the Delaware territory for many years," she looked at Harrison inquisitively.

He nodded, "Yeah. I know that."

"And about every two years they realign our territories so the zip codes we cover change."

"Right."

"Well after one of my territory realignments, I had all three of Dr. DiStefano's office zip codes again. So I go to his office in north Wilmington and wait for him in the sample room. He finally bursts into the room, the way he always does, and he sees me and laughs. We joke around for a couple of minutes and then I state the obvious, which is that I'm back to calling on him again. Then I tell him the products I'm promoting. And suddenly Dr. DiStefano's expression changes to a serious look and he says, 'Deb, I love ya like a sister after all these years. But I'll never write for your products because . . . off the record . . . you know how I felt about Diane. And I swore to her if she left the territory I would never write for Inhaber-Taft products again.' My mouth dropped open and I couldn't even hide that I was shocked. Then I finally said, 'You're kidding, right?' and he shakes his head and says, 'No Deb. I'm sorry, but I'm absolutely serious.'"

Harrison said, "Wow. That really sucks."

"I know. I tried to joke around a little bit after he said that but I have to admit, after I left his office, I stopped in the restroom in the lobby of the medical building and just started to cry. I mean, he's got a huge practice and I knew I would never be able to increase my market share or even make my sales numbers if I couldn't get him to write for CARDIOPLEX or anything else for that matter. But I kept calling on him and one day he finally said, 'For you Deb, I'll write some charity scripts for CARDIOPLEX.'"

Harrison said, "Hey, don't forget I'm working on him now too."

"Oh, I know. Sorry about that Harrison. I'm sure he's writing scripts because of you too. I just wanted to give you the back-story. Hey, come to think of it, does he say the same thing to you about writing a few 'charity scripts' for Inhaber-Taft products?"

Harrison's eyes lit up. "Yeah, he says that all the time and I figured it was because everybody knows he's owned by Prescott-Williams. I mean, hell, if you look at the sales reports, he writes almost exclusively for their products. He's always bragging about how much of their stock he owns, and somebody told me that Prescott-Williams sends him a big, fat check every month. They call it something like a Specialist Consultation fee."

Debbie said, "It's such a bummer that so many doctors are so unethical, isn't it?

Harrison made a grimace and shook his head in agreement.

Debbie said, "I don't doubt for a minute that what you've heard is true. And let's face it, it sucks."

"Really," said Harrison somberly.

After a moment he added, "Prescott-Williams is the only pharmaceutical company DiStefano speaks for at dinners and conferences. And when you think about it, most of the docs on the speaker circuit are doing it for at least five or six different companies. They just spin their presentations to promote the drug of whichever company is paying them for them to talk that night."

Debbie laughed and said, "If only their patients knew how creepy most of them are. Hey speaking of docs, I hope this meeting ends soon because I want to get out on territory."

Harrison said, "Yeah, this is another meeting that's turning into a real mess." He looked over to where Rose had been sitting and said, "I guess Rose slipped out for a cigarette."

"Probably."

"Hey, what was Diane's last name again?"

"Harrington. Diane Harrington. She's been promoted a couple of times and now she's a district manager in the Midwest somewhere."

Harrison said, "Wow. That kinda creeps me out. I mean, it seems like the more ruthless people are, the further they go in this business."

"Yep. And the irony is that every time we get a new manager, they look at the sales reports and ask what the problem is with Dr. DiStefano. Then they swear they're going to bring him around and get him writing for our products. But nobody ever changes him."

Harrison said, "I know. Katie McDonaugh was on that again when I worked with her last month. By the way, what about this in-your-face talking thing with Dr. DiStefano? What's that about?"

Debbie rolled her eyes and said, "When he rushes into the sample room, he walks right up to you — like about two inches from your face. Then he says something like, 'Hey Deb, how's it going? Do you need any TRIAGRA for Mark?' and then, because I don't want to look like a prude, I just smile and say 'No. Things are going just fine but thanks.' And then he wiggles his eyebrows and says 'Oh, really? Tell me more about it, Deb.' I just smile and act like it doesn't bother me. And then I change the subject and start to talk about CARDIOPLEX, and then he drops the whole pervert thing for a couple of minutes."

Harrison shook his head and grinned.

Debbie said, "One time, just after DiStefano signed for samples of CARDIOPLEX, he reached up to the shelf with TRIAGRA samples, and grabbed a bunch. Then he tosses them onto my sample signature pad and says, 'Here, give these to Mark and see if things get a little hotter.'"

Harrison furrowed his brow and said, "Now that's not right."

"I know. But what I really don't get is — why does a Cardiologist have tons of samples of TRIAGRA? I mean, TRIAGRA is for erectile dysfunction and, oh by the way, it can cause adverse cardiac events in men with a history of heart disease. And here's this Cardiologist whose patients all have heart disease, and he's pushing TRIAGRA like it's water!"

Harrison leaned in closer to Debbie and said quietly, "I asked him about that one time. We were joking around and he was in a rowdy mood, so I decided to ask him. He said he knows his patients well enough to know who can tolerate TRIAGRA. He said a guy usually wants it because the beneficiary of the drug's effect is not his wife. They aren't going to tell their wives they're taking it, if they're running around. So it's a matter of doctor/patient confidentiality."

Debbie said sarcastically, "Oh that's just great."

Harrison said, "And he's always giving *me* samples of TRIAGRA and trying to sell me on using it. Then he says, 'But I've heard African American men don't need it,' like that's going to get him on my good side."

Debbie looked surprised, "He said that?"

"Oh yeah. I love it when white people insult black people with some stereotype and then they use the term 'African American' like somehow that makes what they just said less offensive."

Debbie said, "I know. What an idiot!"

After a minute she said, "Let's face it, DiStefano pushes TRIAGRA because it's another Prescott-Williams' product."

"Oh sure. But really, how does Prescott-Williams get away with all this shit?"

Debbie said, "They get away with it because they're based in England. There's so much more political pressure on pharmaceutical companies based in the United States. I mean, Inhaber-Taft doesn't do a third of the stuff that Prescott-Williams and all these other internationally based companies do to get the business. But, of course, the media sensationalizes everything and they never bother to learn the distinctions between U.S. and internationally based companies. They don't care to know because they can grab more headlines by demonizing the entire pharmaceutical industry. Meanwhile, what about the doctors? The companies wouldn't be doing this stuff if the docs weren't standing there with open pockets.'"

Brad stood up straight behind his chair and said loudly, "I just need your attention for a couple more minutes and then we can get out of here. Look, we all co-promote MELAVOX, and Marketing thinks this Blitz campaign will help to bring up our sales. And if we increase our sales and market share, we'll all get a bigger bonus."

Meredith interjected, "We all want to increase MELAVOX sales, but what happens if we spend all of our time on this, and then our sales numbers drop for CARDIOPLEX or FLAGIT?"

There were disgruntled mumblings of agreement.

Blaire said, "If your lead product is not MELAVOX, but it's CARDIOPLEX, for example, then you still have to call on the MELAVOX targets. But, you can arrange your week so that you hit the offices of your top physicians for CARDIOPLEX."

There were sighs of exasperation.

Blaire had enough. She said, "Alright you guys. Let's not get too anal about this. Everybody knows that some days are much easier than others. You can find a way to get this done and still be home in time to watch the Oprah show!" Most of the group laughed and Blaire smiled with relief.

Brad said, "Just review the information that we've covered. If you have any burning questions, you should send a voicemail to Katie or Michael. Otherwise both Katie and Michael will be reviewing this information again next week at the district meeting."

Rose said, "Oh good. Katie always makes this stuff a lot easier to understand." She laughed and added, "She translates marketing language into English."

Slowly they filed out at 11:00 a.m. Molly and Blaire stopped to use the restroom.

Brad picked up the check. He thought to himself, "I like the way everybody just assumes that I'm paying, since it was a meeting about MELAVOX. Oh well, just one more receipt for my monthly expense report."

By 5:00 p.m. on that same Friday, Meredith made two more sales calls after her luncheon; went to her manicurist to change her French manicure to a pink shade, and picked up her dry cleaning.

Blaire had a luncheon with a group practice of three physicians and thirteen staff. Afterwards, she made six more sales calls. The day before, she had worked her PT job, so she had to make enough sales calls on Friday to meet her weekly quota. She had time for a light workout at her fitness club, before she showered and drove to Kelly's Pub. Blaire and Steven always went there on Friday nights to party with their friends. It was Steven's job to stop by their house first and walk Parker and then feed him. He met up with Blaire by 6:00.

Molly made three sales calls after the meeting. It was that time of year again when she got up a little earlier on Fridays to pack her stuff for the beach. She hid her duffle bag on the floor of the car's backseat. She covered it up with detail pieces (promotional brochures). She and her friends rented a beach house from March through October. It was really cold this time of year, so they spent the weekend barhopping. She was on her way to Dewey Beach by 2:30 p.m. She arrived at 4:30 and was sipping her first Margarita by 5:00.

Harrison made four sales calls and then went home and fell asleep watching a movie. He was still asleep at 5:00.

Rose made ten sales calls, all within the same medical office building. By 3:30 her back was aching, so she drove home. Her husband saw her pull into the driveway. As she slowly wound around the long sloping half circle that ended near the front porch, he let the dogs out of the house. They were barking incessantly as she got out of the car and bent down to pet them. Her posture was still slumped as she walked into the house. She opened a kitchen cabinet and took out the Ibuprofen bottle. She swallowed a couple of tablets with a big glass of water and asked her husband to make her a cup of tea. By 5:00 she was napping in her favorite chair with her legs propped up on the ottoman. One of her Jack Russell Terriers was asleep on her lap and another one was stretched out in front of the roaring fireplace across the room.

Ken left the meeting and made two sales calls. Then he called his girlfriend and they met for martinis at Longhorn Steakhouse. By 5:00 he had ordered his third martini.

Brad drove three hours to Hagerstown, Maryland, to attend another cluster meeting. He re-lived the entire experience. Only the names and faces had changed. By 5:00 he began his three-hour drive back home again.

Debbie made eight sales calls after the meeting and pulled up to her townhouse just after 5:00. While she was still in the car, she picked up her cell phone and dialed the 800 number for the Inhaber-Taft voicemail system. After several prompts, she began her message to her manager, Katie McDonaugh.

"Hi Katie. I hope you're having a good Friday. I'm looking forward to our district meeting next week. Our cluster meeting went well today, but there was some general confusion about the specific details of the MELAVOX Blitz. Everyone on our team said they were looking forward to you clarifying this for us. I'll see you on Monday at the Annapolis Marriott. Have a great weekend." She listened to her messages, and then gathered up her paperwork from the passenger seat and got out of the car. She stretched and then sighed. She could hear Harry barking on the other side of the door. "Hi Sweetie. I'm home."

Chapter 14: Grant Preston

BLAIRE WAS RIGHT. After the cluster meeting, Grant *did* go back home again. He watched television and then napped for a couple of hours. He woke up at the sound of his phone ringing. His heart beat a little faster when he realized it was his home phone and not his cell phone. It could be "Big Brother" checking up on him. There were rumors that Inhaber-Taft randomly called reps at home, or paid detectives to drive by their house, in order to catch them at home when they should be on territory.

He checked the time. It was 4:30 p.m., which was an acceptable time for a sales rep to be found in their home office. If it had been earlier, he would not have answered the phone.

He took a deep breath and relaxed on the exhale before he said, "Hello."

"Hi Grant. What are we doing tonight?" Jillian asked.

He was happy to hear her voice. Grant let out a comfortable yawn. "Ahh . . . excuse me."

"Were you sleeping?" Jilly asked.

"For a little bit. I was down in Dover today after our cluster meeting, and the drive back gets me so sleepy." Grant yawned again. He lied because he didn't think Jilly needed to know too much information about his job.

"How long does it take?" Jilly never went down to "slower Delaware" as it was called. Those who lived south of New Castle County were thought of as country hicks because the area quickly became rural and there wasn't much to do if you enjoyed cultural activities, expensive restaurants, and a sophisticated bar crowd.

"It's just an hour's drive."

"Oh. Well, that's not too bad."

"Yeah but it's monotonous driving all the way up Route 1 with nothing to look at but the road and grass on either side."

"Yeah, I know what you mean. So where do you want to go tonight?"

"Let's go to Kelly's Pub. Dr. Goldman's band is playing and there's a bunch of people going."

"OK that's cool. What time will you be at my place?"

"Let's see. It's 4:30 now. I'll be over in about an hour."

"Good. Why don't you stop for some take-out and we can eat here first." Then she added in a flirtatious tone, "I'll give you a massage before we go out."

"Oh, I'm definitely up for that Jilly. In fact, I'm getting in the shower right now."

Jillian laughed. "Alright I'll see you soon."

"Bye Jilly." Grant felt refreshed after his long nap and he was excited to see Jillian. He didn't know yet that his mother was missing . . . He didn't know yet that his mother had been murdered.

As they expected, many of their friends were already there when Grant and Jillian arrived around 7:30.

By 10:00, they were still laughing and drinking, when Dr. Goldman's band, Rendezvous, started their first set. The band played covers of soft rock music from the 60's through the early 90's. They drew an eclectic following of college students, baby boomers, hospital and office staff, and of course, the pharmaceutical sales reps who called on Dr. Goldman.

Ira Goldman was a partner in Dr. Friedman's group. He was the only Internist (Internal Medicine physician) and M.D. in the practice. The other physicians were family practice doctors and D.O.'s (Doctors of Osteopathic Medicine). Internists had one or two additional years of training that usually included a concentration in a subspecialty such as cardiology, which was Dr. Goldman's area of expertise. Both of his parents were physicians — his mother, a Pediatrician and his father, an Internist. But he didn't come by his medical school training easily. Although he was extremely intelligent, Ira never really applied himself to the task of rigorous study. In college, he took pre-med and did well enough to pass all of his classes. But Ira was more interested in pursuing his musical interests and women, than in getting A's and B's in his classes. As a result, he had trouble getting accepted into some of the better medical schools. Ira's parents decided that, rather than delay his medical school education while waiting and hoping for acceptance each year, they would pay for Ira to attend medical school in another country.

There are many physicians, born in the United States, who are not accepted into a medical school in the States. However, many of them are accepted into med schools in different countries. After graduation, they return to the U.S. and are eligible to complete a residency program affiliated with a U.S. medical school.

Dr. Goldman attended medical school in the Caribbean Islands. He came back to the States and was accepted into the residency program of Thomas Jefferson University Medical School. Physicians are required to display their diplomas in their offices. But Ira prominently displayed his diploma from his residency program at Jefferson. His medical school diploma from the Caribbean was obscured from view by a high back side chair in his office. Most people just glance at the diplomas with the fancy scrolling letters and never bother to read them.

Dr. Goldman's easygoing nature put people at ease. He was only 36 years old and he told all of the reps to call him Ira. He was average height with a thin frame. He had bright blue eyes and dark brown hair. All of the female reps wanted to date him, and all of the male reps wanted to party with him. The women rated him as one of the best looking doctors in their territory, and he was single. But he had a reputation as a player, who lived life in the fast lane, and only dated women of the same ilk.

Jillian moved closer to Grant and spoke loudly, "Hey Grant, there's Blaire and Steven."

Grant looked in the same direction. He caught Blaire's eye and waved to her. Blaire and Steven each gave a quick wave and then headed in their direction. Although she didn't like or respect Grant, Blaire, like all the other reps, was nice to him because of his connection to Dr. Friedman.

"Here they come," Jilly said.

Blaire also knew it was good for business to "see and be seen" whenever Dr. Goldman's band played in Wilmington. She gave Grant a hug when she reached him and Steven hugged Jilly. "Hey you guys! How are you?" Blaire hugged Jilly loosely after they shared an air kiss.

"Good, good. Can I get you a beer?" Grant asked, as he looked to see if Blaire and Steven had a drink.

They each held up their beers and said, "No thanks. We're good."

Blaire moved closer to Jilly so they could hear each other. Ira was wailing away on his bass guitar during a brief solo interlude. Blaire looked in the direction of Ira and said, "Ira is so talented and he's so hot."

Jilly said, "I know. He's really good looking. But I guess you see a lot of good looking doctors in your job."

"No. Not at all!"

"Really?"

"Oh, I'm telling you. When I was working as a PT at Pennsylvania Hospital, there were a few good looking Orthopods and some of the primary care docs weren't that bad. But I don't know. Maybe I picked the wrong territory. There's really only a handful of good looking ones around here. I thought it was just me but the other reps I talk to say the same thing."

"Wow, I didn't know that. I'm surprised. I guess it's just a stereotype that doctors are good looking — or maybe it's all of those hospital shows on TV with all the hot looking doctors. Everybody thinks that's reality."

"Oh that's definitely what it is. But it certainly works out to Ira's advantage. I mean all of the reps go crazy over him."

"Does he go out with any of the reps?"

"I know he's dated a few of them but I think he prefers women who are a little bit older than the average rep. You know he went out with Katie McDonaugh for about a year. Do you know Katie?"

"Yeah, I've talked to her many times at the Inhaber dinners, but I didn't know she was dating Dr. Goldman."

"Well, not anymore. They just broke up recently after she found out he had been seeing somebody else on the side."

"Really?"

"Yeah. A nurse told me he's seeing a friend of hers. I think she's a lawyer who does corporate counsel for Dupont."

"Poor Katie."

"Yeah, but what does she expect. Most of the doctors I've met are players. Katie must know that by now. I mean, how could they be anything else, really. Hell, even ugly residents turn into rich doctors and the money is all that matters to a lot of women. So, of course, the good looking doctors can basically get any woman they want."

"Yeah I guess so." They both looked in the direction of the band. Blaire hoped that Ira would see her in the crowd so she could score some points for coming to see his band.

The room was getting louder with the noise of the rowdy, partying crowd and the blaring music. Everyone stood shoulder to shoulder around a small space that had been cleared in front of the band for dancing. But the ripples of their movements and the push of the crowd made it difficult to stand still. Blaire looked around toward Steven. He and Grant were talking to a couple of women standing next to them.

Blaire leaned toward Jilly, anxious to share some more gossip. She said, "Dr. Friedman told me that Ira was once arrested for cocaine possession."

"Are you serious?"

"Yeah. It was a few years ago though, and Friedman said he thinks that Ira slowed down a lot after that."

"I guess he had to."

"Yeah. Dr. Friedman said it really scared the shit out of Ira."

Blaire looked again in the direction of Steven and Grant. She realized the women they were talking to were nurses from Dr. Goldman's office. She made a beeline for them.

"Hi Angie! Hey Jennifer!" Blaire hugged each of them.

"Hi Blaire. Is this your husband?"

"Yes. This is Steven."

Angie smiled and spoke loudly enough for Steven and everyone else to hear, "Blaire talks about you all the time."

"Oh really?" Steven smiled and raised his eyebrows.

"All good things. It's nice to meet you." Angie smiled flirtatiously.

Blaire looked over and saw that Jennifer was talking to Grant with a very serious expression on her face. She could only see Grant's profile, but he was listening very intently to Jennifer. Angie must have noticed the same thing because she and Blaire simultaneously moved over toward them to find out what they were talking about.

Blaire had always thought of Grant as a shallow, pretentious guy. But when she got closer to him, there was a genuine look of shock on his face.

"I'm sorry Grant. I thought you knew." She heard Jennifer saying.

"Knew what?" Blaire asked.

Jennifer gave Blaire and Angie a blank stare. Something was seriously wrong. Finally Grant said indignantly, "Jen was just telling me that my mother has gone missing."

"Missing? What are you talking about?" asked Blaire.

Angie's eyes grew big and she cupped her mouth as if suppressing a cry. She moved her hand from her mouth and said, "Grant, what happened?"

By now Grant looked like he might cry. He blurted out, "I don't know what happened, but Jen said that everybody at the office was talking about it."

"What do you mean — everybody was talking about it? How did I *not* hear about it?" Angie asked.

Jennifer said, "Angie you said you left early today so I guess the news didn't reach the office in Newark until after you left."

Jillian walked over to Grant and put her arm around him. "Sweetie what's going on? You look upset."

Blaire watched Grant turn his face into Jillian's neck and it looked as if he started to cry.

Jillian leaned toward Blaire and said, "I think we better go."

Grant lifted his head and turned toward the group. He had tears in his eyes and could only manage to say, "I'll see you guys later." Then he quickly turned and led Jillian by the hand, as they slowly weaved their way through the crowd.

Blaire turned to Jennifer. "Did I hear you right? Did you say that Grant's mother, Lee Young, is *missing?*" It seemed to Blaire that she needed to confirm the name of Grant's mother because she thought there must be some mistake.

Jennifer said, "Yeah. Joan said as soon as Dr. Friedman got in yesterday, he went into Dr. Margotitis's office and told her and Joan that Lee didn't come home on Wednesday night. He called the police and they're investigating it."

"And she's still missing today?" Angie asked.

"Yeah, as far as I know, she's still missing," Jennifer said.

"Oh that's terrible. I can't believe it. I wonder what happened," Blaire said. Then she asked, "Where was she last seen?"

"Joan said Dr. Friedman told them Lee went for a run on Wednesday afternoon. You know she's a marathon runner?" Jennifer asked.

"Yeah. Yeah." Angie and Blaire both nodded their heads.

"Dr. Friedman said he talked to Lee on Wednesday afternoon just before she left for her run. But then she never came home."

Grant and Jillian held hands as they walked in silence toward their car in the parking lot across from Kelly's Pub. Grant opened the door for Jillian and then climbed in on the driver's side. He shivered nervously from the cold and the shocking news.

"Maybe your mother got a call from her parents and left for an emergency," Jillian said.

For a moment, Grant felt optimistic and said, "Hey, maybe you're right Jilly. I didn't think of that. My mother might have gone to my grandparents' house." He took out his cell phone and started to punch in their phone number. Jill grabbed his arm.

"Wait!"

"Why?"

"Well . . . it's late and . . . what if she isn't with them? Maybe it's not a good time to break the news to them."

Grant stopped for a second and looked at Jilly. Then he looked at his watch. "It's only 11:00. That's not late." He looked at Jilly and put his arm around her and pulled her closer. Then he buried his face in her hair and said, "I'm worried Jilly. I have to know what's going on. And why didn't Donald call me? Jennifer said he has no idea where my mom could be!"

Jilly moved back just far enough to look into his eyes. "This *is* really scary." She moved over so Grant could reach his cell phone. He called his grandparents out of desperation. He knew his mother was never close with her family because she wanted to deny her roots. She came from a hard working Korean family. Her father's restaurant in Philadelphia had evolved into a successful business, but only after many years of struggling. Her father moved his family to the suburbs for better schools and a safer neighborhood. Lee had been the perfect child--smart, obedient, and beautiful. But by the time she entered high school, she felt like an outsider because she wasn't white skinned and blonde. She complained to her parents about feeling alienated. They happily complied with anything she asked for, with the hope that it might make her feel more comfortable. They paid for tennis and skiing lessons and bought her the latest fashions. They allowed her to attend any parties that she wanted to and even gave in to her pleas to become a cheerleader. As long as she achieved good grades in school, they let her do anything she wanted to do. Eventually, Lee became friends with the popular crowd and solidified her position in *the* clique when she started to have sex with the popular, athletic boys.

By the time she attended the University of Delaware, she had happily denied her Asian roots and continued to seek out friendships with only white, upper class women and men. She majored in Marketing and when she was a senior in college, she started to work part time in real estate. She worked at an office in Greenville, Delaware, because she surmised (from her sorority activities at the university) that Greenville was where the old money families of Delaware lived. Some of the Dupont family still resided there, as well as physicians, lawyers, Dupont executives, and the good old boys of the banking industry. It was through this job that Lee met Mason Preston, an older man with rugged good looks and wealth attained from his real estate sales and holdings. Mason was immediately attracted to Lee and he offered to be her mentor. He spent every Saturday working with Lee and taught her about the local real estate market. Gradually he sensed a mutual attraction and decided to ask her to escort him to a holiday party at Helen Carpenter Dupont's estate. Lee did her best to impress Mason and his wide circle of friends. She succeeded and, after only six months of dating, they became engaged.

After they married, Lee moved to Mason's house in Greenville and maintained minimal contact with her family. When her son was born, she gave him a proper, upper class name--Grant. And as he grew older, she was grateful that he looked more like his father than her Asian family. A couple of times a year, Lee and Mason visited her family in Pennsylvania. Lee's father worked so many hours at the restaurant that it was more convenient for them to visit at *his* home. But the visits became sporadic over the years, until they finally stopped.

Lee's parents were sadly aware of her feelings about her heritage. They had seen it as early as her high school years. But they wanted nothing more for Lee than for her to assimilate herself into the society that their generation would never be a part of. They had to be satisfied with her rare visits and occasional phone calls.

"Hello?"

"Grandma . . . Hi . . . it's me . . . Grant."

"Hello Grant! How are you?"

"I'm good Grandma. Well, not exactly so good right now. I was wondering . . . is my mother with you or have you heard from her?"

"No. No. She's not here. She hasn't called us for a long time. Is she OK? Is something wrong?" Her voice was suddenly filled with panic.

Grant looked at Jilly, who could hear his grandmother's worried voice on the phone. He frowned with regret. He covered the phone and whispered to Jilly, "You were right. I shouldn't have called her."

He uncovered the phone. "Ahh . . . what's that grandma? I didn't hear you."

"Is she OK? Is something wrong?"

Grant decided it wasn't a good idea to tell her much more. "Everything's fine Grandma, and Mom is doing great too." He knew he had to calm her down. He had to think fast. He decided to make something up. "My mother said she was going up to Pennsylvania tonight and I thought maybe she was going to your house."

"Oohh . . . oh . . . ha ha . . . oh Grant, you're so cute. No honey. She didn't come here. She probably went to visit some friends."

"Oh, OK Grandma. I'm sure you're right. Hey, how are you doing?"

"Oh good, good."

"How's Grandpa?"

"He's good too . . . still at work . . . you know."

"I'll have to come and visit you soon. I want you to meet Jillian."

"Jillian?"

"Yes Grandma. She's my girlfriend."

"Aahh . . . good . . . yes I want to meet her. When are you coming?"

"Maybe in a couple weeks . . . is that OK?"

"Yes, yes, sure. Come soon. Come anytime."

"OK grandma. I'm sorry I called so late. I went out dancing with Jillian and we didn't realize how late it was."

"Oh, that's OK. It's OK Grant."

"Thanks Grandma. Well . . . you take care. I'll call you soon OK?"

"OK. Call soon."

"I love you Grandma."

"I love you too Grant."

"Bye Grandma."

"Bye bye."

As soon as he ended the call, Grant punched in Donald's phone number.

"Who are you calling now?"

"I'm calling Donald."

He put the phone to his ear and then turned the ignition key. He revved the engine and backed out of the parking space. "There's no answer." Grant dropped the phone into his lap. He looked angry. The car wheels screeched as he accelerated and turned out of the parking lot.

When Jilly saw they were not headed in the direction of her apartment, she asked, "Where are we going?"

"We're going to see Donald," Grant said. "He better have some answers about my mother. I mean, what the hell is going on?"

"Just calm down Grant. I'm sure everything is going to be all right. There must be some misunderstanding."

About ten minutes later, Grant pulled into the driveway of Lee and Donald's house. The lights were on downstairs. Grant parked the car and jumped out. Jilly followed him to the front door. He rang the doorbell twice. Instantly, they saw Donald through the veil of curtain as he entered the foyer. He didn't check to see who it was, he just opened the door.

"Grant! Hey, how are you? Hi Jilly." Donald shook hands with Grant and he hugged Jilly, as they entered the foyer.

"What brings you two here at this time of night?" Of course he knew the answer, but he still wasn't ready for all this.

"We were just at Kelly's Pub and ran into Jennifer and Angie from your office."

Donald's heart skipped a beat. Now it was time for Grant's interrogation.

Grant said, "They told us that you told everyone in the office my mother has gone *missing?*" Grant sounded angry and Donald resented the insinuation in his tone.

Donald rubbed his forehead and pretended to be upset. "I'm afraid she is, Grant. I'm sorry. I should have called you."

"Yeah. You should have," Grant said indignantly.

"I've just been so upset and distracted."

"Well, what happened? Do you have any idea where she could be?"

Donald put his hand on Grant's shoulder and motioned toward the living room. "Why don't you come in?" The three of them walked into the living room and Grant slumped into a chair.

"Do you want anything to drink?"

"No. Well, yeah. I'll have a beer," Grant said.

"Jilly, how about you?"

"Ah, OK. I guess I'll have a glass of wine."

Donald left the room and Jilly sat on the arm of Grant's chair and rubbed his hand. "Don't worry sweetie. Everything will be alright."

"I hope so." Grant rubbed his upper lip and looked around the room. He stood up and Jilly followed him into the great room, where Donald was pouring wine into a glass.

"So what happened? What's going on?" Grant asked.

Donald held up the wine glass and a bottle of beer. He motioned for them to retrieve them from him. Then he poured himself a brandy and led them back into the living room. It was just too awkward to have Grant sit on the same couch where Lee had been.

They sat down and Donald said, "I called Lee on Wednesday afternoon . . ."

Grant interrupted, "So did I! She was just getting home from work."

Donald said, "I guess I talked to her shortly after you did because she was getting ready to leave the house for her run. She sounded fine. We just said we would see each other later that night when I got home from my parents. I wanted to visit them because they had just returned from wintering in Florida."

Grant tried to be cordial, "Oh right. How are they?"

"They're fine."

"So then what happened?" Grant asked impatiently.

"I called Lee around 8:30, when I was on my way to my parents. She didn't answer her cell so I assumed she was in the middle of dinner with a client or a friend." Donald looked at Grant and Jilly. He didn't want Grant to be angry with him. That could lead to suspicion. He was relieved to see they were both listening intently and seemed to be relatively calm at this point.

He continued. "I called her around 9:30 from my parents' house and again about an hour later, while I was driving home. I started to think something might be wrong because she wasn't answering her phone. When I arrived home at 11:30 and she wasn't home and she still hadn't returned my calls, I decided to call the police."

Grant welled up with tears. He said nothing for a moment while he tried to compose himself. The three of them sat in silence. Then Grant asked, "What did the police say?"

"They're looking into it. They said they normally don't file a missing person report until someone is missing for 48 hours. But I called again on Thursday morning and insisted they assign a detective and start an investigation."

"Good!" Grant's expression changed. He looked hopeful.

Donald continued with his version of the truth, "The detective's name is Healy — Detective Healy. I talked to him yesterday and he came over here last night and I told him every detail that I could think of. He assured me he would find Lee." Donald rubbed his forehead again and then threw back a swig of brandy. "I'm sorry Grant. As I said, I should have called you but I've been so upset and I just haven't been thinking straight. You should never have found out the way you did." He looked at Grant with an apologetic frown.

Grant made the same expression and said, "It's OK. I understand. I can imagine you were upset and just didn't think about it."

Donald looked down at his glass and swirled a finger around the rim. Then he looked up with a pleasant expression . . . as if just thinking about Lee made him happy. He said fondly, "You know, your mom was preparing for another marathon."

"Yeah, she told me about that."

Donald said, "I told her it was probably too soon after her last marathon to do another one, but you know how she is once her mind is made up about something."

Grant gave a half smile and said, "Yeah, I know." Then his expression became serious and he said, "Come to think of it, Mom was a little aggravated when we talked on Wednesday."

Donald swallowed hard. He was almost afraid to ask, but he did. "What was she aggravated about Grant? That could be important."

Grant pushed his hand through his hair, and his hopes of an important clue diminished when said, "Come to think of it, it was just about a house that was on the market for a couple months. She was frustrated because it wasn't selling right away."

"Hmm." Donald was relieved but pretended to be disappointed that it was apparently superfluous information.

After a silence, Grant put his beer bottle down on a side table and then stood up. "It's late. We better go."

Donald stood up and walked over to Grant. He gave him a consoling embrace and said, "I hope we hear something soon."

"Yeah. Me too." Grant looked closely at Donald. He had no doubt that Donald was as upset and worried as he was. "Call me as soon as you hear anything."

"I will," Donald said. He patted Grant on the back and the three of them walked toward the door.

Grant opened the front door and then turned to Donald. "Stay in touch."

"You too. Let me know right away if your mom calls you."

"I will Donald."

"I'm so sorry Donald," Jilly said, as she reached up and hugged him.

"Thanks Jillian. Goodnight." Donald held the door open and watched Grant and Jillian walk to their car. He caught himself grinning as he shut the door and thought, "That went well . . . so far so good."

Chapter 15: The Search Party

THE IDEA OF a search party was Grant's. Saturday had shaped into an oddly uneventful day for Dr. Friedman. He worked at the office in Newark and by 2:00, he had seen 19 patients — most of whom were walk-ins, which was typical for the Newark office. He had called Detective Healy in the morning and again after lunch just to appear overwrought.

But then Grant called him at 3:00.

"Hey Donald. How are you?"

"OK, I guess."

Grant could hear the distress in Donald's tone, and it emboldened him to share his feelings. "I woke up in the middle of the night and felt this sense of panic that Mom could be lying by a roadside with a broken ankle or a broken leg . . . I knew I had to do something. So this morning Jilly and I decided we want to organize a search party for tomorrow."

Donald tensed up with anger and thought, "I knew this little prick was going to be a problem."

"Donald?"

"Oh yeah, sure. That's a good idea. How are you going to organize it?"

"First I need the name of the detective you're working with. I think you mentioned his name last night, but honestly I don't remember."

"Detective Healy. His name is Detective Healy."

"OK. Do you have a direct phone number for him or should I just call the main number for the police department?"

Donald resented Grant's mention of police and detectives. But he said, "Ah . . . just a minute Grant . . . I'm looking for the number. I should remember it by now because I've called him twice today already." Donald was pleased that he could report his follow-up with the detective.

"Here it is. Do you have a pen?"

"Yeah, sure."

"302-646-1233"

"Is that his direct line?"

Donald thought, "What an idiot this kid is." But he said, "Yes. I told you I called him twice today." Donald heard the irritation in his voice so he quickly added in a pleasant tone, "What can I do to help?"

"I guess, just be there."

"Where are you guys going to meet and when?"

"We thought it made sense to follow mom's latest running route."

Donald felt his heart seize in his chest. He knew Lee would be found eventually. He even *wanted* her to be found, but now that the time had come, he wasn't sure he was ready for it. He worried, "What if I forgot something? What if I neglected a detail?" He tried to sound casual and asked Grant, "How do you know her latest route?"

"She told me about it when I talked to her on Wednesday. She said she discovered that if she ran from Greenville to Wilmington and then to New Castle, she could wind up at the base of the Delaware Memorial Bridge."

In an instant, Donald's feelings of paranoia dissipated and he thought, "This could actually work to my advantage." He listened intently.

Grant continued, ". . . then she runs across the bridge on the footpath and winds up on the back roads of Salem County."

Donald pictured the scene where he left Lee's body. He said, "Yeah, I know about that route as well. In fact, when Lee told me about it, I told her it was an awfully long run."

It almost seemed as if Donald and Grant were competing with each other in terms of how close each of them was with Lee.

Grant said, "She told me it was 16 miles. She said she runs that route three days a week to build up her long distance endurance."

Donald said fondly, "She's amazing. I'm just concerned because it's too much wear and tear on her joints."

There was a moment of silence. Both Grant and Donald were becoming self-conscious about using the present tense when they referred to Lee--but for different reasons.

Donald heard Jilly say something in the background. It seemed that Grant was distracted for a minute and then he said, "We called a bunch of our friends and they're willing to help. We told everyone to meet at the Hockessin Sunny Side Up restaurant. Then we'll split up the group. Some people will walk along Route 141. We'll start where it intersects with Route 72. The others will drive to New Jersey and walk along Route 29 into Pennsville. We thought if we contacted the detective, he might be able to provide some police support with the search."

Donald tried to sound sincere, "That's a great idea Grant. What time should I be there?"

"Jilly and I thought 11:00 a.m. is a good start time."

"Alright." Donald knew Lee was not inclined toward close female friendships, but he asked, "Do you want me to contact any of Lee's acquaintances, or people from her office, to help out tomorrow?"

Grant said, "I already called Susie and Ashley and I left a message for Sandy."

"OK good." Donald decided it would be more convincing to show a little emotion. "You know Grant, I'm impressed that you thought of this and I don't know how to thank you."

"You don't have to thank me. We both love my Mother and we have to find out if she's been injured . . . or maybe . . . at least find some clue about what's going on."

Donald heard Jilly talking to Grant again. Then Grant said, "Donald, I know this might sound kind of crazy but . . ."

Donald was immediately uncomfortable and thought, "Now what?" But he sounded fatherly when he asked, "What is it Grant?"

"Jilly and I were wondering . . . do you think it's possible that my mother was kidnapped?"

Donald was caught off guard. He said, "Oh, I don't think so. Why?"

"I don't . . ." Grant was becoming emotional. "I guess I . . ." Then he started to cry.

"Take it easy Grant. I understand." Donald's tone was uncharacteristically soothing.

After a minute, Grant sniffled and continued hesitantly, "I don't want to consider the possibility that Mom may have been . . . harmed in some way . . . but I thought that maybe . . . well, after all, you guys have a lot of money and people are crazy and . . ."

Donald knew he had to support any plausible set of circumstances in order to show his unwillingness to consider the worst possibility--that Lee had been murdered.

He interrupted Grant, "We have to consider every possibility that might help us to find Lee and bring her back home again. So don't ever feel embarrassed to be direct with me and tell me your ideas." He feigned humility and said, "I just don't think a kidnapping happens to your average family doctor." Then he quickly added, "But you're right about one thing Grant, we have to keep our eyes and ears open. Think back to anything that may have occurred over the past several weeks that might seem unusual in retrospect."

"Alright Donald. I will."

"Think about every conversation you've had with Lee recently and try to remember details that might be pertinent." Just then his beeper went off.

Grant heard the loud sound and said, "I'll let you go now."

"Yeah, it looks like I better get back to my patients. But call me back after you talk with Detective Healy."

"OK. I'll call him right now."

"Good. I'll keep my cell phone on me and wait for your call."

"Thanks a lot Donald."

"You're welcome Grant. You know . . . I think of you as my son." When Donald heard this come out of his mouth, he thought it was a little over the top. There was a moment of silence.

These were words Grant thought he'd never hear. He choked up with emotion and finally uttered, "Thanks Donald. I'll call you back soon."

Donald could hear the emotion in Grant's voice. "Brilliant move," he thought to himself as he ended the call.

About twenty minutes passed, and he had not yet heard from Grant. He started to feel a little paranoid about what might have transpired in the conversation between Grant and Detective Healy; until his cell phone began to vibrate. He felt immediate relief when he saw that it was Grant's number.

"Hello?"

"Hi Donald. It's Grant."

"Hi Grant. Did you catch up with Detective Healy?"

"Yes, I did. He seemed a little bit apprehensive about the search party at first, but I assured him we would instruct the group to stay clear of highway traffic as they walked. Then he said he was concerned about . . ." His speech faltered with emotion, but he continued, "he was concerned about people touching any possible evidence that might be found. He said I would have to instruct everyone, if they find anything suspicious, to stay at the location and use their cell phone to call me. I will then alert the police who are going to help us with the search tomorrow."

Donald said, "That sounds like a good way to coordinate it. How many policemen will the detective assign to the search party?"

"He said he'll assign two for the Delaware portion of the search — one in Wilmington and one in New Castle. He'll contact the Pennsville and Carney's Point police departments to get their approval of the search party on the Jersey side, and ask for officer assistance."

Donald asked, "When does he think he'll get approval from their police departments?"

"He said it won't take long . . ."

Donald heard a beeping sound coming from Grant's phone.

"Hold on Donald. I have another call coming through. It might be the detective."

"Sure. I'll hold." As he waited, Donald thought, "The Pennsville Police Department . . . They know the back roads and I guess once they're on board it will only be a matter of . . ."

"Donald?"

"Yes, I'm here."

"That was Detective Healy. He said Pennsville approved the search and they'll schedule one officer to assist. He said Carney's Point approved the search but they don't have the manpower to assign an officer to help."

"Alright, well, that sounds about as good as it can get. Great job Grant. I can't tell you how much this means to me, and your mother would be very proud of you. I'm sure it will be very soon when she can tell you that herself."

Grant sighed and said, "Thanks Donald. I hope you're right."

But it wasn't meant to be. Lee was not found on Sunday, nor were any clues. However, it definitely aroused greater interest in the case. A local news reporter approached members of the search party. By Monday, Dr. Friedman was afraid to turn on the television or radio, and he ignored the local newspaper by his front door. He feared it was only a matter of time before a reporter ran up to him outside of his office or even his home.

He thought, "It won't take long before the story is picked up by Philadelphia television and radio stations. Once they report it, all hell will break loose." But then he had a revelation. His eyes grew wide, "Wait a minute . . . that's it! I'll call Detective Healy and tell him I want to offer a reward to whomever finds Lee . . . or, wait . . . no . . . I can't say that. It sounds as if I know they'll find a dead body. . . I have to appear as though I refuse to acknowledge the possibility that Lee has been harmed. I'll say I want to offer a reward to anyone who reports information that leads us to Lee." He called Detective Healy.

"Good morning detective. This is Dr. Friedman."

"Good morning Dr. Friedman."

"Listen, I have a great idea. I want to offer a reward to anyone who provides information that enables us to find Lee and bring her home."

Detective Healy was intrigued. "What kind of a reward did you have in mind?"

"I was thinking maybe . . . $50,000?"

"That's certainly a generous amount, and we appreciate the incentive because it does get people talking to the police. The only downside for the police is that we're often bombarded with a lot of erroneous phone calls. People report what they think are tips and more often than not, they lead us nowhere. I'm not trying to upset you Dr. Friedman, I just want you to have a realistic expectation of what this will add to the investigation."

"Detective, I appreciate your candor but I also agree that a reward will get people interested and talking. There must be someone out there who knows something. We just need to provide the incentive to get them to come forward."

"Oh sure, I agree with you. Somebody out there knows something about this case."

Hearing the detective say those words made Dr. Friedman uneasy. He thought, "Why do I get the feeling he's keeping something from me." A moment later he asked, "How does this work? Do you notify the media or should I contact someone?"

"We'll handle the media contacts from here. Are you certain about the $50,000?"

"Yes. Absolutely."

"$50,000 it is then. You may want to check out the news this evening. I'm sure they'll report about the reward money by then. By the way, did you notice the news reporter along the search route yesterday?"

"No," he lied. But I was told about it later. Did you contact *The News Journal* to do a story?"

"Yeah, I thought it was a good idea to get the word out. Did you see the story they ran on the local news last night?" the detective asked.

"No. What did they say?"

"It was just a brief piece with some details about Lee and of course they mentioned that she's been missing for four days now."

Donald pretended to be upset. He said, "It's surreal to me. I feel like I'm living a nightmare . . . but I appreciate your efforts detective. Call me as soon as you hear something . . . anything."

"I will Dr. Friedman. You have a good day."

For some reason, Monday mornings always presented Dr. Friedman with a cascade of problems when he arrived at the office. This Monday was no different. When he walked into the sample room, the bins with MELAVOX caught his attention and he remembered something else that he had to take care of — Debbie Kaminski. He recalled their conversation at the pharmacy on Thursday night. His feelings slowly escalated into the same sense of panic he felt that night. He thought, "She overheard me say that I didn't need Lee's prescription *now* . . . and she saw me reach for the prescription bag from the pharmacy tech . . . it was obvious my arm was in pain . . . Jesus, why did I have to run into her? . . . I'll just get her in here and kind of check out her demeanor . . . see if she behaves any differently toward me now that she's heard the news about Lee."

He looked at the sample bins and thought, "I'll tell Joan to call Debbie and ask her to bring us more samples of MELAVOX. Wait a minute . . . all the Inhaber-Taft reps have samples of MELAVOX so that won't work. Joan doesn't like Debbie so she'll probably call one of the other reps to ask them to bring the MELAVOX samples to the office. What else does she sell?" He perused the sample bins, ". . . CARDIOPLEX. That's it. I'll tell Joan to call Debbie and tell her we need more samples of CARDIOPLEX." He heard Joan talking to Joyce at the reception desk.

"Hey Joan."

She grinned as she walked up to Dr. Friedman, "What's up?"

"Call Debbie Kaminski and tell her we need more CARDIOPLEX samples." He had an afterthought, "Tell her I need an additional carton of it for Larry Berman's mother."

"Sure. No problem."

Dr. Friedman liked the way he could make the sales reps jump through hoops to please him because they all wanted his business. He turned toward Joan and gave her a devilish grin. "And tell her I need it today or I'll start writing scripts for LIPOPLEX instead."

Joan laughed. She liked his style. She knew she could make the reps jump too because she was his office manager. "Gotcha!" And she walked over to her desk to look up Debbie's voicemail number.

Chapter 16: Windshield Time

Monday, March 14

BY 7:15 A.M. DEBBIE was cruising down I-95 south on her way to Annapolis, Maryland for the district meeting. The early morning rain had given way to bright sunshine and she loosened her scarf and unbuttoned her coat. She had plenty of time to think for the next two hours. She felt much better after taking FLAGIT for the past three days. It had managed to stop the pain and discomfort of her urinary tract infection.

That reminded her of last Thursday night. "That was odd," she thought, "I never knew doctors picked up their own prescriptions. I just figured they took whatever meds they needed from the office sample closet. I didn't think they would actually go to a pharmacy like the rest of us. And of all people, *Dr. Friedman?* He wheels and deals his way to get as many freebies as possible. Why wouldn't he just ask one of the reps to give him a carton of MELAVOX for Lee . . .it's weird."

When she came home from the pharmacy that night, she had called Mark. She always dialed his cell phone because he always had it with him. It was faster than calling around to his phones at the cabin or his office. The phone rang once, then twice, then three times. With each passing ring, her mood changed. She went from happy and upbeat to worried and anxious by the time it rang six times. She kept hoping that at any second, Mark would answer the phone. But it didn't happen. Then again, it *always* happened. Mark would tell her to call him, but he rarely answered his phone. Sometimes Debbie thought he did it on purpose so she would think he was always busy working. She started to worry that he had driven to Gretchen's house after all. But, within minutes, Mark returned her call and it gave her the reassurance she needed.

It wasn't the first time Debbie had struggled with her insecurities about a lingering relationship with another woman. Debbie's ex-husband had a female friend named Bonnie, who lived within walking distance of their house in Wilmington. Bernard and Bonnie worked together at an insurance company in Philadelphia. Bonnie was pretty, intelligent, and a math whiz, which made her well suited for her position as an actuary. Bernard often talked about Bonnie and when Debbie finally met her at a party at Bonnie's house, Bonnie had said, "It's so nice to finally meet *the wife*." That was the last effort she made to speak to Debbie all night. Debbie felt threatened by Bonnie because she could see that Bernard was very impressed with her. But little did Debbie know that her competition was not Bonnie but a more formidable opponent — alcohol.

Debbie used to pick up Bernard at the Wilmington train station every night at 7:30, when he returned from his daily commute to Philadelphia. Each night, as he started to get into the car, he would say he had a stressful day and he wanted to go to Cavanaugh's bar. Debbie used to go with him, but she began to feel guilty about drinking during the week. She had no problem with a little partying on the weekends, but during the week, just a couple of beers left her feeling tired and groggy the next day. She argued with Bernard about it, but there was no changing his mind. Night after night he wanted to stop at Cavanaugh's, so Debbie stopped picking him up at the train station.

Every night he walked home from the bar between 9:00 and 9:30. He was always drunk enough that he slurred his words. Debbie yelled at him, but he yelled back even louder. They began to fight every night. Debbie knew the only way to save their marriage was to get Bernard to stop drinking.

One Friday morning, while they were still in bed, Debbie said to Bernard, "I have an idea. Why don't we just have a cozy weekend at home, instead of going out?" Before he had a chance to respond, she moved her body closer to his. "We can have wild sex and I'll cook, and we can take Harry for long walks."

Bernard rolled over to grab his cigarettes from the night table and lit one. He took a quick drag and said, "Alright." He smiled and stroked Debbie's hair. "That sounds like a plan."

When Debbie got home from work that day, she found a parking space on the same block as their house, which was very unusual in the congested city neighborhood. "This must be a good sign," she thought.

She changed into her tight jeans and a flattering yellow, sleeveless shirt. She put Harry on a leash before she opened the front door.

They lived in Bernard's house in Wilmington. They were the only White people in a twelve-block radius. The majority of the residents were Black, with the exception of the Chinese people who lived there and ran a restaurant. Debbie and Bernard were among the few people who bought take-out food at the restaurant. Most of the patrons were young kids who went in to buy cigarettes and harass the Chinese people. Bernard bought the house because the realtor assured him of the ensuing gentrification of the neighborhood. But gentrification occurred in pockets of cities that had the right mix of affluent, liberal minded people, who could afford to renovate their houses and enjoyed the diversity around them. Unfortunately, they never bubbled up in Bernard's neck of the woods.

Debbie led Harry over to her car. Just then she heard Mrs. Harris yell over, "Hi Miss Debbie!"

"Hi Mrs. Harris. How are you?" Debbie asked.

Mrs. Harris was only in her late sixties but she looked like she was 80. She was not well and suffered from diabetes, among other things. But she always smiled and said, "I'm doing fine. How bout you?"

"I'm good. We're going to pick up Bernard at the train station," Debbie said.

"Oh, OK. I'll let you go then."

"Alright. Bye Mrs. Harris," Debbie yelled as she got into her car.

She pulled up to the train station just as Bernard walked out onto the street. He had just lit a cigarette. Debbie leaned into the windshield and waved to him. She pulled to a stop at the curb.

"Hey! How's everybody doing tonight?" Bernard said as he got into the passenger seat. "Good. How bout you?" Debbie leaned over and kissed him.

"I'm good too."

"I'm going to make spaghetti and meatballs for dinner."

Bernard took a long drag on his cigarette. Debbie felt nervous because she sensed that his mood had changed from that morning. She dreaded that he might suggest going to Cavanaugh's.

And then Bernard asked, "Can we stop by the liquor store on Tenth Street?" Debbie's heart sank.

Bernard quickly added, "I just want to buy a lottery ticket."

"Oh, OK, sure." Debbie said. She exhaled and relaxed. Tenth Street was one block over from their house on Eleventh. In this part of the city, there was a liquor store on every corner.

When they reached the store, Debbie couldn't find a parking space. Finally she said, "You know what? Why don't I just drop you off and I'll see if that space is still available across the street from our house? Then I'll just walk over and meet you here."

Bernard was annoyed by her suggestion. He thought to himself, "She probably wants to make sure I don't buy any alcohol." But he was also tired of the yelling and fighting and he wanted to have a peaceful weekend, so he said, "OK. That's a good idea."

Debbie stopped the car and let Bernard out. "I'll see you in a minute" she said.

She had to drive two blocks north to make a right hand turn because Eleventh Street was one-way going west. She was surprised to find the space still open when she turned onto Eleventh Street. "Another good sign," she thought. She let Harry out of the car and the two of them started to walk over to the liquor store on Tenth Street. Debbie felt incredibly happy. Maybe it was because she hadn't felt happy with Bernard in so long that the feeling was so deep and full, and it consumed her.

She could see Bernard up ahead. He was standing outside of the liquor store talking to their neighbors — John and Lizbeth. Debbie whispered out loud, "Oh shit." She remembered a party at their house when she found Bernard in the kitchen smoking pot with Lizbeth. Since then, Debbie referred to Lizbeth and John as "the aging hippies."

As they got closer, Debbie could see that John and Lizbeth were each holding a six-pack of beer in their hands. Bernard had a cigarette in one hand and lifted a bottle to his mouth with the other. Debbie's heart sank. She thought, "Oh no. He's standing there drinking a beer — on the sidewalk!" Drinking in public was against the law, but in this neighborhood, the cops had bigger fish to fry. And Debbie wasn't really worried about him drinking in public. She was worried about him *drinking*.

As she approached them, she smiled and said, "Hi Lizbeth. Hi John."

"Hey, how's it going Deb?" John asked.

Lizbeth said, "We were just asking Bernard if you two want to come over tonight for a few beers. We haven't gotten together in a long time."

Debbie looked at Bernard, but he avoided eye contact with her. He slowly dragged on his cigarette and said nothing, while he discreetly held a bottle of beer by his side. There was a brief awkward silence until Bernard exhaled and said, "Yeah, Deb. What do you say?"

Debbie felt a twinge of heartache but her feelings of anger were stronger. She thought to herself, "Bernard just wants to go to their house to get drunk and, who knows, maybe they'll even smoke pot." But she heard herself say, "Well, OK." She looked directly at Bernard and decided to make one last attempt to save the evening. She added in a sheepish tone, "But I told you I was going to make spaghetti and meatballs tonight." She hoped he would get the hint.

Bernard was obstinate. "Can't we have it tomorrow night instead?"

Debbie knew there was no turning back. Bernard had been rescued from a night without drinking. She said quietly, "Yeah, I can make it tomorrow night instead." For a moment she felt as if she was going to cry, so she pretended to be distracted by Harry. Then she slowly inhaled to make the feeling go away, but tears were already welling up in her eyes.

Fortunately, Lizbeth started to say something so Debbie raised her glance and tried not to blink. It worked, and the tears subsided.

Lizbeth said, "OK good. Why don't you come over as soon as Bernard gets out of that work suit?" The three of them laughed and Debbie forced a smile. Lizbeth motioned toward a house further down the block and said, "We're just going to check in on Josie for a minute, so we'll see you at our place."

Bernard and Debbie said, "OK." They turned to walk toward their house.

Debbie couldn't contain herself another minute. She blurted out, "I don't believe you Bernard! We just talked this morning and said we would have a cozy weekend at home!" She felt like a desperate child as she said it.

Bernard stopped short and turned toward Debbie. His face was contorted with anger and he said loudly, "Oh come on Deb. A cozy weekend at home? Who are you kidding? You're just anti-social and you're afraid of life!"

Debbie was exasperated, "What? Afraid of life? What are you talking about? You said this morning that . . ."

Bernard interrupted her, "You just want to hide me from other women so you don't have to be jealous. You're sick!"

Debbie cried out, "Sick? Sick? How dare you say that! You're the one who's sick. You're an alcoholic!"

Bernard lifted his right hand that still held his cigarette and smacked Debbie in the face.

Debbie screamed, "Oww! Oww!" Then with a wail she cried out, "You bastard!" Just then she smelled her hair burning. She jumped back and saw Bernard's cigarette fall from her hair. Without thinking, she let go of Harry's leash and tossed her hair around with her hands to make sure it wasn't burning.

"Oh God! I hate you Bernard!" she cried out.

"I hate you too Debbie! You stole my life!" Bernard screamed as he walked away.

Debbie threw her head back and looked up at the sky and cried out, "Oh God! I can't take this anymore!" Suddenly, she looked down and saw that Harry was gone!

"Harry! Harry!" she screamed. Harry was nowhere in sight. "Harry! Harry!" Debbie looked around and saw Harry in the distance. He was running away from both of them. She started to run. She was crying and screaming, "Harry! Stop! Harry!"

Harry turned a corner and she lost sight of him for a minute. A little girl stood on the sidewalk outside of her house. Debbie shouted to her, "Help me! Help me find my dog!"

The little girl started to point to the right and began to walk to the corner when her mother shouted from the doorway, "Don't you help her! Don't you help that white bitch!"

Debbie couldn't believe what she was hearing. The woman didn't want her daughter to help her because she was *white?* She kept running and screamed, "Harry," as she turned the corner. Harry had stopped to smell a pile of trash in the street. Debbie caught up with him and grabbed his leash. She bent down to hug him, as she sobbed uncontrollably.

"Oh Harry. I love you. Don't ever do that again! I'm sorry. I'm sorry. You're sick of all this fighting too. Don't worry. It's over. I can't take it anymore. I promise. It's over."

She felt relieved, as she straightened up and walked back to the house. She unlocked the front door and went inside. Bernard was standing by the small table in the corner, leafing through his mail. It was quiet. They were all quiet. It was the silence of change in the air — drastic change.

Bernard said nothing and went upstairs. Debbie walked over to the couch and sat down slowly. She knew what she had to do. After a few minutes she walked upstairs.

Bernard had just finished changing his clothes in the bedroom. Debbie remained on the opposite side of the room and spoke in a solemn voice. "Bernard . . . Bernard, I think we should get a divorce."

Without hesitation Bernard said, "I think you're right," and he walked out of the room and ran down the stairs.

Debbie sat down on the bed and started to cry. She heard the front door slam shut. She thought, "Nothing matters more to him than drinking. Jesus! I just told him I want a divorce and he heads out the door to party! Of course he's not going to turn down an opportunity to get drunk. I'm sure he'll get totally wasted with John and Lizbeth. They'll celebrate Bernard's newfound freedom!"

She stood up and walked into the bathroom and looked at herself in the mirror. All of the crying had washed her mascara from her lashes and onto her face. There were big blotches of black under her eyes that streaked down her face. Her upper lip was swollen from Bernard's blow to her face and the skin around it was red and would later turn black and blue. She started to cry again and then bent down to the sink to wash her face.

"Ouch!" She stood up and looked in the mirror again. Her nose had a bruise on one side that she hadn't noticed. She touched it with her fingertips and it hurt. "Thank God he didn't break my nose," she thought.

She gently dried her face and went back into the bedroom to change into loose fitting shorts and a t-shirt. She felt a little bit better when she went downstairs, until she looked at Harry. It seemed as if he knew something was wrong. He was lying in front of the sofa with his head resting on his paws. He didn't move. He just glanced over at Debbie with big, sad eyes. Debbie walked over to him and sat down on the floor and petted him. "It's OK Harry. We're going to be much happier now."

By 9:10 a.m. Debbie slowed her car into the steady stream of traffic that cruised through downtown Annapolis. Traffic snarled around the center of the shopping and dining district. As she turned left into the roundabout, she was just a stone's throw from the Annapolis Marriott. She could see the beautiful yachts lined up around the marina.

She looked to the right and spotted an attractive, older man in khaki pants, a navy blue blazer, and a sparkling white shirt.

The car in back of her beeped the horn. It jolted Debbie's attention back to the road. She pulled her car off the street and onto the safe oasis of the hotel driveway.

Chapter 17: District Meeting - Day 1

AS DEBBIE APPROACHED the front desk in the lobby, she recognized the back of Ken Welder's head with his collar length, wavy white hair. She waited until he turned around. He bent down to zip something into his suitcase and then looked up.

"Hey Debbie!" Ken Welder gave her a big smile and opened his arms to Debbie.

"Hey Ken!" Debbie smiled and patted Ken on the back as he hugged her. They were genuinely excited to see each other, which was odd since they had just seen each other at the cluster meeting on Friday. Only a weekend had passed between them. Yet this is one of many puzzling phenomena in the life of a salesperson. No matter how competitive they are, they can't escape the kinship they feel for their comrades in arms.

Each day the pharmaceutical sales rep charms his (or her) way past the gatekeeper at the front desk, who allows them to enter the door from the waiting room and into the exam room hallway. They wind their way further up the hallway to the sample closet or to the doctor's office to reach the ultimate goal: a face-to-face encounter with the physician. Along the way, they chat with medical assistants, lab techs, file clerks, and nurses. They make it their business to remember a daughter's graduation or prom, a son's new braces, an athletic triumph, a new boyfriend, or a worrisome surgery. And not just for one doctor's practice, but for a couple hundred on average, multiplied by the office staff and the number of physicians at each practice. Salespeople have the energy and personality that makes their job look easy. They have patience and tolerance in the face of rude behavior and cold-hearted rejection. They are great talkers and eager — if not attentive — listeners. But they share a secret they seldom talk about — it's lonely out there. A sales rep is alone in the car all day, every day, with the exception of the one to two days each month when their district managers work with them to evaluate and critique everything they say and do. They work out of offices in their homes — alone. And all of the preparation for, and reporting of, sales calls is done alone. So whenever they attend a meeting, whether it is at the territory cluster level or at the district, regional, or national level, sales reps are always excited to see each other. However, the sentiment is short lived. After an eight hour meeting on Day 1, followed by a mandatory group dinner, followed by a stop at the local bar or dance club; Day 2 already begins with an upset stomach for some and a distaste for their coworkers for most. Maybe if the first day didn't evolve into being too close for comfort, the mania would last a bit longer. But by the morning coffee break on Day 2, most of the group is depressed about unmet goals and envious of the district overachiever, who makes the rest of the group look sluggish, inept, and dull. And by lunchtime on Day 2, the sales reps are surreptitiously swapping stories about the legend salaries and bonuses provided by other pharmaceutical companies. The sales reps who had lackluster sales numbers in the previous quarter, mask their worry about job security with egotistical trash talk about headhunter calls and alleged indecision about which offer to seriously consider.

"Kenny! Debbie!" Todd Benjamin called out as he entered through the revolving front door, dragging his rollerboard behind him.

"Hey Todd!" shouted Kenny. They rushed toward each other and clasped hands with a hearty shake and a backslapping shoulder butt.

Debbie was right next to Todd awaiting her turn. "Hi Todd!"

"Hey Debbie!" Todd pulled her toward him and they hugged. Todd Benjamin was the Specialty Sales Manager for the reps who sold only one product--MELAVOX. Debbie knew Todd because he had been a sales rep in her district three years ago, before he was promoted.

"How long did it take you to get here?" Ken asked Todd.

"About 2 hours and 20 minutes."

"How bout you Deb?" Ken asked.

"Just over 2 hours."

"That's not bad."

One by one, as the reps arrived and approached the front desk, they each heard the same phrase, "Your room has been taken care of by your company, but I'll need a credit card imprint for all incidental charges."

Incidental charges might as well be referred to as sin taxes. They were fees for nibbling on snacks or drinking alcohol from the wet bar or renting pay-per-view adult movies. The sinners in the group were shrewd enough to have the front desk swipe their personal credit card because they didn't want the charges for these incidentals showing up on the detail of expenses for their corporate credit card.

Debbie looked over at Blaire, Molly and Grant. The three of them were huddled together in the hallway by the front desk. She walked over to say hello.

"Hi guys."

Blaire glared at Debbie as if she had just interrupted a serious and personal discussion.

Molly ignored Debbie's presence and said to Grant, "I can't believe you came to the meeting! You should have stayed home."

Grant looked at Debbie and said, "Hey Debbie," with a frown and very little enthusiasm.

It was obvious that something was seriously wrong. Debbie moved closer to Grant and asked, "Are you OK? Is something wrong?"

The three of them were silent for a minute and Debbie felt like an intruder.

Finally, Molly spoke up and said in a somber tone, "Grant just found out this weekend that his mother is missing."

"What?" Debbie asked in horror. "What happened?"

Grant said, "She went for a run on Wednesday and Donald hasn't seen or heard from her since. And I haven't either."

Debbie could see Grant's eyes fill with tears. Without hesitating, she put her arm around his shoulder. "I'm sorry Grant." She added in a low voice, "I'll keep you and your family in my prayers."

"Thanks." Grant forced a grin and then wiped away a tear.

There was an awkward silence and then Blaire tried to change the subject. She looked at Molly and said, "We're meeting in the Wheelhouse Room over there." She pointed to the hallway to the right of the front desk. She hoped that Molly would get the hint and they could escape to the conference room.

But instead Molly asked, "What room is your district meeting in Debbie?"

"The Galley Room." She pointed to the hallway to the left of the front desk and said, "Down that way."

Grant finally said, "I guess I'll see you guys later."

They all responded at once, "OK Grant." And they watched him walk over to Ken and Todd.

Molly lowered her voice and spoke with gossipy fervor, "Did either of you see the news last night?"

Debbie said, "No."

"Oh my God — you should have seen it!"

"What?"

"Grant and Jilly; and I guess Dr. Friedman, organized a search party to look for Lee."

"Really?"

"Yeah. It's so unbelievable," Blaire said.

"I know," Debbie said. "Where did they search?"

"They showed them walking along Route 141 near Hockessin and then around New Castle."

Blaire added excitedly, "Did you see it on the news this morning?"

Molly and Debbie both said, "No."

"They said they were also searching over in Pennsville and Carney's Point."

"Really? Why?"

"They did a short little story about Lee Young and how she's this incredible real estate sales woman and also a marathon runner. They said she was training for another marathon and she had all these different training routes, including parts of Salem County, New Jersey."

Molly said, "Oh my God. That is just so creepy. I drive through Salem County to take the back roads to the shore."

In fact, they all knew the area of Salem County because their territory used to encompass Salem County, New Jersey; New Castle County, Delaware; and part of Delaware County in Pennsylvania. But a year ago, their territory geography was realigned. They lost responsibility for those slices of Pennsylvania and New Jersey, and now they covered the entire state of Delaware.

Debbie asked, "Do they have any idea what happened to her?"

Molly said, "According to what Grant just said, they still don't know anything."

"This is really awful," Debbie said, as she watched Meredith walking over to the three of them.

Blaire said, "I wonder how Dr. Friedman is taking it."

Meredith walked up just as Blaire finished her sentence. She asked, "Taking what?"

Molly excitedly started to retell the whole story. Debbie saw Katie McDonaugh walk into the lobby. She said, "Hey I'll talk to you later. I want to catch up with Katie."

By the time she reached Katie, she was already surrounded by three other reps. Debbie walked up to the group and listened. They were talking about Lee Young, Grant and Dr. Friedman. It was the hot topic of the day.

Katie said, "It is really terrible. I was just listening to a report about it on the radio. I just hope that we can get everybody calmed down about this because we have a lot to cover during this meeting."

The reps were silent for a minute, until Katie broke the silence and said, "I'll see you guys in the conference room."

She started to walk away from the group but stopped and turned to Debbie and asked, "Can you start to move everybody along and get them headed into the conference room?"

"Sure."

"Hey winner!" Rose shouted as she walked over to Debbie.

"Hey Rose!" Debbie hugged Rose and Rose whispered in her deep smoker's voice, "What the hell is going on with Grant's family? Did they arrest Friedman yet?"

They both started laughing. Debbie leaned toward Rose and whispered in a half laugh, "Leave it to you Rose to say what everybody else is thinking!"

Just then Debbie had a flashback to Thursday night . . . Dr. Friedman's face flushed when his arm ached with pain . . . she heard the pharmacist ask, "Do you want your wife's prescription?" . . . He said, "No, I don't need that *now*." Her eyes widened. Her imagination ran wild and she thought, "Oh my God, what if his arm was in pain because he injured it when . . ."

She wanted to blurt it out to Rose but she stopped herself and thought, "Maybe it's better to keep this to myself for now."

Gradually, everyone made their way into the Galley Room by 10:00. But the business of Inhaber-Taft was the last thing on their minds. Everyone was whipped into a frenzy over the news of the strange and tragic disappearance of Lee Young.

"Good morning everyone," Katie said in a loud voice in an attempt to quiet the group and direct attention to herself. There were still some conversations going on when she said, "We have a lot of material to cover today, as you can see from the agenda that I emailed to you. Tomorrow we will spend the entire day with Michael Poong's team to focus on MELAVOX. That means we only have today to cover our Group A products." She hesitated for a moment and then added, "Oh and Michael Poong will provide us with an overview of the MELAVOX Blitz campaign."

There were grumblings from the group and Rose and Harrison were laughing. Katie said, "I know. I know. I've heard from some of you that you were really confused about the MELAVOX Blitz after your cluster meetings on Friday."

Meredith said, "I think most of us understand it now. It's just that we're worried about what's going to happen to the sales of our Group A products while we spend an entire month running around focusing on MELAVOX." There were murmurs of agreement.

Katie said, "I don't want to get into that now or we'll wind up spending an hour on the topic. Just believe me when I tell you that you don't have to worry that the sales of your Group A products will suffer."

Harrison was brave enough to ask, "How is that possible?"

It was one of those questions that everyone was both happy to hear, and relieved that it came from somebody else. It was politically incorrect to take an issue too far. Once a decision was made on a sales strategy, there is no more room for discussion on the matter. Questions are allowed, but frowned upon.

There were cardinal rules within the corporate culture of Inhaber-Taft and, for that matter, all other pharmaceutical companies.

1) Say yes with a smile to all assignments.
2) Don't question the wisdom of management.
3) Never, never go outside the chain of command; that is, never go above your manager's head.

Katie gave Harrison a tolerant grin and responded, "As I said, we will address all of the issues around MELAVOX tomorrow. So, let's get started." She pressed a button and the slide on her laptop was projected onto the screen in the front of the room.

An hour and a half later, Katie got to part they were all waiting for — the sales results for each territory within the district.

Katie said, "Now let's take a look at the top performers for each product." Everyone tried to keep their cool. Nobody wanted to look too excited. "The top performer within our district for CARDIOPLEX was Rose Heinrich."

Everyone applauded. Some were more enthusiastic than others. Debbie turned to her and said, "Congratulations Rose."

"Ah . . . .thanks, winner. Not bad for an old gal huh?"

Katie said, "That's really impressive Rose because we had a lot of competition and a lot of challenges."

Rose laughed and said, "Yeah, like when I had to explain to my docs why I didn't have any samples to give them . . . that was fun."

Katie smiled and said, "Yes, it was a difficult challenge for us during those two months when Manufacturing was short on samples of CARDIOPLEX. That's why Rose should be commended for her ability to, not only maintain, but increase her sales volume and market share for CARDIOPLEX. Let's have another round of applause for Rose."

Rose shook her head modestly and smiled.

Katie said, "OK. Now the results for PEPLIN."

Rose squeezed out of her chair, in between rows of long and narrow tables. She quietly slipped out of the conference room. Katie pretended not to notice, but everyone knew Rose was headed outside for a cigarette.

Katie changed the slide and announced, "The top performer for PEPLIN was Harrison Johnson."

Harrison said, "Thanks," and gave a wave of his hand and a big smile to the group.

"Great job Harrison. Keep up the good work," Katie said, as her cell phone rang loudly. She was initially embarrassed because she had cautioned everyone at the start of the meeting to shut off their cell phones. She looked at the number of the caller. It was her boss, David Clarke. "Excuse me for a minute. I have to take this. It's David Clarke." And she stepped outside of the conference room.

When Katie returned, she wore a neutral expression on her face. She knew everyone would try to read something into it. She said, "And finally, FLAGIT. The top performer in our district for FLAGIT was also the top performer in the region."

She looked around the room and made a silly grin as she tried to build up excitement. Finally she said, "Debbie Kaminski!"

Everyone cheered and clapped. It wasn't so much that they were happy for Debbie, but because it was the last item on the agenda before lunch. While Katie continued to talk, they rudely gathered up whatever they wanted to bring with them to lunch. Some even stood up and stretched while they waited for Katie's final word.

"It looks like you guys are ready to eat," Katie said. "We're having lunch in the Maritime Room. It's a served luncheon, so you can head over and make yourselves comfortable. Michael Poong's team will join us for lunch. We have to be back here at 1:00 sharp. Enjoy your lunch."

The conversation at each table included some discussion of the news about Lee Young. Dr. Friedman was known by all of the managers in the region, as well as the marketing team. His practice, Better Health Physicians, was one of the top sales targets because of its tremendous prescription writing potential. Even the reps who covered other territories knew who Dr. Friedman was, and had at least seen his wife, because they had attended so many functions sponsored by Inhaber-Taft.

Dr. Friedman and Lee were known as members of "the diner's club." That was the term the sales team gave to the group of doctors in each territory, (usually a dozen or more) who attended every dinner sponsored by the pharmaceutical companies.

While most physicians were open to any marketing campaign that included money or free trips, some of them only made time for meals that were brought to their office; whereas the "diner's club" always responded *Yes* to a dinner invitation.

It was mutually beneficial because these doctors, in turn, dutifully wrote prescriptions for the products of the companies who wined and dined them. Somehow they knew how to juggle their prescription writing habits effectively, in order to keep everybody happy.

Additionally, Dr. Friedman was classified as an early adopter of new pharmaceutical therapies, which meant he tried all of the latest drugs to hit the market, as long as he was "paid" in some fashion. The reps had a word to describe these doctors too — whores. They could be bought by anybody for the right price and their loyalty ran as shallow, which was exactly until their prescription writing requirements were met, at which time they switched to prescribing the next company's drug. Even other physicians knew who the whores were, but they were still influenced by these physicians because there had to be some merit to their experience.

Maryland crab cakes, julienne vegetables, and roasted red potatoes adorned each plate that was hastily placed in front of each sales rep.

"Alright. Dig in winner," Rose said to Debbie.

"It looks good." Debbie started to eat heartily. "Umm . . . now these are good crab cakes. Look at that . . ." Debbie held up a forkful from her plate and said, "They have chunks of real crabmeat in them — imagine that."

Rose laughed and said, "Only in Maryland."

When they finished, Rose said, "I'm going outside for a cigarette."

"I'll go with you," Debbie said.

It was a little bit chilly because neither of them was wearing a coat. But the fresh air and sunshine felt good. "Congratulations on your CARDIOPLEX sales Rose."

"Same to you on FLAGIT," Rose said and then took a long drag of her cigarette.

"Thanks. I'm really happy about it but I know it won't have a major impact on my career."

"Why not?"

"Because FLAGIT is not a strategic product for the company. It's a drug for a smaller market segment, so it generates much less revenue than CARDIOPLEX or MELAVOX."

"You're right about that. You shouldn't feel bad though, because it's a big accomplishment. There's lots of other products out there that treat UTI effectively."

"That's true."

"But you're right about one thing winner — it's all about visibility. You'll be noticed if you exceed plan for the big products that make the big bucks."

"Yep." Debbie stretched her arms and then looked at her watch. "It's quarter of one . . . we better get back to the conference room."

Rose took one last drag from her cigarette. She exhaled a little bit and said, "I have to hit the restroom first."

"Me too."

Grant was noticeably absent from the lunch group. He correctly assumed that, by lunchtime, everyone would be talking about his missing mother. He was able to get into his room early because Michael Poong told the hotel manager that Grant had some personal matters to attend to and he needed the privacy of his room. Grant ordered a room service lunch but was only able to eat a few bites.

At 1:00 only three quarters of the reps were back in the Galley Room. Katie was tapping away at her keyboard and didn't seem to notice.

At 1:15 she got up and flipped the light switch. She directed everyone's attention to the slide. It was an overview of Inhaber-Taft's sales strategy for 1996, which ranked each product in terms of its potential effect on the company's bottom line.

There were currently eight pharmaceutical products actively being promoted by the national sales force, thus the ranking started with #1 through #8. Once again MELAVOX was at the top of the list, followed by CARDIOPLEX. These two products were expected to generate a tremendous amount of revenue. The other Group A products, PEPLIN and FLAGIT were ranked at numbers 4 and 7 respectively.

Katie announced the sales goals for 1996 for the nation and then their region, district, and individual territories.

Everyone gasped in unison when the numbers jumped out at them from the screen. The numbers were astronomical in terms of the projected dollars in sales volume and percentage increase in market share. Every year the numbers seemed to increase exponentially to the point of absurdity.

The new reps worried and the tenured reps shook their heads. Experience tempered the anxiety because it was typical that the annual sales goals set by Marketing were often revised by mid-year. Marketing wanted to set the goals high enough to motivate the sales force. But this was trumped by the executive leadership who had to consider how Wall Street interpreted their sales results.

If results were achieved, the value of the company's stock went up. If sales results were markedly lower than expected, the price per share decreased. Companies like Inhaber-Taft knew that Wall Street would put the blame on the heads of company executives for a failed strategy.

In order to avoid this, if sales were much lower than anticipated by the second quarter of the year for a strategic product, pharmaceutical companies quietly adjusted their projected sales numbers and thus, the percent to planned objective achieved, became a much larger number.

The opinion of Wall Street was essentially a performance evaluation of the company CEO and his or her executive team. CEO's and executives cared because it affected the value of the company stock and their next corporate move. However, the amount of their bonuses was contractual and could not be altered by poor performance.

By 5:00, Katie could see that she was losing the interest and attention of the group.

"OK, let's wrap things up for today. You guys were great. Thanks for your attention and congratulations again to our top performers."

"What time are we meeting for dinner?" Mike asked. His territory covered the eastern shore of Maryland. He had driven three hours to get to Annapolis for the district meeting.

Katie said, "We're joining Michael Poong's team for dinner. Everyone should meet in the lobby at 6:15."

"Where are we going for dinner?" Pete asked. He was one of Mike's territory counterparts and his unofficial mentor. Pete was 33 years old with blonde hair and a perpetual tan. He worked out regularly to maintain his svelte physique. Born and raised on the eastern shore of Maryland, Pete had a good 'ole boy swagger. He was married with children but his flirtatious nature lead women to question his spousal devotion. That was enough to arouse the interest of the many nubile, young women who worked in doctors' offices. Even the older women appreciated one of Pete's discreet winks. He was also very well liked by the doctors. The physicians who chose to live in the secluded woods or quiet beaches of Maryland's eastern shore usually shared the interests of the locals. Boating, fishing, hunting, and fast cars were interests of both the "haves" and "have-nots."

Pete was comfortable when he was in his element. He was a big fish in a small pond. He was even comfortable at district meetings. But at regional and national Inhaber-Taft meetings, he felt a little insecure among the polished pretty boys from up north. His popularity was trumped by the smart, savvy, handsome young fellas from corporate marketing. Pete disguised his insecurity by muttering cynical and sarcastic comments during their presentations. Those within earshot giggled at his antics, but some were simply annoyed by his sophomoric humor.

Katie proclaimed, "We're going to Maria's for dinner."

"Is that the one just down the street — across from the marina?" Harrison asked.

"Yes, that's the one. They have the best homemade pasta I've ever had," Katie declared. She was pleased with her planning for the meeting thus far. She and Michael took turns making arrangements for their district meetings.

Katie quickly added a cautionary note, "And remember, everyone has to meet in the lobby because we will walk over together. I don't want you to go there by yourselves."

"Why not?" Mike asked, playing devil's advocate.

"Liability issues," Pete said. "They don't want Inhaber-Taft to get sued because some idiot rep manages to get hit by a car."

A couple of people laughed. Katie heard what Pete said and agreed. "That's right. Like it or not, Michael and I are responsible for your safety and wellbeing when you attend a meeting."

Pete added sarcastically, "Ahh . . . that's touching Katie."

Katie smiled at Pete and said, "Now get going if you want to try and get a run in before we meet for dinner. See you at 6:15."

Debbie always figured out a way to squeeze in a workout. This meeting was no exception. Once she was in her room, she heaved her suitcase onto the bed and took out her workout gear.

She was happy to see an empty room when she arrived at the hotel's fitness center. She chose one of the two treadmills. She wasted five precious minutes by the time she entered her height, weight, age, length of workout and all of the other vital statistics that the machine required before it started. Ten minutes into her run on the treadmill, she was surprised to see Grant enter the room.

"Hey Debbie," Grant said with a smile.

"Hi Grant. How was your meeting?"

Grant immediately began to hoist a couple of free weights into the air, as he watched himself in the mirror. He said, "Oh, it was good. How was yours?"

"Good. We covered all the usual stuff with sales results and then planned objectives." Grant grinned and they both fell silent.

At 6:00 she stepped down from the treadmill. She had fifteen minutes to shower, get back into her work clothes, and meet everybody in the lobby.

Grant had progressed from lifting a series of free weights to the rowing machine. Debbie was surprised that he was still working out at this hour. She thought to herself, "Maybe he's not going to the group dinner. I can't blame him if he just wants to be by himself."

"Are you going to the dinner?" she asked.

"Yeah." Then, as if he read Debbie's mind, he added, "I'm sure we won't leave by 6:15. You know it'll be at least another ten minutes after that, before everybody winds up in the lobby."

"That's true. I'll see you later then."

"Bye Deb."

As she made her way back to her room, she was pleased with herself for behaving so nonchalantly around Grant. Not only was the disappearance of Lee enough to make her uncomfortable, but Debbie was always a little self-conscious around Grant because she had casually dated Dr. Friedman several years before. She always wondered if Grant knew; not that it mattered because it was far from a steamy romance. The extent of their physical contact was a kiss on the cheek at the end of the night.

Around the same time that rumors started to circulate that he was dating Lee Young, Dr. Friedman seemed to change. He began to take himself more seriously as an eligible bachelor. He lost weight, bought stylish frames for his glasses, and touched up what was left of his graying hair. As always, he bragged about his tennis game, but he began to play other sports like squash and racquetball. Debbie remembered him saying to her once, "I can't believe somebody like Lee is even going out with me!"

Debbie laughed. She was relieved by his candor. "Maybe he hasn't changed that much after all," she thought. She said to him, "Well, I guess that says a lot about me!"

Dr. Friedman caught himself and said, "Oh Deb, you know what I mean."

Of course she knew exactly what he meant. He was surprised that someone as glamorous and gorgeous as Lee Young would go out with him — a frumpy, out-of-shape, balding guy. Behind his back, everyone was saying that Lee was a gold-digger.

Debbie finished a quick shower and then rushed out of the bathroom to check the time. It was 6:12. "Oh my God! I'm going to be late!" She threw the wet towel on the floor and shoved one foot at a time into the same pantyhose she had worn all day. It was faster work now because the stockings were stretched from wear and even maintained a limp mold of her feet. She discovered her back was still wet as she buttoned her blouse and it stuck to her.

Finally she pulled her coat from the hanger, causing the rest of the metal hangers to clang against each other in the closet. As she ran down the hall toward the elevators, she started to wonder if Grant would be in the lobby before she was. When she got on the elevator two other reps said hello and then continued their intense conversation ". . . maybe he realized she didn't really love him and just married him for his money . . . what if he found out she was going to leave him and take half his money and he decided to get rid of her!" Debbie knew who they were talking about, but she self-consciously looked down at the floor and then pretended to remove lint from her coat sleeve. But, like most people, as they heard the news about Lee Young's disappearance, she too was growing suspicious about Dr. Friedman. And the timing couldn't have been worse because it was only recently that the state of Delaware received national media attention for a notorious murder case. The mistress of a married lawyer went missing. Eventually the lawyer became a suspect and, when the case went to trial, the lawyer was found guilty of murder. A television movie was made about it, and the case set a precedent in the eyes of the public. Now, every time a wife, girlfriend, or mistress went missing, the husband or boyfriend became the prime suspect.

When the elevator doors opened, the lobby was bustling with laughter and chatting. Judging from the size of the crowd, it looked as if all the reps were present. Debbie glanced over at Katie, who had apparently spiffed up the same outfit. She added a black and gold silk scarf and teardrop diamond earrings. She was engrossed in conversation with Michael Poong. Debbie looked at her watch and thought, "At least she didn't notice I arrived six minutes late."

Inhaber-Taft was very strict about punctuality. In sales training they even referred to it as "Inhaber-Taft time," which meant that your watch should be set ten minutes early figuratively, if not literally. That way, as an Inhaber-Taft sales rep, you were always ten minutes early to an appointment with a physician and never, never late. There were a lot of attributes necessary to be a successful sales rep for the long term, but showing up early was still half of it.

However, the managers were more lax about timeliness at sales meetings. It was good for morale to cut the reps a little slack and allow them some time to socialize and catch up with other reps living hours away from them. They felt the socialization built and nurtured a team spirit which was vital to their success.

Debbie noticed when Grant discreetly joined the group at almost 6:30. Katie and Michael never looked in his direction but, as soon as Grant arrived, Michael said in a loud voice, "OK everybody, let's go. Follow me." Michael made his way to the head of the pack and led the group to the restaurant.

The night air was cold, and they entered through the heavy, wooden door of Maria's, one by one. Everybody shivered and shrugged deeper into the necks of their coats until they felt the warmth of the dining room. The waitress led them to their private room. There were no place cards for assigned seating. But everybody tried to subtly position themselves next to their buddies and away from their managers. Only those on the fast track to promotion were brazen enough to intentionally position themselves next to their bosses. They wanted to take advantage of the opportunity to build rapport. They were willing to invest their emotional energy into making conversation with their managers, whereas most reps took the easier road. They were happy to sit back and relax on Inhaber-Taft's tab. It was a nice change to be out to a dinner that didn't require them to chat it up with doctors and their wives or husbands.

As the dinner progressed from appetizers to the main course, the wait staff kept the wine flowing. They didn't even ask if someone wanted a refill. The assumption was that everyone did. That made it more comfortable for all. The conversations didn't have to be interrupted and no one had to be embarrassed by asking for more wine. The new, young reps viewed the group dinners as a chance to party late into the night. Some of the older, married reps and managers looked forward to a night of freedom from their spouses and children.

After dessert was ordered, coffee and tea were served. By now, those who wanted to continue the party were brazen enough to ask for more wine. Molly Proctor was one of them. She was sitting to the left of Blaire, who had managed to get one of the seats next to Michael Poong.

"Would you like another one too?" The waitress asked Blaire.

Blaire knew better than to order another glass of wine. She gave the waitress a patronizing grin and said, "No thanks."

Everyone knew that Michael and Katie were both partiers. They usually went out with the gang after dinner. But Blaire also knew that the managers had to turn in their receipts for dinners at district meetings. They didn't want the liquor portion of the bill to be inordinately high — Michael had told her this. So they cut themselves off once dessert was ordered and expected their reps to do the same. But later, the "in crowd" would drink like fish, when they barhopped after dinner. By then everyone was buying each other drinks with cash, instead of using their company credit cards.

But Molly was one of the reps who didn't always follow protocol. There were times when the morays of her social class took precedence over present company. In the social circles of Molly's parents, it was ironically as virtuous to imbibe as it was to hold one's liquor. Molly knew a lot about wine and she often enjoyed a glass or two when she got home from work. She had an innate sense of security and confidence that the monied class enjoyed, as part of their insular existence. Drinking was natural and worry about repercussions never even crossed her mind. Her upper class roots made her popular with physicians of the same background. However, physicians came from families that ran the gamut from upper middle class to lower income. Some were only able to go to medical school with financing from the Army or another branch of the military. They owed the Army years of service, as payback for their education. Other physicians had many years of school loans ahead of them.

Once their debts were paid, very few physicians chose to stay in low income, or rural areas. Most of them moved on to urban or suburban areas where they quickly gained financial stability and wealth. While some physicians were demure and guarded about their income level, others enjoyed flaunting it. This was easily discerned by noticing the cars they drove to the office.

Grant was sitting to the right of Michael Poong, and Katie was flanked by Brad Arnold on her right and Todd Benjamin to her left. For a moment, there was an uncomfortable silence at the table while they waited for the waitress to bring the check. In this little clique, no one dared to broach the subject of Lee's disappearance, even though it weighed heavily on their minds. Each of them caught themselves in a lingering stare at Grant and then prudently adjusted the direction of their gaze. It was as if they were trying to detect any nonverbal cues or emotions, on his part, that might shed some light on the mystery. There was a tiny thread of suspicion of foul play, but no one breathed a word of it.

No one had ever witnessed any ill will between Dr. Friedman and Lee. There were no rumors about affairs and no second-hand accounts of arguments between the two. Larry Berman was the only one who knew about Lee's affair with Dr. Schaeffer, and even Larry had assumed the affair had ended because Donald and Lee were still together. As for Lee, none of her friends knew about her affair with Edgar. Lee was hard wired to protect herself. She never shared her innermost feelings. And like Donald, she disclosed her plans to no one. It seemed there were no revelations to be found that could bear witness to her guilt . . . or his.

Before the meeting, Michael had declared to Katie that he would vigilantly watch over Grant. He didn't want Grant to become an object of salacious gossip. But as with everything he did, Michael had selfish motivations. He knew that if he treated Grant with fatherly concern, the word would eventually get back to Dr. Friedman.

"I don't know why I'm drinking coffee at 8:30 at night," Debbie said.

Pete was sitting across from Debbie. He said, "You should have another drink Deb." He gave her a sly grin.

Debbie smiled at him and said, "I'm too old for that Pete."

Pete laughed and said, "I don't think so Deb. You look as good as the rest of these gals and I'm sure you could go toe to toe with any of them if you wanted to."

"You're probably right about that," Debbie said with a laugh.

Once Michael signed the check, Katie stood up. Everyone had been courteously awaiting her cue to leave. Pete and Mike charged in her direction, which happened to be toward the exit.

"Where are you guys headed to?" Katie asked when they stopped next to her.

"We're going over to the Anchor Room first. How bout you Katie?" Pete asked.

Katie looked at Michael. They had all partied in Annapolis many times whenever they had meetings there. They even had their favorite bars. Usually, everybody started the night at the more subdued and clubby Anchor Room. After that, they headed to Jack's Flat for dancing and more drinking.

It was an awkward moment, as Michael waited to see how Grant reacted. Grant sensed this and spoke up, "I'll join you guys for a little while." He wanted to have a couple of drinks and hoped that would help him to get some sleep.

"Sounds good," Michael said.

Katie clasped her hands and touched her fingertips to her mouth. With a coy grin, she looked at Pete and said, "Looks like we'll see you guys in a couple minutes."

"Alright Katie," Pete said with a wink and a smile.

At the other end of the second table, Debbie asked Carol, "Are you headed back to your room?"

Carol shared her territory with Mike, Pete, and six other reps who covered the eastern shore. She said, "Yeah, I'm tired. I'm going to call my husband and kids and then enjoy watching whatever I want on television. It's nice to have a bed all to myself. How bout you Deb?"

"I'll walk back with you. I'm going to call Mark and then I might even go to the fitness room again."

"You're kidding? Why? I thought you already worked out before dinner." Carol said this in the slightly overdramatic tone that her southern accent imparted. She was born and raised in North Carolina.

Debbie grimaced and said, "I know it's a little irrational, even for an exercise addict like me. It's just that I can't sleep well when I go to these meetings. If I exercise enough, I fall asleep from sheer physical exhaustion. I guess I just miss Harry and Mark."

"Wait a minute Harry *and* Mark?" Carol asked. As soon as she said it, she remembered that Harry was Debbie's dog. She laughed and said, "Oh Harry — your doggie! How is Harry anyway?"

"Harry's great. And so is Mark," Debbie said with a big smile.

Debbie and Carol were at the tail end of the group when they finally left the restaurant. It had gotten much colder outside and everyone walked quickly. The group started to divide and separate, as some walked toward the hotel and others walked in the direction of the Anchor Room. Katie yelled over, "You guys are headed back to the hotel right? And you're OK?"

The answers to her questions were obvious. But the questions hinted at the legal ramifications. Katie was clearly bearing witness to the fact that they were willingly returning to the hotel unescorted by management. Debbie thought it was juvenile and an insult to her integrity but she was used to the patriarchal style of Inhaber-Taft's management.

Carol and Debbie shouted back to Katie, "Yes. We're fine, thanks."

In her accent that managed to sugar coat even a catty remark, Carol said, "I guess all this legal stuff is necessary, given the fact that most of the salespeople were living in dorm rooms before they landed their jobs." They both laughed.

When Debbie got back to her room, she immediately picked up the phone on the bedside table to call Mark. At the end of the fourth ring, a recording told the caller to leave a message. "Hi Mark. I just got back from our group dinner and I wanted to catch up with you. I'm going to the fitness room and I'll be back in my room by 10:00. I just want to ride the bike for about a half hour or so. I love you. Bye."

Next she called Karen. This time the phone was answered on the first ring.

"Hi Karen. It's Debbie."

"Oh hi Debbie. I was just on my way out the door to your house to let Harry out one more time before I go to bed."

"How is he doing?"

"He's doing great. I threw the ball to him a bunch of times in your yard this afternoon, and then I sat with him and watched TV for a little while."

"Oh good. Thanks Karen." Debbie hesitated for a minute but then reassured herself that Karen would understand, so she said, "I miss him."

"I know how you feel Debbie. It's hard to be away from our little buddies."

Debbie smiled and said, "Thanks Karen. I should be home tomorrow night by 8:00 at the latest and maybe even as early as 6:00. It's hard to tell. Sometimes they let us go early and other times we stay until 5:30 or 6:00."

"Don't worry Debbie. I'll plan on doing the usual walking and feeding schedule and if you're home when I get there, then we're all set."

"That sounds great. Thanks Karen." Then she added, "Oh Karen!"

"Yeah?"

"You have the phone number for the hotel where I'm staying right? The Annapolis Marriott?"

"Yes. I have it. You included it in the instructions that you printed out for me on the kitchen counter."

"OK. Thanks Karen."

"Sure thing. Goodnight Debbie."

"Bye."

As soon as Debbie hung up the phone, she started to undress. She changed back into her exercise bra, shorts, and a t-shirt. She began to tie her sneakers when the phone rang. "That has to be Mark," she thought.

"Hi my love."

Debbie smiled, "Hi Mark."

"How's the meeting going?"

"Good. I was just getting ready to go work out at the fitness room."

"Yeah. I listened to your message. Isn't it a little late for that?"

"It is, but you know I overdo the exercise at meetings so I can sleep and . . ."

Mark interrupted, "I can think of a better way to make you fall asleep. How about if I come over there and keep you company?"

"Now that sounds good," Debbie twisted the phone cord in her fingers and swayed back and forth as she stood there. She and Mark both knew that he wasn't going to drive to Annapolis at this hour but it made them both feel good to imagine it.

Mark started to talk through a yawn, "Uhhh, I'm tired."

"Are you still at the office?"

"Yeah. I'm going to get out of here now though." It sounded to Debbie as if Mark had stood up from his chair. She pictured him standing by his desk . . . his tall, lean body; probably dressed in navy blue pants and an oxford blue shirt. His tie was most likely still neatly in place.

Debbie asked, "Did you eat dinner?"

"Yeah. I walked down the street and grabbed a slice of pizza." Mark yawned again, "You'll be home tomorrow night right?"

"Yeah."

"What time?" As soon as Mark asked the question, he knew the answer. He quickly added, "I know. I know. It depends on when they let you guys go."

"Yeah."

"Alright, well, call me on the way home and let me know what time I should come over."

"OK. I'll call you on my way home."

"I love you Debbie."

"I love you too Mark. Goodnight."

Debbie looked at the clock. It was 9:35. She thought, "I better hurry. I forget whether they close the fitness room at 10 or 10:30."

It was about 10:30 p.m. when Debbie walked across the lobby to return to her room. Something caught her attention, and she looked toward the revolving front door. She couldn't believe what she saw! Brad was carrying somebody over his shoulder as he made his way into the lobby. Debbie thought it looked like Michael Poong. Molly and Blaire were laughing as they squeezed into the next pie-cut of a door opening. Katie, Todd and Pete were next. Everyone was laughing as Brad lowered a very drunk Michael Poong to the floor. He wobbled a little when his feet touched the floor. Debbie was shocked but she didn't show it on her face because she didn't want them to think she was a prude. She walked toward the group and asked, "What happened to him?"

Pete said, "Oh, Michael just had one too many margheritas." Everybody laughed. Debbie looked at Michael. His eyes were bloodshot and he looked at Debbie with a blank stare.

Todd said loudly, "Hey, does anybody want to hit the hotel bar for a nightcap?"

Michael grunted something and everybody started to laugh.

"No Michael. I think I better deliver you to your room," Brad said. With that, he threw Michael over his shoulder again and walked toward the elevator. Molly, Blaire and Pete headed to the hotel bar with Todd.

"Aren't you coming Katie?" Todd shouted back.

"No. I have to do a little bit of homework, so I'll see you tomorrow."

Debbie got onto the elevator with Katie, Brad and Michael. Katie said to Debbie, "Boy you're working out kind of late."

"Yeah, well, it helps me to sleep." Debbie felt a strange mix of emotions. She thought to herself sarcastically, "Great role model — the professional female! But look at her!" She boldly glared at Katie's face in the harsh light of the elevator and thought, "She looks like 'ten miles of bad highway.'" She could smell the alcohol spewing from Michael's breath as he hovered over Brad's shoulder right next to her. The elevator stopped at the third floor. Apparently Inhaber-Taft employees were all on the same floor because everybody exited the elevator.

Katie giggled and asked Brad, "Do you know his room number?"

"Yeah, it's 302 — right here." He bent down slightly and Michael slid down onto the floor, only this time instead of landing on his feet, he just kept going.

"Ooops . . ." Brad said, as he collected Michael into his arms and threw him over his shoulder again. Katie was laughing hysterically. Debbie forced a laugh, but she was obviously uncomfortable.

Katie said, "Oh Deb, don't look so worried. You know Michael will be a hundred percent in the morning."

Debbie looked at Katie and thought to herself, "She must be high or something." Rumors had always swirled around Katie. There were stories about her drug use and her affairs with everyone from reps to doctors--even the region director. But, in an odd way, the rumors about her bad behavior managed to prop up Katie's image in the eyes of her young subordinates. It seemed to fulfill a fantasy that it was possible to be happy and successful while burning the candle at both ends.

Brad easily managed to hold Michael on his shoulder with one arm, while he slid the cardkey into the slot on the door with his other hand. He pushed the door open and Katie leaned against it to prevent it from closing. Debbie stepped into the doorway. She had to see how this ended.

Brad flopped Michael onto one of the queen size beds and said in a breathless tone, "I wonder if he arranged a wakeup call."

Katie had stopped laughing and at least made the appearance of straightening herself up. She said, "Why don't you call the front desk and ask them for a wakeup call at 6:00 a.m."

"Good idea."

"Then maybe as a backup . . . well, I don't know."

"What Katie?" Brad asked.

"Would you mind checking in on him in the morning somewhere around 6:00 to make sure he's up? I mean, after all, he's running the meeting tomorrow so . . ."

"Oh no problem. Sure I'll do that." Brad was more than happy to take on a task beyond the call of duty. He knew Michael would owe him for helping him out in this precarious situation. Todd was his manager, but Michael and Todd were close buddies, so Brad only stood to gain from his involvement.

After Brad set the alarm and called the front desk, the three of them left Michael's room. Katie and Debbie made a left and Brad walked to the right. "Goodnight" they said simultaneously. Debbie's room came up first and Katie continued down the hall. "Goodnight Deb."

"Goodnight Katie." Debbie shut her door and walked over to the bed and slumped down onto her back. As she stared at the ceiling she said out loud, "What's happening to this company?" She thought to herself, "It used to be so professional and conservative. Now all the managers are just wild partiers. It doesn't pay to be professional and just do your job. You have to be a partier if you want to join the "in crowd." It's like high school! It never ends. The popular, wild kids just keep getting their way — even in the business world."

She got up and went into the bathroom and looked at herself in the giant mirror. She thought she looked old and tired, and thought, "The younger women wear provocative clothes to show off their boobs and their butts, while I run around in my wool skirts and blazers."

As she got ready for bed she thought cynically, "I guess Stacey was right after all."

Stacey had been an Administrative Assistant in the Marketing department at Inhaber-Taft. Like Debbie, she had aspirations of becoming a pharmaceutical sales rep once she graduated from night school. Stacey was proud of her reputation as a party girl. She hoped it would help her to get ahead. She had gotten an interview with Prescott-Williams and spent a couple of days "in the field" with their reps. One day at lunch, she told Debbie the Prescott-Williams reps partied with physicians all the time. She said one of the reps told her she slept with a couple of the doctors.

Stacey had laughed and said, "Yeah, one night after partying at Hannigan's in Philly, they all ended up getting naked and jumped into the hot tub at the doc's house." Debbie began to wonder if she still wanted to be a pharmaceutical sales rep.

Soon after that, she went on a day "in the field" with an Inhaber-Taft sales rep. She decided to relay Stacey's stories to find out if that was a typical part of the job. She had already decided the job was not for her if it was true.

She was relieved to hear, "Pharmaceutical sales is like any other sales job. It's what you make of it. Look at me. I'm successful, and I don't sleep with the docs. If you're smart and have a good personality and you know your products, you don't have to get involved in any of that. Sure there are docs who like to party and they'll like you better if you party with them. But going down that road can get you into a lot of trouble — not just professionally but in your personal life. Trust me, there's just as many docs, in fact more, who are interested in the information you have about your products." Then she added with a laugh, "And of course what kind of perks you can offer them."

Debbie had laughed with relief. She felt like a weight had been lifted from her. And over the years, she had always maintained her integrity. Some doctors were flirtatious and some even made passes at her. But she rebuffed them politely and they respected her wishes, although that didn't stop them from trying again but only until they found someone who wanted an affair.

As Debbie lay in bed that night, she thought, "It wouldn't have been so bad if it had just been one of the reps who got totally wasted . . . but a district manager! . . . and not just any manager, but Michael Poong — on the career fast track . . . not that he doesn't have a reputation, but to get so drunk that a rep has to carry him back to the hotel?"

Suddenly she sat up, "Wait a minute, David Clarke is going to be at the meeting tomorrow . . . I'm going to find a way to talk to him for five minutes and tell him what happened tonight. I'm sure he'll be happy if I tell him about the behavior of the managers who report to him. He'll straighten them out."

When she was initially hired by Inhaber-Taft, she worked in the pharmaceutical manufacturing technical services department. David Clark, her current region director, was one of several pharmacists who worked in the same department. At that time, everyone was working on a project to transfer product manufacturing formulas into a new computer database. The pharmacists proofread the formulas, which were lengthy specifications, and Debbie typed them into the computer. In those days, David Clark was not a popular guy. He wore thick glasses and his nose protruded in a shape resembling a shark fin. He was quiet and reserved and fairly young to be married with a child. Debbie liked him and his wife, whom she had talked with on a few occasions at social functions for the department.

Over the years, a few of the men and women who had worked in the much more conservative and much less glamorous Manufacturing Division, managed to cross the divide and land a job in the Marketing and Sales Division.

All it took was a visit to the company cafeteria and an employee could be identified, by division, based on physical appearance. The dark, navy blue suits and crisp shirts held together with a spiffy tie were worn by the remarkably good looking Marketing group.

The Marketing women were much fewer in number in those days, but also very attractive. They dressed in demure female versions of a marketing man's suit.

Other than top management in the Manufacturing Division, most of the men and women wore blue lab coats over their clothes. The lab coats were required in the manufacturing and packaging areas, and most people just left them on when they went to the cafeteria. Those who didn't, probably should have, in order to cover up their ill-fitting suits in dull shades of brown and gray.

It seemed that those who managed to cross over into marketing or sales did so only after a discreet metamorphosis. One day David Clarke was no longer wearing glasses. Laser surgery improved his vision and he tossed away the thick lenses. Plastic surgery chiseled his nose and chin into an aristocratic profile. And somewhere along the way, he divorced his wife and shared custody of his child, which allowed him considerable more time for dating. Suddenly, he landed a job in the Sales Division, and was soon showing off his new trophy wife at cocktail parties.

Debbie knew that David had changed, but she was naïve enough to think that a good guy still lurked beneath the surface.

Just before midnight, Katie heard a gentle tapping at her door, as she expected. She closed the drawer where she hid her coke and checked her nose in the mirror. She didn't see any white powder under her nostrils but she wiped them with her fingertip out of habit. The tapping started again. She was light on her feet as she dashed over to open it.

"Hi Pete," Katie whispered.

"Hey Katie."

They didn't waste any time. Pete shut the door behind him and grabbed Katie and kissed her passionately. She groaned as he moved her backwards through the bathroom doorway. He flipped the switch for the light and then picked Katie up and sat her on the bathroom counter. She lifted her blouse over her head. Pete undid her bra and slid his hands around to her breasts and squeezed them as she moaned. Then Katie ripped open his shirt and sent a button flying. She was tiny enough that Pete easily turned her around so she faced the big mirror. They both watched Pete slide his hands up her thighs and in between her legs. "Ahh. . .do it Pete. Do it." When they were finished, they laughed breathlessly, as beads of sweat ran down their bodies. As they walked out of the bathroom, Pete said, "Now I get to do the walk of shame." That's what everybody called it when one person sneaked over to another hotel room to have sex and, afterwards, had to walk back to their own room.

Katie laughed. "You're leaving already?"

"Yeah. My wife didn't answer the phone when I called her earlier. I know she's going to call back and if I'm not in my room at this hour, she'll hassle me about what I'm doing. She doesn't trust me."

Katie laughed again.

Pete said, "I think she doesn't answer the phone on purpose so she has an excuse to call me late at night. That way she can check up on me."

"Poor Pete," Katie said coyly. Then she added, "Hey, maybe we can hook up at that bed and breakfast in town before you drive home tomorrow."

"Sounds good to me," Pete said. He kissed her and then said, "I'll see you tomorrow morning boss."

Katie smiled and said, "Goodnight Pete."

Chapter 18: District Meeting - Day 2

Tuesday, March 15

DAVID CLARKE WAS about an hour south of Annapolis when he called Katie at 6:30 a.m. on Tuesday morning.

"Did you get it?" David asked.

Katie recognized David's voice. She was expecting his call. "Hi Dave. Yeah. I stopped by Tim's place before I left town yesterday morning."

"Good. Just put it in an interoffice envelope as usual."

Katie yawned nonchalantly and said, "Sure, same as usual."

David added, "Hey, I'm sorry I couldn't talk when I called you yesterday but my assistant burst into my office the minute you answered your cell phone."

"No problem Dave. I assumed something like that happened."

She could hear the smile in his voice when he said with relief, "Alright, I'll see you soon."

"Bye Dave."

For the most part, the rumors about Katie were right. She did sleep around, and she did have an affair with the region director--her boss, David Clarke. But it ended just a few months after he promoted her to a district sales manager. They had met at a symposium in Hilton Head, South Carolina, when Katie was working as an analyst in the market research department. Their affair started and ended within six months. David quickly lost interest in the women he had affairs with, and he always managed to detach himself before things got complicated. He had no plans to end his marriage because he loved his wife. He simply enjoyed the excitement of his trysts. He had two young children with his second wife, Alexis, who happened to be the daughter of a member of the Board of Directors for Inhaber-Taft.

Katie's affair with David won her two things — a promotion and information about David that would assure her job security as long as he was her boss. He confided in her one night after they had sex in his hotel room. "Katie, I've been suffering with a bad back for a while now. The only thing that helps is TOXYCONTIN. I've been having trouble getting it lately from my usual source." He hesitated for a moment and then continued, "You confided in me about doing some coke, so I wondered if you know anyone who would be a reliable supplier."

Katie smiled. She knew her fate was sealed. She immediately thought of Tim Peyton. He was a Running Back for the Philadelphia Eagles, and Katie had dated him for about four months, until their relationship started to sour. One night, Tim had a party at his house with a live band. It was Dr. Ira Goldman's band. Katie met Ira that night and they hung out together during the band's breaks because Tim was nowhere to be found. Eventually, Katie found Tim--in one of the bedrooms with two women. Tim and his friends used prescription drugs for pain and, as professional athletes, they had no problem getting a steady supply of any drug they wanted. Katie knew Tim would be cool about it. She said, "Sure Dave. No problem. What strength do you need and how much?"

Ever since then, Katie had been delivering TOXYCONTIN to David at meetings. He always wanted the same amount — four bottles of sixty tablets in an inconspicuous interoffice envelope. David didn't want to risk sending it through the mail. Michael Poong eventually found out about his boss's affinity for TOXYCONTIN once David realized how desperately Michael wanted to be on the career fast track. David asked Michael to help him out and, of course, he said yes. Interestingly, Michael's supplier was Dr. Ira Goldman. But Katie and Michael never found out they were providing the same service. Instead, each of them held the secret closely, like a marker they would use when the time was right. The day would come when David would return the favor by signing off on the next promotion along the fast track.

Throughout the hotel, in the early morning hours, alarms went off and showers rained. Fitness buffs exercised, while partiers swallowed aspirin and hit the snooze button. Eventually hair was coiffed, faces were shaved, cologne dabbed and perfume sprayed. Some reps opted for the 7:30 breakfast in the hotel restaurant. It was usually set up buffet style with eggs, bacon, sausage, pancakes, and home fries. Hot grits, gravy and biscuits were always on the menu for the native Maryland folks who considered themselves southerners. Although the region's reps who hailed from Virginia contested the notion that geography south of the Mason-Dixon Line was reason enough to include Maryland as part of the south.

Debbie sat on the edge of her bed in her blouse and underpants. She was waiting for the coffee pot in her room to perk up a cup. At first, she was afraid to use it when she held it up to the light and saw the layer of dust on it. "When was the last time this thing was used . . . or cleaned?" But she washed it out with soap and hot water and then checked the expiration date on the complimentary coffee pouch. "Good. It still has a year to go."

She still felt angry about the night before. "It'll be interesting to see what kind of shape Michael Poong is in this morning."

The hotel's daily events were displayed on the television of each room via channel 2. There was also an easel with a big poster by the front desk in the lobby that displayed the same information. Still, a few of the reps went to the wrong conference room because they returned to the room where they had been the day before. Day 2 of the district meeting combined both Michael Poong's and Katie McDonaugh's teams in one, large conference room. They were going to spend the entire day focused on Inhaber-Taft's number one product, the blockbuster drug, MELAVOX.

Many of the reps had already seated themselves at one of the long rows of tables, adorned with the customary white tablecloths, water glasses, and pitchers of ice cold water. The table at the front of the room was reserved for management. Today, David Clarke would give a brief presentation, so everyone seemed to "take it up a notch" in terms of their dress and professional demeanor.

Carol and Debbie were chatting when Carol said, "Hey Mike, hey Pete," as they moved into the row in back of them.

"'Mornin' Carol and Deb. You ladies are looking fine today," Pete said with an exaggerated southern accent.

"Well thanks Pete," Carol said.

"Good mornin' ladies," Mike said in the same tone as Pete.

"Good morning fellas," Debbie said with a smile. She was intrigued by the way Mike followed Pete around like a puppy dog. He mimicked his mannerisms and even his good 'ole boy style. Mike was a young rep with less than a year on the job. It didn't take him long to find out that Pete was deeply entrenched in the medical community of the eastern shore. Mike knew the docs thought that any friend of Pete's was a friend of theirs. And female reps, like Carol, fit in perfectly with her southern charm and simple good looks.

"Hey winner!" Rose dropped her briefcase onto the floor and her books onto the table simultaneously.

"How was your night Rose?" Debbie asked.

Rose laughed and said, "Good. I hung in traction." Debbie had heard Rose say that at every meeting. She usually just laughed in response, even though she could only imagine what that looked like. This time, she decided to ask.

"How do you hang in traction?"

Rose laughed and said, "Ahh winner . . . you're funny."

Debbie gave her a big smile. Then she said, "No. I'm serious. I don't know."

"Well you know by now that I have a bad back right?"

"Yeah," Debbie said. In fact, there was an urban legend that Rose once laid on the floor at the back of a conference room, during a meeting, because her back was in such pain.

"I bring an inversion table with me when I go to these meetings," Rose said.

"What's an inversion table?" Debbie asked, although she could sort of visualize it.

"It's a collapsible table." Rose leaned in to Debbie and said in a stage whisper, "I usually have the bellhop set it up for me after he carries it up to my room. Then I just lie down on the table and push a motorized gear that raises and lowers the table to any position I want. I like to position it so I'm upside down."

"Are you really completely upside down?"

"Well almost. I set it at about a 70 degree angle since I put on a few pounds."

"Are you strapped into it?"

Rose giggled and said, "You have to be, otherwise you'll land on your head. I strap in my ankles, waist, and one of my wrists. I have to leave one arm free so I can change the gears."

Just then Katie McDonaugh walked up to the table in front of them and said loudly, "Hi everybody." Rose turned toward her and said, "Hey girl. How are ya today?"

"Good." Katie said and then turned to put her belongings down. Michael Poong and David Clarke were in deep conversation but stopped as soon as Katie approached them. Debbie watched as they greeted each other.

"Why do women wear sunglasses on the top of their heads at these meetings?" Rose asked. "I mean it's not like they were just outside. They came from their hotel rooms!"

Debbie laughed a little and then said, "So when you hang upside down, does it help your back to feel better?"

"Oh yeah."

"How long do you do it?"

"Usually for a half hour or forty five minutes. But at these meetings, I use it off and on during the night."

"Do you sleep on it?"

Rose laughed, "Not intentionally, but I have been known to fall asleep on it. It's usually not a good idea. I try to get into my bed before I crash for the night."

Grant Preston entered the conference room and walked up to Michael, David and Katie. Rose whispered, "I wonder if Grant is going to stay for the meeting." Just then, Michael Poong put his arm around Grant's shoulder.

Rose laughed and said, "Look at Michael. That young buck is such a sycophant."

Debbie laughed. She wasn't sure what the word meant but assumed it summed up pretty much what she thought of Michael — a brownnoser. She leaned closer to Rose and said, "You know he was so drunk last night that Brad actually carried him into the hotel and up to his room?"

"You're kidding?"

"No. I was walking across the lobby . . ."

When she finished telling Rose about the night before, Rose seemed unfettered by the gossip. She had seen lots of bad behavior among the residents at the hospital when she was a nurse. Ironically, it was her laissez faire attitude that unintentionally invited people to confide in her.

Carol leaned toward Debbie and said, "I wish we would get started."

"Me too."

Carol whispered, "You know, I work as hard as anybody — in fact probably harder than most — and yet the reps at these meetings are always clicking away on their computers and making cell phone calls and . . . I mean it makes me uncomfortable because I feel like I should be doing something too — instead of just sitting here."

Debbie smiled and said, "I know what you mean. But I think all these frenzied displays of work are just for show. The reps just want their managers to think they're constantly busy. I always get caught up on my paperwork before I go to a meeting. That way I'm not distracted by a lot of loose ends."

Carol said, "Yeah, me too."

But there was one nagging thought bothering Debbie now. It was the same thought she had just before she left her room that morning. "I should have checked my voicemail for messages. I always forget to check at these meetings."

For the most part, voicemail messages were from other Inhaber-Taft reps or a district manager. Occasionally a physician's office would call to ask for more samples or to confirm a lunch appointment. In fact, her hesitancy to pick up a phone and check for messages was the dread of the inevitable "on hold hell" that she would suffer when she called the doctor's office.

When a sales rep called a doctor's office, it was just as frustrating as it was for a patient calling the office. She was immediately put on hold for five or ten minutes. Finally, a receptionist got back on the line, only to interrupt once or twice to take another call. It could take half an hour just to return two telephone calls to doctors' offices.

The reps knew the sampling habits of the physicians they called on. Some physicians gave out a lot of drug samples to each of their patients, while others did not. The reps knew approximately how many samples of each product the office would need on each visit. This allowed the reps to stock their trunks with the appropriate amount of samples each day, depending on which offices they planned to call on. The reps are required to keep records of all the samples they distribute. They re-order an appropriate quantity of samples each month in order to maintain a proper inventory. At the end of the month, a UPS truck delivers about 35 to 40 cartons of drug samples, which are usually stored in the reps' basements or garages.

Michael tapped at the tiny microphone on the lapel of his jacket. "Good morning. How are you guys today?" He gave everyone a big smile and there were various responses of "good" or "great." Somebody said, "tired" and everyone laughed, including Michael. He said, "I think everybody had a good time last night and we owed ourselves a little celebration for a great year." He flipped a slide onto the screen that had the names of the reps with the highest sales and market share for each product. "Congratulations to our top performers."

Michael put his hands together and said, "Let's give ourselves a hand for a job well done." Everyone applauded.

Michael took a deep breath for dramatic effect and said, "Well guys, today is a new day and now we must move forward to take on the challenges we are facing this year. The objectives have been set and we are being paid not only to meet these objectives, but to exceed them. Each one of you is a skilled professional representative. You know your products. You know the science behind them. We've armed you with the information you need for obstacle handling and presenting your products' features and benefits. But it's a competitive market and each year the competition gets tougher."

Michael stepped away from the podium and slowly approached the first table of reps. After a pause, he said to the group, "You know there are reps out there who want your job. Inhaber-Taft is one of the top five pharmaceutical companies in the world . . . in the *world!*"

Someone in the audience clapped, so Michael followed suit and everyone responded with more applause.

Michael continued, "Each one of you is in the unique position of being able to chart your own course. You can sit back and feel confident in your product knowledge, in the reputation of Inhaber-Taft, and about your job security. But you risk becoming complacent. This year, I challenge each and every one of you to shift the paradigm. I want you to think of yourself as a *sales* person. Years ago, the medical community called you *detail* men and women. Your business card says 'Professional Representative' or 'Senior' or 'Executive' Professional Representative." Again he paused and then continued, "Now . . . we're not changing your job title. But from now on, I want you to look at your business card and see the words, 'Professional *Sales* Representative.' More importantly, I want you to internalize that perception. It's not enough anymore just to *promote* MELAVOX and CARDIOPLEX and PEPLIN and our other great products. There's just too much competition because there are other good products out there. We have to *sell* our physicians on why they should prescribe our products instead of our competitors' products. Today, we will spend the entire day focusing on MELAVOX. But the take-away message from this meeting is that you have to *sell* each and every one of your products — not just *promote* them. Starting right now, think of yourself as a *sales* person."

Michael pushed for a response from the reticent audience, "Are you ready?" A few people mumbled yes.

Michael cupped his ear with his hand and said, "I can't hear you. Come on guys." He looked at his watch and said, "It's 9:08. You guys are typically out on territory at this hour and I don't hear the enthusiasm that I should." He smiled because he didn't want to appear too heavy handed. Once again he said, "Are you ready?"

Everyone shouted loudly, "Yes!" and there were some who added, "We're ready."

Michael laughed a little and led everyone in applause, as he said, "You guys are great!" For Michael, it was important that the reps liked him. In fact, it was important to all of the managers to be well liked, if they planned to advance their careers. It was part of the corporate culture. Executive management promoted sales managers who achieved their goals and gained the respect of their team. Likeability was essential.

Michael returned to the podium at the front of the room and said, "Today we are fortunate to have David Clarke with us."

David stood up and walked toward Michael. The group applauded. When David reached Michael, they shook hands and slapped each other on the back.

"David wants to say a few words about your fantastic performance last year and the challenges that await us this year."

Michael pinned his microphone onto David's lapel and then sat down next to Katie.

"Thank you Michael. Good morning everyone," David said with a genuine smile.

For the next ten minutes, David gave a "rah rah" speech to rally the troops. He likened them to athletes because their performance each day had to exceed that of the previous day. He finished with, ". . . so our top performers should take a moment and enjoy their achievements, but all of us must now turn our attention to the new challenges that await us each day. Each win calls for celebration, but we must move on from that as swiftly as we move on from rejection, because there is another opportunity that awaits us just around the corner. Again, congratulations and let's achieve even greater things this year."

Everyone applauded and cheered. Michael returned to the podium and again shook hands with David. There was another handoff of the microphone and then Michael said, "Let's take a five minute break. Just five minutes please, and then return to your seats."

Debbie saw that David Clarke started to gather up his things. She thought, "Is he leaving already?" She lingered for a minute. If he was leaving, she didn't want to risk a dash for the restroom and then miss the opportunity to talk to him. David shook hands with Katie and seemed to be saying goodbye. Debbie thought, "I better step outside of the conference room and then catch him as he walks out."

As Debbie waited, she knew it would take a few minutes before David Clarke exited the conference room because, as the region director, he was like a celebrity among the reps. A few of them managed to stop him for a moment and fussed and fawned about his inspirational talk and their readiness for the new year.

Debbie wasn't the only rep waiting to pounce on David when he walked out of the room. Blaire and Brad were trying to be nonchalant as they chatted just outside the room. Neither of them was actually listening to the other, but they shared the unspoken bond of a shared purpose — to ensnare David as he walked toward the lobby doors. Debbie could see they were positioned for better access than she was. But it didn't matter because she was determined. There was no way David was going to exit the hotel without her catching him.

Blaire and Brad rushed up and the three of them were all smiles, laughter, and chatting. After a moment, they followed David's lead and began to walk toward the revolving door in the lobby. Debbie followed a few paces behind. They lingered by the door and Debbie stood a respectable distance away, but it was obvious that she was waiting to lunge at him. David Clarke looked at Debbie and smiled. Blaire and Brad could see that their time was up and David was ready to move on to the next person.

David said, "Alright, thanks." He shook hands with Brad and then with Blaire. He said, "Good luck. And let's get those MELAVOX numbers up."

"Oh, no doubt," Brad declared.

"We will," Blaire said confidently. Then the two of them walked away and to Debbie's surprise, David started through the revolving door, so she pushed through the door behind him. She felt a little embarrassed by her desperation. The thought even crossed her mind to forget the whole thing. Then she heard herself calling out, "David." He stopped short and turned around. Debbie bumped into him. The brown interoffice envelope that he was carrying fell to the ground. They both recognized the sound of tablets rattling in plastic bottles. Debbie assumed that David had asked someone to get him samples of an Inhaber-Taft product for his personal use. This was taboo because the reps were cautioned again and again that taking drug samples for personal use was grounds for termination. But sometimes discreet exceptions were made for upper management.

As she picked up the envelope and handed it to David, she said sheepishly, "Sorry."

David couldn't hide the fact that he was both embarrassed and annoyed. He felt his face flush and he grabbed the envelope from her. Debbie felt uneasy and diminished, like a child who pretended not to notice something very bad. It was an awkward moment, until David finally composed himself and said, "What can I do for you Debbie?" And before she could answer, he quickly added, "Congratulations on your FLAGIT sales performance."

"Thanks David." She thought, "It's now or never," so she blurted out, "David, I think you should know about something that happened last night."

"What's that?" David felt a sense of relief, rather than apprehension, because apparently Debbie's focus was now on something other than whatever might be in his envelope.

"Well, the group went out to dinner last night and a few of them went out afterwards." Debbie started to get nervous when David shifted his weight impatiently, but she continued. "I was walking across the lobby around 10:30 or so, when Brad and Katie and some other people walked into the lobby." She was certain the next part would shock him. "Brad was carrying Michael Poong over his shoulder because Michael was too drunk to walk."

David was obviously taken aback. He furrowed his brow and said in a very serious tone, "That's definitely not good."

Debbie was heartened by his reaction. She felt a kinship with David, as she thought to herself, "Good, he's still the same old David at heart. He believes in the professional standards of the old Inhaber-Taft, just like me . . . Michael is in trouble now."

She decided to push the issue a little further to make sure Michael didn't get away with it. She said, "David, you and I have worked for this company for a long time and I just don't think that managers getting drunk — I mean totally trashed drunk — should be acceptable behavior. This would never have been acceptable in the Manufacturing Division and I'm afraid that if we just let it go that . . ."

David interrupted Debbie. He thought she had gone a bit too far when she said "if *we* just let it go." After all she was a rep, not a manager. He resented her assumption that just because they had worked together years ago, they shared a bond of any kind. David knew he had changed a great deal since then, both personally and professionally. He didn't want to be haunted by someone who clung to the memory of his past. But he said what she wanted to hear. "You're right Debbie. It is not acceptable behavior. I'm going to have a talk with Michael."

Debbie was happy and thought naively, "I knew I could count on David." And when he smiled at her she dared to think, "Maybe he'll see me differently now. Maybe he'll even think of me as a potential manager because of my integrity. He won't care that I was once just an Administrative Assistant."

In reality, the only bond they shared was simply the desire to bury their pasts. David didn't like having Debbie in his region. When he looked at her, he saw his past reflected back at him.

David said, "Don't give it another thought. I'll take care of it and you just concentrate on your job." He thought that sounded a bit too patronizing, so he added, "I'm really happy that you told me about this, but don't give it another thought." Then he shifted the items he was carrying so that he could shake her hand.

Debbie smiled and said, "Thanks a lot David."

He grinned at her and the valet walked up to him and asked, "Do you have your ticket sir?"

"Yes I do," David replied.

He turned away and Debbie went back into the hotel. She slipped back into her seat in the conference room. The reps were listening intently as Michael Poong talked at the front of the room. He had an unimpressive, slight frame and rose to a height of only five feet, five inches. But his posture was perfectly straight as he stretched his spine for every inch of height. He was speaking in a clear, deliberate tone that had the affect of diminishing his Vietnamese accent. He was able to captivate the group for two reasons. One, he was passionate and two, everybody knew that a friend on the fast track meant a contact in the network to promotion.

Michael said, "Inhaber-Taft has made the mistake of letting our competition sell *us* on the deleterious effects of MELAVOX 75 mg. It's time to take back ownership of this great product and the superior pain relief that MELAVOX 75 can provide. We have to *sell* physicians on the importance of titrating up to 75 mg of MELAVOX. We tell physicians to use MELAVOX 75 mg for the treatment of acute pain for 5 to 10 days. Why are we specifying 5 to 10 days? I'll tell you why. Because Prescott-Williams has sold us on the idea!"

Brad led the group in applause. He said loudly, "You're right Michael!"

But not everyone was comfortable with the idea. They were thinking about the METAPO study results.

Michael continued in a fervent tone, "There is nothing in the prescribing information for MELAVOX that specifies the duration of treatment for acute pain. So we have to change the paradigm. I want you to tell your physicians that MELAVOX is the drug of choice for the treatment of *pain!*" He said emphatically, "Let's break free of the habit of specifying *acute* pain. Pain can be chronic with acute flare-ups of worsening pain. But you know from your own experience that when you occasionally suffer from pain, you don't describe it to your doctor as acute pain or chronic pain. You simply say that you're *in pain* and that you want him or her to prescribe something that will stop the pain. So, the number one change in our strategy is to change our vocabulary. We are dropping the word 'acute.' I don't want to hear any of you using the word 'acute.'" The second change is that we tell physicians that MELAVOX 75 mg once daily is the appropriate dose for the treatment of pain and it *can* be used as long term therapy. We are eliminating the phrase 'for five to ten days of therapy.'"

Debbie felt her heart beating wildly in her chest. She thought, "I can't believe he's saying this! What about the METAPO study! This is unethical.m MELAVOX is only supposed to be used for five to ten days for the treatment of acute pain. It's the only safe way to use the max dose of the drug. I have to say something! I can't believe that nobody else is objecting to this bullshit!"

Her heart was beating faster with the anticipation of speaking up. She practiced her comment in her mind before she said it out loud. But she was full of nervous anxiety at the thought of contradicting him.

Michael continued, "MELAVOX is the most effective non-narcotic medication for the treatment of pain. By the time we leave here today, I want each and every one of you to be convinced and confident that MELAVOX 75 mg can be used for long term treatment of pain. I want it to roll off your lips as naturally as 'MELAVOX 25 mg is the appropriate dose for long term treatment of osteoarthritis.'"

Debbie sat up straight and then slowly contracted her stomach muscles to relax her breathing. She was ready. She half raised her hand and got

Michael's attention. In those few seconds, she started to get nervous again, but she took a shallow breath and again contracted her stomach muscles. She wasn't sure if Michael would stop long enough to let her speak. He did.

"Yes Debbie," he said in an abrupt tone, insinuating, "this better be good."

"Michael, I think it is unethical to tell physicians that MELAVOX 75 mg can be used as long term therapy."

Michael didn't flinch.

Debbie continued, "I don't think that we're being sold or brainwashed by Prescott-Williams and our other competition. The METAPO study is a valid clinical study that showed that MELAVOX 75 mg taken every day for six months caused thromboembolic events like heart attack and stroke."

Silence hung in the air for a few seconds. Absolutely no one dared to back up Debbie's statement. It was career suicide. The young reps cared more about spending their salaries than evaluating the ethics of a manager's style. The older reps had bills to pay and children in college. They were wise enough to ignore the sleazy tactics of a yuppie manager. Besides, the tenured reps knew they would do it their own way once they were out in the field. They knew meetings were mostly about showing up early with a smile, a positive attitude, and a ready "yes" to whatever management asked of them. For the sake of job security and potential promotion, it was more expedient to ignore the guerilla in the room.

Michael remained poised. He looked at the floor for a moment. He had a grin on his face that turned into a half smile before he spoke. His tone was disparaging. "Debbie, you don't understand the science behind the nature of pain."

Debbie was embarrassed and insulted, but she maintained her composure as he continued.

Michael said, "But I'm glad you raised this point because I have a slide that will help us out." With that, he pressed the remote control and a new slide popped onto the screen. In big, bold letters the word **ACUTE** lurched forward from the screen.

"By definition, acute pain is an intense flare-up of pain that requires immediate treatment. Unfortunately for our purposes, acute pain is transient, so duration of treatment is limited. It amounts to a script for just ten tablets.

Now, are we going to exceed our sales objectives for MELAVOX if our docs are writing scripts for ten tablets at a time? I think you know the answer to that question. And remember, we are going to think of ourselves as salespeople from this day forward." He paced around in silence and then clasped his hands behind his back. He slumped his shoulders and looked at the floor as if in professorial deliberation.

Finally he said, "Let me be blunt. As pharmaceutical salespeople in today's competitive environment, we can only keep our jobs if we meet our sales goals. And you, my friends, can only get promoted if you *exceed* your planned objectives. We are going to sell our physicians on MELAVOX as the drug of choice for the treatment of chronic pain. We will tell them to use the MELAVOX 75 mg dose, with no qualifier as to how long they can use it. If the physician asks 'How long can my patient take the 75 mg dose of MELAVOX?' then we respond, 'as long as needed."

Debbie sat there quietly indignant. She knew she had already done enough career damage by speaking up and contradicting Michael. And it was clear that Michael had no intention of changing his course.

Michael continued to preach to the reps. Debbie tuned him out thought to herself, "His logic is flawed and he's selling a load of unethical bullshit to these reps!" But she could see that most of them were nodding in agreement.

Michael said loudly and authoritatively, "There are nuances that you must learn. A successful sales person recognizes the moment when he or she can sell the product with what they *don't* say."

Debbie fidgeted in her seat. Since no one had spoken up to concur with her comments, she was the outsider. She no longer felt brave but anxious about the fallout from her comments. She looked at the back of Katie's head at the table in front of her. She worried about what Katie was thinking and what she would say to her later. She wondered if Michael would confront her at the break.

She wasn't listening anymore until Michael said, "As you know, Prescott-Williams started a program called Physician Consultant Forums in November of last year. Now, initially, there was a lot of discussion about the pros and cons of Inhaber-Taft conducting these programs. Some people argued that it wasn't Inhaber-Taft's style, and others said we have to change with the times in order to compete. Now, I guess you know which camp I'm in." Michael laughed a little and bowed his head in mock humility.

The reps laughed as Michael switched to a slide that enumerated the steps of the program. He said, "This is how a Physician Consultant Forum works." And then he read from the slide:

1. You, as the territory rep, ask six of your physicians to participate in a new Physician Consultant Forum for Inhaber-Taft. These six physicians have to be your highest volume writers for MELAVOX. Explain to the physician that they will be paid $300 if they attend a dinner program regarding a new marketing campaign for MELAVOX. The dinner will be held at a local restaurant and the Inhaber-Taft reps for that territory will be present during the cocktail hour. Since it is not a sales event, the reps will have to leave before the dinner program begins. At that point, the physicians are brought into the dining room where they are joined by two or three members of our Market Research team, one person from the MELAVOX product management team, and the district sales manager.

2. A member of our Market Research team will present our latest promotional pieces. These promotional pieces have not yet been distributed to our sales force. We will consult the physicians for their feedback about the clinical data presented in the pieces. We want to know if the promotional pieces touch on the product features and benefits that really matter to them.

3. Just so the physicians don't think that we're asking for too much of their time, you must explain to them that the presentation will occur *after* they have ordered their dinner. The ensuing discussion will take place *while* they eat dinner, so the entire program should take only two and a half to three hours of their evening.

Michael asked the group, "What do you think?"

Everyone applauded. Then Ken Welder spoke up, "Michael, I have a concern about this." Everyone turned to look in Ken's direction.

"What's that Ken?"

"I've heard from the Prescott-Williams' reps that these forums have set a precedent. Now physicians want to get paid every time they go to a dinner, even if it has nothing to do with being a consultant."

A few of the reps meekly agreed.

Ken continued, "I mean, it hasn't affected us yet because Marketing pulled back our expense money right around the time that Prescott-Williams started doing this at the end of last year. I haven't had a dinner yet this year, but I'm concerned that, down the road, I might have trouble getting docs to come out for a dinner for one of my other products when they find out they're not going to get paid for it."

Harrison decided to speak up. He said, "Yeah, Michael, last week I started to invite some physicians to a dinner program for PEPLIN. Dr. Knowles said to me, 'why should I come out to a dinner if I'm not getting paid for it.' At first, I thought he was just kidding. But he was serious."

Michael knew he had to jump in quickly to extinguish the negativity. "Alright. Look, you guys remember the old rule of thumb: you can't worry about things that are beyond your control. Look at the positive. Now we have the opportunity to compete on the same playing field as Prescott-Williams. It's all in the way you present it. You make it clear when you invite them that they're not getting paid just to come out to a dinner. They are getting paid for their services as a Consultant. And the good news is, soon we will be rolling out another opportunity for physicians to be paid as Consultants when we initiate our own post-marketing clinical trials."

Michael quickly flipped through some slides and stopped at the one that gave the new sales objectives for MELAVOX. He said sternly, "Take a look at these numbers — both volume and market share."

Everybody gasped in shock, as he expected. He said with exasperation, "These numbers are huge!" He paced around a bit and then stopped short and spoke in an emphatic tone. "There is no way we can achieve these sales objectives if we go about doing business as usual."

He moved closer to Katie McDonaugh and said, with intimidating authority, "The time is now to stop doing business as usual. If anyone here does not think they are up to the task, then you need to step aside."

His next words were uttered in the feverish crescendo of a preacher. "And let me tell you something, *my* team is going to exceed our sales objectives in both volume and market share. We will sell more MELAVOX than any other district in the region and the nation!"

Suddenly everyone broke out into thunderous applause. Michael's words gripped them and his invincible spirit was contagious. His team clapped and cheered the loudest, and Katie's team wished he was their manager. But not Debbie Kaminski; however, she clapped dutifully and managed to summon a grin to her lips. She looked around and saw the other tenured reps doing the same. Rose, Frank, and Ken also clapped — not because they believed what Michael preached was possible, but because they knew it was how they were expected to react.

As the day went on, there were moments when Debbie found herself lost in thought. It was true that the pharmaceutical industry was changing. The cut throat culture of some of the giants in the industry was permeating the high standards of even the old, stodgy companies. Inhaber-Taft was still at the top of the industry, but no longer the number one pharmaceutical company. That honor now went to Prescott-Williams, which proved that effective pharmaceutical products were no longer enough to make a company successful. Prescott-Williams proved that money and other perks were the driving force to motivate physicians to write millions and millions of prescriptions for their products.

Inhaber-Taft's strategy and culture had to change with the times. "David" was now leading "Goliath." Sales managers like Michael Poong were able to steer a corporate giant down a very dangerous path. As long as sales objectives were exceeded, executive management looked the other way.

It was time for the lunch break. Debbie wondered if Michael was going to say anything to her about contradicting him during the meeting. She looked at Katie, who was standing up and stretching, apparently very relaxed and casual. Debbie hoped it was possible that Katie agreed with her.

"Are you headed to lunch winner?" Rose asked.

Debbie said, "I never miss a meal." They both laughed and walked out of the room together.

Rose whispered, "I agree with what you were trying to say to Michael."

"Thanks Rose," Debbie said sincerely. She wasn't surprised that Rose decided not to get involved in the controversy during the meeting. Deep down, Debbie knew that Rose was right not to contradict Michael. It wasn't the first time Debbie had been brave enough to speak up with a different opinion. But the result was always the same. Nobody backed her up during the meeting. You could have heard crickets chirping in the room. But several people discreetly approached her in the ladies room or in the hallway during one of the breaks and secretly told her they agreed with what she had said and they were glad she spoke up. Debbie used to think that her courage to speak up with a differing opinion would get her promoted. She hoped her peers, and even management, would see her as a leader. She still had a shred of hope that she was right. But there was a little voice inside her that said it was better to remain silent and agreeable. And now that same little voice told her she was probably in trouble because she hadn't.

Rose said, "Michael's just a young buck trying to make a name for himself. He's definitely wrong to coach the reps to tell docs to prescribe MELAVOX 75 mg as long term therapy."

Debbie said, "I know Rose. It's unethical because it's not safe for the patient to take the max dose long term."

Rose made light of it and giggled, "He's definitely playing with fire on that one."

"So what should we do?"

"Listen Debbie, just keep telling your docs that MELAVOX 75 mg should be prescribed for five to ten days for acute pain. You know how this works. Michael is a short timer. He's going to get promoted into marketing soon and we won't have to worry about him anymore."

Debbie said, "You're right Rose. I don't know why I let myself get so fired up about this stuff. I should keep my mouth shut."

Rose grinned in silent agreement, and Debbie's stomach did a flip-flop but she tried not to show it.

By 3:30 they were finally wrapping up the meeting.

Michael said, "Alright, so . . . is everybody ready to hit the ground running tomorrow?"

There were muted responses of agreement.

"Come on guys, you can do better than that." Michael smiled. "Let's try that again. Are you ready to hit the ground running tomorrow?"

This time, nearly everyone shouted, "Yes, we're ready." Everybody laughed and clapped. A moment later, they charged the doors and made a quick exit to get on the road.

Chapter 19: Heroic Efforts Backfire

ONCE DEBBIE WAS on the highway, she thought about her planned sales calls for the next day, when suddenly she said out loud, "I forgot to order lunch for tomorrow!" She knew if she waited until morning, she would have to get *pizza.*" All the reps knew that hospital residents were the only docs who were happy to see pizza on the lunch table. Their normally discriminating tastes were clouded by a haze of interminable exhaustion and hunger. However, physicians' office practices preferred full course meals for lunch, but they would tolerate gourmet sandwiches.

There was a time when the office staff appreciated a free lunch. But they managed to up the ante over the years with menu preferences that went in and out of vogue. Veggie wraps were all the rage for a short time, but eventually they went the way of pizza. Wraps were added to the list of forbidden menu items. The staff had no qualms about telling the sales reps where to buy their lunches and what to order. Dr. Friedman's staff in Newark was still in their Greek food phase. Debbie knew she didn't even have to call to ask if that's what they wanted for lunch the next day. The past three times she brought lunch to them, they insisted that she bring Greek food.

She reached over for her cell phone. The phone rang just once. A man with a thick Greek accent said, "Diego's Greek Specialties."

"Hi Diego, this is Debbie Kaminski . . . yeah, Debbie . . ." She smiled and said, "No, no, I'm driving home from a meeting." She was responding to one of Diego's predictable comments. If it was after 3:00, Monday through Thursday, he would say, "Oh, are you home now doing your paperwork while you watch the Oprah show?" And on Friday's, he always said, "It's Friday. That means lunch and then sneaking off to the beach."

But Diego was very accommodating to the pharmaceutical reps. After all, they put his Greek Specialties and Pizza Shop on the map. Without their business, five days a week, he would never have made so much money. Diego and his wife still lived in a small, split-level house in north Wilmington, but by 1990, he had finally saved enough money to buy a house at the beach in southern Delaware. It was a gorgeous, two-story Victorian home in Rehobeth Beach. His children and grandchildren took turns visiting every weekend from April until October. Diego had even begun to take off from work every other weekend in July and August to spend it with his family at the beach. So, even when the reps called at the last minute to order lunch for 25 people, Diego was charming and eager to please.

Diego had once estimated that his shop averaged six catered lunches per day for pharmaceutical reps. On Friday's that number doubled to an average of twelve. Each lunch was for an average of 20 people. Everybody loved the trays of moussaka, spanakopita, and Greek salad and of course baklava for dessert. About half of the reps picked up the food and schlepped it to their cars and then to the physicians' offices. It was worth the extra effort because then the reps were certain the food arrived on time, and they didn't have to worry about a delivery person getting lost or running late. But the other half of the sales force simply requested that the food be delivered and they took their chances on whether or not it arrived on time.

Debbie said, "I'm sorry to call so late, but I . . ."

Diego interrupted her, "No problem. No problem Debbie. What can I get for you? The usual?"

"Yeah that's great."

"For how many?"

"Well, let's see, tomorrow is Wednesday. There should be five doctors in the office and about twenty or so staff people . . . twenty five, enough for twenty five people."

"OK and what about drinks?"

When Debbie finished the order she asked, "Can you have it ready by 11:30?" She had to allow plenty of time to load the food into her car, drive to the office, unload the food, and set it up on the table in the office kitchen.

"11:30 is good. No problem."

"Thanks Diego. I'll see you then."

Debbie slowed down as she neared the traffic that crawled toward the toll booths in Havre De Grace, Maryland. The cars and trucks fanned out into eight lanes, and Debbie was behind a backup of about twenty cars for one of the lanes marked "cash only."

"Now's a good time to check my voicemail messages," she thought. She had just four messages. The first one was from Joan, from Better Health Physicians. It was sent on Monday morning at 8:30 a.m. She asked Debbie to come by the Wilmington office and leave samples of CARDIOPLEX. She told her to bring an extra carton of CARDIOPLEX because Dr. Friedman wanted it for a close friend.

The next message was a five-minute motivational speech from Dean Wallace, the Vice President of Sales. He commended the reps on their outstanding performance for the previous year. He immediately transitioned to the rote phrases of "This year brings even tougher challenges . . . our sales objectives are much bigger . . . our competition is much greater. I know that each and every one of you can exceed . . . and beat the competition . . ."

The next message was a reminder from Katie McDonaugh to her team. She told them to submit their travel expense reports for the district meeting by the end of the week.

The last message was another one from Joan. She said, "Debbie, it is now 3:00 on Tuesday. I am very disappointed that you have not yet responded to the message I left for you first thing Monday morning. We are still waiting for our CARDIOPLEX samples. We are completely out. Dr. Friedman said to tell you that he will start to write prescriptions for your competitors if you don't get in here to restock our samples. I don't know why you tell people to call you any time, when two days go by and we don't hear from you!"

Debbie's heart skipped a beat. She said out loud, "Oh, my God! I don't believe it. I *knew* I should have listened to my messages." She rubbed her forehead. "Shit! . . . That's it! From now on I'm going to check my voicemail five times a day, even when I'm at a meeting!" She looked at the clock on the dashboard. It was 4:45 p.m. "I'm going to call the office right now and tell them I was at a meeting and . . . oh shit!" Debbie was just one car length away from the tollbooth. She fumbled around for her wallet and quickly took out some money.

"Three dollars please miss," said the man at the tollbooth.

"Here you are sir."

He smiled and said, "Thank you miss."

She picked up speed and edged in front of a truck. Another truck approached her on the right and then slowed to keep pace with her car. Debbie had seen this game before. It always happened when she traveled by herself on the interstate highway.

The truckers liked to flirt with women who were driving alone. First the trucker beeped two short beeps to try to get her attention. If she didn't look over at him, he revved his engine and maintained just the right speed to sort of float in the lane next to her car. The first time it happened, she was naïve enough to look out of her passenger side window so she could see up to the driver of the truck. She was disgusted when she saw him looking at her with his tongue out, as if he was panting, and then he simulated masturbation by moving his arm up and down really fast. After that, she never looked over again.

Debbie increased her speed enough to get in front of the truck. But then he flashed his high beams so they blared through her window, and a blinding light bounced off of her rearview mirror. She made a gesture with her middle finger in the mirror, and she was surprised and relieved to find that this worked every time. Apparently, the truckers got the message that she wasn't interested. They simply proceeded down the highway, looking for their next opportunity to break up the monotony of the road.

Debbie pulled off at the exit for the Perryville outlet shops. She always enjoyed the sudden burst of quiet, as she steered around the winding exit turn-off. She cruised toward the giant parking lot and pulled to a stop, but left the motor running and the heat on. She called the Wilmington office of Better Health Physicians. The receptionist blurted out, "Can you hold?" It wasn't a question. It was a warning. Debbie knew she would be on hold for a long time, as she burned up her cell phone minutes. But, she always put a smile in her voice when the call was finally answered.

"Thanks for holding, can I help you?"

"Hi . . . Laurie?" Debbie guessed.

"Yeah this is Laurie." She was a file clerk and, occasionally she filled in at the reception desk. Oddly enough, she was always put off by people calling the office or approaching the reception desk!"

"Hi Laurie. This is Debbie Kaminski with Inhaber-Taft."

There was no response. Laurie was nonplussed. Debbie continued, "Can I talk to Joan? I'm returning her call."

"Joan is busy right now. Can I give her a message?" Laurie was annoyed. She just wanted to end the call and finish with her work day.

Debbie persevered, "Joan left me a couple of messages that your office needs samples of CARDIOPLEX. I was at a district meeting yesterday and today. In fact, I'm just driving home now."

Again there was no response. In fact, there was no acknowledgement that she even knew who Debbie was. But of course, she knew exactly who Debbie was.

Suddenly, Debbie had a brilliant idea. She thought, "I'll just go to the office now. I'm sure they're open for a while yet." It was just before 5:00.

Debbie asked, "What time is your office open until tonight?"

"We're seeing patients until 7:00."

Debbie thought, "I'll show Joan what a great rep I am after all. I'll drive to the office now, before I go home and leave her the CARDIOPLEX samples."

Debbie said, "Can you please tell Joan that I'm on my way over there now, and I'm bringing the samples of CARDIOPLEX?"

"OK."

"And can you please tell her that I was at a district meeting and that's why I . . ." Suddenly, Debbie heard the empty sound of no one listening. "Hello?" She held her cell phone in front of her. "Did she just hang up on me? Well, maybe our connection was dropped. Oh, well. I wouldn't be surprised if she just hung up. It was obvious she wanted to get rid of me and go home."

As Debbie drove onto the ramp for I-95 north, she straightened her posture and thought proudly, "I'll definitely impress Joan by showing up at this late hour. I can be there by 6:00 or so if I don't hit a lot of traffic."

After a while, she thought, "What should we have for dinner? I don't feel like cooking . . . maybe Mark will be in the mood for Chinese food." She picked up her phone and called Mark.

"Hello?"

"Hi Mark."

"Hi Deb. I was wondering when I'd hear from you. I guess your meeting went late."

"No. It wasn't bad. I just wanted to wait until I was on the highway to call you."

"When should I come over? Where are you now?"

"I'm almost in Elkton."

"Why don't you stop by my office?" Mark's office, in Newark, was close to Elkton.

"I'd like to, but believe it or not I have to drop off samples to an office in Wilmington."

"You're kidding?"

"No. I got two messages from Dr. Friedman's office, while I was at the meeting. His office manager said I better get in there right away or Dr. Friedman will start writing scripts for my competitors."

"That's obnoxious."

"Well, you know how he is."

"Yeah, from what you've told me, he's a real ball buster."

Debbie laughed a little and said, "Well, he's not going to stop writing for CARDIOPLEX if I don't get there tonight, but I think it will impress them if I do."

"That's a good idea."

"I should be home by 7:00 at the very latest."

"What about Harry? Do you want me to go over and . . ."

Debbie interrupted him. "Don't worry. Karen will take care of him. She said she'll just keep up her routine with him until she sees my car at home."

"What about dinner?"

"I was thinking about Chinese. Are you in the mood for Chinese food?"

"Yeah. I can pick it up on my way."

"Good. Can you go to the restaurant in Lantana Square?"

"Sure. That sounds good. I like their food."

"Can you do me a big favor and call in the order about twenty minutes or so before you leave your office?"

"Sure. What do you want?"

"I'll have my usual — shrimp with cashew nuts."

"Alright. Sounds good. Hey Deb, I missed you."

Debbie smiled. She was excited about seeing Mark and it sounded like he felt the same way. "I missed you too. I'll see you at 7."

Debbie reached the next toll booth. She said, "Mark, I just got to the toll booth in Elkton."

Mark said abruptly, "OK. I'll let you go. I'll see you soon."

"Alright, bye."

Debbie arrived at the Wilmington office of Better Health Physicians at 6:08 p.m. She got out of the car and stretched a little bit. Her lower back ached from the long drive. She looked around the parking lot and there were still quite a few cars in the lot. She thought, "I wonder if Dr. Friedman will be here. What if they found Lee?"

She opened the rear door of her car and flipped through some hanging folders that hung from the sides of a plastic container that looked like an old milk crate. There it was — her sample signature pad. She shut the door and walked around to the back of her car. She opened the trunk and lifted out one carton of CARDIOPLEX samples and rested it on the bumper, while she placed another carton on top of it. She propped the boxes against her left hip as she closed the trunk and then headed for the office.

There were only a couple of empty chairs in the waiting room. Apparently, they still had a few more patients to see. Debbie walked up to the reception desk. There was no one there, but a moment later, Joyce walked up and reached over to slide open the plexiglass window. "Hi."

"Hi Joyce. I called earlier and talked to Laurie. I told her that I would come by tonight to bring you samples of CARDIOPLEX."

Suddenly Joyce's pleasant expression changed and she glared at Debbie.

Debbie thought to herself, "Maybe they just got some bad news about Lee!"

Then Joyce started to speak softly, so Debbie poked her head through the open reception window to listen. Joyce said, "Laurie told me you called. She said you told her you were at a meeting and you didn't appreciate getting a bunch of messages about samples."

Debbie was dumbfounded. Her jaw dropped for a second and then she said in a pleading tone, "Joyce, you've known me for years. You know I would never say something like that."

Joyce grinned and shook her head. "Don't worry about it," she said. "Come on in."

Debbie didn't feel any better after Joyce's response. It certainly wasn't the reassurance she was looking for. After closing the door to the waiting room, she walked into the sample room. She opened one of the cartons and started to unload the CARDIOPLEX samples into a plastic bin. She turned, with a start, when she heard someone enter the room. She was relieved to see Joan.

"Joan. Am I glad to see you!"

Joan grinned and said, "Well, it's about time!"

Debbie felt miserable again because she could see that Joan wasn't kidding around.

Joan said, "I didn't expect to see you so soon after what Laurie told us."

Debbie said in an apologetic tone, "Joan, Joyce just told me what Laurie said, and it's just not true. I would never say something like that."

Joan moved closer to Debbie and snarled, "Are you calling Laurie a liar?"

Debbie was surprised to smell alcohol on Joan's breath. It wasn't that she was surprised that Joan was a drinker; after all, she always had a haggard look on her face and her eyes were often glassy. But it was one thing to wonder and another to *know* that Joan was drinking at work. Normally, Debbie would have felt sorry for someone like Joan. But the two of them never managed to strike up any chemistry between them. Joan was always cold toward Debbie and she could never figure out why. It wasn't as if she was one of the young, beautiful reps who tended to inspire envy.

Debbie said calmly, "Joan, maybe we should start from the beginning."

Joan shifted her weight to the other hip and sighed with impatient disinterest. Her eyes were red and glassy when she finally focused on Debbie.

"I don't have much time. I'm busy," Joan said. More alcohol breath floated into Debbie's face.

Debbie spoke quickly, "OK. I just wanted to let you know that I was at my district meeting yesterday and today. I don't check my messages everyday when I'm at a meeting. But believe me, I'll never do that again. I'm sorry. It was obviously a mistake on my part. I finally checked my messages late this afternoon while I was driving home from the meeting."

"So why do you tell people to call you any time and you'll get right back to us?"

"Believe me. I've learned my lesson. As I said, it was a mistake not to check my messages. I'll never do that again. But, Joan, it's important for you to know that as soon as I listened to your message, I called right away. When I talked to Laurie, I asked her how late your office would be open. Then I told her I would drive over here tonight."

Debbie could see from the hard look on Joan's face that she wasn't getting through to her.

Joan said, "Well Laurie told us you said you didn't appreciate getting a lot of messages about samples."

"Joan, I swear to you, I did not say that and I would never say that. Never."

Joan's expression didn't change. Debbie could see that Joan didn't believe her. She felt anxious. It was the second time that day that she worried she may have endangered her job. For a moment, Debbie felt like she was starting to well up with tears.

But then something strange happened. Joan shifted her weight again and it was as if she suddenly started to feel the effects of the alcohol and whatever else she might have taken. Her eyes closed slowly and, for a second, she swayed forward. Now, she was so close to Debbie that, as she lifted her head back in a jolt, her hair brushed across Debbie's face.

Debbie thought with horror, "My God, she's drunk! It would be bad enough if she took a few nips at work, but she's drunk!"

Joan abruptly stood upright and blinked a few times very deliberately. She looked into Debbie's eyes and slowly opened her mouth before she spoke . . . Just then Dr. Bichotti walked into the sample room. Debbie was relieved to see him. She wanted him to see that Joan was drunk, in case Laurie and Joan repeated the lie to him, although Debbie was certain he would never believe it anyway. After all, she had called on him for a few years now.

"Dr. Bichotti!" Debbie exclaimed with relief.

He looked at her through his thick glasses and spoke in his usual nervous tone, "Hi Debbie."

Joan straightened her posture again. She spoke in an angry voice, "Dr. Bichotti, we've got a problem here."

Dr. Bichotti pushed his glasses up to the bridge of his nose and asked nervously, "What . . . what seems to be the problem?"

Joan said, "This rep is way out of line."

Debbie couldn't believe her ears. Her heart started pounding. Now she was angry, and worried at the same time. Her eyes widened and she sounded desperate when she said, "Dr. Bichotti, I was not out of line. I just drove here from my district meeting in Annapolis to drop off samples of CARDIOPLEX. Joan had left me a couple of messages but . . ."

Joan interrupted, "But she didn't want to be bothered with messages about samples."

"What?" Debbie said loudly in exasperation.

"Well that's what you said!"

"Dr. Bichotti, I did not say that and I would never say that."

Joan said, "Oh and so it's her word against mine. Now she's calling me a liar! First it was Laurie, now it's me. I want her out of this office or I'm going to call the police."

"Is she crazy? Dr. Bichotti, do you see what's going on here? Can't you see that she's drunk?"

Joan said loudly, "Drunk? How dare you?" Then she shouted to Joyce at the reception desk, "Joyce, get me the police!"

Joyce came running into the sample room. "What happened?"

Joan said, "You heard me. I said, call the police! Now!"

Joyce ran back to her desk.

Debbie implored, "Dr. Bichotti, this is insane. I feel like I just walked into the twilight zone. I don't know what's going on. I came here with the best of intentions, as a professional sales rep, to bring you the samples you needed. Now, I'm being accused of saying things I never said."

Debbie's voice was cracking and she was shaking. But Dr. Bichotti was no help at all. He appeared to be frightened by the situation, and he didn't know which side to take.

Debbie pleaded, "Dr. Bichotti, you've known me for years. You know that I would never say those things."

Joan shouted, "Get out of this office now!"

Dr. Bichotti was overwhelmed, but he tried to take charge. He said nervously, "OK . . . OK . . . Joan, come with me."

But it was clear that Joan was in charge. She said, "Why should I go with you Dr. Bichotti?"

He repeated, "Just . . . just come with me Joan." He looked at Debbie and said, "Just stay here. I'll be right back."

Debbie's heart was pounding but somewhere inside, a voice told her that everything would be all right. After all, she had done nothing wrong!

Dr. Bichotti was only gone for a moment. When he came back into the room, he gave Debbie a nervous half smile and she was relieved to see that he was on her side. But to her great surprise he said, "Debbie, I'm going to have to ask you to leave now."

Debbie's heart leapt to her throat. "But Dr. Bichotti, please believe me. Joan is obviously drunk. Can't you smell the alcohol on her breath?" But she already knew her pleas fell on deaf ears.

Dr. Bichotti continued, "Debbie, Joan is the office manager. She asked that you leave the office, so I'm going to have to go along with that. Please leave."

Debbie welled up with tears. "But Dr. Bichotti . . ."

He cast his eyes downward for a somber moment. Then he took a step toward her and pursed his lips into a grimace. He put his hand on her shoulder and led her to the door. Debbie was numb. Then suddenly she remembered the samples and said, "I can't leave the samples if you don't sign for them."

Dr. Bichotti lifted his hand from her shoulder and said softly, "Alright, then take them back."

Debbie's hands were shaking as she took the samples from the bin and put them back into the carton. She heard Joyce shout to Dr. Bichotti, "I have the police on the line. What should I tell them?"

Dr. Bichotti said, "Just tell them it was a false alarm." It seemed as though it was the only solace he could give Debbie. He opened the door to the waiting room for Debbie. She looked at him with tears quietly rolling down her face.

He said, "I'm sure we'll get all of this straightened out."

With one last effort, Debbie started to say, "But . . ."

For the first time, Dr. Bichotti seemed to be in control of the situation. He gave her a stern look that immediately silenced her.

Debbie felt humiliated as she walked through the waiting room. She opened the front door of the office and felt a rush of cold air. By the time she got into her car, she was shivering uncontrollably. She turned the ignition key and started to cry. "What just happened?" she said out loud. "This is a nightmare! Wait til Katie hears about this! I can't imagine what Joan is going to tell Dr. Friedman . . . more lies . . . God this could get worse!"

She cried some more and when she finally calmed down a bit, she longed for home.

It was just after 7:00 when she pulled up next to Mark's car, in front of her townhouse. She gathered up a few things and got out of the car. She thought about her luggage and paperwork as she shut the car door. "I'll just get it later." She could smell the Chinese food when she opened the front door. Mark and Harry charged at her.

"Hi guys. I'm so glad to see you." She was suddenly filled with emotion and started to cry.

"Debbie, what happened?"

After she told Mark everything, he said, "Now I understand why you were so upset. But honestly, I think it was a bizarre comedy of errors and I'm sure everything will get straightened out."

"How?" Debbie looked incredulous.

"I think you have to take the high road. I mean, the office manager and Dr. Biscotti . . ."

"It's Bichotti."

"Whatever. OK. Dr. Bichotti and . . . what's her name . . . Joan?"

"Yeah Joan."

"They both handled things badly. But after all, you're the sales rep and it is *their* office. If you want to get back in there, you have to appease them."

"Even if Joan was *drunk?*"

"Debbie, it's your word against hers. I know it's not fair. I know it's frustrating and upsetting. Believe me, I would be upset too. But, the only way out of a he said/she said argument is for somebody to take the high road and apologize."

"But if I apologize, then everyone will think that I really said the things that Laurie accused me of. And they may even think that I did something wrong tonight at the office."

"Debbie, I'm telling you. You have no choice. You said this is one of the most important practices in your territory."

"Unfortunately, it is *the* most important practice in my territory. If I can't get back in there, I might as well pack it in."

Suddenly Debbie said, "Wait a minute!"

"What?"

"How could I forget? I guess I've been so upset I just forgot all about it."

"About what?"

"I have a lunch with Dr. Friedman's group tomorrow!"

Mark interrupted, "Well that can't happen."

"No. It's not at their Wilmington office. It's at their office in Newark. Dr. Friedman sees patients at the Newark office on Tuesday's and Wednesday's."

Then Debbie remembered about Lee Young. "Wait a minute, maybe he won't be there tomorrow."

"Why?"

"That's another story."

Mark said, "I think I need a glass of wine. How about you?"

". . . and that's why I'm not sure if Dr. Friedman will be in the office tomorrow. But I guess I'll just go ahead with the lunch as if nothing has happened."

"Well, I hate to tell you Debbie, but I think the staff at the Wilmington office will talk to the staff at the Newark office before lunchtime tomorrow."

"No. Believe it or not, I don't think so. Half the staff at the Newark office doesn't get along with the people at the Wilmington office. Tomorrow is Wednesday and Joan doesn't go over there on Wednesday's. This could be my perfect opportunity to talk to Dr. Friedman before Joan or Dr. Bichotti gets to him. Then I can straighten everything out."

"I hope you're right."

By the time they got to bed, they were too emotionally drained to think of anything but sleep. It certainly wasn't the romantic night that they had hoped for. But once they snuggled under the warm blankets, Debbie whispered to Mark, "Thanks for believing me. I don't know what I would have done without you."

Chapter 20: Lunch with Better Health Physicians

Wednesday, March 16

DEBBIE CALLED THE Newark office of Better Health Physicians at 9:00 a.m. to remind them she was bringing lunch. Donna answered the phone and seemed pleasant. She said everybody knew about the lunch and they were looking forward to it. Debbie was relieved because she didn't sense any animosity toward her. "Thank God," she said out loud when she ended the call. Then she thought, "Should I call Katie McDonaugh and tell her about what happened last night? I really don't want to, but what if one of the doctors calls her . . . no . . . I think I'll just lay low until after the lunch today and see what happens there. I'd rather tell Katie after everything is straightened out. Then the whole thing won't seem so bad."

By 12:15 p.m., Debbie had managed to carry one of the bags of soda and the tray of mousaka up two flights of stairs to Dr. Friedman's office in the Newark Medical Building. She didn't take the elevator because there were already a few people standing in front of it waiting. Besides, she didn't mind the exercise of using the stairs. Fortunately, a patient was leaving the office as she arrived. He was able to hold the door open for her. "Thanks a lot," she said with a smile.

"No problem."

Debbie made eye contact with one of the receptionists, who smiled as soon as she saw the food tray.

"Hi. I'm here!" The tray was getting heavy by the time Donna opened the door leading to the exam rooms and the private offices of physicians. The rest of the staff sat in rows of desks that looked like an old-fashioned secretarial pool.

Donna turned to Debbie, who was following her toward the kitchen. In a low voice she said, "We're running behind as usual."

They entered the kitchen, which was the size of three exam rooms put together. The size of the kitchen in a doctor's office, relative to the rest of the office space, is a good indicator of where the doctor's priorities are. There was a huge, wood laminated table with a dozen chairs staggered around it. At least a dozen more chairs were stacked in a corner of the room. An expansive set of kitchen cabinetry hung over counters crowded with a microwave, two coffee makers, a toaster, a blender, and empty donut boxes. The dish rack next to the sink was empty. All of the dirty coffee cups were stacked in the sink, along with some miscellaneous silverware and a long cake knife that was crusted over with chocolate cake and blue and white frosting. Dispensers for antibacterial soap and paper towels hung on the wall above the sink. Next to the spigots were two partially filled containers of dishwashing liquid that were smudged with dirt and dried up clumps of soap around the nozzles.

There was a water cooler next to a small buffet table that was crowded with plastic cups, plates, napkins, straws, and about a dozen half-opened soda bottles that had long since lost their fizzle.

The table had a few sets of salt and pepper shakers. Little wicker baskets were littered with half open sugar and sweetener packets. Newspapers and gossip magazines had traveled from the waiting room to the exam rooms; followed by a detour into the bathroom, before they finally rested on the kitchen table with matted edges and torn pages.

Debbie said, "I have to run back down to my car and get the rest of the food."

Donna said, "OK. No problem. We'll be here."

Debbie squeezed past file clerks, patients and a nurse, as she made her way down the hall to the waiting room. Just as she opened the door, she glanced over to the reception desk and saw Dr. Goldman looking at a patient chart. In a loud voice she said, "Hi Dr. Goldman. Can you join us for lunch today?"

He looked up and smiled at Debbie. "Yeah, sure. I'll be back there a little later on."

"OK. Sounds great."

Denise jumped up from her chair at the reception desk and approached Debbie just before she opened the door to the waiting room. Suddenly, Debbie's heart jumped to her throat and she held her breath. She thought, "Oh no. Here it comes . . . she talked to Joan or somebody else at the Wilmington office."

Denise asked, "Debbie, can you enter the office through the private side door when you come back up?"

Debbie exhaled with relief and then breathed again. "Oh, OK. I'm sorry, I forgot to enter that way the first time."

Denise said, "Oh, it's OK. No problem."

Most of the physicians' offices asked the sales reps to enter through an alternate private entrance when they brought lunch. They didn't want their patients to know they were fed by the pharmaceutical industry every day of the week.

Whenever they brought food, sales reps were always given special treatment by physicians and their staffs. They were given private office phone numbers, which meant the call was answered right away. Instead of being put on hold, the reps were immediately given the food orders for the office staff. The reps were also given access to private entrances and conference rooms. But they learned quickly that the exceptional hospitality began and ended with lunch. Once everyone was fed, the reps were again relegated to exit and entry via the general patient doorway. And the staff was appalled if a rep called on their private line for any reason other than lunch.

Debbie made a second and then a third trip to her car. She wanted the third trip to be the last, so she grabbed the last two bags containing more giant soda bottles. They were heavy, but she decided to string one bag on each arm and then gingerly leaned into the passenger seat to grab her briefcase. The soda bottles in the bag on her left arm bumped against the rear passenger door, which caused the balance of her right arm to falter. She removed the bag from her right arm and gently dropped it onto the passenger seat. She didn't want to jostle the bottles too much, otherwise they might spray all over the kitchen once they were opened. She used her free right hand to slip the shoulder strap of her briefcase over her left arm. Somehow she managed to twist her right side just far enough into the car to grasp the plastic bag she had just thrown onto the seat. Then she stood upright and backed away from the car door. She lifted her right foot and pressed it against the bottom of the car door and gave it a quick shove. She pressed her automatic key lock and listened for the thud.

She walked in a brisk but lop-sided fashion to the door of the medical building. This time she was going to take the elevator. She pressed the "up" arrow with the back of her finger joint. She never used her fingertips on an elevator button. She had read that an elevator button was one of the top five public access objects for harboring bacteria.

The elevator was empty. When it stopped at the second floor, Debbie lurched forward and raced down the hallway to the private side door. She gingerly bent down to grasp the doorknob. She turned the knob. "Oh, my God. I don't believe it. It's locked!" She tapped at the door with the back of her right hand. The bags of soda bottles had slipped to her wrists. She knocked one more time. Now the plastic straps of the bags were stretching from the weight of the contents and Debbie's wrists were turning red from the strain. Again, no one answered. By now, her wrists were in pain. She thought to herself, "They must have thought my second trip up was the last one. But why would they lock the door if it was just open five minutes ago?"

Then her heart started pounding. She thought, "Oh my God. What if Joan called them from the Wilmington office, while I was unloading the food and told them that I should be banned from the office?"

By now the straps of the plastic bags hung like threads, from stretching. She bent her knees and lowered herself toward the floor and let the bags slip off onto the carpeted floor. "Oww. That hurts." She looked at her wrists where the heavy bags had pressed against her bones and created a red bracelet of skin against bone. "Oh great. Now I look like I tried to slit my wrists. That'll be the next rumor."

She saw a patient walk down the hall in her direction.

"Are you OK?" she asked.

Debbie realized her mouth was open and she was still breathing heavily. She said, "Oh thank you. I'm fine. I just locked myself out," she lied.

The patient smiled, "Ooops. I've done that myself."

Debbie changed her expression and tried to look cool and calm, as she started to walk down the hall to the main entrance of the office. Before she reached the reception window, she made immediate eye contact with Donna.

"Oh no!" Donna said, when she saw Debbie walking toward the reception desk window. "I thought you were done, so I locked the door."

Debbie smiled and gave a little laugh. She said, "Oh, that's OK. I tried to knock but. . ."

Donna walked around her desk and flung open the door. "Come on in Debbie. Sorry about that."

"Oh, it's no problem" Debbie said. "I just have to get the rest of the food in the hallway."

Donna said, "Oh, sure."

Debbie felt a little embarrassed when she saw the bags lying on the hallway floor. She said, "It was just getting too heavy, so I just left them there."

Donna laughed and said, "Debbie, I am so sorry. You must think I'm such a ditz!"

"No, I don't," Debbie lied again.

She made small talk with the staff, as they each filed into the office kitchen to load up their plates with gobs of food. Many of them said a quick thank you and then quickly left the room. They preferred to spend their lunch break with their office buddies. They didn't have the energy or the good manners to strike up a conversation with the sales rep.

Instead they would quickly eat yet another free lunch and then slip out of the office to spend the remainder of their break outside smoking. They all congregated near the front entrances and back doors of medical office buildings and hospitals.

Doctors are notoriously cheap when it comes to staff salaries, so they typically hire three types of high school graduates. The first type is a working mother who is poised, professional and trying to provide or supplement the family income. The second type is the young, single, gum-chewing doctor groupie with big, brassy hair, little class and little money. The third type is at the other end of the spectrum. The 50-something woman with class and a couple of years of college education. She wants to work for physicians because she thinks there is a certain cachet to it.

The staff at each of Dr. Friedman's offices consisted of the big hair, doctor groupie variety of young women. They always gave the reps the once-over to check out their clothes, hair, nails, and jewelry. They hated most of the reps because they knew the doctors liked some of them, respected a few of them, and were rumored to be sleeping with others. And it was always the unscrupulous ones who had the instincts to sniff out the ones like themselves. The medical assistant who was sleeping with one of the doctors hated the drug rep rumored to be doing the same. It was a figurative catfight, but the big secret was, there were no winners.

Debbie found herself alone in the kitchen after about fifteen people had attacked the food. Once in a while, she welcomed these moments because it was her chance to catch her breath and gobble up some food before the physicians came in. But today she was feeling a little paranoid and insecure about the staff's reaction to her. She decided to be happy that apparently no one had gotten a gossip call from their Wilmington office.

She went over to the sink and pumped a blob of antibacterial soap onto her palm. She was rubbing her soapy hands together when the stale smell of coffee, with a hint of hazelnut, caught her attention. She looked at the coffee makers. They were splattered with coffee stains and there was a heap of sugar spilled on the counter in front of them. She turned on the water and gazed into the filthy sink. She felt guilty washing her hands amid coffee cups and silverware. But they looked as if they had lingered in the sink for days or weeks without being washed. She had seen doctors enter their kitchens hundreds of times, after treating patients, and proceed to wash their hands over the office dishware.

She walked over to the food and took a scoop of moussaka and decided to skip the Greek salad after she had seen one of the file clerks pick at the black olives with her fingers. She walked over to large table and sat down. Somehow, even though she was apprehensive about talking to Dr. Friedman, she had a hearty appetite.

She quickly finished her food and put on some lipstick. She popped a breath freshening mint into her mouth. "Umm, perfect," Debbie thought. "That's what I like--a chance to eat and freshen up before the doctors come in."

It wasn't that she was uncomfortable eating with the doctors. But many times, she had to delay eating because she knew it was her only opportunity to talk about her products, while the physician was chewing.

Now that her hunger was satisfied, Debbie realized that she had not gone to the bathroom for a few hours. Somehow this awareness increased her sense of urgency. She thought, "Should I go now or should I wait?" The staff bathroom was just outside the kitchen. Debbie started to walk toward the doorway that led to the bathroom.

Just then, Dr. Chercovich entered the room. He gave her his typical nervous, geeky half smile and quietly said, "Hi Debbie." He shirked away as she neared him and shyly diverted his path. Debbie was used him by now. He joined the group about a year ago. She thought it was no coincidence that Dr. Friedman hired physicians who were nerdy and nervously submissive types. After all, Dr. Friedman had a domineering personality and, as head of the practice, he only wanted to work with physicians who went along with his ideas and let him run the show. The exceptions were Dr. Margotitis and Dr. Goldman. But they had been the first two physicians to partner with Dr. Friedman. He appreciated their confident, take-charge attitudes during the tough, early years of starting up the practice.

"Oh, good. Greek food." Dr. Chercovich said, as he filled a plate.

Debbie decided to jump right into a product discussion.

"Dr. Chercovich, you have told me on several occasions that you are happy with the blood pressure lowering effects with CARDIOPLEX."

Dr. Chercovich shook his head to indicate agreement and continued chewing.

Debbie said, "Well, you're probably familiar with the CIVIC Study: CARDIOPLEX Improves Vascular Integrity and Cardiac Function Study."

Dr. Chercovich shook his head and swallowed. "Yes, yes. I'm familiar with it."

"Great. Well, as you know . . .

A little while later, Dr. Goldman sauntered over to the table.

"Hi Dr. Goldman. I'm glad you could join us," Debbie said.

"How are you Deb?"

"Good."

Dr. Goldman stood next to Dr. Chercovich and said, "Dr. Friedman seems to be OK today, but can you stay later tonight to finish up for him, in case he has to leave early?"

Without hesitation, Dr. Chercovich said, "Oh sure. Of course I can. He seemed fine when he came in this morning but. . ."

Dr. Goldman rubbed his chin and said, "I know. He puts on a good show, but I can tell he's hurting."

Debbie was happy to hear that Dr. Friedman was in the office. She thought, "Great. I'll be able to straighten everything out."

Dr. Chercovich and Dr. Goldman had stopped talking and were looking in her direction. She said, "I'm so sorry to hear about Lee. Everyone is so worried about her. I can only imagine how difficult this is for Dr. Friedman . . . and for Grant."

Dr. Chercovich recognized the connection and said, "That's right. You work with Grant. How is he doing?"

"I'm sure he's really upset, but believe it or not we just had a district meeting in Annapolis and Grant was there. I guess he looks at it the same way Dr. Friedman does, which is that it's better to stay busy."

Dr. Chercovich shook his head in somber agreement.

Dr. Goldman said, "You're right about that Debbie." Then he turned to leave the room.

Debbie hesitated for a second and then asked, "Dr. Goldman, can you take a break for lunch?" She felt uncomfortable when she heard her own question. She thought, "Maybe I should back off a little today given the situation with Lee."

But Dr. Goldman didn't seem to mind. He said, "I'll stop back a little later on," and he left the room.

Debbie shifted her glance back to Dr. Chercovich. She thought of something to say that would help her to determine whether Dr. Friedman or Dr. Chercovich knew anything about last night. She said, "I guess there's a lot of stress on everybody in the practice these days." She knew that Dr. Chercovich was well tuned into the rumor mill. The first time Debbie realized this, she was quite surprised. It didn't seem to fit his shy and retiring demeanor. But the more she thought about it, the more it made sense. Dr. Chercovich lacked social skills and he was always awkward when he tried to make conversation. But keeping abreast of the latest gossip in the rumor mill, provided him with fodder for conversation.

Dr. Chercovich leaned into the table and spoke tentatively, as if he were about to reveal a big secret. Debbie thought, "Oh no — here it comes."

Dr. Chercovich said, "Dr. Friedman is still keeping up with his heavy patient load, but I can see that it's really taking a toll on him. We're all working extra hours just in case he needs us to cover for him at the last minute. But so far, he continues to work his usual long hours."

Debbie was silent for a minute. She didn't know what to say.

Dr. Chercovich added in a whisper, "You know, it's been a week now that Lee's been missing." He folded his arms against his chest and slowly leaned back into his chair, as he held her gaze.

Debbie wondered what he was insinuating. Was it possible that he might be thinking what she dared to think, "What if Dr. Friedman killed Lee?"

Finally, she said, "It's really scary. I mean, the longer it takes to find her, the worse the outcome may be."

"I know. I agree. Hey, you said that Grant was just at your meeting?"

"Yes. There were moments when I looked at him and he was obviously distracted but there were other times when he seemed fine."

Debbie asked, "Do they have any ideas yet about where Lee is? Or what happened to her?"

"No. But Dr. Friedman said he's been pushing the investigating detective for answers."

Debbie nodded in agreement, but she had an eerie feeling they were both feeling guilty about their unspoken suspicions.

Dr. Chercovich looked at his watch and said, "I have to get back to my patients."

"OK Dr. Chercovich. Thanks for coming in and joining me for lunch." She hesitated for a moment and then said, "I feel awkward about this, but I have to do my job. Please remember to write for CARDIOPLEX 10 mg b.i.d. for your post MI patients."

Dr. Chercovich smiled and said, "I already do."

Debbie was right behind him as he left the room. She couldn't wait any longer. She made a quick right from the kitchen into the bathroom and carefully shut the door. The staff bathroom was clean and smelled fresh, as opposed to the messy and slightly odorous patient bathroom. As she washed her hands, she looked at herself in the mirror and was suddenly panic stricken. She worried about what would happen when the physicians in the practice found out about the incident with Joan. And then she had another worry, "Oh God! Why did I have to open my big mouth at the meeting yesterday and disagree with Michael Poong! When Katie tells him about the whole mess with Joan, maybe he'll use it as a way to get rid of me!"

Debbie had every reason to be worried because she knew Inhaber-Taft would not tolerate a rep who endangered their business with a top writing physician by aggravating the office manager. They were not interested in hearing both sides of the story. All they needed to hear was the physician's side of the story. And if a physician was angry or upset with a rep, the rep was either transferred or terminated.

As she left the bathroom and went back into the kitchen she thought, "I hope Dr. Friedman comes in soon for lunch . . ."

A moment later, Dr. Goldman came in for a quick meal. Since it was easy to be candid with Dr. Goldman, Debbie asked, "Why aren't you writing as many scripts for FLAGIT for your patients with UTI?"

He gave her a coy smile and said, "Deb, your biggest competitor, Jamie, just took me to a Rolling Stones concert."

Debbie smiled and then pleaded, "Dr. Goldman, you know I can't compete with that. Inhaber-Taft doesn't do entertainment."

Dr. Goldman shrugged his shoulders and said, "I know, and that's too bad. It makes your job tougher."

"Dr. Goldman, Inhaber-Taft may not be providing entertainment, but we have excellent products. And you know from the feedback you get from your patients that FLAGIT is a very effective and well tolerated drug. Comparative studies with all of the drugs in this therapeutic class showed that women who took FLAGIT at the first symptoms of UTI experienced faster and more complete pain relief."

"Debbie, I have seen good results with FLAGIT, but your competitors' products are also good. Sure, there are some patients who don't get immediate relief. And when that happens, I write a script for FLAGIT."

Debbie felt frustrated but she persisted, "But Dr. Goldman, if FLAGIT became your drug of choice for the treatment of UTI, you wouldn't have to worry about its potential effectiveness. There is so much clinical evidence that shows FLAGIT provides fast relief of symptoms while it treats the infection. So why write for another drug first, and then be bothered with patient calls to your office because the drug didn't work?"

"Debbie, there's a 95% chance that your competitors' drugs will work. That's a risk I'm willing to take because my patients will get another drug if it doesn't work. Eventually, everybody's happy, including me because Jamie can take me to concerts and Heather can send me on ski trips." He winked at her and smiled. She smiled too because she naively believed her persistence could change him. She had listened to Dr. Goldman explain the logic behind his script writing habits a hundred times before. But she planned to chip away at him over time, visit after visit to his office.

He had finished eating and stood up. "Thanks for lunch Deb."

"You're welcome Dr. Goldman."

"I have to run."

It was almost 2 hours after her arrival when Dr. Friedman finally rushed into the kitchen. "Hi Deb."

He sounded as if he was in a good mood as he dashed over to the sink and wet his hands under the spigot. He grabbed a paper towel and then turned toward Debbie with a smirk on his face and said, "I thought they gave you guys a quota to meet everyday. How can you do that if you're still sitting here?"

Debbie was happy to see he was his usual sarcastic self. She said, "I decided to stick around in case you stopped by to get something to eat. And yes, they do give us a quota to meet everyday so I'll just have to work late tonight."

He grinned and walked up to the table. As he was sizing up the array of food he said, "I've seen sixteen patients so far today. Each one is crazier than the one before. Oh, this looks good." He scooped some food onto his plate and stopped to taste it with his finger. "Oh good, it's cold — just the way I like it."

"Sorry. I forgot the chafing dishes," Debbie said sarcastically. It felt good that they were getting along so well. In fact, it even felt like old times — like "before-Lee" times. He hadn't been this relaxed and jocular for a long time. Debbie figured that either he didn't know about what happened last night with Joan, or he didn't care because he had bigger worries on his mind.

But the irony was that they were each worried about what the other was thinking. Debbie didn't know that, for the first time, Dr. Friedman was genuinely concerned about the impression he made on her. He had to know if their meeting at Wilmington Pharmacy the week before had made Debbie suspicious at all.

He sat down at the table and spoke with a practiced ease. "So, what do you have for me today?"

This was a question Debbie had heard hundreds of times before. It was a nice open ended question that bought the physician time to do something else like eat their lunch, open the mail, or look for a patient's chart, while the sales rep rambled on.

Although she was afraid she might alter the fraternal mood, Debbie felt compelled to say, "I'm very sorry to hear about Lee. I hope she's alright and I hope they find her soon."

Dr. Friedman stopped chewing, cast his eyes downward, and sat still. Debbie panicked for a second. She thought, "Oh my God. Maybe I shouldn't have said anything!"

Then Dr. Friedman swallowed and looked at Debbie with an intense focus. "Thanks Debbie. You're a very nice person. I'm glad you said something. So many people just act awkward around me and they don't say anything to acknowledge what's going on. I know it's uncomfortable for people, but when you're in a situation like this, you really appreciate it when people empathize with your pain."

Dr. Friedman could see that he put Debbie at ease. He asked, "So what's new in your life besides Inhaber-Taft?"

Debbie smiled coyly and said, "I've been spending a lot of time in Maryland these days."

"Maryland? Why Maryland?"

"My boyfriend Mark lives in Maryland and I stay there on the weekends."

Debbie found out long ago that doctors expected the reps to talk about their personal lives. It was a way to build rapport with the reps and it was a natural extension of the way physicians and nurses related to one another. They sought it out as a way to escape from the intensity and stress of dealing with sick people all day long.

"Where in Maryland?"

Debbie knew Dr. Friedman asked for the name of the town because it would give him an idea of how well Mark was doing financially. She wished she didn't have to tell him the name of the city because it was known to be a generally low income area. She said, "Elkton," and then quickly added, "He has a nice, wooden cabin on the Elk River. He's actually closer to Chesapeake City but his zip code is Elkton."

Dr. Friedman asked, "What's his last name?"

Debbie thought to herself, "Oh no, just when things were going so well." She had purposely avoided saying his last name because she knew how prejudiced Dr. Friedman was.

She tried to appear nonchalant and said, "Reinhardt." She was relieved to see his expression didn't change. But, just as he was about to speak, Amy, one of the file clerks entered the kitchen.

"Dr. Friedman, I have Joan on the line and she said it's urgent. She's been trying to reach you all morning."

Debbie froze. "Oh my God! Joan is going to tell him about last night, while I'm sitting here having lunch with him! She probably planned it that way. Somebody in this office must know about what happened and they tipped her off."

Dr. Friedman walked over to the phone on the wall. "What line is she on?"

Amy looked nervous.

Debbie thought, "She knows! . . . I can tell from her expression . . . she can't even look at me . . . she's the one who's in cahoots with Joan . . . I just hope Dr. Friedman realizes everything Joan tells him is a lie!"

Now Amy seemed emboldened. It seemed she wanted Debbie to know she was consorting with Joan. She said, "Joan wants you to take the call in your office so you have privacy."

Dr. Friedman grinned at Debbie and threw his hands in the air in mock frustration. "Alright. I guess I have to take this. I'll be right back."

Amy left the room too. Debbie worried, "What if he believes her? He might just come in here and tell me to leave the office . . . no . . . he knows me better than that. He won't believe her."

She stood up to shake off the nerves. She rubbed her forehead and thought, ". . . we were getting along so well today . . . he didn't even say anything rude about Mark's last name . . . although he was interrupted just as I said it." Now she was worried again. "Oh God! . . . talk about bad timing! With everything going on right now with Lee, maybe this will be the last straw . . . maybe he'll freak out and overreact. Who knows?"

As Dr. Friedman walked into his office he repeated Mark's last name to himself. "Reinhardt. Another German bastard! What is it with these women? Goddamn anti-Semitic . . ."

Joan found out that Debbie was bringing lunch to their Newark office when she called to review their daily patient census with Donna. Her next call was to Amy. Now she hoped Dr. Friedman might do something impulsive. She thought, "He'll be so pissed off, he'll call her boss and have her fired on the spot. That fucking bitch . . . telling Dr. Bichotti I was drunk!" She watched her hand shake in a nervous tremor as she reached for her cigarettes. "I should've stepped outside for a smoke before I called." She had worried for some time now that somebody might find the bottle of whiskey she kept hidden in the back of her desk drawer. She had three teenage boys at home and her husband just lost another job. He sat at home and watched television all day and spent the night at the local tavern. She usually joined him there after work for a few hours. But Joan was the breadwinner for her family. She thought, "There's no way I'm going to get fired. I'll do whatever it takes to make this fucking rep look bad. It'll be her sorry ass that goes--not mine."

Suddenly she heard, "Hey Joan, what's up?"

"Hi Dr. Friedman. I'm so sorry to have to tell you about this now. I mean, with everything else you have on your mind. I hate to add to it but . . ."

Dr. Friedman worried, "Did Detective Healy stop by the office? Maybe he called Joan and . . ." He stopped himself and summoned a calm tone to his voice and asked, "What is it Joan?"

"I have to tell you about an incident here last night at the Wilmington office regarding Debbie Kaminski."

"Hold on a minute." Dr. Friedman was intrigued. It was the last thing he expected Joan to say. He shut his office door and picked up the phone again. "Alright, so what happened?"

Joan did her best to describe the events of the previous night in a manner that would make her look like an innocent victim. She changed the facts and embellished the details. She wanted to get Debbie fired.

As the story unfolded, Dr. Friedman sat back in his chair with a delighted grin and thought, "Now I have a chip to play with Debbie."

But he wasn't sure how to play it. His immediate reaction was to have her fired. "Perfect," he thought, "I'll have her terminated and she'll be out of the picture."

As Joan continued, he thought, "Wait a minute. She'll be more inclined to suspect me if she sees me as the brute who got her fired. No, I can't risk that. I have to do the opposite. She knows I can pick up the phone right now and tell Michael Poong I want her terminated and he'll make it happen. He won't even care why. So I just have to give Debbie a scare and then tell her I decided to save her neck. She'll be so grateful that she'll want nothing more than to stay in my good graces."

When Joan finished, he said, "You're not going to believe this, but Debbie is sitting in our kitchen right now. I was just having lunch with her when you called."

"You're kidding?" Joan lied.

"No. I'm sorry you had to go through this Joan. You handled it very well. I'm happy to hear that Dr. Bichotti backed you up. I'll talk to Debbie right now."

Dr. Friedman knew there had to be more to the story, but right now it was in his best interest if Debbie looked like the bad guy.

Joan thought, "Dr. Friedman doesn't sound as pissed off as I thought he'd be." She decided he needed a little push, so she blurted out, "I think we should ban her from our offices — maybe even get her fired." It was easy for Joan to wield her influence over the physicians in the practice because they saw her as a buffer between themselves and administrative hassles, whether it was with patients and their families, insurance companies, or sales reps.

But given the circumstances, Dr. Friedman resented Joan's assumption of power. He thought, "She needs to be taken down a few notches. She's feeling a little too self-important. She needs to know I'm running the show — not her." But just as he was about to respond, he visualized Joan walking into his office as he was wrapping an ACE bandage around his right arm — the arm he fell on after he dumped Lee's body in the field.

Joan noticed he hesitated. She wondered what he was thinking. "What if he's smelled alcohol on my breath too? . . . I have been a little careless lately.

I used to wait until late afternoon but anymore I start around lunchtime . . . well . . . sometimes in the morning too but . . ."

Dr. Friedman thought, "The tactic of fear will work with both of them. I've got to make Joan nervous and desperate too."

Finally he said, "Joan, you've been our office manager for what, ten years now?"

"Nine," Joan said with trepidation.

"Alright, nine years. You've always done a great job for us. But Joan, I want you to tell me the truth now. You can trust me. This is between you and me — nobody else will know we talked about this. I promise. You're not just my office manager, you're a friend, and you're also one of my patients. So I know you've had some problems in the past with alcohol addiction."

Now Joan had tremors rushing through her whole body. "Should I tell him the truth? I know Laurie has walked in on me a couple of times when I was taking a swig. What if he decides to secretly ask the staff about it? She promised she would never tell, but who knows. Maybe it's better if he hears it from me."

Dr. Friedman asked the question she dreaded hearing. "Have you been drinking at work Joan?"

He knew there was a risk of Joan simply lying and saying no. But instead, he got just what he wanted.

Her voice was shaking. "Dr. Friedman, you know that Charlie lost another job. We have three teenage boys to feed at home. The bills keep piling up with these kids. I guess I've just gotten a little bit friendly with the bottle again, if you know what I mean."

There was silence for a few seconds. She panicked. "Maybe I said too much . . . or . . . oh, wait a minute . . . good . . . I didn't actually say anything about drinking at work. She quickly added, "I mean, I meet Charlie at the tavern after work but . . ."

Dr. Friedman winced and thought, "I almost had her. She just about admitted it . . . I can't let this happen." He persisted, "Joan, come on. It's me. I can get you some help and nobody will know about it. But if you lie to me and I find out otherwise . . ."

That was all Joan needed to hear. She said, "It's just been too much lately." Then she broke down and cried a little bit. It was somewhat genuine because she was afraid of losing her job, but she also knew she could play on his sympathy.

She said, "A few times at work lately. . . I . . . I mean only late in the day. . . I took a couple of sips. Sometimes I bring one of those little bottles. You know . . . the kind you get on airplanes but they sell them at the liquor store too. I put one in my pocketbook sometimes."

Dr. Friedman made a satisfied grin and thought, "Good. Now it's all under control. After I talk to Debbie, they'll both be in dire straits. And the best part is, they know I hold the strings."

He spoke in a terse manner, "Alright. Thanks Joan. Tomorrow when I'm back at the Wilmington office, I'll give you the name of somebody I want you to see. He can help you beat this thing before it gets out of control."

Joan said in the most humble and demure voice she could muster, "Thanks Dr. Friedman. Thanks for helping me."

"Alright Joan. Just take it easy. Don't worry. I'll take care of it from here."

Joan thought, "Shit. I blew it. I don't think he's going to get rid of Debbie." Her mind felt fuzzy and confused. She thought, "God, I need a drink! Oh well, at least I still have a job."

She said, "Thanks Dr. Friedman." Then, as an afterthought she asked, "Any news about Lee?"

"No. Still no word." Then he added, "Hey listen, I better go now."

"OK. I'll talk to you tomorrow."

Dr. Friedman sat back in his chair, clasped his hands behind his head and sighed. He made a smug grin and thought, "I couldn't have asked for a better twist of fate. Joan and Debbie were the only two people who had me worried. What are the chances they would each do something to turn the tables in my favor?"

Debbie heard Dr. Friedman's voice in the hallway. She felt like she was waiting for dental surgery. She calmed down for a minute and thought, "What am I worried about? He's probably going to side with me anyway."

Suddenly, her mood changed again. "Who am I kidding? He still resents me because I wasn't the typical wench who jumped into bed with him. And I know he can be an evil and cruel person."

She would never forget what Dr. Friedman had said to her about Bernard, which would have been even more disturbing if she didn't already know how much he hated Germans. It was at an Inhaber-Taft dinner program, shortly after the word got around about her engagement to a guy from Germany. That night at the cocktail reception, Dr. Friedman said to Debbie, "I heard you got engaged." Debbie smiled and said, "Yeah, I'm very happy about it. All of his family still lives in Germany, so I'm trying to learn the language so I can impress them when we visit." Dr. Friedman smirked and said, "Let's just hope he doesn't teach you how to say, 'Send them to the showers.'" Debbie was shocked. She immediately understood the reference.

Debbie kept her eyes on the kitchen doorway. Dr. Friedman walked in, and it seemed he had the same smirk on his face. He walked over to the table and asked, "Can I talk to you for a minute in my office?"

"Sure." She began to worry again about what Joan might have said to him.

They walked into his office and he shut the door and motioned toward a chair. "Take a seat for a minute."

Debbie sat down and watched him walk around to the other side of his desk. She didn't take her eyes off of him. She was trying to read what he was thinking from the expression on his face and the look in his eyes.

Dr. Friedman had a pleasant look on his face when he leaned forward to rest his elbows on his desk.

Debbie leaned forward in her chair.

He said, "I just got off the phone with Joan. She's pretty upset about what happened between you and her, and some of our staff last night at the Wilmington office." He paused for dramatic effect. Then he made a half laugh and joked, "It looks like I'm going to have to get rid of you first and then our boy Harrison."

Debbie knew he expected her to find humor in his bizarre comment. She thought, "It's so ironic that Dr. Friedman is so prejudiced. He doesn't like Harrison because he's black, and yet he has the audacity to complain that so many people are anti-Semitic!" She felt indignant. She tried to smile but her nervous facial muscles collapsed into a grimace. Still, she had to plead her innocence. She said, "Dr. Friedman, I certainly hope you know me well enough by now to take whatever Joan said with a grain of salt."

He didn't answer. He offered no reassurance.

She continued, "I don't know if you talked to Dr. Bichotti about this yet but . . . "

"No, I haven't."

"Dr. Bichotti doesn't know what actually happened. He just happened to walk into the sample room when things were getting way out of hand with Joan. Then Joan proceeded to lie about the situation."

Dr. Friedman gave a dismissive wave of his hand, "Don't worry about it. I know there are two sides to every story. I didn't even bother to call Dr. Bichotti yet because it sounded like he was just there for the tail end of the altercation. Besides . . ." Then he lowered his voice and said, "There are two things I want you to know: first, I know that Joan has a drinking problem but we're going to take care of that; second, if what happened was as bad as Joan described it, I would have gotten a call last night from Dr. Bichotti. As it is, I still haven't heard from him. So that tells me there is gross exaggeration on Joan's part and, let's face it, she knows she was in the wrong to drink alcohol at work. There's no excuse for that in a medical practice. It is not only unprofessional, it is dangerously negligent because patients' lives are at stake."

Debbie felt vindicated. Apparently Dr. Friedman had made a fair assessment and decided that Joan was in the wrong. It sounded as if Dr. Friedman wasn't even going to take the time to hear her side of the story because his mind was made up. She thought, "I think he's going to fire Joan." But she felt no remorse. She thought, "She only has herself to blame."

She said, "Dr. Friedman, I want to tell you the truth about what happened last night."

He stood up and said, "It's not necessary Debbie. I've known you long enough to know you would never tell Laurie, or anyone else on my staff, not to bother you with phone calls."

Debbie smiled and stood up. She said, "Thanks Dr. Friedman."

He said, "Look, just lay low for a little while and don't call on my practice for a couple weeks. I think it's a good idea to put some space between you and Joan. Just ask one of the other reps to leave extra samples."

"That sounds like a good idea. And I'll ask Harrison to make sure you have enough CARDIOPLEX and FLAGIT samples."

It wasn't until then that Dr. Friedman remembered his plan to get Debbie into the office. He had to pretend that Larry Berman needed samples for his ailing mother. He said, "I almost forgot, can you leave a carton of CARDIOPLEX for my friend's mother?"

Debbie was more than happy to oblige. She pretended that it hadn't slipped her mind. "Of course Dr. Friedman. I'll leave the carton in your office after I drop off the other samples."

With that Dr. Friedman opened his office door and said, "Alright. Time to get back to my patients."

Debbie was about to leave his office when he turned to her and asked, "Did you tell your manager about all this?"

Debbie stuttered, "No, I . . . I . . . was going to wait until after I talked to you today and . . ."

He interrupted her and said emphatically, "Look, I know Inhaber-Taft takes these things very seriously." Then he grinned and said, "It looks like your fate is in my hands. Now, fair or not, it looks like both you and Joan have a potential credibility problem. It's all in the way I spin it."

Debbie swallowed hard. She didn't know what to say.

Dr. Friedman said, "I'll cut you a break this time and give Michael Poong a call to let him know everything is fine."

Debbie smiled and said, "I appreciate it Dr. Friedman but Katie McDonaugh is actually my manager."

"That's right. I forgot. What's her phone number? I have Michaels' but I don't have Katie's."

Debbie gave him the phone number. "Dr. Friedman, I had planned to tell you about this today at lunch. It's just that Joan got to you first."

"I know. I know." He looked at his watch and said, "I have to go."

Debbie reached out to shake his hand. She said, "Thanks again Dr. Friedman for believing me. I'm sorry you had to deal with this now, when you have so much else going on." She cringed inside when she heard the trite phrase come out of her mouth.

Dr. Friedman didn't say anything. He just grinned before he headed toward an exam room.

Chapter 21: The Shoe Dropped

Wednesday afternoon

DEBBIE RETURNED THE food trays to Diego's shop and then drove to Dr. DiStefano's office. On her way there, she thought about her conversation with Dr. Friedman. "I wonder what Katie McDonaugh will think about everything after Dr. Friedman talks to her." She agreed with Dr. Friedman's suggestion that she lay low for a while before she called on their offices again.

She found an empty parking space close to the front door of Dr. DiStefano's office, which was really lucky since it had started to rain. She thought, "Hey this day isn't turning out so bad after all."

There were half a dozen older men in the waiting room. As usual, the reception desk was cluttered with forms and files. Although Natalie was the office manager, she sometimes covered for the receptionist. Natalie held the phone near her ear, "Cardiology Care, can you hold please." A medical assistant, Liz, stood next to her with an open chart, as they conferred about a patient's insurance update. Natalie smiled when she saw Debbie approach the window, "Hey Deb."

"Hi Natalie. Hi Liz."

Natalie turned around and strained her neck to catch sight of another medical assistant. She asked her, "Is there anybody back there?" (Natalie was referring to pharma sales reps).

Debbie heard a voice in the background shout, "No. The last one just left."

Natalie turned back to Debbie and said, "You can go back."

"Thanks." Debbie didn't take up Natalie's time making small talk. She credited some of her success as a sales rep to her own experience as an administrative assistant. She remembered vividly how uncomfortable and annoyed she was when sales people forced her into idle conversation while they waited for her boss to show up for an appointment. Worse yet, was when they didn't have an appointment and just stood by her desk chatting it up just so they could buy time, figuring that eventually her boss would walk through the door. If she wasn't particularly busy, she enjoyed a little conversation. But most of the time, she was very busy. She could never understand why her body language and the paperwork on her desk didn't deter their persistence.

Debbie was about to open the door to the sample room when Susie, one of the medical assistants, rushed up to her with a mischievous expression, "Hey Deb! Did you hear any updates about Dr. Friedman's missing wife?"

Debbie felt awkward getting involved in gossip about Dr. Friedman, given what had just happened. But she forced herself to sound interested and said, "No. Did you hear anything?"

"Are you kidding? In this madhouse? We have no idea what's going on in the outside world." She looked around her and then whispered, "Besides, we don't want to piss off Dr. DiStefano by talking about it because he's really close with Dr. Friedman. The other day Natalie asked if any of us saw the news the night before. She started to tell us about what they reported on channel 5 about Lee Young. All of a sudden, DiStefano gets all scary serious and says, 'It's not appropriate to discuss that here.' So Natalie clammed up and we all just went back to work."

Debbie said, "Yeah I guess Dr. DiStefano feels pretty bad about it . . . but no . . . I've had NPR on in the car all day and there's nothing new so far. They just repeated that the search continues."

Susie looked disappointed. "Oh well, maybe something will happen by the time I watch the 11:00 news tonight."

"Yeah, maybe."

They heard Liz call out, "Susie, I need a hand here."

She smiled and shrugged her shoulders, "Gotta go Deb. I'll see ya next time."

"Alright. Take it easy."

Ever since the news broke about the disappearance of Lee Young, it became the hot topic of conversation among all of the business and personal acquaintances of Lee and Donald. The general public was slowly drawn into the story with each morsel of news. And as the daily updates in the newspapers, radio and television began to include every tidbit of salacious gossip, their audience was not only hooked but addicted.

Debbie walked into the large sample room and checked out the bins for her products to see which ones required a refill. Whenever Dr. DiStefano prescribed a drug, he loaded his patients up with free samples. He wanted his patients to like him. He knew they would get their prescription filled, but no matter how generous or how slight their pharmacy benefit was, everybody liked a few freebies.

Debbie stepped out of the room and saw Liz in the hallway, "Is he going to be a while?"

"Yeah."

"OK, thanks. I'll be right back." The rain was much heavier now. She didn't keep an umbrella in the car because it was just too impractical. Her hands were usually full with samples, detail pieces and her briefcase. In heavy rain or snow, she wore a baseball cap to and from her car and took it off before she entered the office.

She ran to the back of her car and quickly opened the trunk and took out a couple of cartons of samples. She ran back into the office and into the sample room. Dr. DiStefano was still not there. She was losing her grip on the sample cartons, as she started to lower them onto the floor. The first carton landed upright but the second one toppled over, and she watched the contents spill across the carpet. She bent down and started to pick up the bottles of tablets. As she stood upright and stepped forward, her coat brushed against one of the shelves and knocked something to the floor. She turned around and saw a pair of running shoes sticking out of a trash bag that had just fallen from a shelf. She squatted down and put her carton back onto the floor. She reached over and picked up the shoes with one hand and the trash bag with the other. The sneakers had the crisp, clean look of brand new shoes, except for the gashes of grass stains and dirt on one shoe. They were gray in color so she didn't know if they were a man's or a woman's shoes. She turned the shoes slightly in order to insert them back into the trash bag. She noticed there were strands of brown weeds in the tracks on the bottom of the shoes. They were a small size, but Dr. DiStefano was a small man. Debbie thought, "I guess Dr. DiStefano is already going to throw them out because they're dirty. Since when did he get into running? . . ."

Just then the door to the sample room burst open. When Debbie turned around, she was still holding the sneakers in her hand. "Hi Dr. DiStefano."

"Hey Deb, what cha doin down there?" Dr. DiStefano said in his usual high energy cadence.

Debbie laughed slightly and stood up. "Well, with my usual grace and poise, I dropped a sample carton and then accidentally knocked this trash bag to the floor with my coat." She held up the sneakers and asked, "Are you throwing out your running shoes because they got dirty?"

"Oh they're not mine."

"I thought maybe you decided to get into running."

"Running? When would I have time for that?" Dr. DiStefano made a funny face and then started grabbing sample bottles out of one of the bins. He said, "You know any free time I have is dedicated to my orchids."

"And what about your lovely wife?" Debbie smiled coyly. Dr. DiStefano was a newlywed and all of the reps liked his wife, Abby. She was unpretentious and they seemed to be genuinely in love.

Dr. DiStefano got up close to Debbie and did exactly what she had talked about with Harrison. He stood about two or three inches from her face and looked into her eyes. He flipped his eyebrows up and down and said, "I always make time for my lovely wife, Deb."

Debbie smiled and tried to subtly step back a little bit from the uncomfortably close position of Dr. DiStefano. She was still holding the trash bag in one hand and the sneakers in the other.

Dr. DiStefano said nonchalantly, "You can put them back on the shelf." Then he turned to grab more samples of a drug sold by one of her competitors.

Debbie dropped the running shoes into the trash bag and wrapped the bag around the shoes a few times and then stuffed it back onto the shelf. She turned around and said playfully, "Now as far as the samples you're reaching for now, why not use CARDIOPLEX instead?"

When she first started to call on him years ago, Dr. DiStefano had told her she was too stiff and old-fashioned. He advised her, "Most of the docs in Delaware are pretty relaxed Deb. You're not dealing with those stuck up MBA's in Marketing anymore. Just be yourself and chill out. You'll be much more successful."

Dr. DiStefano moved close to Debbie's face again and said, "Deb, you know I can't write for CARDIOPLEX now that Diane is gone."

Debbie said, "Dr. DiStefano, I know I can convince you that CARDIOPLEX is an effective and well tolerated treatment for your patients with high blood pressure. And now, as a result of the CIVIC study, the FDA has approved CARDIOPLEX 10 mg b.i.d. for your post MI patients."

"Alright Deb. I have to get back to my patients. But just for you, I'll write a few scripts for it now and then."

Debbie tried to keep things light and said, "Thank you Dr. DiStefano. I appreciate your business and I'm sure the patient outcomes you'll see with CARDIOPLEX will convince you to write more of it over time."

"Ah Deb, you're sweet." Dr. DiStefano made a motion with his pen as if writing on the air, "Do you need me to sign for the samples?"

"Yes."

While he was signing, he asked, "Hey Deb, when are you getting married again?"

Debbie smiled. "I don't know yet." But she thought, "Oh no, here we go again."

Dr. DiStefano asked softly, "Does he need any TRIAGRA?"

Before Debbie could say anything, Dr. DiStefano was scrambling for samples of it. He dropped a couple bottles into her open briefcase.

Debbie forced a laugh and pretended to be shocked, although there wasn't much he could do that would shock her. She said, "Dr. DiStefano!"

"Just take it. He may not need it now, but just keep it for a rainy day." Again he raised his eyebrows up and down.

Debbie smiled and shook her head.

"Hey have a good day Deb," Dr. DiStefano flung the door open and was gone in a flash.

As she bent over to pick up the empty cartons, the trash bag caught her eye again. She thought, "I guess the running shoes belong to somebody on his staff." It wouldn't be the first time that she had seen all sorts of things in a sample closet.

As she walked out of the sample room, Dr. DiStefano raced down the hall toward her, "Hey Deb, have you seen my new plaque?" He asked excitedly.

"No."

"Follow me." Dr. DiStefano led her down the hall toward his office. As they entered, he turned to the right and straightened out a frame on the wall. "There it is," he said proudly.

Debbie moved closer to read it, "On this thirteenth day of January, 1996, Dr. Joseph DiStefano has been inducted into the Royal Orchid Society of the United Kingdom."

"Wow! Congratulations. I guess it doesn't get any better than that in the world of orchids."

Dr. DiStefano said with a dash of bravado, "No. It doesn't Deb. All my years of hard work with my orchids has finally paid off . . . seven different species and one hundred seventy five orchids in my own greenhouse." He moved closer and said dramatically, "No, seriously, this is a rare honor. There are only thirty-two people in the entire United States who have been inducted into the Royal Orchid Society of the UK."

Debbie made a fuss about it, as she knew Dr. DiStefano wanted her to do. But she had already heard about it through the grapevine. Eventually, he brought every sales rep into his office to have a look at his newest plaque, just so they could lavish him with compliments.

Everyone knew about his passion for orchids. In fact, many of the reps had bought him orchids. Still, it was surprising that he had qualified for such a rare honor. But it took just one rep to take a closer look at the matting around the plaque while Dr. DiStefano took a phone call. Sure enough, the honor was bestowed upon him courtesy of UK based Prescott-Williams. Debbie looked closely and saw, in very small print, the Prescott-Williams' name and icon.

Natalie rushed into the office and said, "Dr. D, I have Dr. Friedman on the line. He's returning your call."

Dr. DiStefano said, "Thanks Nat. Gotta go Deb."

"Alright, I'll see you later Dr. DiStefano."

"Hey Deb, shut the door on your way out please."

"Sure." As she slowly pulled the door closed, she heard Dr. DiStefano say, "Hey, Donald let me call you back from my cell phone."

Debbie caught up with Natalie and said, "Hey Natalie, thanks for letting me catch up with him today." They were both walking at a brisk pace down the hallway. There was something about being around Dr. DiStefano that made people emulate his frenetic pace. It was as if the buzz of his energy was contagious and those around him began to talk and move more quickly.

Natalie said, "You're welcome Debbie. Have a good one," as she veered off to the right to return to her desk.

Debbie settled into her car and shivered from the cold rain, when her cell phone rang.

"Hello this is Debbie Kaminski."

"Hi Debbie, it's Katie."

Debbie's heart skipped a beat. "Hi Katie. How are you?"

"Good, good. Listen Deb, I just had a conversation with Dr. Friedman. He called to tell me about your visit to their Wilmington office last night." Katie paused for a minute to get Debbie's reaction.

Debbie became uncomfortable in the momentary silence but she forced a confident tone and said, "Yes. I talked to him today and fortunately he was very fair in his assessment."

Katie said, "Debbie, I want to commend you on your effort to get to their Wilmington office on Tuesday night on your way home from Annapolis. You and I both know that most reps would have let it slide and waited until the next day. It's obvious to me, and I think to Dr. Friedman too, that you never would have said what this girl Laurie claims you said."

"Thank you for believing in me Katie," Debbie said sincerely. "I wanted Dr. Friedman's group to know that I'm the kind of rep who goes above and beyond the norm. I wanted them to know that Inhaber-Taft is not just about great products, but about great service too." Debbie thought she sounded a bit heavy handed, but she knew the sales managers remembered this kind of stuff when they completed a performance evaluation.

Katie said, "But I do agree with Dr. Friedman's suggestion that you lay low from their offices for a few weeks."

"Yes. I think it's a good idea too."

"It seems that Joan and Laurie have it in for you."

"I'm glad you see that Katie. I just don't understand why they dislike me."

"I know it's irrational, and it's not fair. But most of us have experienced it. And keep in mind, sometimes people really *like* you for no apparent reason. The unfortunate part is that it works both ways, and sometimes a person dislikes you for no good reason."

Debbie said nothing. She was just relieved to know that Katie trusted her and believed in her.

"Let's just move forward. We have too much work to accomplish to let something like this get in the way. Just make sure you remind Harrison to get to their offices more frequently to pick up the slack with samples."

"Sure I will."

Katie asked, "So how is your day going otherwise?"

Debbie laughed slightly, "Well, as a matter of fact, I just came out of Dr. DiStefano's office."

"Oh boy! How did that go?"

"He showed me his new plague. He's been inducted into the Royal Orchid Society of the United Kingdom, courtesy of our friends at Prescott-Williams."

". . . son of a gun! . . . that *is* frustrating. But we'll continue to be persistent and tenacious and arm ourselves with the evidence that supports superior clinical outcomes with CARDIOPLEX." It sounded like a recorded message.

But in the same spirit, Debbie said, "You're right Katie. We can never give up."

"Alright Debbie. I've got to run. But again, thanks for your superior efforts and professionalism."

Debbie ended the call and said out loud, "Wow! Friedman really did back me up!" She was surprised at her next thought, "It's almost out of character for him to be so unbiased and fair . . . I wonder . . . oh well, just leave well enough alone and thank God it's over."

"Hey, what's up Joe?"

Dr. DiStefano answered grimly, "Don, I think you need to know something."

Dr. Friedman knew it wasn't good news. "OK, what is it?"

"I didn't have a chance to get rid of the shoes yet."

Dr. Friedman was speechless. He had entrusted Dr. DiStefano with his horrible secret. He told him why and how he killed Lee. The running shoes were the only physical evidence of the crime. He asked Joe to get rid of them because he couldn't risk putting the shoes in his own trash or dumping them at a landfill, where they might be discovered by the police. His only concern about asking Joe to do it, was knowing that Joe always overextended himself. He remembered being at dinner with Joe when his beeper went off; it was his nurse at the hospital telling Joe she had a patient prepped and waiting for him to insert a cardiac catheter. He had said, "Jesus, I didn't know I still had one more procedure. I thought I just had the three cases today. I'll be right there." And with that he fled the restaurant.

Dr. DiStefano had enthusiastically agreed to help him and, almost immediately, he devised a clever plan to dispose of the shoes. He was a member of the exclusive garden club at Winterthur Museum in Greenville and, as a primary benefactor; he had access to the entire property. Funding had been secured to construct a new building to house the Japanese gardens. As luck would have it, the project was postponed due to severe winter weather that kept the ground frozen throughout January and February. The project finally got underway at the beginning of March. The installation of a fountain, at the center of a valet parking rotary, required contractors to dig a very large and very deep hole in the ground. Dr. DiStefano intended to dump the running shoes into the hole in the ground where they would be buried under the fountain.

Dr. Friedman wasn't sure he wanted to know why Joe was suddenly calling him in the middle of the day to tell him that he hadn't disposed of the shoes yet. He took a few seconds to calm himself, before he spoke. After all,

Joe was doing him a big favor and he didn't want to put him on the defensive by sounding upset.

Finally, he said, "I thought you were going to get rid of them the other night after your office hours. How could you . . ." He stopped himself. Instead he asked, "Can you get over there tonight?"

"I think I have to," Dr. DiStefano said dramatically.

Dr. Friedman's breathing stopped for a few seconds. Now he had to know. "Why? What happened?"

"I stashed the shoes in my office, as you know. I figured I would just grab them on my way out of work and head over to Winterthur on my way home."

"Right? So what happened?"

"Well, today a rep was in the sample room and . . ."

Dr. Friedman interrupted, "You put them in the sample room?"

"Yeah, yeah. But don't worry; they're still in the trash bag. I just stashed the bag on one of the shelves."

Suddenly Dr. DiStefano regretted his call to Donald. He thought, "Why the hell am I telling him all this? I should have just gotten rid of the shoes and he would never be the wiser." But it was the nature of his manic personality to stir things up. It usually worked to his advantage because it enabled him to motivate his staff and even provoke his patients to comply with their recommended medication and lifestyle changes.

Dr. Friedman was anxious for him to get to the point. "OK . . . so?"

"Look, maybe it's not such a big deal, but today one of the reps . . ."

"Which rep?" Dr. Friedman asked.

"Debbie Kaminski."

"Debbie Kaminski? You've got to be kidding me!"

"What? Why?"

Dr. Friedman propped an elbow on his desk and cupped his forehead in his hand. Finally he said, "It's a long story Joe. I'll tell you later." He straightened his posture and said, "Just tell me what happened next."

"I rushed into the sample room between patients, and there was Debbie picking up the running shoes from the floor and putting them back into the trash bag. Apparently she knocked them off the shelf by accident, when she was unloading sample cartons."

"What!" Now Dr. Friedman was really upset.

"Relax Donald. As I said, I don't think she'll give it another thought, but I just wanted you to know about it."

"Well, did she say anything about the shoes?"

"She asked me if I had started running."

"So she thought they were your shoes?"

"Yeah."

"Well that's good."

But Dr. DiStefano was silent for a moment, which made Donald uncomfortable. Regretfully, he asked in a low tone, "There's more, isn't there?"

"I told her the shoes weren't mine."

"Why did you do that?"

"I don't know. It was a gut reaction."

"Who did you say they belonged to?"

"I didn't. And she didn't ask. She just put them back on the shelf. Well, actually, she asked if I was going to throw them out — I guess because they were in a trash bag. And I said no. I told her she could just put them back on the shelf. She probably thinks they belong to one of my staff."

"I don't believe it!" Donald stood up and shoved his chair against the wall. He paced around his office.

"Look Donald, we think it's a big deal because we know the story behind those shoes. But to anyone else, there's nothing odd or out of the ordinary about a dirty pair of running shoes."

Dr. Friedman regained his confidence. "You're right Joe. I'm just being paranoid. How could Debbie Kaminski ever piece anything together?"

They were both silent for a moment. Then Dr. Friedman said, "Just do me a favor Joe, and get rid of the shoes tonight, or would it seem odd if somebody saw you walking around the grounds of Winterthur at night?"

"No. No. Don't worry. I'll get over there while it's still light out. The only problem is that it's raining heavily right now."

"Is it raining?"

"Yeah. I'm looking outside right now, from my office. But listen, it looks like it's slowing down. Don't worry Donald. It's payback time buddy. You've covered for me many times when I juggled a few different women at once. I won't let you down. In fact, as soon as the rain stops, I'll just slip out of the office and get it over with. I'll tell Natalie I have to run home and she can just stall my patients."

Donald relaxed and said, "Thanks Joe."

"Consider it done. I've got to run."

"Alright, thanks. Just give me a quick call tonight to let me know how it went."

"I will."

Dr. DiStefano saw three more patients and two more sales reps by the time he looked out the window in the reception area and noticed the rain had stopped. Natalie was still sitting at the front desk because the receptionist called during her lunch break and said she wasn't coming back — ever.

Dr. DiStefano bent down to whisper in Natalie's ear, "Hey Nat, listen, I have to run home for a few minutes but I'll be right back." He started to walk away.

Natalie thought, "Oh shit! Now I'm going to be stuck here while he sees patients until 8:00 tonight. She took a deep breath. She knew if she whined playfully, it would get her further than complaining. She got up from her desk and followed him down the hallway to the back door. As she neared him, she raised her voice just enough so he could hear her. "Dr. D, it's 4:00 and we still have six patients to see. Do you have to . . ."

He did an about-face and walked toward her. He put his arm around her shoulders and said in a stage whisper, "Just cover for me."

Natalie smiled and said wistfully, "Alright Dr. D."

Dr. DiStefano had already put the trash bag containing the running shoes into his briefcase. He slipped out the back door of his office and fired up the engine of his Porsche. Within twelve minutes, he turned right into the entrance for Winterthur Museum. He cruised around to the administration building on the back of the property. It was far enough away from the general admission museum to provide the administrators and curators with a comfortable distance from public access.

He parked his car in front of the building and left his briefcase on the passenger seat. The administrative assistant for the Gardens Curator looked up from her desk. She smiled when she saw him.

"Hello Dr. DiStefano. How are you?"

"Good. Good. Listen, is Madeline in today?"

"Dr. DiStefano, I'm surprised at you. How could you forget?" Her tone was playfully disparaging.

Of course he knew where Madeline was. It was just a ruse in case he was seen on the property at this hour. He gasped dramatically, as if he had just remembered. Then he said inquisitively, "Maybe she's in London . . . for the Royal Orchid Society's annual symposium."

Her assistant was charmed by his affable manner. "Yes, of course Dr. DiStefano. In fact, we had hoped you might be able to attend as well."

"No. No. I'm so busy right now it would be impossible for me to get away. But for some reason I thought it wasn't until next week. That's why I came by today because I wanted to catch up with Madeline before she left for London."

"Well, I can certainly get in touch with her for you."

"Ah no . . . no. That won't be necessary. I have her email address. I'm sure she's checking her email while she's away."

"Yes, of course Dr. DiStefano."

"Good. Hey how's the construction going on the new building?"

"It's finally moving along. They dug the foundation for the fountain and they were going to fill it today. But with all the rain, they decided to wait until tomorrow when it's supposed to be sunny for a change."

"Maybe I'll drive back there and check it out before I go."

"You should Dr. DiStefano. As one of our most generous benefactors, you should check out the progress."

He smiled and said, "Have a good evening Susan."

"Thanks. You also Dr. DiStefano."

He drove around to the construction site.

First, the road peaked in a dramatic incline to highlight the majestic evergreens. Then there was a progressive descent in the shape of a hairpin turn. It was lined with shrubs that were sculpted into topiaries. The contrast of the tall evergreens and the decline of the road that sloped into a valley, created a visual perspective that made the topiaries appear smaller at first glance. The effect simulated bonsai plants that led to the main entrance of the Japanese gardens.

The setting was serenely quiet. Dr. DiStefano glided to a stop and reached over to the passenger seat and opened his briefcase. As he pulled out the trash bag, the plastic caught on one of the brass locking clips. At the same moment, he opened his door to get out of the car. He tugged at the bag when he realized it was stuck and managed to rip an even bigger hole. He stood upright and the running shoes fell out onto the road. "Shit!" He picked up the shoes and tossed the trash bag into his car. He thought, "I'll just throw that out at the office."

He walked to the edge of the hole that would be filled with concrete the next day. Fortunately, no one could see him from this vantage point. He was about to drop the shoes into the hole, when he suddenly hesitated. He thought, "What if one of the construction guys notices them tomorrow and decides to check it out? It's not like we're in the middle of an urban area where people just toss stuff into the middle of construction digs. Shit! This isn't going to work." He didn't want to take the chance that somebody would find the shoes. After all, it was all over the news that a wealthy Greenville woman was missing and her last known whereabouts were on an exercise run. If somebody found a pair of running shoes tossed into a construction site in the same town, the police would be very, very interested.

The excavator and bulldozer sat in ominous silence on the opposite side of the hole. Then he spotted a shovel. "That's it!"

The sun was starting to set, which made it less likely that anyone would spot him. He carried the shovel, as he walked about seven or eight feet from the road. He didn't want to go much further because his shoes were already muddy. He shook his head in disgust when he saw some rain soaked trash and garbage, apparently tossed away by the construction workers. He immediately began to dig a hole large enough to fit the shoes. "That should do it," he thought. He dropped the shoes into the hole, covered them with dirt, and then tamped it down. He checked the time on his watch. "That took longer than it should have."

He quickly returned the shovel to the spot where he found it. When he got to his car, he opened the passenger door and popped open the glove compartment. He took out some tissues and wiped off his shoes and then his hands. He wrapped the tissues in what was left of the trash bag and placed it on the floor of the car. He drove slowly as he exited the museum grounds and headed back to Wilmington.

Dr. Friedman was finishing up with a patient when his cell phone rang. "Excuse me Neal, I have to take this call. I'll be right back." He shut the door to the exam room and stepped into the hallway, "Hello?"

"Donald, it's Joe."

"Hey, Joe. Just give me a second to get to my office." He was just about to shut his door when Joyce poked her head in, "Dr. Friedman, I just have a quick question."

"Not now, Joyce." He shut the door and said, "Joe, how'd it go?"

"No problem. It's done." Dr. DiStefano decided not to tell Donald that he changed the burial site. The important thing was, the running shoes were buried and no one was going to find them.

"I owe you Joe."

"I'll keep that in mind when the time comes."

Dr. Friedman asked, "Are you sure nobody else, other than Debbie Kaminski, saw the shoes?"

"Absolutely sure."

"And you don't think she thought there was anything odd or suspicious about them being in your sample closet?"

"Donald, relax. Do me a favor. After we end this call, go to your sample room and take a look at all of the miscellaneous shit that's floating around in there. All the reps know that our sample closets are a catch-all for all kinds of stuff. It's not unusual for somebody on the staff to store an umbrella there or a change of clothes or whatever."

"You're right Joe. I just have to calm down."

"You'll get through this Donald. Don't become your own worst enemy. Just play the role of the distraught husband and wait it out and go the distance. This time next year, you'll be counting your money from Inhaber-Taft."

Donald laughed, "I like the way that sounds."

"Gotta go, Don."

"OK. Thanks."

PART III

Cause of death . . .

Chapter 22: Lee's Body is Found

Thursday, March 17

"HAVE THERE BEEN any changes in your diet that might be causing the constipation?" Dr. Friedman asked. There was a knock on the door and then Joan poked her head into the exam room. "Dr. Friedman, I have an urgent call for you." She didn't want to say the detective's name in front of the patient.

"Excuse me Mrs. Cacchio, I'll be right back." Dr. Friedman followed Joan. "Who is it?"

She walked toward his office and stopped just outside. She said quietly, "It's Detective Healy, and he said he has urgent news."

Dr. Friedman shut the door behind him. His thoughts raced as he stared at the phone. He hesitated to pick it up. He felt the need to rehearse his reaction to whatever the detective might say. "Maybe they found her," he thought, "I don't know if I'm ready for this." Then he pictured the scene where he'd left Lee . . . and then Grant coming over to his house after he heard the news . . . and the whole debacle with the running shoes at Joe DiStefano's office.

Finally, he took a deep breath and reached for the phone. "Hello this is Dr. Friedman."

"Dr. Friedman, this is Detective Healy. I have some news for you, but I'm afraid it's not good."

Dr. Friedman began to shake and his body weakened. He slumped into his chair. "What is it?"

"We received a call from the Pennsville Police Department in Salem County around 3:30 this afternoon."

"And?"

"A group of teenagers drove down one of the back roads off of Route 29 today. One of the girls thought she saw a body in the weeds just a couple of yards from the road. They pulled over and the kids got out of the car and, sure enough, there was a body of a woman lying in the weeds . . . in a running outfit . . . I'm afraid it was your wife Dr. Friedman."

"Is she . . . alright? Is my wife . . . OK?"

"I'm sorry Dr. Friedman, but Lee is dead."

"Oh God! What happened?" Adrenalin surged through his veins and his heart pounded heavily. He was stricken with anxiety over his own demise, until he realized he could take advantage of the emotion. He wanted the detective to hear the hysteria in his voice. "Why? My poor Lee . . . why?"

"We don't know yet. We will of course let you know as soon as the Medical Examiner provides us with his findings."

"Where is she now?"

"The body . . . or . . . ah, I'm sorry Dr. Friedman. She's at the Medical Examiner's office in Wilmington Hospital. Can you get away to meet me there?"

"Of course. I'll leave right away."

"Good. It's 6:00 now. Can you meet me there in twenty minutes or so?"

"Yeah sure. Where should I meet you — in the lobby of the hospital?"

"Yes. That would be the best place to meet. I'll see you there shortly."

"OK . . . oh, ah, Detective, did you contact Lee's son Grant yet?"

"No. I thought it would be better if you did that."

"Thanks Detective. I agree. I'll call Grant on my way to the hospital."

"Good idea. Dr. Friedman . . . I'm very sorry for your loss."

"Yes . . . me too . . . ah, thank you Detective." Dr. Friedman sounded despondent. Even before he hung up the phone, he was already running through every detail of that night. He pulled his coat from the hanger on the back of his office door. "I hope I didn't leave anything behind in that field."

He opened his door and saw Joan talking to a patient on the other side of the office. He called out, "Joan!" He knew a little hysteria would be perceived as normal for a man who just found out the police discovered his wife's dead body.

Joan turned around and knew immediately, from the look on his face, that it was bad news. She rushed over to Dr. Friedman. "What is it?"

"They found Lee. She's . . ." His face wrinkled into tears, which surprised him.

"What? What? Is she alright?"

"No. She's dead." Dr. Friedman hugged Joan and shed a few tears.

"Oh God! Dr. Friedman, I'm so sorry."

He stepped back from her and wiped his face with the back of his hand, like an adolescent boy. "I have to go."

He stopped and turned to Joan again, "Who's here to cover for me?"

"Don't worry about it. Go. I'll take care of it. Dr. Bergman and Margotitis are here."

He didn't say another word. He let the tears roll down his face. "This is good," he thought. "Everyone in the office will remember seeing me upset. I'm putting on such a good show; I almost believe it myself, although it's a lot easier to cry and be a blithering mess when your ass may be on the line."

When he got into his car he thought, "How am I going to tell Grant? What do I say? Well, now's a good time to do it when I'm so emotional. He'll hear it in my voice." He punched the number into his cell phone.

"Hello?"

"Grant, hi it's Donald."

Grant heard the dire tone in Donald's voice. He asked sheepishly, "What is it?"

"I'm on my way to meet Detective Healy."

"Did they find Mom?"

"Yes. But I'm afraid it's not good." He was not crying now but he sniffled to make it sound like he was. "She's dead Grant."

Grant cried out, "No! No! What happened?"

"I don't know!" Dr. Friedman said emphatically. He turned the key in the ignition. "I'm on my way to meet the detective right now."

"Where?"

"At Wilmington Hospital — in the lobby. We're going to meet with the Medical Examiner."

"I'm going there too."

"Grant, I don't think that's a good idea." Dr. Friedman pulled out of the private physician parking lot in the back of the office building.

"Why not?"

"Because I . . . I don't know what kind of condition Lee is in . . . maybe it's not a good idea for you to see her."

Grant cried, "Why? Why?"

"Grant, is Jillian there?"

"No, but she should be home any minute now."

"Alright. Do me a favor. Wait for Jillian and tell her what we know so far. I'll come over to your place as soon as I'm done with Detective Healy." There was a moment of silence. "Grant? Did you hear me?"

Grant sobbed, "Yes. I heard you. I'm going to wait for Jilly to get here, but then we're going to Wilmington Hospital."

Donald was about to say something, but he stopped himself. He suddenly thought, "If Grant is there, he'll create an unnecessary distraction. These are pivotal moments . . . when I meet Detective Healy in the lobby . . . when we meet with the Medical Examiner. They are going to evaluate everything I say and every emotion I express. I have to be very careful and very conscious of my words and actions. Grant will only distract me."

Donald said, "Grant, Detective Healy asked me to contact you. He would have called you himself if he thought it was a good idea for you to be there now. Let me be blunt. Lee was found in a field in New Jersey for God's sake!"

Grant became hysterical. "Oh God! No. Was she murdered?" Tears, mucous and spit ran down his face.

Donald was getting sick to his stomach. He couldn't take another minute of this. He took shallow breaths and swallowed repeatedly. Now he recognized the urge to vomit. The more Grant sobbed, the more nauseated he felt. He looked into his rearview mirror. He let an oncoming car pass him on the right and then quickly pulled over to the side of the road. He thrust the gear shift into first and let go of the clutch too soon. The car jerked to a stop. He pulled back the emergency brake and jumped out of the car. He fumbled around the front of the car and started to vomit. He raised his right hand to wipe his face and was surprised to realize that he still clutched his cell phone in it. He could hear Grant saying, "Hello? Hello?" Donald started to heave again at the sound of Grant's voice. He thought, "This kid is going to be the death of me. I've got to be careful though because I'm going to have deal with him for a while. I have to treat him delicately so he doesn't get suspicious."

"Yes Grant, I'm here," he said breathlessly.

"What happened?"

"What happened? . . . I just pulled over to side of the road and threw up — that's what happened." He was careful to sound upset, not angry. It must have worked because Grant finally relented.

"I'm sorry Donald. I know this is terrible for you too."

"It *is* Grant. I love your mother very much."

"I know that."

Donald got back into his car. Now he could hear Jilly's voice in the background.

Grant said quietly, "Donald, Jilly's here now. I'll talk to her and we'll both wait for you here."

"Thanks Grant. I'll be there soon. I just hope Detective Healy can make some sense out of all this. Goodbye Grant."

Donald thought, "It's a terrible thing for a son to go through. But maybe Lee should have thought of that before she started having an affair with Edgar Schaeffer. But of course she wouldn't do that. She was a spoiled brat. No, she was much worse than that — she was a whore — going from one husband to the next — upgrading for financial gain. I'm sure she had her sights set on Edgar as the next husband."

He pulled into the physician-parking garage at Wilmington Hospital. He was feeling better now that he had gotten his conversation with Grant out of the way. He thought, "It's really no loss. What did Lee add to the world other than another gold digger? The only person who'll miss her is Grant. Edgar won't give a shit. He'll just move on to the next bimbo."

As Donald neared the front entrance of the hospital, he did his best to change his facial expression and his mood. "Show time," he thought.

When Dr. Friedman entered the lobby of Wilmington Hospital, he was surprised to see about four or five policemen standing in a huddle. Without realizing it, his eyes widened and his mouth opened. Fear and panic were building inside him. "Why all the police? Where's Detective Healy?" He noticed two of the policemen look over in his direction. They said something to each other and then began to approach him. One of them said, "Dr. Friedman?"

"Yes, I'm Dr. Friedman." He wondered, "How did they know I'm Dr. Friedman. This can't be good."

"Follow me please, Dr. Friedman," one of the officers said.

"Sure."

They walked into an office just beyond the front lobby, and Dr. Friedman was relieved to see Detective Healy. Apparently he had managed to temporarily commandeer an office shared by two billing clerks. He was on the phone. With his mouth and finger he motioned, "One minute." The police officer said, "Have a seat Dr. Friedman."

"Thanks."

Just before he sat down, another officer asked, "Can I take your coat?"

"Ah, yeah, sure. Thanks." Dr. Friedman stood up and slipped off his coat. He hadn't bothered to button it. When he sat down in the chair, he saw that he was still wearing his white lab coat. He was relieved. "That's how they knew I was Dr. Friedman. They don't suspect me." He felt his confidence flooding back.

Detective Healy finished on the phone and immediately stood up and walked around the desk toward him. He reached out his hand and said, "Dr. Friedman, I'm very sorry about your loss."

Dr. Friedman was careful to give the detective the handshake of a dead fish. He wanted to appear drained. His face was sullen and he asked, "Do you know anything about what happened?"

"I'll tell you what we know so far. But we'll know more after we talk with the Medical Examiner." The detective asked the police officers to leave the room. "Can you fellas give us a couple of minutes?" With that, they shut the door behind them. He sat on the edge of the desk, and spoke in a low voice. "As I told you on the phone, we received a call from the Pennsville Police Department around 3:30 this afternoon. They reported that an officer responded to a call about the discovery of a body in a field off Route 29. Their police chief called us after they confirmed the body fit the description of a missing person — Lee Young. Shortly after 4:00, I was on the scene with our

Crime Scene Investigators. It appears that Lee had been jogging because she was wearing a running outfit. She was bruised up a little bit and our initial findings indicate that she took a fall while she was running."

It didn't take great acting ability for Dr. Friedman to appear upset. As soon as the detective said the words, "Crime Scene Investigators," he felt the contents of his stomach leap to his esophagus. It required an intensely focused effort on his part in order to halt the process of regurgitation. He felt a wave a warmth pass through him and once the beads of sweat felt cold against his skin, he knew he had subdued the urge to vomit. But, now that he was listening again, he found the slow cadence of Detective Healy's speech unnerving. He thought the story was at the perfect juncture for him to ask, "Was she . . . was she . . . attacked?"

The detective said in a reassuring tone, "Dr. Friedman, our initial findings show no signs of a violent attack."

Dr. Friedman sat back and sighed. He wiped his forehead and said, "Thank God for that much."

"Would you like some water or anything? You look very pale."

"Ah, no. I'm OK now, but I must admit I was feeling ill a moment ago." He leaned forward in his chair and said, "I called Grant on my way here and . . ."

Detective Healy interrupted him, "Good. Good. I was hoping you would do that."

Donald said dramatically, "Well of course. I think of him as my son." He rested his head in his hands and squinted hard in an effort to shed a few tears.

Detective Healy saw a box of tissues to his left. He grabbed a couple and handed them to Dr. Friedman. "Here, please. Take a moment."

Dr. Friedman blotted his face and then continued, "Naturally Grant was hysterical and I tried to comfort him but . . . at the same moment, I think it really hit me . . . you know?" He looked at the detective as if pleading for empathy.

"Of course. I understand."

"When I heard the words coming out of my mouth about Lee, that's when . . . that's when I realized the truth of the matter and well . . . I had to pull the car over because I got sick."

"This is a terrible shock for you and for Grant."

Dr. Friedman shook his head in despair and blew his nose. Finally, he said, "You said something about Lee taking a fall. Did she twist an ankle or . . ."

"Well, that's the strange thing. There appeared to be no broken bones, which might have caused a sudden fall." Detective Healy looked at his watch. He reached for the phone on the desk. "Let me call down to the Medical Examiner's office. He might be ready for us now."

Dr. Friedman thought smugly, "Come on guys. No violent attack. No broken bones. What else might have caused Lee to fall?" Then he heard Detective Healy saying, "Hi. Yes, this is Detective Healy. Do you know if the Medical Examiner is ready for us to come down?"

"OK. Fine. We'll be right there."

He looked at Dr. Friedman and said, "We can head down to see the M.E. now."

Dr. Friedman stood up and followed the detective out of the office. One of the police officers joined them on the elevator, which alarmed Dr. Friedman.

Detective Healy said sternly, "Dr. Friedman, this isn't going to be easy for you."

Dr. Friedman looked at the floor and said, "I know."

They were silent until the elevator's computerized voice announced, "Basement level" and there was a slight pinging sound.

The police officer got off first, followed by the detective and Dr. Friedman. They walked down a corridor with sickly, green tiled floors and walls. Dr. Friedman hadn't been to an autopsy room or pathology lab since he did his residency at Riverside Hospital in Wilmington.

They stopped in front of a door with a plaque that read "Pathology Lab." The police officer opened the door for the detective. He entered first, followed by Dr. Friedman. The officer stayed in the hallway. They walked through the lab and then through a second door that opened into one of the autopsy rooms. The room was the same austere, floor-to-ceiling stainless steel, as the ones at Riverside Hospital. They were struck by a malodorous fusion of cleaning fluid and formaldehyde, which seemed to dissipate immediately when their eyes fell on the focal point of the room — a gurney.

A shrouded body rested underneath bright fluorescent lights, and a gowned and gloved pathologist stood over the body with probing instruments at the ready. Dr. Friedman heard Detective Healy say, "Here, put these on." He was referring to a box of plastic gloves. The detective reached in and grabbed at the wilted blue plastic. He snapped on a pair of gloves and Dr. Friedman did the same.

"Follow me."

The Medical Examiner had covered the body completely when he heard them enter the room. He had been through this before. He knew that Detective Healy wanted to observe Dr. Friedman's reaction when he was exposed to the corpse of his wife for the first time.

"Here Dr. Friedman. Could you stand here please?" Detective Healy motioned to the side of the gurney that was opposite the Medical Examiner. For the moment, the detective stood next to Dr. Friedman. He motioned toward the other side of the gurney and said, "This is Dr. Pagoshi."

Dr. Pagoshi respectfully lowered his head a bit, as a greeting. Dr. Friedman could only see Dr. Pagoshi's eyes because he was gowned from head to toe and wore a surgical mask. He said, "Hello Dr. Pagoshi." They both knew enough not to extend hands in greeting.

Then the detective turned slightly toward Donald and said, "And this is Dr. Friedman." Now the detective walked around to stand next to Dr. Pagoshi. He could get a good look at Dr. Friedman's face from this vantage point.

Dr. Pagoshi looked to his left and asked Detective Healy, "Shall we get started?"

"Please."

Without hesitation, Dr. Pagoshi pealed the sheet away from Lee's face.

Dr. Friedman gasped and covered his mouth with his gloved hand. "Oh God!" He turned away and was pleased to feel tears welling up in his eyes. He turned toward the gurney again and said in an exasperated tone, "Oh my beautiful Lee. What happened?" He extended his hand to touch her hair.

Detective Healy said loudly, "Dr. Friedman, please!"

He pulled his arm back.

"I'm terribly sorry Dr. Friedman, but I can't let you touch her right now."

Dr. Friedman sniffled, "I understand."

Detective Healy asked, "Are you OK?"

Dr. Friedman said nothing. He just nodded his head to indicate he was ready.

"Dr. Pagoshi, can you tell us about your findings?"

"Of course. The corpse has been identified as one Lee Young. Rigor mortis has subsided. It is my understanding that Lee Young was reported missing eight days ago. Pallor and muscle atrophy, due to the progression of decomposition, indicate that she has been dead since the day she went missing."

Detective Healy watched Dr. Friedman back away from the gurney. He said, "Excuse me for a moment." He walked toward the door but did not leave the room. He took a tissue out of his pocket and wiped his eyes and his nose. He stood still for a moment and then turned to walk toward the gurney again. Out of the corner of his eye he noticed a metal table that rested against the wall. On top of it were Lee's clothes and running shoes. He stopped for a few seconds and did nothing to hide his gaze. He knew it would appear natural that he was struck by the sight.

Detective Healy said, "I'm sorry Dr. Friedman. If you want to leave I understand."

Dr. Friedman said resolutely, "No. I want to know what happened to her."

The detective said, "Please continue Dr. Pagoshi."

Dr. Pagoshi said, "Given the circumstances, I submitted lab samples for a toxicology study as soon as they brought her in." He pulled the sheet down further until it rested at the end of the gurney. They now had a complete view of Lee's naked body.

Dr. Pagoshi continued. "She has a few bruises that are consistent with a fall. And there is no sign of blunt force trauma. Apparently she was not attacked." He stepped back and walked over to an X-ray board and turned on the back light. He pointed to the panel of X-rays of her feet, ankles, and shins. He said, "And as you can see, there are no broken bones or fractures which would have caused a sudden fall." He returned to the gurney as he said, "In the absence of external trauma, the cause of her sudden death may be attributed to an aneurysm or embolism, a heart attack, or perhaps a brain tumor. I'm afraid the only way I can determine this is to conduct an internal examination."

Without hesitation, Detective Healy said, "I think you should move forward with the internal examination." Then he directed his attention to Dr. Friedman, who was despondent. His eyes were cast down and fixated on Lee's face.

The detective said, "I'm sure we have your concurrence on that Dr. Friedman."

"Yes . . . yes of course," he said as he held his gaze.

The detective said, "Let's get you out of here Dr. Friedman. We can meet with Dr. Pagoshi tomorrow to discuss his findings. I'm sorry. I know this is terrible for you."

The detective directed a question to both of them, "Can we meet in Dr. Pagoshi's office tomorrow morning at 9:00?"

They both answered, "Yes."

Detective Healy said, "Good. Let me walk you out Dr. Friedman."

Dr. Friedman said grimly, "Thank you Dr. Pagoshi."

Dr. Pagoshi said, "I'm very sorry for your loss."

Dr. Friedman and the detective didn't speak until they stepped onto the elevator. Dr. Friedman said, "I promised Grant that I would stop by to see him tonight and let him know what you've learned so far."

"That's a good idea."

Dr. Friedman was grateful that it was a short ride to the main lobby. He needed to get some fresh air. He turned to Detective Healy and shook his hand loosely. "Thanks Detective. I'll see you at 9:00 tomorrow morning."

"I'll see you then Dr. Friedman."

Detective Healy returned to the autopsy room. This time he didn't bother with the plastic gloves. He stood in the doorway and saw that Dr. Pagoshi was using a scalpel to open Lee's chest. He said, "Excuse me Dr. Pagoshi, how long will the autopsy take?"

Dr. Pagoshi did not look up. He answered, "I know which organs I need to assess, so I should be able to make a determination within a couple of hours at most."

"Alright then. You know my home phone number. Can you give me a call when you're finished?"

Dr. Pagoshi remained focused and simply said, "No problem."

"Thanks. I'm getting out of here."

Dr. Friedman approached the front door of Grant's townhouse. He hesitated for a second and then knocked gently. Jillian answered the door. "Hi Donald. Come in please." She immediately reached out to him and clasped his hands. "I'm so sorry about Lee. This must be awful for you."

Donald held her hands for a moment in solemn silence. He finally said, "Thanks Jilly. It really is awful."

"Would you like some dinner?"

"No thanks."

"Are you sure?"

Dr. Friedman followed her into the dining room. Grant heard him come in but he stayed seated at the table. He finally stood up when Donald entered the room.

They embraced. Grant cried for a few minutes and then asked in a pained voice, "What did they tell you?"

Jilly pulled a chair back from the table and said, "Here. Sit down Donald."

"Thanks." Donald sighed and shook his head. "The Medical Examiner said that Lee apparently died the same night she went missing."

Grant burst into tears and dropped into a chair. He rested his head on his arms on the dining table and sobbed. Jilly knelt beside him and patted his head. Donald felt badly for him but he was in no mood for more demands on his emotional energy. He forced himself to appear sympathetic. He reached across the table and put his hand on one of Grant's arms. He even managed to work up a few tears himself. Then he said, "Apparently Lee had fallen to the ground as a result of a heart attack or maybe a pulmonary embolism. The pathologist isn't sure. He's going to conduct an internal examination of the suspect organs. I'm going back tomorrow morning to meet with Detective Healy and Dr. Pagoshi — he's the M.E.

Grant sat up, "Let me go with you tomorrow."

Donald knew he wouldn't take no for an answer this time. "I don't see why not. But Jilly, I think you should go with him and do the driving."

Jilly said, "Of course I will."

Suddenly, Donald stood up and said, "Look, I hope you can understand, but I'm going to head back to the house. I need some time to myself."

Jilly said, "Of course I understand." She and Grant walked Donald to the front door. Nobody knew what to say. Jilly reached over to hug Donald and impulsively, Grant did the same. Donald thought, "It must be a terrible thing to lose your mother this way." And it was his profound narcissism that obscured the irony of that thought.

Donald said, "I'm so sorry Grant."

Grant touched Donald's shoulder, "It's every bit as horrible for you Donald."

As he started out the front door, he turned and said, "Oh, try to be at the hospital a little before 9:00 tomorrow morning. Goodnight."

Detective Healy's head bobbed up and down on the edge of the pillow, until he finally succumbed to sleep, on the couch in his living room. The light on the table next to him had gone out thirty minutes ago. It was set on a timer to protect his family from burglars. The bright lights from the television commercials suddenly flickered in front of him and teased his eyes open. But in seconds, the softer lighting of black and white reruns caused him to drift off again into a cozy stupor. The beer bottle in his right hand was almost empty. His loose grip tightened each time he was partially awakened. Now the bottle slipped through his hand onto the rug.

"Patrick," his wife called from the kitchen.

He was startled into wakefulness and his thoughts raced, "What did I do now? She always calls me Patrick when she's pissed . . . I think I heard the phone ring." He sat up and pushed down on the couch cushions with his hands as he shoved his ankles against the wooden frame for momentum. He winced from the slight pain in his ankles and hoped that someday he would remember not to do that. And, as sometimes happens when he stands up suddenly, the momentary low blood pressure caused him to stagger. Just then his wife entered the room. She saw the empty beer bottle on the rug, as she walked toward the couch. This time she spoke in a quieter tone for fear of waking the kids. "Pat, it's Dr. Pagoshi on the phone. He said you're expecting his call."

"Oh yeah. Sure. Thanks honey." He rubbed his forehead and cheek, as he walked toward the kitchen.

"Dr. Pagoshi?"

"Hello Detective. The cause of death for Lee Young was a heart attack."

"Wow, that's shocking! Are there any signs of foul play?"

"Not at this point. There is damage to the structural integrity of the heart muscle that is consistent with a heart attack. But that's why the toxicology report is important because I have to rule out the presence of any acutely administered chemical agents that may have induced a myocardial infarction. And conversely, there is additional deterioration to the heart that may be the result of prolonged exposure to a chemical agent."

Detective Healy asked, "Are you saying that it's possible she was poisoned slowly over time?"

"Anything is possible, but I don't want to speak out of turn. I can assure you that the toxicology report will clarify which chemical substances were in her body. Then it's my job to assess the duration of exposure and any possible link to her death."

Detective Healy said, "Do me a favor please, Dr. Pagoshi. Since the cause of death is relatively suspicious given Lee's age and otherwise healthy condition, I would appreciate it if you did not mention to Dr. Friedman that we've already spoken."

Dr. Pagoshi had worked with Detective Healy before on several cases. They appreciated each other's no-nonsense approach.

Dr. Pagoshi asked, "Are you suggesting that Dr. Friedman had something to do with the heart attack?"

Detective Healy said, "Quite honestly, until now, I was convinced Dr. Friedman wasn't guilty of any wrongdoing. Now I wonder if I've been too careless, too naïve."

Dr. Pagoshi said pensively, "I see."

The detective said, "When we meet with Dr. Friedman tomorrow, let's just begin the conversation as if we've never spoken. It will give me an opportunity to evaluate his reaction more carefully."

"I understand. I'll see you tomorrow morning then."

"Thank you Dr. Pagoshi. Goodnight."

Chapter 23: Suspicion

Friday morning, March 18

JUST BEFORE 9:00 A.M., Dr. Friedman stood in the lobby of Wilmington Hospital. Jilly and Grant arrived five minutes later.

Detective Healy saw the three of them through the glass of the billing clerks' office, which served as his ad hoc quarters for one more day. He frowned with empathy as he approached them. "Thanks for coming back Dr. Friedman." Then he turned to Grant and said, "You must be Grant."

"Yes, yes. I'm Lee Young's son."

The detective shook Grant's hand warmly and said sincerely, "I'm very sorry for your loss."

"Thank you." Grant looked as if he was going to burst into tears again.

Jilly quickly reached out her hand and said, "Hi Detective. I'm Grant's fiancé, Jillian."

They shook hands. "I'm Detective Patrick Healy. It's nice to meet you. I'm sorry it's under such dire circumstances."

Jilly frowned respectfully, "Yes detective."

Then he moved closer to the three of them to create a sort of huddle. He said, "I appreciate that all of you came down here this morning. But I'm afraid I have to ask Grant and Jillian to wait in my temporary quarters over there." He motioned toward the office across the lobby.

Grant protested, "But I . . ."

Detective Healy interrupted him, "I'm sorry, but I think it's best right now for Dr. Friedman and I to meet with the Medical Examiner. We will certainly discuss his findings with you afterward."

Jilly spoke up, "It's OK Detective Healy." She slipped her arm under Grant's arm.

"Alright then, follow me."

After Grant and Jilly were seated in the billing office, the detective asked, "Can I get you a cup of coffee, water, anything?"

They both said, "No thanks."

"Alright. Just sit tight and we'll be back shortly."

Jilly said, "Thanks detective."

When they were in the elevator, Detective Healy said, "Dr. Friedman, I forgot to tell you last night that we found a key in Lee's pocket, which is probably your house key. We also found a cell phone."

Dr. Friedman was pleased with his clever planning. He had called her cell phone several times in anticipation of this. He appeared concerned. "Did she try to call me? Did she call 911?"

Detective Healy said, "I'm afraid we don't know just yet. But we've contacted her service provider. They're going to fax me a list of outgoing and incoming calls over the last billing period. We'll see what turns up."

Dr. Friedman said, "Good. Good idea."

Suddenly a thought flashed through his mind, "Shit! They're going to find phone calls to Edgar Schaeffer . . . and from Edgar Schaeffer."

They got off the elevator and followed the same hallway as they had the night before. But this time, instead of entering the Pathology lab, they continued past it and stopped in front of a door with a plaque that read, "Chief of Pathology – Dr. Pagoshi."

Detective Healy turned and saw the pained expression on Donald's face. He looked pale. "Dr. Friedman, are you alright?"

"Yes, I'm fine. I'm just . . ."

He interrupted, "I understand. Are you sure you're ready for this?"

Dr. Friedman exhaled heavily and then said, "Yes. I'm as ready as I can be."

The detective knocked gently on the door and then opened it. Dr. Pagoshi was sitting at his desk. "Please come in."

"After you." Detective Healy motioned for Dr. Friedman to sit in the chair next to the wall. The detective moved his chair a little off center and to the right so he could have a good view of Dr. Friedman, without the loss of subtlety.

Dr. Pagoshi said, "Good morning gentlemen."

Dr. Friedman spoke first, "Good morning Dr. Pagoshi. Please . . . tell us what you found."

Like most pathologists, Dr. Pagoshi did not mince words. He said, "The cause of death is myocardial infarction." He remembered the detective's request to give the impression that they had not already spoken. Dr. Pagoshi directed his next comment to Detective Healy and said, "In laymen's terms, she suffered a heart attack."

"What? How can that be? She was an athlete?" Dr. Friedman cried out in disbelief.

Dr. Pagoshi said, "It is certainly unusual for a woman her age and in her apparently excellent physical condition to suffer a heart attack. It does happen, however rarely. The structural damage to the heart is consistent with that which is caused by a myocardial infarction. However, the extent of tissue necrosis had to be the result of decreased blood flow due to prolonged vasoconstriction and platelet aggregation."

Detective Healy had been watching Dr. Friedman, but now he looked at Dr. Pagoshi and said, "In English please, Dr. Pagoshi."

"Sorry detective. Given Lee's otherwise good health, and the extent of damage to the heart muscle, we cannot rule out the possibility that the event was initiated by some chemicals on board that slowly and insidiously damaged the integrity of the heart."

Dr. Pagoshi leaned forward and looked intently at Dr. Friedman. "Do you know if Lee was taking any prescription medication?"

Dr. Friedman thought, "Now we're getting to the good part." He was careful to use the present tense, "Lee takes MELAVOX for her osteoarthritis and back pain."

Detective Healy asked, "What's MELAMOX?"

"MELA-VOX." Dr. Pagoshi corrected the detective's pronun-ciation and then continued, "It's a COX II Inhibitor."

"A what?" asked Detective Healy.

Dr. Pagoshi said, "I'm sorry. Have you heard of non-steroidal anti-inflammatory drugs?"

"I don't know about the first part, but I've heard of anti-inflammatory drugs, yes."

Dr. Pagoshi continued, "There are a few that are available over the counter. But most are still classified as prescription drugs. Anyway, a COX II Inhibitor is an NSAID or non-steroidal anti-inflammatory drug. MELAVOX is the first drug in this therapeutic class, and it's only available by prescription."

Dr. Friedman remained silent and listened to the exchange, while he assessed his next move.

Detective Healy asked, "Dr. Friedman, did you prescribe this MELAMOX or MELAVOX, or was your wife seeing another physician?"

Dr. Friedman thought, "If only you knew the irony of that statement." He said respectfully, "It's MELA-VOX Detective, and yes, I prescribed it for her. My clinical experience with MELAVOX has shown it to be an effective and well tolerated drug." He sat forward in his chair and said, "Detective, Lee is in . . . I'm sorry . . . Lee *was* in very good health. Her osteoarthritis was simply a manifestation of normal aches and pains for a woman her age who still manages to run marathons. And to answer your other question, the only physician she saw was her Gynecologist for annual checkups."

Dr. Pagoshi asked, "Was she taking any other medications that you are aware of?"

"No." He lied. He knew she was taking the birth control pill, EFFAMIN, which can cause a dangerous increase in potassium levels; but he would wait until the time was right to play that card.

Dr. Pagoshi said, "That's helpful for evaluation, but I must ask you Dr. Friedman. Forgive me, but in light of the circumstances, it would be helpful to know if your wife used any recreational drugs."

"No. Absolutely not. She's very health conscious. She eats right, runs marathons, she . . ." Suddenly, Dr. Friedman put his hand to his mouth. He shook his head. "I'm sorry" he said, "this is just so . . ." He lowered his head and his eyes filled with tears. When he looked up again, Detective Healy took note of his apparently sincere emotions.

After an awkward silence, the detective said, "Dr. Pagoshi, you'll contact me as soon as you get the results of the toxicology report?"

"Yes detective. I certainly will."

Dr. Friedman thought, "Now is probably a good time to say . . ."

Suddenly, Detective Healy stood up and said, "Let's get you out of here."

But in a dramatic turn, Dr. Friedman remained seated. He looked up at the detective and said, "There is something I'm worried about."

Detective Healy immediately sat down again and asked, "What is it?"

Dr. Friedman spoke as if he was in a trance. "Dr. Pagoshi said that Lee had a heart attack."

"Yes?"

"As I told you, Lee had been taking 25 mg of MELAVOX for her osteoarthritis. But several weeks ago, she asked me to bring home some samples of the 75 mg dose. She wanted it for breakthrough pain." He looked at the detective and explained, "For the days when her pain flared up. She got the idea because she goes to all the drug rep dinners with me. The reps who sell the drug are promoting the max dose--75 mg--as safe for long term treatment of pain. So I had no concerns about Lee taking the max dose occasionally. In fact, I prescribe the 75 mg dose for several of my patients." He paused for a moment and then added, "I mention this now because, initially I had some trepidation about prescribing MELAVOX 75 mg because of a clinical study that showed a risk of adverse cardiovascular events."

Detective Healy rubbed his chin and said, "I must be missing something. Are you suggesting that a prescription drug might have caused her heart attack?"

Dr. Friedman had a look of chagrin on his face. He said, "God, I hope not. As I said, Lee was taking the lowest dose of MELAVOX for a long time, and I'm sure she only took the max dose occasionally. But in any case, I'm sure Dr. Pagoshi will be able to elucidate the cause of the M.I."

Dr. Friedman was planting the seeds for his lawsuit against Inhaber-Taft. He knew the lawsuit would be much more damaging to Inhaber-Taft if they proved that Lee was taking the lowest dose of the drug chronically and only taking the maximum dose for breakthrough pain.

Detective Healy furrowed his brow.

Dr. Pagoshi said, "It *is* possible. There was a study published in the New England Journal of Medicine that showed MELAVOX caused thromboembolic events in some patients."

"What's a thrombo . . . whatever event?" The detective asked in frustration.

Dr. Pagoshi started to answer, "It means . . ." and then he slowed his speech as if he became more enlightened as the words came out of his mouth, "It means a stroke . . . or a heart attack."

The two doctors looked at each other. Dr. Friedman sprung to his feet and said angrily, "Inhaber-Taft stood behind MELAVOX as being appropriate for healthy patients with no history of cardiac disease. Michael Poong and his reps *all insisted* that the max dose of 75 mg could be used as long term therapy!" He purposely dropped Michael's name knowing the detective was bound to think of it later. Then he said, "They were all coming to my office *assuring* me that the METAPO Study was poorly designed and fraught with errors. Of course I wouldn't just go by their word. It's also my clinical experience with a drug that guides my judgment. But I consider companies like Inhaber-Taft and Prescott-Williams to use the highest standards of truth and ethics in the promotion of their products."

Detective Healy motioned with his hands and said, "Dr. Friedman, please slow down."

Dr. Friedman calmed down a bit and said, "Maybe I *am* jumping to conclusions. After all, I have many of my patients on MELAVOX 25 and 75 and none of them have had a thromboembolic event."

But the truth was that none of his patients had been taking the 75 mg dose of MELAVOX for as long as Lee did. Nor were his patients ingesting the quantity of MELAVOX that he had made certain Lee was.

Dr. Pagoshi said, "This is all very important for me to know Dr. Friedman. But please, don't blame yourself. As physicians, we use our best judgment based on clinical outcomes and experience with a drug. And every patient is different." He shook his head in disgust and continued, "All of this mass marketing of medicine is wrong. We know better now that a drug that works for some patients may not work for others. The same is true of tolerance and adverse events. Some patients have an idiosyncratic reaction to a drug that leads to a disastrous outcome."

Dr. Friedman drew his hand across his forehead and then rubbed his temples with his fingers and said, "This is all just too much."

The detective motioned to the empty chair and said, "Please, sit down."

It was apparent that Dr. Pagoshi was inclined to agree with Dr. Friedman's theory as to the cause of the heart attack. He said, "It's a disturbing possibility, but the cardiac event may have been precipitated by MELAVOX. I'm certainly familiar with the study you referred to that created a lot of controversy among physicians about the safety of COX II Inhibitors."

Detective Healy asked Dr. Pagoshi, "Can you get me a copy of that study?"

Dr. Friedman jumped in, "I can probably get it to you more quickly. I'm sure we have copies in our office." He shook his head in despair, "My God! To think that I may have prescribed the medicine that led to this!"

Dr. Pagoshi said, "Dr. Friedman, don't despair. The toxicology report will enlighten us as to which chemical is likely to be responsible."

Detective Healy was unconvinced. It seemed the two doctors had agreed on the cause of death based on a theory about a legal, prescription drug.

Dr. Pagoshi said, "Now that we know what we're looking for, I'm sure I'll be able to get back to you later today with the toxicology report."

"Good. Thank you Dr. Pagoshi."

They both turned their attention to Dr. Friedman. He looked exhausted. "I'll be in touch with you after I hear from Dr. Pagoshi," the detective said.

Dr. Friedman made a resolute sigh and then stood up. He had been tossing around the idea of whether or not to ask about her wedding ring. He thought, "It's probably a good idea to ask about it. They'll think it has sentimental value for me."

"Dr. Pagoshi, I noticed you have some of Lee's personal effects. Did you by any chance find . . . do you have Lee's wedding ring?"

Detective Healy jumped in, "I'm sorry Dr. Friedman but there was no jewelry found. Unfortunately, the parties who discover a body have been known to remove such items. But in any case, we're working with the

Pennsville Police Department as we continue with all aspects of the investigation. I will certainly alert them to the missing ring."

Dr. Friedman stood with a faraway look in his eyes. The detective said, "Please, Dr. Friedman, you've been through enough." He motioned toward the door. "Please, after you."

Dr. Friedman shook his head in agreement. But first, he turned toward the M.E. "Thank you Dr. Pagoshi."

"You are most welcome."

Dr. Friedman followed Detective Healy into the office where Grant and Jilly awaited them. Grant jumped up and walked over to Dr. Friedman. He asked, "What did they tell you?"

"Unfortunately Grant, it's going to take some more time before we can definitively say what happened to Lee."

Grant thought they were hiding something from him. He said, "They must have told you something!"

Dr. Friedman could not withstand another hysterical reaction from Grant. He said grimly, "Detective Healy will tell you what they know so far. I'm sorry, but I've got to get out of here."

Detective Healy said, "Dr. Friedman, I can have one of my officers give you a ride home."

Donald was caught off guard. He had planned to drive to the office. Then he thought to himself, "Should I go home? Maybe it would appear odd, or even suspicious, if I'm able to just pick up the pieces and go back to work." He appeared confused and troubled. He said, "No. I can drive back to the house . . . or . . . actually maybe I should go to the office. I don't know. I guess I'll decide when I get to my car." He looked at Grant and said, "I'll call you later."

He started to walk out of the office when Detective Healy said, "I'll contact you later today about that issue." The detective did not want to refer to the toxicology report in front of Grant.

Dr. Friedman stopped in the doorway and said, "I have my cell phone with me. It's best to call that number."

"I will do that."

As he walked to his car, he was careful to maintain a sullen expression because he had an eerie feeling he was being watched. Once inside his car, he leaned back on the headrest and thought, "Maybe it would look better if I go home now. I guess it's just not typical for a guy to go to the office while he's in the thick of things like autopsies and toxicology reports on his dead wife. Besides, I called Joan this morning and told her I wasn't sure if I'd be in. She said Bichotti can cover for me." He rubbed his forehead and then dropped his hand to his lap. He thought, "Jesus, my whole life is at stake here! . . . shit! . . . I had no idea how difficult it would be to live through this whole mess . . . I have to regroup . . . . . . I have to think about how I'm going to react once Detective Healy inevitably discovers cell phone calls between Lee and Edgar Schaeffer . . . and then there's the toxicology report . . . well, at least I have that in my favor."

Dr. Friedman was startled when he saw someone walk past his car in the rearview mirror. But the man continued toward another car. He turned the key in the ignition and shifted into reverse, "I better get the hell out of here."

When he arrived home, Dr. Friedman poured himself a Remy and then sat down in one of the chairs at the far end of the dining room. He liked the view from the side windows. He thought, "It's hard to believe it was just nine days ago." He threw back a mouthful of brandy and felt the burn. "Nine days since the last day of Lee's life . . ." He settled back in the chair and reminisced about Lee's last day.

He had instructed Joan to limit his patient schedule that day because he wanted to leave early; ostensibly to visit his parents, who had just returned from their winter sojourn in Florida. He would do this only after he made Lee her last meal.

He had called Lee on her cell phone at 4:00 that Wednesday afternoon. She said it had been a hectic day and she was just about to leave the house for her run. She neglected to mention her rendezvous with Edgar Schaeffer earlier that day.

Donald said, "I have seven more patients to see and then I'm outta here."

Lee asked, "Would you rather go out to dinner tonight?"

Donald laughed and said, "Are you kidding? Go out to a dinner that's not paid for by a drug rep?"

Lee laughed and said, "You're right. Silly me. What was I thinking?"

Donald added, "Besides, Ira burned me a copy of 'A Winter in Tuscany.'"

"Oh good. I want to see that movie."

"Great. I'll make pasta and broccoli rabe — it's quick. Then we can watch the movie."

"OK. So it sounds like you'll be a little early tonight."

Donald said, "Yeah, I should be home around 6:30 or so."

"Oh, that's perfect. That'll still give me enough time to take a longer run today. I want to stay on schedule with my marathon training."

"Good. I'll see you later then."

When Dr. Friedman got home at 6:20 that night, he quickly began to prepare dinner. It was important that he had dinner ready before Lee had a chance to shower, so that she was still in her running gear.

At 6:45, he heard Lee walk in the front door. She immediately walked into the kitchen and gave him a kiss on the cheek. Breathlessly, she said, "Oh, that was a great run, but I'm hurting. I think I overdid it." She was pacing around to cool down and Donald said, "Why don't you sit down for a minute?"

Lee said nothing but walked over to the kitchen island and began to munch on a carrot. Donald poured her a glass of slightly chilled pinot grigio.

"Thanks Donald." She held her glass up and said, "Cheers."

Donald reached for his wine glass and smiled, "Cheers."

Lee took one sip and then another. She sat down on one of the bar stools and sighed. Donald said, "This won't take long. The water is almost at a boil for the pasta." He had just rinsed the broccoli rabe and pressed the leaves to remove the excess water. He set it down in the sink and walked over to the range and turned the gas on high under the frying pan. He grabbed the olive oil and poured it liberally into the pan. Next he took some bulbs of garlic from the dish on the counter and expertly stripped away the skin with a sharp knife. He used a garlic press to squeeze slivers into the heated pan. The garlic hissed as it struck the hot oil and Donald breathed deeply and sighed, "Ahh, the only thing better than the smell of fresh garlic is the taste!"

Lee smiled and asked, "Do I have time to take a quick shower?"

Donald tossed some pasta into the boiling water and said, "This should be done in about four minutes . . . Just relax. You can shower after dinner, before we watch the movie."

"OK, Donald. I'm easy." She sat down and sipped her wine.

"Oh, Lee, a rep brought some fantastic tiramisu to the office today."

"Did you bring some home?"

Donald turned around from the stove and gave her a sly grin and said, "Of course I did. I know it's your favorite." He opened the refrigerator and took out the bakery box containing the luscious dessert. He said, "I don't like it when it's too chilled, so I'll let it sit out while we eat dinner."

Actually, a drug rep had not brought the pastry to the office that day. The truth was, Dr. Friedman called the bakery across the street that morning and ordered the tiramisu. He said he wanted to bring it to his parents and would pick it up later. The bakery owner, Patty DiCola, offered to deliver it to his office but he said his staff might devour it if they found it. Patty laughed and said, "No problem. I'll see you later then." Patty's business had increased three-fold after Donald told the drug reps that he loved her pastries. Every day they brought Patty's delicious treats to Dr. Friedman and his staff, and to other practices in the area.

With attention to every detail, he had opened the pastry box in his car that night and used his pen to cut out a big slice of the tiramisu, which he discarded on the roadside. He did this because he knew Lee would expect that some of it would have been eaten by him or his staff.

Lee was careful about every calorie she put into her body, but she often gave in to the temptation of chocolate--if only in small doses. She opened the pastry box and studied the dessert. "Umm. It looks fantastic."

Donald grabbed a bunch of broccoli rabe into his hands and tossed it into the frying pan. Without turning around, he asked Lee, "Hey, can you change the CD? I've been listening to Bruce for a while now, and I'm ready for something mellow."

"Yeah, sure. I think Bruce Springsteen is a little bit much for dinner music."

Donald turned to watch her walk to the other side of the room. He quickly took a tranquilizer capsule from his pocket and then reached into the cabinet for the little plate with a crushed MELAVOX tablet. He lifted up one of the ladyfingers in the tiramisu and peppered the chocolate with the MELAVOX granules. He then opened the capsule and poured some of the contents into the chocolate mixture. Lee was known to take a tranquilizer now and then to help her get to sleep. For the purpose of the inevitable toxicology report, he knew he had to be careful. Otherwise, the Medical Examiner or the police would wonder, "Why did Lee take a tranquilizer before running?" Donald knew that Lee's petite frame would only require a small amount to make her sleepy after some wine--enough to serve his purpose and too little to be detected; whereas the high concentration of MELAVOX would undoubtedly be discovered. He put the empty capsule into a paper towel and slipped it into his pocket. He turned back to stove and lifted a pot from the burner. He strained the pasta in the colander.

Lee startled him when she snuck up behind him and said playfully, "Sneaking a taste of the dessert huh?" Fortunately for him, she had only seen Donald pull his chocolate-covered finger from the box.

Donald smiled and said, "Oh, you caught me!"

Lee said, "Well, two can play that game." She took a spoon and plunged it into the creamy dessert. With a flirtatious wink, she opened her mouth and ate a heaping spoonful.

Donald laughed and said, "What are you doing? You won't eat your dinner."

"Oh yes I will, just watch me." She ate one more spoonful and then sauntered playfully into the dining room. She swayed to the music of a jazz CD and then sat down.

Donald entered the dining room with two plates of steaming broccoli rabe over pasta. He hesitated for a minute and gave a careful listen. "Excellent choice. It's a good night for some Grover Washington."

As he set a plate down in front of Lee, she started to push back her chair and then stood up. She said, "Let me just run upstairs for a second and grab a sweatshirt. My clothes are still damp from sweating."

Donald worried that she might quickly change clothes. But a moment later, she returned to the dining room saying, "Donald, I feel like a slob--schlepping around in my sweaty clothes."

"Lee, just relax. After dinner you can take a hot bath instead of a shower. You'll feel terrific."

"Donald, you are so good to me." She rubbed his arm affectionately before returning to her seat.

For a moment, Donald felt weakened in his resolve.

As Lee sat down, she said, "Oh, by the way, on Sunday Susie and I are going to brunch and then shopping."

Donald's guilty feelings quickly dissipated. He knew Lee was lying. She was really going to spend the afternoon with Edgar Schaeffer.

As they finished dinner, Donald was edgy. He was afraid Lee would change her mind about having dessert. She finished chewing her last mouthful of dinner and said, "That was just what I needed. I'm really going to have to do more carb loading to sustain me on these long training runs. The truth is, I have so much more energy when I eat lots of carbs. I can really feel the difference."

As he stood up from the table, Donald said, "Oh sure, protein increases your muscle strength but you need a balanced diet with carbs to be healthy."

Lee drank some more wine and soon Donald returned with two crystal dessert cups filled with tiramisu. She smiled and said, "Now this is good for my mental health."

As she began eating, Donald said playfully, "You drive me crazy with your worries about your weight. I should be so lucky to be able to eat like you do and not gain an ounce."

Lee laughed and said, "We're innocent victims Donald. How can we stop eating so much when we're wined and dined all the time by the drug reps."

Donald held a spoonful of dessert in front of him and said, "You're right about that."

Lee's spoon made a clinking sound against the empty crystal bowl. She leaned back in her chair as she stretched her arms into the air. "Wow! That was really delicious. And you are such a good cook Donald."

"Thanks Lee. You know how much I. . ." and before he finished his sentence, he noticed that Lee was beginning to look peaked.

She said, "I don't know what's wrong, but I feel so tired suddenly. I think I need to lie down."

Donald stood up and walked around to her chair. He helped Lee to stand up. She began to sway and groan by the time he helped her onto the couch. Donald said, "Here. Just lie down for a minute and I'm sure you'll feel better."

Lee was losing consciousness and said, "I don't know what's wrong, I . . ." and with that she passed out.

Donald said, "Well, I know what's wrong . . .you lying bitch!" He knew she couldn't hear him, but it still felt good to say the words out loud.

He hurried out of the room and into his home office. He walked behind his desk and flung open the middle drawer and fished out a key for the side cabinet. He opened the cabinet and felt for the lacquered box. It was hidden in between some files toward the back of the drawer. He grabbed the box and put it in the middle of his desk and opened it. His hands were shaking as he ripped open the plastic bag containing a syringe and one vial of potassium. He thought, "I better sit down and take a deep breath, or I won't be able to fill the syringe."

He sat in the chair and realized he was panting. He wiped his sweaty forehead with the back of his hand. He reached over to turn on the desk lamp. "I can do this," he coached himself. Then he tore at the sterile packing of the syringe, pierced the tip of the vial with the needle and withdrew the vial's contents, filling the syringe.

He pushed back from the chair and bumped his thighs on the half-open middle drawer as he stood up. "Ouch!" he cried out loudly when he felt the pulsating pain that subsided instantly. Then, in a deliberately cautious manner, he held the syringe upward in his right hand and quickly returned to Lee. She was fast asleep on the couch. Donald pushed the coffee table aside and knelt down in front of Lee. He shoved the sleeve of her sweatshirt up above her elbow. The light was too dim. He got up and reached over to the table lamp and turned it to a brighter setting. He knelt down again and grasped her arm in the light. That was much better. He found a vein immediately and gently punctured her arm with the needle. He emptied the contents of the syringe into her vein. He pulled out the needle and suddenly stood upright. He backed away from her, as if her death might be contagious.

His heart was pounding and his adrenalin rushing. Dr. Friedman was a well trained physician and, even in this circumstance, he was able to think methodically, "Now the potassium bolus will accelerate the electrical activity of the heart." He envisioned Lee's arteries and veins, the plasma and bones. He saw her heart pumping faster and faster. He could almost hear the pounding! He crouched a bit, as he moved closer again, until he hovered over her. He stood there wide-eyed with his hands clenched. Suddenly Lee's body stiffened, as her heart seized and then stopped.

His hand reflexively grabbed the sweat from around his mouth and he uttered a brief, exasperated cry, "Oh God!" he shrieked in anguish. He moved toward one of the chairs and then slumped into it. Suddenly, he felt his innards gurgle and he rushed into the powder room. He unbuckled his belt and opened the button and zipper of his pants in one continuous motion. He pounced on the toilet seat and relieved himself.

When he finished, he sat for a minute, hunched over and panting. His nose was running and a tear rolled down his cheek. He thought, "I better get moving. I still have a lot to do."

He had dropped the syringe near the couch. He glanced at Lee matter-of-factly before his eyes searched the floor. "There it is!" He bent down to pick it up and looked over at Lee again, as he stood upright. Whether he was numb from shock or ambiguous from hatred, this time, when he looked at her, he felt nothing. But suddenly he said out loud, "The sweatshirt!" He gently pulled the sweatshirt over her head. She didn't wear a sweatshirt at this time of year, while she was running.

He returned to his office with the empty syringe in his hand.

He sat down and opened the drawer. This time, his hands were not shaking. He felt around on the bottom of the drawer, under the hanging folders, for the thick plastic bag. "Oh good, here it is." He took it out of the drawer and opened the red bag.

Donald was pleased with himself for his forethought. He had taken the bag from the office weeks ago and stashed it in his desk. It was a waste bag for hazardous materials including "sharps" or, needles and syringes. These bags were collected each day at the office and disposed of according to OSHA (Occupational Safety and Health Act) standards.

After putting the syringe, vial and plastic wrap into it, he opened his leather briefcase where he tossed the bag. He shut his briefcase and locked it. He reached over to the lacquer box and peered into the empty red velvet cavity. He thought of all the times he secretly peaked into the box and thought about this moment. "And now it's done."

He moved the box to the side of his leather desk blotter where it again served its original purpose as an innocently decorative object.

He left the room and took a coat from the closet in the foyer, but quickly decided to put it back. He thought, "It'll be cold tonight but I don't want the coat to get anything on it that might incriminate me later. My clothes I can wash or even throw away if necessary."

He returned to the living room and picked Lee up from the couch. Then he hoisted her over his shoulder. He thought, "Man, she is a lightweight — lucky for me." He squatted down so that he could move the coffee table back toward the couch. He stood up and made his way to the door that led into the garage. He popped open the trunk and let out a grunt as he let her body slither down the front of him until her feet touched the garage floor. He then cradled her body in his arms and gently placed her into the trunk. He reminded himself, "Easy does it." He didn't want to scratch her skin and risk any traces of blood in his trunk or on the garage floor.

He slammed the trunk shut and got into the car. He opened the automatic garage door and listened to the engine purr as he backed out slowly. He cruised out of the neighborhood and onto Route 52. He drove into downtown Wilmington, and another traffic light turned green as he approached. He relaxed his posture and pushed his lower back into the leather seat. He sighed and felt oddly relaxed. He eased the car into a right turn for the exit to I-95 south. He downshifted and slowed almost to a stop as he yielded for traffic. Then, with his right foot firmly on the gas pedal, he let the engine roar as he cruised down the interstate.

He felt empowered. He had taken back control of his life and he felt the buzz of freedom. His satisfied grin stiffened to a frown when he reminded himself that he had to watch his speed. He had to slip unnoticed over the Delaware Memorial Bridge and into Salem County, New Jersey.

Suddenly, the ringing of his cell phone broke the silence and a spasm of nerves caused his glass to flip out of his hand and drop onto the carpeted floor. He didn't bother to pick it up but, instead, reached into his left pocket for the phone.

"Hello?" Dr. Friedman felt a burning sensation in his throat and then, oddly, a pang of hunger.

"It's Detective Healy, Dr. Friedman."

"Any news?" He glanced at his watch. It was 12:30 p.m.

"Yes. I have some new information from the toxicology report and the cell phone calls."

Dr. Friedman was speechless. After an uncomfortable silence, the detective asked, "Can I stop by your house to talk with you?"

Dr. Friedman said, "Sure, absolutely. When will . . ."

Detective Healy interrupted, "I'd like to drive over there now if I could."

"Alright Detective. I'll see you soon."

After Dr. Friedman ended the call he thought, "How does he know I'm at home? At the hospital I said I wasn't sure if I was going home or to the office. He didn't even ask if I was at home. He *knew!*"

He jumped up and walked to one of the windows in the living room. On the other side of the street, just beyond his property, there sat a black Chevy Lumina. The windows were tinted so he couldn't see if there was anyone inside. He thought, "That bastard had me followed. Shit! Am I a suspect? Why would he have me followed if he didn't suspect something? Did they think I was going to sneak home and load up my car with suitcases and leave town? Oh shit! This is bad! . . . wait a minute . . . I have to pull myself together. I'm sure the toxicology report found MELAVOX, which is exactly what I wanted them to find . . . and as far as the increased potassium levels . . . well, I've got a good story for that too. Maybe he's coming over here because he wants to break the news gently about the phone calls between Lee and Edgar. Little does he know . . . now all I have to do is remain calm."

He used the bathroom next to the kitchen and patted his face with the towel after he washed his hands. He looked at himself in the mirror. "I don't look too bad for a guy who's trying to get away with murder." He straightened his glasses and turned his thin lips into a grimace as he examined his receding hairline. He pulled on a fleshy jowl, but then straightened his posture and murmured victoriously, "You might have to be good looking to get the girl, but all you need is brains to bring down a major pharmaceutical company." Just then, the doorbell rang and he shut out the light and closed the door.

Dr. Friedman appeared solemn as he opened the front door. "Hello detective. Come in." He looked down to the street and saw the Chevy Lumina pull away very slowly.

Detective Healy asked, "How are you holding up?"

"As well as can be expected detective. Do you want a drink or a cup of coffee?"

"No. I'm fine. I had some lunch earlier."

"Now that's something I seem to have forgotten to do today."

"What's that?"

"Eat."

The detective said, "That's to be expected under the circumstances. But you really should try to keep your strength up."

Dr. Friedman said, "I think I can afford to miss a couple of meals." The small talk made him uncomfortable. He started to have that burning sensation in his throat again. He motioned to the next room, "Why don't we have a seat?"

As soon as they sat down, Detective Healy asked, "Dr. Friedman, do you think it's possible that Lee was having an affair?"

"No. Not at all. Why?"

"I received a copy of Lee's cell phone calls during the last billing period." He paused for a moment. "There were a number of calls to another cell phone in north Wilmington."

He watched Dr. Friedman very carefully as he said, "The calls were to Dr. Edgar Schaeffer. He's an Orthopedic Surgeon."

Dr. Friedman said, "I know who Dr. Schaeffer is but . . ." He moved to the edge of his seat and looked directly into the detective's eyes and asked, "Are you suggesting that Lee was having an affair with Edgar Schaeffer?" The tone of his voice grew more incredulous as he finished the sentence.

"Dr. Friedman, as a detective with a dozen years of experience, I have seen it all. This is certainly not the first time that I've had the unpleasant task of telling someone the evidence suggests their spouse was having an affair. It's never something that anyone wants to hear. Even if they suspect that it may be true, no one wants to have a relative stranger say the words to them. So I understand the news is either devastating or embarrassing. It's rare that a spouse is ambivalent about it."

"Detective, you don't know Lee. She was very confident, independent, and even strong willed, but she loves . . . or . . . loved me and I loved her." He sat back in the chair again as if he'd gotten something off his chest. Then he added, "Lee was a beautiful and attractive woman. As a real estate agent, she had a lot of male clients who were looking for a house after a divorce or because they were new to the area. It's only natural that a guy or two would try to make a play for Lee. Maybe Edgar Schaeffer was one of her clients. You know how it is when you're looking for a house; you exchange a lot of phone calls with your realtor."

Detective Healy said, "I'll find out if he was one of her clients. That would certainly have something to do with the unusual number of phone calls that were exchanged between the two of them. Do you know if Dr. Schaeffer is married?"

"No. I don't." But of course, Dr. Friedman and the detective both knew that Edgar Schaeffer was indeed married.

"I'll look into it."

Dr. Friedman said, "I can understand that you've become a bit cynical about people as a result of your experience as a detective. Hell, as a physician, I've become cynical about my patients, insurance companies, other physicians, pharmaceutical companies--you name it! But fortunately, there are a lot of people who are simply genuine and what you see is what you get. And that, detective, is how I would describe Lee . . . and even myself for that matter."

The detective was listening intently. Dr. Friedman said, "In fact, another thought just occurred to me. Maybe Dr. Schaeffer wasn't one of her clients. Maybe Lee went to see him about her knee pain."

The detective gave him an inquisitive look. Dr. Friedman said, "As I told you, Lee was taking MELAVOX for osteoarthritis and back pain. But just recently she complained about a sore knee."

"Did she tell you she was going to see an Orthopedic Surgeon about her knee?"

"No. But that doesn't mean she didn't decide to make an appointment and go. And Edgar Schaeffer is reputed to be one of the best Orthopods in Delaware. The phone calls could have been a follow-up about treatment options. I'm sure if Edgar Schaeffer recommended even a minimally invasive procedure such as arthroscopic surgery, Lee would have argued against it."

Detective Healy spoke with a halting cadence. "Dr. Friedman . . . keep in mind that your wife also *received* many phone calls from Dr. Schaeffer . . . now, you and I both know that it's not typical for a physician to call a patient on a regular basis."

Dr. Friedman grinned and said, "You and I both know how difficult it can be to catch up with a specialist. It's typical that the patient and the specialist wind up playing phone tag."

The detective said, "You've got a point there." He decided not to tell Dr. Friedman that the length of the frequent calls suggested brief conversations and not just phone tag messages. He continued, "But in any case, the toxicology study results came back and Dr. Pagoshi confirmed that MELA . . ." He sighed in frustration and said, "Wait a minute. I highlighted a section of Dr. Pagoshi's report, and I have it right here."

He opened the manila envelope that he had carried in with him. He took out some papers and read from one, "MELAVOX was found in the bloodstream in a quantity indicative of chronic use of the drug. The extent of damage to the structural integrity of the heart exceeds that which is typically incurred as a result of an acute event, such as a myocardial infarction. Microscopic observation reveals insidious tissue damage mediated by a chemical agent that, in this case, was MELAVOX. The damage precipitated a fatal thromboembolic event. A slight elevation in serum potassium prompted further testing. The drug EFFAMINE . . ."

Dr. Friedman interrupted, "EFFAMIN. It's pronounced EFFAMIN. But I thought Lee had stopped taking EFFAMIN quite a while ago. In fact, she told me so."

The detective had learned from Dr. Pagoshi that EFFAMIN is a birth control pill. But he didn't understand why Dr. Friedman seemed upset now that he heard Lee was taking it. He thought to himself, "If he was still having sex with his wife, wouldn't they have to agree on whether or not to use birth control."

Dr. Friedman observed the detective's puzzled expression. It was what he expected. He explained, "I would not have prescribed MELAVOX for Lee if I knew she was still taking EFFAMIN."

"Why not?"

"Because MELAVOX is an NSAID, as Dr. Pagoshi mentioned earlier today. This therapeutic class, whether it's a traditional NSAID or a COX II inhibitor, can increase the risk of hyperkalemia in some patients due to inhibition of prostaglandins and thus impairment of renal function."

Dr. Friedman was delighted to see that Detective Healy was further confused. He continued, "You see, potassium is mainly excreted via the kidneys. If normal renal function is compromised in a patient taking an NSAID or a COX II inhibitor, the result is an electrolyte imbalance. For some patients the imbalance presents as hyperkalemia, which is to say, very high levels of potassium . . . long story short, Detective . . . NSAID's or COX II's taken in conjunction with another drug that has the potential to spike potassium levels is just not a good idea. The concomitant administration of the two drugs is not contraindicated, however I tend to be conservative in my approach to certain drug combinations."

Detective Healy gave him an uneasy grin. He shifted his glance back to his papers and continued from where he left off, "EFFAMIN is one of the newer birth control pills on the market. One of the possible side effects is the elevation of serum potassium."

Detective Healy looked at Dr. Friedman with a blank stare.

Dr. Friedman thought to himself, "That takes care of the potassium issue." All he needed to win his lawsuit against Inhaber-Taft was evidence beyond a reasonable doubt that MELAVOX caused Lee's heart attack. He had that now, in black and white, in Dr. Pagoshi's report. He felt giddy inside because it actually seemed possible that it would all be over soon . . . but somehow the detective seemed unconvinced. He phrased the question as if the answer was obvious, "So it *was* MELAVOX that caused Lee's heart attack?"

Detective Healy said, "That's what Dr. Pagoshi determined." Again, he searched for his place in the autopsy report, "Let's see . . . here it is . . . based on physical findings of an internal examination, as well as the results of a toxicology report, it is my final determination that Lee Young's myocardial infarction was induced by the drug, MELAVOX."

Dr. Friedman self-consciously suppressed any evidence of the great relief he felt. Instead he said, "These goddamn pharmaceutical companies!"

Now the detective moved forward in his seat and said, "With all due respect Dr. Friedman, one thing I don't get is, if you and Lee were getting along OK, then I presume you were having sex."

Dr. Friedman fidgeted in his chair. He had anticipated this line of questioning. He knew what the detective was getting at, but he wanted to appear uncomfortable.

Detective Healy continued, "I guess what I'm getting at is, wouldn't you and your wife be on the same page about birth control?"

Dr. Friedman pretended to be embarrassed. He said, "As I told you, I'm surprised to hear that Lee was taking birth control pills, not only because of possible drug interactions . . . but because we haven't had sex in . . . well . . . for quite some time . . . uh . . . maybe even close to a year." He looked at the floor and shook his head. After a moment, he looked directly at the detective and said, "I wasn't happy about it, but I tried to be patient and understanding. And it was obvious to me that her episodic acute pain was very real. It seemed to me that Lee was as disappointed about it as I was."

He paused for a moment and then continued, "I first prescribed MELAVOX for Lee because I heard the Orthopods and Rheumatologists rave about it as the new wonder drug for pain. I wanted to relieve Lee's pain for the sake of her health, but . . . I have to admit there was a selfish component. I didn't want to push her but . . . you know . . . I missed the sex." Dr. Friedman grinned coyly, "I don't want to be graphic but we . . . well, there was a time when we did pretty well in that regard." His grin dissolved into sadness. It appeared as if he missed her terribly already. And with the confidence of a trusting spouse, Dr. Friedman said, "As far as the birth control pills — the EFFAMIN — the only thing I can imagine is that maybe she asked her Gynecologist for a birth control pill because she was starting to feel better and wanted to be on birth control when we started to have sex again. And if her Gynecologist prescribed the drug, she would have taken it religiously. Lee was like that. I mean, she was a marathon runner for God's sake. Every day was structured around her routines and habits. She went to bed at a regular time and got up at a regular time. She started her daily run at the same time each day and followed a training regimen. So, naturally she would take her birth control pills out of habit--not because of an affair."

Detective Healy shifted in his seat. He said, "I'm afraid there's more." He looked squarely at Dr. Friedman. "I'm sorry to have to tell you this but, Dr. Pagoshi found traces of semen when he did the internal examination." He kept his eyes fixed on Dr. Friedman and continued, "There was no sign of trauma or force. Lee apparently had consensual sex the same day she went missing."

Dr. Friedman's mouth dropped open and he sat motionless.

Then the detective added the final blow, "Dr. Friedman, just now you said that you and Lee had not had sex for almost a year. I'm sorry, but based on what I've put together at this point, I'm certain your wife was having an affair with Dr. Schaeffer."

Dr. Friedman put his face into his hands and shook his head. He knew he had to appear devastated. He waited a moment and then looked up and said, "I'm embarrassed by my naiveté."

Detective Healy noted that Dr. Friedman's reaction appeared to be genuine. But he knew from experience that if a husband kills his wife in a jealous rage, there is anger seething beneath the surface. It dissipates over time, so the closer it is to the event, the easier it is to antagonize the perpetrator and bring out those raw feelings of rage. And he wanted to draw it out of Dr. Friedman, if it was there.

He said, "I can only imagine how devastating this is for you. I mean, our findings just keep going from bad to worse. There was no evidence of rape and yet we found semen on Lee. And then there are the phone calls between Lee and Dr. Schaeffer . . . and the birth control pills . . ."

Dr. Friedman stood up and waved his hands back and forth, as if raising a flag of surrender. "Alright. Alright. Enough Detective. There's no need for you to pour salt on the wounds. I suppose anything is possible, but I hope you can understand that it's difficult to believe it."

The detective said nothing because, sometimes, silence is the most effective way to get someone talking.

Dr. Friedman sensed the detective was putting him on the spot, and he resented it. Finally he said resolutely, "Detective, I need to be alone now."

"Of course. I understand. But as a matter of standard procedure, we'll still need a DNA sample from you."

Dr. Friedman looked surprised. He didn't appreciate the insinuation that he might be lying. But he said, "Of course. That's not a problem."

The detective added, "I can assure you that we will also collect a DNA sample from Dr. Schaeffer."

Dr. Friedman said nothing for a moment. Then he asked, "How do I go about getting the sample to you?"

"Can you come down to the station this afternoon?"

Dr. Friedman was surprised by the urgency, but he said, "Of course. I can drive to the station now . . . or do you want me to go with you?" He nervously awaited the detective's response.

He was relieved when Detective Healy said, "Give yourself a few minutes. I really dumped a lot on you all at once. Just try to get there today please. The lab is on the first floor of the Wilmington police station on Market Street."

"OK, no problem. I know where the station is and I'll head down there in a few minutes. Thanks Detective."

They walked to the front door in silence. The detective turned and looked at Dr. Friedman with the pretense of an afterthought, "I almost forgot. You said you would get me a copy of the study that showed the possibility of heart attacks with MELAVOX. For whatever it's worth . . . I guess just my own curiosity . . ."

Dr. Friedman interrupted nervously, "Oh right. I almost forgot. I'll call the office now and ask them to fax a copy to you. What's a good number to send it to?"

Detective Healy took a business card from his pocket. "Have them send it to the fax number on my card. I'm headed back to the station now in fact. Just have them fax it there."

"OK. I'll call Joan right now. Just call me if you have any questions about the study."

"Thanks Dr. Friedman."

He shut the door slowly and thought, "A DNA sample? Shit! . . . And if the cause of death has been determined with certainty, why is he so interested in the affair with Schaeffer? . . . At least he wants a DNA sample from Schaeffer too. Hell, maybe he suspects *him*. But why does he still want a copy of the study about MELAVOX? Something's not right . . . but I better give Joan a call and ask her to fax the study right away."

He started to walk away from the door and stopped. He turned and slowly crept back. He looked out of the glass panel and gasped. The Chevy Lumina was back and parked across the street from his house.

Detective Healy was almost convinced there was no foul play involved in Lee's death. Yet somehow, it all pieced together too neatly. Then again, the detective had to remind himself that it was the first time he had a case in which the cause of death for a young, healthy woman was a legally prescribed medicine. He decided to call his deputy and tell him about his conversation with Dr. Friedman.

The man in the Chevy Lumina picked up his cell phone. "Hello?"

"Hi Mike, it's Pat."

"Hey, how'd it go?"

"Good. But that's the problem. All the pieces are fitting together and you know how that bugs me."

"I hear ya. It's pretty much the same on my end. There's nothin' odd or suspicious about any of the good doctor's comings and goings. He's not home much, but all he does is go to work. A couple of days a week he works at the Newark office of . . . hold on, what's it called, I got it written down here somewhere . . . oh yeah, Better Health Physicians, and the rest of the week he goes to his office in Wilmington. He even works on Saturday."

"Hmm. Has he had any visitors at the house?"

"No. There's no hot babes stopping by and he doesn't drive to any bimbo's house either. Unless he's doin' somebody at the office, I don't see any evidence that this guy's having an affair. He's not driving to Delaware Race track to bet on the horses and he's not hitting the casinos in Atlantic City. So we know there's no women or gambling going on that would have motivated him to get rid of his old lady. What's he like when you talk to him?"

"Believable. He's genuinely hurting over the death of his wife."

"Death? So you *don't* think she was murdered?"

"According to Dr. Pagoshi's autopsy and toxicology report, she had a heart attack that caused her to stumble and fall in the middle of her run. And if that's not weird enough for somebody her age and in her physical condition, Pagoshi says the heart attack was caused by her prescription medicine!"

"Holy shit! That's messed up."

"Yeah. It's pretty scary, especially since it's the latest, greatest drug that's splashed across the television every night."

"Which one's that?"

"MELAVOX."

"MELAVOX . . . what the hell's that for?"

"It's for arthritis pain. I'm sure you've seen the commercials. There's one where they show this former Olympic ice skater . . . I can't remember her name . . . anyway, she's skating across the ice and talking about how the drug relieved her aches and pains, and then there's one with a guy bicycling through God's country . . ."

"Oh yeah. I know the one. Hell they show the commercial fifty times during the game. It's the one where the guy's all aches and pains and then by the end of the commercial he's doing a freakin Iron Man contest!"

The detective laughed a little. "Yeah, that's the one."

"Hey, my friend Joe is taking that for his bad knee. He says it's awesome. He's back to running again. The guy's a maniac. Personally, I think these runners are all nuts . . . beating up their bodies all the time. But it's like they're addicted to it. You know what I mean?"

Detective Healy was no longer listening to Mike as he rambled on. He was thinking about some of the methods he had used in the past to push a suspect enough to rattle his nerves. Unless he was dealing with a hardened criminal, a guilty person usually cracked under pressure. He tried to think of some other way to antagonize Dr. Friedman, which would force him to drop the façade. He visualized the field where they found Lee. He could see the crime scene investigators inspecting the position of her body . . . the bruises from her fall . . . her tousled hair . . . her shoes . . . He thought, "That's it! Her running shoes and the location of the body . . . a few simple nuances to change the truth . . . a couple of lies just to see how the good doctor reacts."

He remembered one of the forensic investigators pointing out the scuffmarks on Lee's running shoes, which were consistent with a staggering fall. The shoes were obviously fairly new because there wasn't much wear and tear on the seams. The investigator showed him that the tracks on the bottom of the shoes had pulled up some weeds, as she dragged her feet before falling.

Mike could tell the detective wasn't listening to him. He thought, "Let me bust his balls with this one . . ." and he asked, "Ya know what I mean Pat?"

"Yeah. Hey listen, Mike, I'll give you a call later. I thought of something to throw at Dr. Friedman just to see how he reacts."

"Does that mean I'm working this weekend?"

"Maybe. If he snaps after I run this by him, I'll give you a holler. The bottom line is . . . I'm not ready to close the case just yet."

"I hear ya."

"Why don't we do this Mike; if I don't call you later today, then you're off the watch for the weekend. And in that case, just stop by my office on Monday and we'll close out the file on this one."

"Sounds like a plan. See ya, Pat."

"Bye Mike."

Chapter 24: Someone at the Window

Friday afternoon/night, March 18

LATE IN THE afternoon on Friday, Debbie settled into her car after her eighth sales call and decided to head back home to her office. "Thank God it's Friday! I wonder what time Mark will finish up." She called him.

"Hey Deb! What's up?"

"I'm just excited to see you and happy it's Friday."

"Me too. What time will you be at the cabin?"

"I guess the usual time — around 7 — unless you're finishing up for the day already."

"Hmm, that's tempting, but I have to finish something here first so why don't we say 7."

"Alright. That sounds good. Do you want to go to the Chesapeake Inn for dinner?"

"Definitely. We can get our usual shrimp Creole pizza and beer."

"Good. So I'll see you at 7:00 and maybe a little before that."

Detective Healy called down to the lab. The clerk recognized his voice when he said, "Let me talk to Bridget Boyle please."

"Sure thing, Detective Healy. One moment please."

After a brief pause he heard, "Hello Patrick James Healy. What can I do ya for?"

"Hey Bridget! How's life treating you these days?"

"You know me Patrick. I'm old enough to know better but young enough to ignore my own advice."

He laughed and said, "Bridget, I'm expecting Dr. Donald Friedman to stop by your lab this afternoon to give you a DNA sample."

"Uh oh, a rich doctor coming in for a DNA sample . . . Hey, can I tell him I need a semen sample? I mean, just think of the possibilities . . ."

Detective Healy laughed again. "Now you behave yourself Bridget Boyle."

"Ahh, you're no fun."

"Seriously Bridget, when he arrives, can you discreetly call my office and I'll stop down to catch up with him."

"You've got it Patrick."

"Thanks Bridget."

Dr. Friedman was pleasantly surprised that the entire process was handled so quickly. There was no waiting in some cold, gray police department lab. The lab manager introduced herself and said that her lab tech was out at a late lunch. She excused herself for just a moment. When she returned, she simply handed him a Q-tip and asked him to swab the inside of his mouth, in order to collect a DNA sample. He was already on his way out the door, when someone opened it from the other side.

"Detective Healy!" Dr. Friedman was taken aback.

The detective didn't pretend it was mere coincidence. He correctly assumed Dr. Friedman would see through that instantly. He said, "Dr. Friedman, I asked Bridget, our lab manager, to call me when you arrived today."

Dr. Friedman's thoughts were racing, "Is it possible . . . no, it can't be . . . what if . . ."

"I just need a minute of your time Dr. Friedman."

"Sure. Sure. No problem."

The detective opened the door to the hallway and said, "Why don't we go up to my office for some privacy."

After a brief elevator ride to his sixth floor office, Detective Healy laid out what he hoped would be a trap. "Dr. Friedman, our crime scene investigators gave me a call this morning about something they found — or I should say — something they didn't find."

"What's that detective?" Dr. Friedman's heart was beating wildly.

"As you know, Dr. Friedman, this started out as a missing person case but, when Lee's body was found lying in a field in New Jersey, the case was reclassified as a criminal investigation."

Dr. Friedman maintained a blank expression, as the detective purposely belabored his point. "It is standard procedure to bring in our CSI team to assess the condition of the body and all physical evidence surrounding it. And as you're well aware, in the final analysis of this case, it was determined that Lee died of a drug-induced heart attack. There is no evidence of foul play. However, our forensics team follows standard operating procedures with regard to the handling of items gathered at a crime scene. This is done in the event that these articles may later be entered into evidence." The detective noted that, so far, Dr. Friedman appeared to be concerned but not threatened. He continued, "Once a case is closed, the CSI team gathers the articles and puts them into storage in accordance with a retention schedule. In other words, we don't immediately discard the items. And it's not unusual for one of the investigators to stop by and decide to conduct a cursory review with the detectives involved, before everything is stored away." Detective Healy paused.

Dr. Friedman said nothing but maintained his intense focus.

The detective continued, "An investigator stopped by to see me with a slight concern." He leaned forward and clasped his hands on the desktop. "You know, it's one of those things that bothers you in the gut for some reason and, in the end, it could very well turn out to be insignificant."

"Sure. I understand." Dr. Friedman furrowed his brow and made his lower lip protrude in a sage gesture.

After a pregnant pause while he watched his fingers tap against the desk, Detective Healy returned his focus to Dr. Friedman and said, "There were no weeds or grass in the tracking on the bottom of Lee's running shoes, even though she had staggered to a fall in the middle of a field."

Dr. Friedman heard himself say, "That *is* odd." Now he was overcome with an absurd fear that the detective might see his heart pounding so violently that it seemed the left side of his shirt was actually moving beneath his jacket. He thought to himself, "He's setting me up! Lee wasn't in the *middle* of a field.

I purposely left her body close enough to the road to be discovered. The good detective actually thinks I'm stupid enough to say something about the location of the body . . . knowing that if I'm innocent, I would have no idea whether the body was in the middle of a field or close to the road."

He tried to calm down. He slowed his breathing by discreetly drawing in his abdominal muscles. Apparently, Dr. Friedman had seized on the point about the location of the body and hadn't paid attention to the detective's point about the shoes.

Detective Healy stalled for time. He had expected more of a reaction from Dr. Friedman, but he seemed to have nothing more to say. He tried to push the issue and said, "It's obvious Lee's running shoes were new because of the lack of wear on the seams, as well as the bottom tracking. I suppose this just made the absence of grass and weeds more obvious."

Now Dr. Friedman thought about the running shoes, but not just the ones the detective had seen. He was also thinking about the pair that Dr. DiStefano had buried for him. Then he visualized Lee's shoes. Maybe it was the stress, but he started to doubt himself. "I thought I made the shoes look like Lee had dragged her feet . . . or am I thinking of the shoes that I wore . . . "

The detective continued, "There's lots of possibilities . . . even when the pieces seem to fit. Have you ever considered the possibility that Lee may have tried to blackmail Dr. Schaeffer? Maybe she threatened to go to his wife. I'm sorry to suggest this, but maybe Lee wanted him to divorce his wife. She may have planned to divorce you and marry Dr. Schaeffer. This is all just speculation, of course, but maybe Dr. Schaeffer wanted to end the affair and Lee would have none of it. If he was desperate enough . . . well, let's just say it wouldn't be the first time that a crime was committed in one location and then the body was dumped at another site. That would account for the lack of weeds in the shoes."

Dr. Friedman needed to swallow, but there was no saliva in his mouth or throat. He thought to himself, "Does he think for one minute that I don't know he's really talking about me, even though he's saying Dr. Schaeffer . . ." He half expected a police officer to walk into the room and handcuff him. Then a thought occurred to him, "Or is it possible he really does suspect Schaeffer? . . . in which case that would rule out the possibility of looking at me as a suspect . . . wait a minute! . . . it's the oldest trick in the book, hell, it's on every television whodunit . . . he's playing me . . .I remember now that I definitely removed one of her shoes . . . I rubbed it against the ground to make sure a couple of weeds got into the tracking." Now he was aware of the silence. He told himself, "Say something. Pull yourself together!"

Finally he said, "Detective, it's one thing to accept that Lee was having an affair but to suggest that she planned some convoluted plot to blackmail this guy and . . ." He shook his head. He was impressed by his own quick thinking. He continued, "It's just too implausible. Lee was not some crazy, evil person. And besides, it just doesn't add up based on Dr. Pagoshi's findings."

Suddenly, he was silent again when he thought, "Wait a minute. I don't want to give the impression that I want the case sealed shut." He rubbed his forehead. He was overwhelmed and he looked it. He decided to appear open to suggestion. He said, "Maybe I'm just being naïve again about Lee. Hell, I guess anything is possible. But there is Dr. Pagoshi's conclusive report that points to MELAVOX."

Detective Healy's thoughts were now as muddled as Dr. Friedman's. It appeared that Dr. Friedman was willing to explore other possibilities. He rubbed his chin and thought, "He never took the bait on the whole business about her running shoes and the location of her body. He didn't ask to see the shoes. If he was guilty, he would have wanted to see them to reassure himself about whether or not he had forgotten a detail." He looked at Dr. Friedman. He was obviously exhausted and yet he did not push to bring closure to the investigation.

Detective Healy thought to himself, "Maybe my nagging feeling was off the mark. Maybe it's as simple as that." But he couldn't reverse his position at this point. He would lose credibility. Instead he said, "I'll talk to our CSI folks and see if they want to take a second look at this."

Dr. Friedman despaired. He thought, "This is going to get ugly." But he had to maintain his composure. In a further attempt to ingratiate himself with the detective, he said, "Detective, I defer to the expertise of your investigative team."

"I appreciate that Dr. Friedman. As you can imagine, we frequently butt heads with some of the very people we're trying to help. They're emotionally charged and that often leads to misunderstandings and worse."

"I know the feeling. As a physician, I frequently find myself in the same predicament with my patients and their families."

"It looks like we both have a tough job."

"You'll call me to keep me updated?"

"Of course Dr. Friedman. Thanks for your time."

"Sure." Dr. Friedman appeared to be spent as he left the detective's office.

Debbie pulled her car to a stop in front of her house and her cell phone rang in the same instant.

"Hello?"

"Hi Deb, it's me."

She knew from the tone in Mark's voice that it wasn't good news. She felt anxious.

"I just got a call from Scott Williamson in Chadds Ford. They're having a problem with their software and they need me to come out tonight." Debbie had met Scott and his wife once on a Saturday afternoon, when Mark stopped by Scott's auto parts store.

She tried to disguise her disappointment with an upbeat voice, "OK. I'll just go to the cabin with Harry and hang out there until you get home."

Mark sounded disappointed. "I'm really sorry. I'll make it up to you. We'll definitely go to the Chesapeake Inn tomorrow night instead."

"What time do you think you'll be home?"

Mark answered in a patronizing tone, "Deb . . . you know how it is. I never know for sure how long it will take."

"Yeah, I know how it is." This time Debbie spoke in a tone that revealed her disappointment.

Mark tried to be patient. "Scott wants me to go over there now because it's after business hours. He knows I'll most likely have to shut down his computer system in order to look for the problem. You see it's . . ."

Debbie's mind started to wander. She didn't listen to him. She thought, "There he goes spouting off a bunch of fun facts about computer software. Maybe he makes half of it up — what difference does it make? He knows I don't know what he's talking about anyway. Well, here goes another Friday night that I'll spend by myself." She felt rejected and somehow embarrassed because she could imagine Blaire or Molly asking in a disparaging tone, "Does he *always* work on the weekends?" And of course, they would manage to convey the insinuation of suspicion. The thought changed her mood in a flash. She was no longer the understanding girlfriend but the suspicious, insecure woman. She worried, "I hope he's telling me the truth." She knew she sounded desperate when she heard herself ask, "Can't it wait until tomorrow morning? We could have breakfast and then . . . "

Mark cut her off. Now he sounded angry. "Deb, I've told you again and again the reason I have to go to some of my customers after normal working hours is because I have to shut down their computer system so I can do my work. Why can't you just be mature about it and accept the fact that I have to be on call to provide troubleshooting support? This is my job Debbie!" He said the last sentence very emphatically.

"I'm sorry Mark. I'm just disappointed that's all."

Mark was calm again. "It's OK. Please just believe that I love you and that you can trust me."

She had to resist the temptation to be petulant. She did her best to sound pleasant. "Alright. I'll get my stuff done and then I'll just pick up something to eat on the way to your place. Should I get you something?"

"Yeah, that would be great. Thanks. I'm going to drive over to Scott's office now and get started. The sooner I get there, the sooner I'll see you at the cabin."

"Alright Mark. I'll see you later." She thought to herself, "Why do I make a big deal out of it? One minute I'm on his case about working and making money to pay for things and then I'm complaining when he has to work." She could see Harry at the kitchen window as she walked to her front door. She smiled and said, "I'll be right there."

When he returned from the police station, Dr. Friedman cruised past the Chevy Lumina parked across the road from his driveway. He strained his vision, hoping to somehow see who it was that sat behind the tinted windows. But he saw no one, as he turned into his driveway. With the garage door closed behind him, he turned off the engine and thrust his head against the headrest. He exhaled heavily and shut his eyes for a few seconds. Finally, he was alone — or was he? His mind flooded with paranoid thoughts, "What if the whole thing about a DNA sample was a ruse to get me out of the house so they could install listening devices while I was gone? Although, that would be better than this whole mess with the goddamn running shoes. Jesus Christ! I can't believe it! So much speculation about whether or not there are any goddamn weeds on the bottom of her shoes . . . But I'm sure he's playing me . . . still . . . what if he discusses any of this with a reporter?"

He went into the house and hung up his jacket and thought, "Jesus, when was the last time I ate anything?" He wasn't in the mood to cook. He opened the freezer and took out one of Lee's frozen pre-packaged meals. He popped it in the microwave and then devoured it. "That's a shameful excuse for a meal."

He went into his home office and sat down at his desk. He turned on his computer and looked around the room for a moment. He wondered again about the possibility of listening devices. "Where would they have put them?" He got down on his knees and looked under his desk. He stood up and looked at the smoke alarm on the ceiling. He returned to his desk and checked his lamps and under his phone. He found nothing. He sat down again and wondered if the stress was making him a little crazy. The silence was uncomfortable. He was rarely surrounded by it, other than those few moments after his head hit the pillow at night, until he fell asleep. It felt strange being detached from his staff, his patients, and the other doctors in his practice. But he knew it was a good move to return home again. It would appear that he was just too upset right now to meet the demands of his job.

He checked his email. There wasn't much going on. He looked around the room again, but this time his mind raced from one scene to the next and then from one conversation to the next . . . conversations with Grant . . . with the detective . . . with Joan. He feared that one sentence or one word he uttered might be the end of his perceived innocence. He remembered saying to the pharmacist at Wilmington Pharmacy, "No she doesn't need that *now*." He remembered reaching for the bag and cringing in pain. He remembered Debbie Kaminski's voice behind him. It seemed she had a knack for being at the wrong place at the wrong time. Suddenly he gasped and his eyes grew wide. "The shoes! Oh shit! Debbie saw the running shoes in Joe DiStefano's office!"

Day after day the television, radio and newspaper reports provided each new detail the police learned about the case. He worried, "What if it's not

Healy, but one of his goddamn CSI investigators that leaks something about the shoes to the media . . . is it possible that Debbie might put the pieces together? . . . no . . . no way . . . it couldn't happen . . . or could it? No. Besides, where's the proof? Joe buried the shoes. They're the only real evidence in the case. And the shoes will never be found!"

He was startled when his cell phone rang. "Where the hell did I put it?" He followed the sound of the ring into the kitchen. He had left it on the counter with his car keys. He looked at the number of the incoming call and felt relief.

"Hi Joan."

"Hi Dr. Friedman."

Before she had a chance to talk he asked, "Hey did you have a chance to fax the METAPO study about MELAVOX to Detective Healy?"

"Yeah. In fact, he called to confirm that he received the fax. But why did he want the METAPO study?"

Dr. Friedman hadn't anticipated the question. "Ah, he said his wife is taking MELAVOX. You know how people are Joan. I can't go anywhere without them trying to get a free consultation. He said a friend of his wife told her about some possible side effects because of something they read in the paper a while ago. I told him I would get him a copy of the study they were referring to and he and his wife could decide for themselves. Of course I reassured him that I think the drug is safe and I've prescribed it for many of my patients."

"Gotcha."

Joan wanted Dr. Friedman to think of her as a friend and trusted confidante, especially after the discussion about her drinking. She wanted him to think of her as indispensable. She couldn't risk that he might think she was suspicious in the least, in spite of the salacious rumors that were circulating. Some of his own staff quietly joked that Dr. Friedman might be sharing a jail cell with the Wilmington lawyer who killed his mistress. They said maybe the lawyer should have told Dr. Friedman where to hide the body so it was never found.

Joan lowered her voice, "Dr. Friedman, the detective also asked me some questions about you and Lee."

"What kind of questions?" Dr. Friedman heard the alarm in his voice, so he repeated the question with only moderate interest, "What did he ask you?"

"He asked what I thought about your relationship with Lee . . . you know . . . like, did you guys get along and how long were you married . . . stuff like that. It kind of felt like he was trying to find out something. You know, like gossip or something."

Now Dr. Friedman was angry. But he remained silent.

Joan said, "I heard he talked to Laurie and Joyce and some of the other girls in the office too."

"Did he stop by the office?" Dr. Friedman asked incredulously.

Joan could hear the anger in his voice. She didn't want him to take it out on her, so she tried to make light of it, "Nah, he just called on the phone . . . Oh and he asked me if I had phone numbers for the Inhaber-Taft reps who call on our practice. I only gave him phone numbers for Brad, Blaire and Molly. I told him to call Inhaber-Taft for the rest."

Dr. Friedman felt a cold chill run through him. He thought, "Detective Healy *must* have doubts about me. Why else would he call my staff? And now he wants to talk to the Inhaber sales reps?"

He asked, "Did he talk to any of the doctors?"

"No. As far as I know he just talked to a few of the girls in the office."

In a voice that sounded as nonchalant as he could muster, he asked, "Did he say why he wanted to talk to the Inhaber-Taft reps?"

Joan resumed the role of trusted confidante and said, "No. He didn't say, but I called Molly this afternoon. She said she would call me after she talked to the detective and let me know what they talked about."

He was afraid to ask the next question because he knew it sounded desperate, but he had to ask, "What did you say about me and Lee?"

"I told him that everybody knows you guys were crazy about each other. And I told him all the reps knew Lee because she went to all the drug rep dinners with you. Come to think of it, I guess that's why he asked me for their phone numbers." There was a moment of silence. "Are you there Dr. Friedman?"

"Yes. Yes, I'm here Joan." He decided it was a good idea to steer the conversation back to business. "How are things going there today?"

"Don't worry Dr. Friedman. Everything is under control. Dr. Chercovich and Bichotti came in early to help out Dr. Goldman and Bergman. We miss you of course. But just take it easy and try to get some rest this weekend."

"What do you mean?"

"Well I assumed that . . ."

"Joan, I'll be in the office tomorrow."

"Are you sure? I arranged coverage for you. That's normally not an easy thing to do for a Saturday but everybody wants to help out Dr. Friedman."

"I appreciate your efforts Joan, but it's actually more difficult to be in his empty house without Lee."

"I didn't think of that. I guess it is tough."

"It is. And I need the distraction of work." He was becoming increasingly agitated. "Joan, I have to go. I'll see you tomorrow."

"Alright. I'll see you then. Bye Dr. Friedman."

Dr. Friedman ended the call and threw his cell phone across the room. It landed on the carpet, which cushioned the impact. "Godammit! Healy thinks I did it! Why else would he call my staff to ask about my relationship with Lee? Jesus! And now he wants the phone numbers for the Inhaber sales reps! That means he wants to know more about MELAVOX, which means he's questioning Pagoshi's findings!" He felt a burning sensation in his gut again. He went into the bathroom to look for some antacid tablets. He threw some cold water on his face and grabbed a hand towel to wipe it. He looked into the mirror and remembered Detective Healy saying, "It wouldn't be the first time that a crime was committed in one location and then the body was dumped somewhere else." He burst out of the bathroom and paced around until he finally dropped into a chair and cried out, "I'm finished!" He put his head into his hands.

Suddenly, he stood up and covered his mouth. His eyes were wild! He worried, "Did I say anything out loud to incriminate myself?" The truth was, his house had not been bugged, but he was overwhelmed with paranoia and guilt. He reassured himself, "No. no. That was the only thing I said out loud. I'm sure of it." He walked into the next room, as if that might give him more privacy. He was furious when he thought, "Why the hell didn't Joe bury the goddamn shoes right away? . . . and he leaves them in his sample closet of all places . . . if Healy's theory about the running shoes gets into tomorrow's newspaper, they'll include a description of the shoes . . . and then when Healy talks to Debbie . . . I'm finished! I can't let that happen. I have to do something."

He imagined the conversation between Debbie Kaminski and Detective Healy. Then the detective would call him. He could hear him on the other end of the phone when he called to say, "I need you to come down to the station," in an authoritative tone. He imagined the cold handcuffs pulled tightly against his wrists when the detective locked them shut.

"I can't let that happen. I can't. I'd rather die than go to prison. But what am I going to do . . ." Suddenly, he stood perfectly still. "That's it! I have to get rid of her . . . I'll just get rid of her! Hell, I did it once. I can do it again. Alright . . . how do I do it? . . . I have to do it tonight . . . OK, it's Friday . . . think! . . ." He rubbed his temples. "Alright. That's it! She said she goes to her boyfriend's cabin every weekend. Where the hell did she say it was? . . . It was somewhere in Maryland. What was his last name? Wait a minute, it was a German name. It's on the tip of my tongue. I remember it was the same last name as . . . Reinhardt! That's it . . . Reinhardt. And his first name is Mark, I think."

He walked over to his cell phone and picked it up. He was going to call Information and ask for Mark's phone number, but he would also manage to get Mark's address out of them. He punched in two numbers and then stopped. He ended the call. "Wait a minute! I have to be careful. I can't just make a phone call, or do anything that could be traced back to me . . . a phone book . . . that's it! I have to find a Maryland phone book. I hope his number is listed. She said he lives in Chesapeake City or was it Elkton? . . . anyway they're both in Cecil County. So I need a Cecil County phone book. So where do I find one? . . . I know. I'll just drive down in that direction and stop at a hotel along the way. They always have the area phone books. I don't have to ask anybody for it. I'll just go to one of the pay phones where they usually have a couple stashed."

He buzzed with adrenalin. He was frantic. He flung open the closet in the foyer and grabbed his jacket. He locked the front door and suddenly remembered the car that was stalking him. He peered out of the glass panel. "It's gone! The goddamn car is gone! Alright, it's now or never." He ran through the kitchen and out the door to the garage. He started his car and revved the engine. "I can't waste a minute. I'm sure that asshole in the Chevy Lumina will come back."

As he eased down the driveway he whispered out loud, "Well he's not here now, so he won't even know I left . . . unless of course, he sees me when I return . . . I can't worry about that now . . . at least he can't follow me . . .that's what matters now."

Fifteen minutes later, he cruised down 95 South toward Maryland. "Should I get off at the Christiana Hilton? . . . no . . . I might run into someone I know. I'll go further south. Oh no! . . . my cell phone." He twisted in his seat and pulled his cell phone from his back pocket. He turned it off. He knew it was possible that Detective Healy would call him. If he answered his cell phone while he was in Maryland, they would be able to trace his location. He couldn't risk that.

Soon he saw a sign for the University of Delaware. "I'll get off here. There's a few little hotels around the university . . . or should I just wait until I get into Maryland? But I don't want to be seen anywhere in Maryland and then risk being connected to Debbie Kaminski's unfortunate accident." He took the exit for Newark/Route 896. Then he worried, "How the hell am I going to do it anyway? I know . . . a fire! That'll work. She said it's a cabin . . . so how unusual would it be for an old wooden cabin to go up in flames? When their lights are out, I'll just sneak up and torch an aerosol can by an outside wall . . . end of story."

Dr. Friedman pulled into the parking lot of a Red Roof Inn and went inside. The young Indian woman at the front desk was helping a customer. Three people were milling around the tiny lobby. There was a sign for restrooms to the left and a sign for telephones indicated that he had to make a right turn from the lobby. Suddenly he was filled with anxiety. He thought, "What if one of my patients happens to be in the hotel and flags me down the way they always do when they see me in public? Ah hell, I'll think of some bullshit excuse. I always do."

He walked past a couple of vending machines to get to the phones. He caught a glimpse of a chocolate caramel covered peanut bar and his mouth watered. "Not now," he thought. There seemed to be half a dozen phone stalls, each covered in cheap wood laminate. Sure enough, there were phone books tossed in a sloppy mess on the shelves beneath the phones. The first book he picked up was for New Castle County, Delaware. Then his eyes widened when he saw a phone book for Maryland in the next telephone stall. He pulled it out, but was disappointed to discover it was for Queen Anne's County. He looked at all of the phone books and not one of them was for Cecil County. "Shit! What do I do now?"

Suddenly, he had the urgent need to urinate. He hurried in the opposite direction, where he had seen the signs for restrooms.

As he headed back to the lobby, the young woman at the front desk caught his eye. "Can I help you sir?"

He made an uneasy grin. He was afraid to speak for fear the woman might remember him if she was later questioned by the police. He thought, "Oh, what the hell . . . she already got a good look at me. It'll save time if I ask." He did his best to appear nonchalant when he said, "I'm looking for a phone book for Cecil County, Maryland."

"I should have one right here." She bent down and looked behind the front desk. Her thin wrists bent backwards, as she heaved phone books to the desktop. She looked at them as if they were puzzle pieces that she moved around to get a better look. "Ah! Here you are. Cecil County."

Dr. Friedman slid the book to the edge of the desk and said timidly, "Thank you." He didn't want to look up Mark's name in front of her so he walked over to the chairs in the lobby, which were now empty. He fanned the book until he could see the R's . . . "Ra . . . Ri . . . whoops." He fanned backwards . . . "Re . . . Rei . . . Reinard." He used his forefinger now. "Reineman . . . Reinen . . . Reinhardt! . . . Reinhardt, Andrew . . . Reinhardt, Evan . . . Reinhardt, Mark! That's it! . . . 913 Buckman Road . . . 913 Buckman Road . . . 913 Buckman Road." He didn't want to write it down for fear he might lose the slip of paper with his handwriting on it. He turned to the front of the phonebook and looked at the area maps. He found Buckman Road and then backtracked. "Alright, once I get to Route 40, I'll make a right onto 40 West and then follow it a few miles to Route 213 . . . and then another left onto Buckman Road. Perfect." He closed the phone book and returned it to the front desk. The young woman was busy on the telephone. She didn't look in his direction. He slipped out of the lobby and got back into his car.

When he stopped for a red light at the intersection, he looked off to the left and stared blankly at yet another string of stores. Then the thought

struck him. "I better stop now and buy an aerosol can of something —
anything, and pay cash for it. The bozos at the counter won't remember
anything that insignificant."

When the light turned green he made a left turn into the shopping
center and drove toward the hardware store. After he purchased a can of azure
blue spray paint, he stopped into a QuikMart and bought a pack of cigarettes
and a lighter. He threw the cigarettes out of his car window when he was back
on the road. He only needed the lighter. He took Route 896 to Route 40 and
looked at the clock on his dashboard. It was 6:39 p.m. and already dark. He
thought, "I'll find the place first, and then park somewhere and wait until 9:00
or so . . . I hope they go to bed reasonably early . . . but what the hell am I
going to do while I wait? . . . Maybe I should just do it now." He glanced at his
speedometer and checked his rearview mirror. He thought, "I better not draw
attention to myself, those goddamn Maryland state cops are always hitting on
cars with out-of-state plates."

Debbie shivered from the cold breeze, as she opened the back door of
her car to let Harry out. She looked toward the river as her eyes adjusted to the
darkness. The quarter moon shed just enough light to illuminate the water.
The river was quiet in March. There were no boaters or jet skis yet, and no
more ice-skaters.

She looked up toward the tops of the tall oak and pine trees that
pierced the starry sky. The shrubbery along the driveway that was illuminated
by her headlights only moments before now formed black silhouettes.
Suddenly the outside lights flashed on, as Harry ran around the cabin. But in a
moment the lights went off again. Debbie decided it was too dark to make her
way down the sloping half dozen steps to the cabin without a flashlight. She
opened her car and pulled out a flashlight from the pocket on the side of the
door. The light pierced the greenery and giant tree trunks. She called out,
"Come on Harry," and immediately heard him running in the distance. In
seconds he was standing by her side, panting. "Come on. Let's go inside."

The door to the cabin opened into the kitchen, with the cabinets and
sink to the left. There was a tiny breakfast room on the other side of the
kitchen, and Debbie used it as her makeshift office when she stayed at the
cabin. It had a beautiful view of the river so Mark didn't want any curtains on

the windows. During the day, the view was exhilarating but when Debbie was alone at night, the surrounding darkness was unsettling.

A couch, two chairs and a fireplace were just beyond the kitchen area. There were two bedrooms and a bathroom on the same floor and a loft at the top of the stairs.

After Debbie turned on the lamp next to the couch, she turned off the bright overhead light in the kitchen. Even at this time of year, it managed to attract a few buzzing insects. In a cabin in the middle of the woods, Debbie learned quickly that she had to desensitize herself to mysterious critters. Once in the heat of a summer night, she was startled by a moth that landed on the screen in front of her as she sat at the desk. It looked like a creature from outer space with a three inch wing span, a bulbous head, and a mint green color. She didn't scream for two reasons: she didn't want Mark to think she was prissy and, fortunately, the moth was on the *outside* of the screen. In the autumn, she had seen a snake slither through the grass and down the hill to the river. And Mark told her he was once surprised by a raccoon standing at the front door.

Once Debbie was inside, the only unwanted visitors she worried about were the ones that scurried around on four legs. But apparently, Harry's presence was a deterrent. She had surmised that mice could detect the odor of another animal and were smart enough to stay away.

She put the takeout platters in the refrigerator and figured she would wait to eat with Mark. She used the bathroom and then stood in the kitchen for a moment, wondering what to do next. She turned and looked at the clock on the kitchen wall. It was 7:20. "I wonder what time he'll be home tonight," she mumbled to herself.

Harry had planted himself on the floor in front of the couch after he finished slurping up the water in his bowl. Debbie walked over to her desk. "I guess I'll do my computer work now. Otherwise, I'll just sit here and worry about what Mark is doing." She pulled the chain for the desk lamp and hit the power button on her computer. In a few seconds, she heard the half dozen welcoming musical notes of her laptop, and the icons waved like greeting flags as they popped onto the screen in synchronized fashion. She clicked on the icon for Call Reporting and began to report her sales calls for the day. After that, she could work on her weekly activity report. The cabin could be a lonely place when Mark wasn't there, so she felt oddly comforted by her connection to Inhaber-Taft. Back in February, she had celebrated 23 years of employment. She still remembered the company's mission statement, which she had memorized before she started to go on interviews for a sales position with the company: "to research, manufacture and market pharmaceuticals to ease suffering, to slow the progression of disease, and to cure infections."

Debbie opened her week-at-a-glance calendar, where she jotted down the names of physicians she called on. She pulled out the 8 ½" x 11" ruled pad where she scribbled her notes after each sales call. She was supposed to do this on her laptop in the car but she found it was quicker and easier to scribble some notes instead of fumbling with her computer in the car after each office visit. She reached for the pink sheets that were her copies of the multi-page sample signature forms. She proceeded to input the information about her product discussions with each physician and the result of her sales close; i.e., did the physician agree to write prescriptions for the product or did he/she object to initial use or continued use.

Dr. Friedman cruised down the heavily wooded, winding curves of Buckman Road. There were no streetlights so he flipped on his high beams. Suddenly he hit the brakes and gasped! Three deer had started to cross the road just a few yards ahead of him. The sound of the screeching brakes frightened them, and they did an about-face and ran back into the woods. He exhaled a sigh. "Phew, that's all I needed was to get my car banged up by a couple of deer. How would I explain that one!"

He proceeded more slowly as he maneuvered further down the seemingly endless road. The houses were all set far back from the roadside. The ones that caught his attention were the ones with lights on inside. Some of the lots were heavily wooded, which obscured the sight of anything beyond the trees. But there seemed to be a regular distance between the houses that accommodated approximately two acre lots. He could read some of the numbers on the mailboxes, but he wasn't even close to 913 yet.

When he finally neared the number, he slowed to a crawl and turned off his headlights. An intense shroud of darkness surrounded him. His car slowly rolled past a mailbox with the number 913 painted in white on the side of the black box. He could see a ranch style house just off center of the mailbox and to the right a little bit. The lights were on in several windows. He felt a wave of anxiety but he reminded himself that Debbie was the only person who could potentially incriminate him. He knew what he had to do and nothing was going to stop him.

He drove past the house and, after a few more lots, he could make out a dead end sign in the distance. He stopped the car and reversed it slowly and then shifted back into first gear to make a u-turn. He could hear gravel stones crackling beneath his tires. He looked for a spot where he could pull off the road and park. He chose a house that sat in darkness, with no cars in the driveway. He parked near the end of the driveway, but not in it. If the people who lived in the house came home, the position of his car would convince them he had parked there to visit a nearby house.

He got out of the car and started to walk toward the house at 913. There were two cars outside, but no sign of Debbie's Ford Taurus. Most pharma sales reps drove a Ford Taurus, but Debbie's was unusual. It was a station wagon style with a roof rack. Dr. Friedman thought, "Maybe Mark has a couple of cars and they went out to dinner in her car . . . but then . . . why are there so many lights on in the house?" He swallowed hard. He wanted to creep up to the house to check it out. He started toward the house when suddenly he heard a car coming down the road. He hurried in between some trees and ducked down. The car's high beams streamed down the road long before the car neared. Finally, there was a sound like a rush of wind, as the car passed.

Again he started toward the house and stopped suddenly. "What if that dog of hers starts to bark?" He looked around him and thought, "Although, out here with all the woods around, I guess a dog is bound to bark at a deer or something now and then. They probably wouldn't even pay attention to it if the dog barked."

He walked around to the back of the house and stopped short. He was startled to find himself in full view of a big, picture window about eight feet wide and four feet high. He quickly ducked behind the shrubbery. When his heart slowed enough so he could breathe again, he peaked out and saw that the room was brightly lit and there was a roaring fire in the big, stone fireplace. He was surprised by the sight of two small children who ran across the room. "Oh no! I don't want to kill a little, innocent kid. But who the hell are they anyway? Does Mark have kids from a previous marriage?" Then he saw a dark haired woman carrying an infant who was swaddled in a blanket near her breasts. "I guess they have visitors." He crept over to a tree that was closer to the house, where he had a better vantage point. He could see a man sitting on the couch and the two children jumped up onto the couch and sat beside him.

Dr. Friedman watched the scene for a few minutes and began to think, "I've been standing here for a little while now and I haven't seen Debbie or Mark. What if this isn't their house? Wait a minute! Now he noticed the siding that covered every inch of what he could see of the house. What was I thinking . . . *house?* . . . Debbie said it was a *cabin.* Shit! This is the wrong place! He made his way around to the front of the house and followed a path just beyond the driveway that forked to the left through more trees and shrubs. He followed the left fork and something caught his peripheral vision. There was a light in the distance to the right. He took a few more steps and realized that he stood at the top of another driveway that sloped down a steep hill.

By now his eyes had adjusted to the darkness, and he could see that the light came from a window surrounded by the wooden panels of a cabin! He could see a van and a pickup truck at the bottom of the hill. And just in front of the little cabin was a Ford Taurus wagon with a roof rack. His eyes widened. "That's it!"

He moved away from the stones onto the grassy side of the driveway, as he slowly made his way down the hill. He was about thirty feet from the cabin when, suddenly, a bright light flashed on and flooded the open area where he stood. He froze for a second and then hit the ground. He crawled over to a tree and curled up behind it. He was panting but he slowed down his breathing so he couldn't be heard. He closed his eyes and trembled with fear. He thought, "Please don't let the dog out to investigate." He had no idea what he would do then. The possibility was just too awful. Then the light went out again. Miraculously, there was no barking dog and everything was quiet. He realized he had set off a motion detector light. "What do I do now? How can I get around it?" Then he remembered that the motion detector lights on his property jut out from the sides of his house. Oddly enough, they can't sense movement directly underneath the lights. The movement has to be at least a foot beyond the lights to be detected. He thought, "I have to get close enough to the cabin to hug the walls and take a peak inside."

He got to his feet and walked further to the right and then slowly made his way toward the cabin. The motion sensor light went on again, but he did a kind of crouching jog until he reached the side of the cabin. He leaned against the cabin and took shallow breaths, as he listened for sound. "Fortunately they ignore their motion sensor lights like most people," he thought. As he shimmied against the wooden cabin, he was grateful that he wore his leather jacket. A wool coat may have snagged against the wood. He crouched down again as he gingerly made his way past two windows and finally reached the one with the light shining through it.

Slowly, he reached his gloved hands toward the windowsill and grasped it as he raised his head just enough to peek through the glass. There was no one sitting on the couch and no one in the kitchen just beyond it. He stretched his neck upward a little and was startled to see a dog sleeping on the floor. He slipped back down immediately.

He crept to the edge of the cabin and turned slightly to the left toward the wall facing the river. About fifteen feet away, a room jutted out further from the rest of the cabin. He could plainly see Debbie's profile as she sat by the window. His heart was pounding. "Should I just do it now? . . . But what if her boyfriend is in the next room and he hears something?"

Suddenly he felt vulnerable when he realized, "All she has to do is look to her right and she'll see me! . . . wait a minute . . . no she won't . . . all she can see is darkness from the inside. As long as the motion sensor light stays off, I'm safe."

He watched her for a minute. He could see that she was looking at a computer screen. He thought, "I guess Mr. Reinhardt is asleep in one of the other rooms . . . he must be here because there's three cars parked outside . . . two of them are obviously his . . ." Dr. Friedman didn't know that the van and pickup truck were just two more of Mark's projects; although at least the truck was in working order.

Again he wondered, "Should I do it now?" He feared he was starting to lose his nerve. "I can't do it now while she's still awake . . . I have to wait until they're all asleep . . . I'll go back to my car and wait."

He slid against the cabin and was once again on the side where the dog slept just beyond the outside wall. When he got past the windows, he stood up and turned, but he caught his foot on a tree root that jutted out of the ground. He lost his balance and bumped into the side of the cabin with his full weight. The dog started barking.

He cringed and closed his eyes in a tight squint. "Shit! Shit!" He stood perfectly still and didn't move a muscle. "If she lets the dog out, I'm done!"

Debbie froze in place. "What was that?" Harry's barking made her more afraid. He came rushing at her. "It's alright. It's alright Harry." For a moment, she thought about letting Harry outside to investigate, but she realized that would just leave her alone, while whoever was out there grabbed her dog. Harry had stopped barking and now wined for affection. Debbie pet him, and as she calmed down she thought, "It must have been a branch that fell from one of the trees." The roof was always covered with leaves and branches. Between the regular shedding from the trees and rain storms, Mark was constantly climbing up on the roof to clear it.

After several minutes, Dr. Friedman slowly ascended the driveway using the same circuitous path, as the motion lights went on and off again. He quickly made his way down the road and spotted his car within minutes. He pulled slowly onto the road and waited until he passed the mailbox for 913, before he flipped on his headlights. Within a few minutes, he spotted a road off to the right and saw a clearing in the woods as he turned. A sign said, "Private Hunting Area. Trespassers will be Prosecuted." There was an area for parking that stretched further into the woods. There were no other cars around. "This is the perfect place to wait it out," he thought.

Debbie poured herself a glass of wine. She knew her preoccupation with Mark was rattling her nerves. She decided to read a little bit and hoped that would relax her. There was no television in the cabin. Mark was against "the senseless drivel of television," as he described it. Debbie was startled when her cell phone rang at 8:30. "Oh good. That's Mark." She sprung up and grabbed her phone from the kitchen table.

"Hello?"

"Hi sweetie, it's me."

"Hi Mark. Are you on your way home?" Debbie squinted with disdain at the sound of her own desperation.

"Not yet Deb." Mark was silent for a minute.

"Hello?"

"Yeah, I'm here." He hesitated again and then said, "I finished up in Chadds Ford, but while I was there, Gretchen called and asked if I could come up and help her with a software problem."

Debbie felt her anger and jealousy bubble up in her throat. "What?" she exclaimed. "What's really going on Mark?"

He was silent.

She yelled, "Why do I even try to make this work? I'm kidding myself. I think you just want me around so that you have something to do while you're waiting for Gretchen to call."

Now Mark was angry. He said, "Debbie, I expect you to trust me by now. I knew you would be upset about this, but that's why I'm calling to tell you now. I figured if I waited until I got home you would be even more angry and jealous about it."

Debbie was indignant, "Oh, so I should be grateful that you decided to tell me the truth about what you've been doing tonight. Did you even go to Scott's office or have you been at Gretchen's house the whole time?"

"Yes, I went to Scott's office. And I told you Gretchen called when I was finishing up so I decided to just drive up there and call you on the way. When are you going to stop this Debbie? I'm tired of it."

"So what does that mean? You're tired of what? Me? Well I guess that's obvious."

"Debbie, stop it."

"No you stop it. When are you going to tell Gretchen to find someone else to solve her problems? What do you expect me to think about all this?"

Mark was silent.

For a moment, Debbie wondered if she was being unreasonable. "Mark, I just . . . I'm sorry . . . I . . . I don't know what to think anymore."

Mark's voice was soothing. "It's alright. But if this relationship is going to work, then you have to trust me."

This time she had a degree of assertiveness in her voice. "Mark, I just don't understand why you have to run up there every time she calls you. I'm sorry but I'm not comfortable with this . . . I think you have to decide if it's me or her." She was proud of herself when she finished. It didn't sound like an ultimatum, even though it was, because she was calm and resolute.

Mark wasn't sure what to think. It was the first time Debbie had taken a firm stand, and he didn't know if he liked it. Finally he said, "Debbie, the sooner I finish there, the sooner I'll be home. Can we just talk about this when I get home?"

She knew she had no choice at the moment. He wasn't going to talk about it now and he would stubbornly go to Gretchen's place. Realizing it might be the end of their relationship, Debbie felt vulnerable. She wanted to believe him. She said quietly, "Alright, I'll talk to you later."

"Thanks. Just let me get this over with and I'll be home soon."

Debbie was silent.

"Hello? Debbie, are you there?"

"Yes."

"Alright. I have to go. I'll be home soon," Mark was abrupt.

"OK bye."

Harry walked into the kitchen and stood by Debbie's side, wagging his tail. "Do you want to go outside for a minute?" He made a short, excited howling sound. She opened the kitchen door and went outside into the darkness. The motion sensor light went on when Harry ran up the steps to the grassy area beyond them. Debbie folded her arms against her chest and shivered. The light went off and now the woods were completely dark. She felt agitated and called out for Harry. "Come on Harry . . . let's go inside now . . . Harry?" There was silence. She thought, "He must have found a mouse or something." She called louder, "Harry. Harry." The leaves rustled as her eyes adjusted to the darkness. She saw Harry running toward her. "Come on buddy. Let's go inside and get warm."

She drank what was left of the wine in her glass. Normally, she would be buzzed after just one glass of wine but she was too nervous and upset to feel anything. She poured another full glass of wine and thought sadly, "I love Mark, but I'm tired of this."

She sat down on the couch and read her book until her eyes grew heavy with sleepiness. She decided to go to bed. Mark always wanted fresh air in the bedroom, regardless of the season, so out of habit, she opened the window just about an inch. Harry jumped up onto the bed and Debbie pulled the comforter up close around her neck and snuggled closer to Harry. She felt warm and comfortable as she turned her face into the pillow. It was completely quiet and she started to fall asleep when she was stirred awake. She heard a rustling of leaves outside. It was more than a simple breeze. It was the kind of rustling sound that footsteps make.

She took short, shallow breaths and pricked her ears so she could hear every sound. The motion sensor light flashed through the window on the other side of the room. Now the rustling was just outside the window above her head! She gasped and thought angrily, "Why isn't Harry waking up?" She peaked over at him snoozing on the bed next to her. She nudged him, but he didn't stir. She tried to calm herself by thinking, "It's probably deer wandering through the property." She remembered other nights when the outside light went on, and she and Mark watched three or four deer stroll past.

It had been quiet for a few minutes, so she slowly got out of bed and crept up to the window on the other side of the room. Sure enough, she saw a deer. She exhaled deeply and began to breathe normally again. She grinned and said to Harry from across the room, "A lot of help you were." He lifted his head and turned to look in Debbie's direction. His snout was droopy and his neck was wrinkled. He seemed to assess that everything was OK and then dropped his head back onto the blankets. He let out a contented sigh, as Debbie climbed back into bed. She was still lying awake when Harry started to snore.

Suddenly, she heard the rustle of leaves again, only this time it sounded like someone was running toward the cabin. Her heart seized! She couldn't move. Then she heard something brush against the screen above the bed! She had an eerie sensation that someone was leaning against the screen. She was lying on her stomach so she pressed the fullness of her weight into the bed. It was as if she was trying to hide in plain sight.

Harry finally jumped up and started barking at the window. Debbie's heart was pounding furiously. She didn't know if she was more afraid of Harry jumping *out* the window or someone else jumping *in* the window! She squeezed her eyes tightly shut and stopped breathing.

Just then, she heard the rumbling of a car engine. It was the familiar sound of Mark's car winding down the stony driveway. "Oh thank God!" Debbie and Harry jumped out of the bed and ran toward the kitchen door. The light went on by the driveway. Harry was barking wildly. Debbie hesitated for a second before she opened the door. "What if it's *not* Mark? No, I'm sure that was his car engine."

She flung open the door and saw Mark's car. She ran up to him and said, "Thank God you're home! I think someone was just outside the cabin!"

"What? Where?"

"I thought I heard somebody outside of the bedroom just now."

Mark walked in the direction of the bedroom to investigate.

"Not there Mark . . . it was coming from the other side of the cabin."

Mark disappeared around the corner with Harry. Debbie ran after them. Mark was sitting on bended knee and petting Harry, "It's OK now buddy." Then he stood up and walked toward Debbie. He said, "Everything's fine. You probably just imagined it." By now they were both standing in the unforgiving harshness of the outside lights. Debbie thought Mark looked pale and tired. She was rattled by mixed emotions. Part of her resented his patronizing tone, but part of her felt relief that he was home. Mark put his arm around her and kissed her on the forehead. "Come on. Let's go inside."

Mark reached for the box of dog biscuits on top of the refrigerator. He took one out and gave it to Harry and asked, "Were you a good boy? Did you protect your mommy?" Debbie smiled at Mark and said, "Mark, I . . . I'm sorry about tonight . . . I"

Mark interrupted her and said with an exhausted sigh, "Debbie, you just have to trust me. I love you. There's nothing going on with me and Gretchen. I promise you. You can trust me . . . but I have to admit you wore me down. I finally told Gretchen she should find someone else to help her with her computer problems."

"Thanks Mark." They hugged and Debbie buried her face in the safety of his chest.

Dr. Friedman drove up 95 North to Wilmington. He shook his head. "It's a dam good thing I snapped out of it! . . . what was I thinking? . . . I wasn't thinking . . . I must have been temporarily insane! . . . It's bad enough that Healy thinks I may have killed Lee, but what if he connected me to a fire that killed two people? . . . and this stuff Healy came up with about there being no weeds on the bottom of Lee's shoes is just bullshit . . . I'm sure I took care of that detail . . . he's just playing with my mind . . . and if the papers report something about the running shoes, and Debbie tells Healy what she discovered in Joe's office, they'll never find the shoes. There's no tangible evidence."

By the time he reached his street, he was regaining his confidence. "Even if the worst happens and this goes to trial, my attorney will be privy to the facts surrounding the discovery area. He can argue against whatever the prosecutors come up with about the minor details. We'll keep the focus on Lee's heart attack and what caused it."

Chapter 25: The Higher the Dose, the Greater the Cost

Saturday, March 19

ON SATURDAY, DR. Friedman went to the office as planned. He called Larry Berman around noon.

"Donald, how are you my friend? I tried to call you several times yesterday after I heard they found Lee. It's horrible. I just can't believe it."

"Yeah, well . . . it's bad Larry. I'm beside myself."

"Of course. Why don't we sit down and talk. Did you eat yet?"

"Ehh, just a little."

"Can you get away for lunch? I assume you're at the office."

"Yes, I'm at the office. But I can't get away. It's crazy busy here."

"Donald, are you taking care of yourself?"

"As much as I can Larry."

Larry felt guilty. "Did you get my messages yesterday? I thought about driving over to your place last night but . . ."

Donald thought, "Jesus Christ! It's a good thing he didn't. How would I explain where I was?" He interrupted, "It's OK Larry. Really. I should have called you but I was just inundated with phone calls from everybody. And to tell you the truth, the only people I called were my kids."

"How are they taking it?"

"They feel bad for me but, as you know, they never really liked Lee — thanks to their mother."

"I know how that works. Did you read the articles in *The News Journal* yesterday or today?"

Donald wasn't sure he wanted to know what was reported. He said, "No. I haven't read the paper or watched the news. What are they reporting?"

"Yesterday morning on channel 7, they showed the site in Pennsville, where Lee was found. And last night they reported that the Medical Examiner did an autopsy and he was going to follow up with a toxicology report. Have you heard anything yet?"

"That's why I'm calling you Larry."

"What is it Donald?"

"The Medical Examiner said Lee had a heart attack."

"What! How could that happen?"

"Believe me, I had the same reaction. I met with the detective and the Medical Examiner on Thursday night, after he did the autopsy . . ." He went on to explain Dr. Pagoshi's findings. ". . . . he confirmed the heart attack was the result of long term exposure to MELAVOX."

"What!" Larry was incredulous. "Isn't that the one they advertise on television that's supposed to be the new wonder drug for arthritis?"

"Yeah, that's the one. Lee took 25 mg each day and only took the max dose for breakthrough pain. I was more than comfortable with that because Michael Poong and the sales reps started to promote the max dose for long term use."

"Who is Michael Poong?"

"Oh, I'm sorry. He's the sales manager for the reps who promote MELAVOX."

"Now which company is that?"

"Inhaber-Taft."

"Son of a bitch! Unbelievable. I'll call my broker right away and sell my shares . . . Now are you telling me that you prescribed the medication according to the FDA approved indications and that this guy Michael and the Inhaber-Taft reps were promoting it for long term use at the highest dose?"

"Yes Larry. That's what I'm telling you. But what's more important is the fact that Lee took the *lowest* dose on a daily basis, and she had a heart attack!"

"It looks like we have a strong case. And don't forget I won a class action suit against Harrington-Beckman. Their sales reps were telling physicians their migraine drug could be used with antidepressants for chronic migraine sufferers. Hundreds of women suffered seizures after long term treatment with that drug combination. A few of them had strokes that killed them!"

"I remember that case Larry. You won a nice settlement as I remember. How much was it?"

"Two hundred fifty million and change."

Donald smiled. "That's why I'm calling bubby. I agree we've definitely got a case against these bastards."

"We absolutely do! When can we meet to talk about this? Iris and I had plans for tonight but I can try to get out of it."

"No, don't do that. I thought we could meet after the service for Lee."

"What service?"

"Lee's son Grant and I just finalized arrangements this morning. You know Lee and I were never religious so we weren't even registered at a synagogue or a church. But Grant suggested Brandywine Chapel in Wilmington. He talked to the minister, and he agreed to perform a remembrance service on Monday morning at 11:00. There's a luncheon afterward at Harry's Grille."

"Good. I'll move some things around on my calendar and Iris and I will be there. In the meantime, I'll start to do some homework. Can you spell the name of that drug for me?"

"Sure. It's M E L A V O X."

"MELAVOX. Got it. And call me anytime bubby."

"I will Larry."

When Grant had called him about a service, he was reluctant to tell Dr. Friedman that his mother had told him once that she wanted to be cremated. But what made him most uncomfortable was telling Donald that he wanted to keep her ashes. Donald was happy to be in the privacy of his office at the time, where no one could see his satisfied grin. He thought, "I can't believe Grant is handing me the perfect opportunity to get rid of Lee's body — for good! Once she's cremated, it's 'case closed.' Detective Healy, or Inhaber-Taft's counsel for that matter, can never exhume her body for further testing." But he said to Grant, "Of course I understand. You're Lee's only son."

Dr. Friedman wondered if Detective Healy had told Grant that it was MELAVOX that caused his mother's heart attack. He thought, "Maybe he just told Grant it was a heart attack and said nothing about the cause." He could never let Grant find out that he planned to sue Inhaber-Taft. Grant might ask to be a partner in the lawsuit, which would mean a possible 50/50 split of the money he hoped to win in the settlement. Donald was certain the case would never go to trial because Inhaber-Taft wouldn't want the bad publicity. He thought, "Grant will find out like everyone else, when it hits the newspapers after an out-of-court settlement. Let him file his own lawsuit, which will surely be part of a class action once the media gets a hold of it."

Edgar Schaeffer finished his shower in the locker room of the surgery lounge at Christiana Hospital. He had participated in three surgeries that morning: a minimally invasive hip replacement, a rotator cuff repair, and a knee arthroscopy. The third and fourth year residents usually start the surgeries in order to practice their surgical technique. This enables Dr. Schaeffer to swiftly progress from one surgical suite to the next with hands-on assistance and the legally required oversight. By the time the residents begin to close the surgical wounds with sutures or staples, he's well on his way to his own personal extracurricular activities.

Edgar checked his cell phone for messages and decided to return Detective Healy's call. He thought, "This must have something to do with Lee. Maybe that prick husband of hers is trying to get me involved in this mess."

"Hello, this is Detective Healy."

"Detective, this is Edgar Schaeffer."

"Oh, thanks for calling me back Dr. Schaeffer."

"Sure."

"Is it possible to catch up with you in person some time today?"

In a pleasant and engaging tone he said, "I just finished my surgeries, so you can buy me lunch." Dr. Schaeffer's manner was charming and charismatic, which allowed him to get away with behavior that would otherwise be considered presumptuous or even rude.

Detective Healy was taken aback. He had anticipated that it would be much more difficult to pin him down. He said, "Lunch sounds good to me. Where are you now Dr. Schaeffer?"

"I'm at Christiana Hospital. There's an excellent deli just across the street on Churchman's Road. It's in a little strip mall with a Borders bookstore next to it."

"Oh, I know the place. Sure. What time is good for you?"

"I have to do a few dictations and a little paperwork, so I can meet you there at 1:30. How about that?"

Detective Healy tried to emulate Dr. Schaeffer's friendly, yet no-nonsense manner. He said, "1:30 it is. I'll see you then."

"Good." Edgar said, and then ended the call. He thought, "At least I'll get a quick lunch out of it."

Detective Healy was having a very productive day. He had spoken with all but one of the Inhaber-Taft reps and was waiting for a call back from Michael Poong. The detective was surprised that he was able to catch up with the reps on a Saturday. He thought, "This must be my lucky day." He jotted down notes after each call. He was hoping that someone could provide further insight into Dr. Friedman's relationship with Lee. He purposely contacted the sales reps, and even Dr. Friedman's staff, by phone. He didn't go to their homes or office because he wanted to be discreet. If anyone wanted to say something unflattering or suggestive about Dr. Friedman or Lee, they wouldn't do it unless they felt their discussion would be held in the strictest confidence. That wasn't very easy to do if they were worried that Dr. Friedman might walk into the room at any moment. If he invited them downtown to the police station, they would immediately be on the defensive. He knew a police station had that effect on people.

For each interview, he asked the same three questions:

1) "How long have you worked for Inhaber-Taft (or for Dr. Friedman)?"

2) "Have you met Lee Young, Dr. Friedman's wife?"

The third question was a bit more provocative. "How would you describe the relationship between Lee and Dr. Friedman, based on what you've observed or perhaps heard through the rumor mill?"

There was a fourth question that he would ask only a few of the reps. He planned to rely on his intuition in deciding whom to ask: "What are the names of the products you sell for Inhaber-Taft?" He had to get to MELAVOX in a round-about way in order to avoid getting himself into any legal hot water. He didn't want to raise any red flags about a particular product. After they mentioned MELAVOX, he would ask, "Do you know if Dr. Friedman prescribed MELAVOX for his patients?" The detective risked a simple yes or no answer. But he thought it was a safe bet that sales people would not stop at a one word answer. "Besides, I think they'll feel safe talking to a small town detective who's just trying to do his job."

He hoped they would provide more details about the dose that Dr. Friedman prescribed and the duration of treatment that he recommended. He wanted to be sure that Dr. Friedman prescribed MELAVOX for several patients, versus singling out Lee. He had to be very careful about asking these questions because, legally, he was not privy to such information. Doctor/patient confidentiality prevented him from accessing pharmacy records or patient charts.

Although the Medical Examiner confirmed that Lee had a quantity of MELAVOX in her blood and tissues consistent with chronic use of the drug; and it was MELAVOX that damaged her heart and even caused a heart attack, Detective Healy was still puzzled. He wondered, "Why then aren't the rest of the people who are taking this medication, dying from heart attacks? Maybe they are and it just hasn't been reported to the general public."

He tried to make sense out of the METAPO study that he had gotten from Dr. Friedman's office manager. He also discovered that apparently he had been oblivious to the media frenzy a few months back. There were television news stories and newspaper articles that warned of the possibility of heart attack or stroke with long term use of MELAVOX. The sensational story eventually faded away. "How could that happen?" he wondered.

So far, Detective Healy found the answers to each of his questions were similar and unremarkable. All of the reps had worked for Inhaber-Taft for at least one year. Not only did each of them know Lee Young, but each had socialized with her at dinners sponsored by their company. They all reported that, from what they had seen, Lee and Dr. Friedman were still living like newlyweds. There were no facts or rumors to suggest otherwise.

Joan, the office manager, reported that they each had busy lives but they made a point to have dinner together every night. She said they either went to the drug rep dinners together or had dinner at home. Joan said Dr. Friedman loved to cook. Even the reps knew that he enjoyed eating and cooking gourmet food.

Detective Healy asked Grant, Blaire, and Brad about the products they sold and Dr. Friedman's use of MELAVOX. He chose Grant because he was Lee Young's son. If anyone had some additional insight into Dr. Friedman, he would. He chose Blaire and Brad because they gave him the impression they were very conscientious about their jobs. Each of them spoke eagerly under the condition of anonymity.

Apparently Dr. Friedman prescribed MELAVOX for many of his patients, and they all knew that Lee was taking MELAVOX. Blaire said that Lee liked to talk about herself whenever she had the chance. What better opportunity than with the pharmaceutical sales reps, all of whom pretended to be captivated by her every word, at their company sponsored dinners.

Blaire said that Dr. Friedman was one of their biggest writers for MELAVOX. Detective Healy asked, "What do you mean by a 'big writer?'" She said it simply meant the physician wrote a lot of prescriptions for the drug.

Detective Healy was on his way to meet Dr. Schaeffer for lunch when he decided to try Michael Poong's number again. "Maybe this time I'll catch him." But just as he reached for his cell phone, it began to ring.

"Hello?"

"Detective Healy, this is Debbie Kaminski. I'm returning your call."

"Hi Debbie. Thanks for calling back. I'm sure you've heard the terrible news about Lee Young."

Debbie said gravely, "Yes, I have."

"I'm calling the Inhaber-Taft sales reps who have called on Dr. Friedman in the last eight months to a year. I want to ask you a couple of questions, if you have a minute."

"Sure. I'd be happy to."

"Great. My first question is . . ."

Her answers to the questions matched those of the other reps, but she was more candid, even verbose. Somehow she steered the conversation into a commercial for Inhaber-Taft and its products. Because of her enthusiasm, he decided to ask her the all-important fourth question.

As expected, she was more than willing to expound on her answer to the question about Dr. Friedman's use of MELAVOX. She said Dr. Friedman prescribed MELAVOX for many of his patients. And she also knew that he prescribed it for his wife. She said, "Lee was a nice person but she was very self-absorbed. She was her own favorite subject. That's why she liked the sales reps because most of us fawn all over the doctors and their spouses. We're more than happy to sit and listen to their wives talk about themselves — or about anything really--as long as we have their attention. We know they'll like us if we listen, and our hope is that they tell their physician spouses how much they like *us*. It's all about relationships."

Detective Healy said, "That's true. It's the same in my business."

Debbie laughed slightly at the irony. "Oh right. You have to be able to get people to trust you so they'll tell you what you want to know."

Detective Healy wanted to return to the topic of MELAVOX. "I don't know too much about MELAVOX, except that I've seen the commercials on television. But I remember it was in the news a few months back because of some serious side effects like heart attacks."

"Yes, I know what you're talking about. The problem is that the information gets reported incorrectly. The journalists who report about it don't know anything about pharmaceutical therapy so they don't even understand the information. But it seems that none of that matters to them because it's all about sensationalizing a story to get people to watch the news. In the study you're referring to there were two big problems . . ."

After she explained the study, Detective Healy said, "You're right about the misinformation." However, he took her viewpoint with a grain of salt since she was obviously on the side of the pharmaceutical company.

Debbie quickly added, "And there are idiosyncratic reactions to every drug."

"What do you mean by an idiosyncratic reaction?"

"It means those rare adverse reactions to a drug."

"And you're saying that it can happen with any drug — in an otherwise perfectly healthy person?"

"Yes. But as I said, it doesn't help matters if physicians are prescribing the wrong dose of a drug."

"How does that happen?"

Debbie felt vindicated. It was her opportunity to tell someone who would actually *listen* to what Michael Poong was doing. She said, "It happens because some sales reps and their managers have no scruples. They want to sell the drug at any cost — no pun intended. The higher the dose of an NSAID, or any pain med, the more expensive the drug is; and the more money the pharmaceutical company makes. That means bigger bonuses for the reps and their managers."

"I see." Now the detective seemed to be rapt with interest.

Debbie sensed this and thought to herself, "But what can a detective do? Well at least someone will know — for whatever it's worth."

However, instinctively, she felt the need to defend the merits of MELAVOX. "Detective Healy, I can assure you that MELAVOX is a great drug. I've heard dozens of patient testimonials about how MELAVOX changed their lives by relieving their intractable pain. Again, the problem is that it is sometimes dosed inappropriately." Now she was on a roll. She had an eager listener, which was rare in the life of a sales person. She continued, "In fact, that reminds me. I bumped into Dr. Friedman at Wilmington Pharmacy when he was picking up a prescription for MELAVOX. Dr. Friedman said Lee was taking MELAVOX 25 mg, but he said Michael Poong and some other Inhaber-Taft reps told him that he should prescribe the max dose of MELAVOX. Now, I know Dr. Friedman is a ball buster, if you'll excuse the expression, but I also know that Michael Poong was in fact coaching his reps to sell the highest dose of MELAVOX--75 mg-- for long term treatment of pain. I want you to know Detective, I had to disagree with what Michael and the other reps were saying. I told Dr. Friedman the max dose should only be prescribed for five to ten days."

Detective Healy asked, "Why would Michael suggest the higher dose if it could cause adverse events?" Then he quickly answered his own question, "Oh, I know. It's because of what you just explained to me--the higher dose costs more, and brings in more money and higher bonuses, etc."

"That's right."

It was obvious to him that Debbie hoped to blow the whistle on this manager. It was a cry for help but there was nothing he could do. He thought, "Hell, I could get into hot water just for asking some of these questions."

After a silence, Debbie said, "It's managers like Michael who lower our standards of ethics. Eventually, they're going to bring down the whole company — no — the whole industry!"

Detective Healy said, "I appreciate your candor Debbie." He was just pulling into a parking space outside of Mike's Deli. He said, "Thanks for taking the time to speak with me. It's been a real eye opener."

"You're welcome Detective Healy." She felt anxious and upset. She thought, "I probably said too much as usual."

Detective Healy said, "I'll be in touch with you if I have any further questions. Goodbye for now."

"Bye."

Detective Healy thought, "Apparently Dr. Friedman has been telling me the truth." He got out of his car just as a shiny, black Mercedes S 500 pulled up next to him. "This must be Dr. Schaeffer," he thought. He was right. Dr. Schaeffer was haughty, egotistical and competitive, and he enjoyed flaunting his wealth.

"Detective Healy?" Dr. Schaeffer walked up to the detective with a big smile on his face, as he reached out to shake the detective's hand.

Detective Healy was immediately charmed. He felt disarmed and relaxed. He got a sense that Dr. Schaeffer was a man's man — the kind of guy who could inspire envy, if he wasn't so charismatic. He was wearing jeans and a tweed sport coat over a white cotton shirt. His height, blonde hair and blue eyes made it easy to understand why women would found him attractive, even before they discovered he was a wealthy surgeon.

"Thanks for coming Dr. Schaeffer."

"You're welcome. No problem." He opened the door to the deli and motioned for the detective to enter first.

Detective Healy had noticed Dr. Schaeffer's slight German accent over the phone. But it was much more distinctive in person. As he proceeded to a booth on the left, he turned around and asked, "Is this good?"

"It's fine."

The waitress came out of nowhere the very second they sat down in the booth. "Can I get you something to drink?" She asked, as she handed them the voluminous deli menus.

Dr. Schaeffer said, "I'll have an iced tea with lemon and no ice."

The waitress turned to the detective and asked, "And what can I get you?"

"I'll take a diet coke."

She scribbled on the pad with her pencil and before she finished, Dr. Schaeffer asked the detective, "Do you know what you want?"

It was obvious to Detective Healy that Dr. Schaeffer wanted to move this friendly luncheon along. He decided to order the first sandwich choice that jumped out at him from the menu. "I'll take an egg salad sandwich with lettuce and tomato."

"Do you want onions and pickles on that?"

"Just pickles please."

"OK and you?" The waitress used a flirtatious inflection in her voice as she turned to Dr. Schaeffer.

"I'll have turkey, provolone cheese, lettuce and tomato on whole wheat toast--and no onions or pickles."

The waitress smiled at Dr. Schaeffer. She said, "I'll be right back with your order."

"Good." Dr. Schaeffer leaned forward with his elbows on the table and hands clasped. He looked directly into the detective's eyes and asked, "What can I do for you today Detective Healy?"

"I was contacted by Dr. Friedman when Lee Young went missing. I led the investigation into her disappearance and, as you know by now, we found her body in Pennsville, New Jersey."

Dr. Schaeffer continued to look him straight in the eyes and said solemnly, "I know. I've caught bits and pieces of the story on the news and of course I've read about it in the paper."

The waitress brought their drinks to the table. "Iced tea with lemon, no ice." She gave the detective a patronizing grin. Then she smiled at Dr. Schaeffer. "And a diet coke for you."

"Thanks." Dr. Schaeffer took a deep breath and continued, "Detective, I think we both know why you're here. Lee and I were having an affair. I'm sure in your line of work you're aware that these things happen. And in my line of work, it's the norm. The important thing is that nobody gets hurt. Neither of our spouses knew about it and I'd like to keep it that way."

Detective Healy was surprised by Dr. Schaeffer's candor. It made him believable. But only part of what he said was true. Larry Berman had told Dr. Schaeffer quite some time ago that Dr. Friedman knew about the affair.

The detective said, "We found Lee's cell phone on her. There were many calls from her husband, and the only other calls of note were the ones to and from your cell phone. It caught my attention because of the frequency. So, you're right. That is why I'm here and you've answered my question before I had a chance to ask."

Dr. Schaeffer smiled and said, "Orthopods are a very direct and no nonsense breed. We're like mechanics. We focus intensely on the problem and figure out how to fix it. Everything else is just extraneous information and a waste of time."

Their sandwiches arrived and Dr. Schaeffer ate heartily. Detective Healy's egg salad sandwich appeared to be more than two inches thick. If he had been at home, he would have managed just fine; but here with Dr. Schaefer, he was careful to wipe egg and mayonnaise from his face after each bite.

Dr. Schaeffer had already finished when the detective still had half a sandwich to go. He put his sandwich aside and asked, "Dr. Schaeffer, do you and Dr. Friedman know each other socially?"

"No. Not at all. We know of each other because it's a small medical community. I've gotten several patient referrals from his practice. But we've never consulted on a patient together or been to the same cocktail parties."

Detective Healy asked, "And what you said before about neither of your spouses knowing about the affair, are you sure that is the case?"

Dr. Schaeffer said, "Yes. I'm absolutely certain. Lee never even talked about her husband. Ironically, that led me to believe there weren't any problems in her marriage. I just think that Lee went after me for kicks. There are a lot of women like that you know."

Detective Healy grinned and then asked, "How did you meet Lee?"

"My wife Emma was a client of Lee's. Actually Lee found our house for us. Emma just called me in for my approval before we sealed the deal. I gave Lee my business card and she started to call me. She came on pretty strong, which didn't bother me. I just don't like it if other people get hurt. But Lee was cool about it. She didn't want to change her life, and she knew I had no plans to change mine."

Detective Healy was suddenly put off by Dr. Schaeffer for the first time. He thought his cavalier attitude about extramarital affairs was disturbing. He wondered if Lee really saw the affair the same way. "Are you saying that Lee never pressured you about leaving your wife?"

"No, she didn't. There was nothing like that going on. We just had some fun together. It was all pretty light stuff."

Dr. Schaeffer knew he had no choice but to lie if he wanted to avoid further involvement in the whole business of Lee's death. In truth, he knew Lee hoped he would leave Emma after she told him she was going to divorce her husband. And likewise, he saw no point in telling the detective about his conversation with Larry Berman. He thought, "It'll just muddy the waters and drag me further into this mess. I'm going to steer away from this one as soon as possible."

The waitress returned to the table. "Can I get you anything else?"

Dr. Schaeffer said, "No thanks. We'll take the check." He was used to running the show, while those around him followed his lead.

"Can I wrap that up for you?" The waitress pointed to the detective's half sandwich.

"Yes please." Detective Healy thought to himself, "Boy these doctors are smooth operators. They really know how to play it cool and take control . . . well . . . now it's my turn." He leaned forward and lowered his voice, "There's one more detail that led me to contact you."

"What's that?" Dr. Schaeffer was unfettered.

"We found semen on Lee. There was no sign of rape. Apparently Lee had sex the day she went missing."

"When was that?"

"Last Wednesday."

"I'll check my schedule. I probably did see Lee that day."

Detective Healy was appalled by Dr. Schaeffer's nonchalance. But it did indicate that he had nothing to hide. The DNA sample was only useful if Dr. Schaeffer had denied an affair. But the detective was so bothered by Dr. Schaeffer's arrogance that he thought the least he could do, for Lee's sake, was to inconvenience the good doctor. He said, "We need a DNA sample. You'll have to go to the lab on the first floor of the Wilmington police station on Market Street. Is there any way you can squeeze that in today?"

Dr. Schaeffer was angry. He resented the implication and, worse, the time it would take to do this. He looked perturbed when he asked, "Are you suggesting that I had something to do with Lee's death?"

"No. It's standard procedure for an investigation like this. I've also asked Dr. Friedman for a DNA sample."

Dr. Schaeffer looked puzzled. Detective Healy added, "Don't worry. Dr. Friedman submitted a sample yesterday so there's no chance that you'll run into each other at the lab."

Dr. Schaeffer grinned. He figured he could extricate himself from this investigation much faster if he simply complied. He said, "It's not a problem. I'll swing by there before I go home."

"I'm sorry for the inconvenience."

"It's practically on the way home. I live in Greenville so I have to drive through Wilmington anyway."

"Good."

Dr. Schaeffer asked, "Do you know what caused Lee's death?"

Detective Healy said, "The Medical Examiner said the cause of death was a heart attack."

Dr. Schaeffer looked shocked. "That's surprising. Lee was a marathon runner and she took good care of herself. She seemed to be in excellent health."

Once again Detective Healy thought there was something honest and genuine about Dr. Schaeffer, in spite of his inflated ego. He said, "The heart attack was apparently brought on by some medications Lee was taking. I'm sorry, but I'm not at liberty to discuss any further details."

"I understand but it's a dam shame . . . such a beautiful, young woman." Dr. Schaeffer wondered if Lee was taking illegal drugs that may have brought on sudden death.

The waitress was back with the check, "Here you go. Have a nice day."

Dr. Schaeffer motioned to the waitress to wait for a moment. He took out his wallet and handed her a twenty-dollar bill. He winked and smiled at her and said, "Thanks. Keep the change."

The waitress smiled coyly. "Thank you."

The two men left the deli and paused to shake hands once they were outside. "Thanks for your time Dr. Schaeffer. I hope you can understand that

I'm just doing my job. I have to tie up all the loose ends before I close out the investigation."

Dr. Schaeffer said, "Of course I understand. Lee was a good woman. I'm happy that you took the time to investigate the cause of death."

Dr. Schaeffer's final words sounded a bit clinical. He was already far removed from Lee Young. She was just another fond memory and the detective could sense this.

Chapter 26: An Expert Opinion

Sunday, March 20

DR. FRIEDMAN HAD left the drapes open on the far side of the bedroom. In the early morning, the sun poured in through the transparent sheers and roused him from his sleep. It was the first restful sleep he'd had in a few weeks.

After he used the toilet, he tugged on his robe and felt comforted by its lush warmth. "I think I need some breakfast."

He finished his omelet in front of the television while CNBC ran updates of the stock market in ticker tape fashion across the bottom of the screen. Prescott-Williams shot up two points, while Inhaber-Taft held steady. He thought, "That reminds me, I have to sell my shares of Inhaber-Taft stock. I better leave a message for my broker today before I forget. He used his last wedge of toast to push a sausage link toward his fork. He got up and put the dishes in the dishwasher and washed out the frying pan. He poured himself another cup of coffee. The food and the caffeine made him feel energized and upbeat. His phone rang and he picked it up without checking caller identification.

"Hello?"

"Hi Donald, it's Jilly."

"Good morning." Donald said in a pleasant tone.

"I'm just calling to ask if you want to join us for dinner tonight?"

Donald was horrified. He thought, "The last thing on earth I want to do is . . ."

Jilly interrupted his thoughts, "Now don't be shy Donald. It's a sad and lonely time for you and it would be good for you to get out of the house."

"Thanks Jilly. You're really sweet. But as you can imagine, I'm behind on a lot of paperwork for the practice and it's only going to get worse because I won't be in the office tomorrow because of the service for Lee." He paused for dramatic effect. "The quiet house isn't so bad right now because I'll be able to get my work done."

"Alright Donald. But if you change your mind, just give us a call or come over."

"I will."

"So, we'll see you tomorrow then."

"Alright Jilly."

"Oh, Donald . . . do you want us to give you a lift to the chapel?"

"No. No thanks. I'll just see you there."

"Alright. I'll see you then."

"Okay thanks. Take care now. Bye."

Donald thought, "The paper . . . I wonder what's in it today." He went to the foyer and opened the front door. *The News Journal* and *The New York Times* were both wrapped in plastic on the front porch. The sun had retreated behind a gray sky and it promised to be a gloomy day. He shut the door and returned to the great room. He flipped the switch for the gas fireplace and returned to his cushiony chair. He snapped the crease out of the newspaper and the front page of *The News Journal* hung in front of him.

Suddenly he jumped out of his chair when he saw the sidebar headline: "Medical Examiner Says Lee Young Died of Heart Attack." His heart was pounding. He scanned the article before actually reading it, and Dr. DiStefano's name popped out at him. His heart beat faster, "What the hell?"

He dropped back into the chair and sat close to the light. He had forgotten that, coincidentally, Dr. DiStefano was on the panel of medical experts for the Delaware newspaper. Apparently the reporter sought his expertise, as a Cardiologist, to explain to readers how it was possible for an athletic woman like Lee Young to die of a heart attack.

Dr. DiStefano was quoted as saying, "Keep in mind that we must respect patient privacy. We don't know the details of what the Medical Examiner found to be the cause of the heart attack; nor is it appropriate for me to speculate about a particular patient. I can only provide information about the detrimental effects of marathon training that can occur in some individuals, albeit relatively rare. Marathon runners can develop left ventricular hypertrophy, or enlargement of the heart. Some long distance runners actually cause structural damage to their hearts via the chronic, sustained oxygen demands that such intense exercise places on the heart. Oddly enough, it is the same damage brought on by congestive heart failure. To put it in laymen's terms, there are two functions provided by the heart. The first is maintaining systolic blood pressure. Systole is when the heart contracts and expels oxygenated blood into the systemic circulation. The second, is maintaining diastolic blood pressure. Diastole is when the heart muscle dilates or relaxes in order to allow it to fill with blood. A marathon runner is continually pumping more and more blood into the left ventricle of the heart because they require more oxygenated blood to be expelled from the heart into the systemic circulation. Fortunately, the physiology of most runners is capable of complying with the increased demands. However, in some individuals, the heart muscle cannot respond to the increased demand in a natural, healthy way. Instead, the elasticity of the heart muscle is weakened because of greater filling pressure. The muscle compensates for this cardiac overload by enlarging and stretching. This causes it to lose elasticity and the ability to maintain a healthy diastolic blood pressure. This, in turn, affects systolic blood pressure. Instead of pumping all of the blood out of the heart during systole, some of the blood regurgitates back and this effects pulmonary circulation. This can result in an acute event such as sudden cardiac death or it progresses into the stages of congestive heart failure."

Dr. Friedman said out loud, "Perfect! Just perfect. Joe, you son of a bitch, I love you!"

The Medical Examiner could not disclose the cause of the heart attack because of patient privacy laws. Additionally, Dr. Pagoshi, the hospital, the newspapers, and the police were all aware they could be slapped with a lawsuit by the pharmaceutical giant, Inhaber-Taft, if they alleged their product had caused the heart attack. All that Dr. Pagoshi could do, in accordance with

FDA regulations, was to report this adverse event to Inhaber-Taft. In turn, the drug company was expected to report this to the FDA.

Dr. Friedman immediately called Dr. DiStefano, but got his message service. He thought, "That's right. Sunday morning he does hospital rounds." He decided to leave a message right away because he wanted him to know how grateful he was.

"Hey Joe, it's Donald." Suddenly he thought, "Wait a minute, I can't say too much on the tape in case it's ever subpoenaed in court." He continued in a more guarded fashion, "I just read the article in the newspaper. It must have been difficult for you to be consulted for this article. But as always, you did a first class job. Thanks Joe. I'll catch you later." He feared he may have sounded too lighthearted, so he quickly added, after a sigh of despair, "I hope to see you at the service tomorrow."

Then he thought about the lawsuit. "Shit! I have to sell my Inhaber-Taft stock. It's only natural that I would sell it now, after learning that their product caused my wife's death. They can't prove there was any discussion of a lawsuit prior to the sale . . . and I couldn't ask for better timing. I'll sell high now. Once the lawsuit is picked up by the media, and hopefully that won't happen until it's settled out of court, the stock will take a nose dive."

He looked up his broker's phone number on his cell and pressed the send button.

"Hello, this is Steve Weinstein."

"Steve. Hi, it's Donald Friedman."

"Hey Dr. Friedman. What can I do for you?"

"I want you to sell my Inhaber-Taft stock and use the money to buy more Prescott-Williams."

"Do you want me to wait until it hits a particular price per share?"

"No. I'm happy with the current share price so you can move forward."

"Good. Consider it done. Anything else?"

"No thanks. That's it."

"Dr. Friedman, I'm very sorry to hear about your wife's passing."

"Thank you Steve."

"I hate to be too practical at a time like this, but do we have to change the beneficiary on any of your investments?"

"No. My children were the beneficiaries on my stock investments, so you don't have to change anything."

"I thought that was the case, but I just wanted to double check with you."

"Thanks. I think we're all set."

"Good. Take care Dr. Friedman."

"Thanks Steve."

Dr. Friedman picked up *The News Journal* to see if there were any more articles about Lee. He checked the obituaries and sure enough, there was a headshot of Lee wearing a big, friendly smile. He thought, "Grant must have submitted this." He read the little blurb stating that "Lee Young's husband, son, family and friends lost Lee suddenly," and there was information about the service the next day. He made a grimace and thought, "Oh well, at least the obit gives the impression that we're one big, happy family."

Detective Healy went to church with his wife and two young daughters. Afterwards, they stopped at the grocery store because, as usual, they were out of milk and bread. For lunch, his wife made them toasted cheese and ham sandwiches with potato chips and pickles as a garnish. When they finished eating, the little girls ran upstairs to play with their Barbie dolls and the detective walked over to his wife at the sink.

He kissed her softly on the neck and said, "Why don't you let me do the dishes?"

She smiled without looking away from the dishpan and said, "It's alright honey. I've got it. Why don't you get your paperwork done now so you don't have to worry about it after dinner tonight."

He slipped his arms around her slender waist and whispered, "Why? Do you have plans for me tonight?"

She slipped her Playtex gloves off and set them on the edge of the dishpan. She turned around and faced him. She grabbed his buttocks in both hands and they laughed. She said, "I think we're about due for some fun tonight."

He hugged her tightly and said, "Why don't we sneak into a nice hot bath together after the girls go to bed."

"Umm, now that sounds good. Maybe I can convince them to go up a little earlier tonight." They smooched a little bit and she added, "Hey, I'll take them to the park this afternoon and let them run around. That should make it easier to get them to bed early."

"I like the way you think."

She gave his butt a tap and said, "Alright, get your work done."

"Alright honey. I'll be in my office." Detective Healy walked into the living room and sat down at his desk in the corner of the room. It wasn't a private office but the girls knew they shouldn't bother their daddy while he was sitting at his desk. But every now and then, they snuck in the room to charm him into a break. He had lots of notes that were neatly tucked into a file labeled, "Lee Young." He had a ritualistic approach to an investigation. At the outset, he jotted down facts and questions as they arose. As he answered questions, they were classified as supplemental facts in the case.

He relied on his training to thoroughly analyze the facts, but experience taught him to trust his intuition. Unfortunately, intuition doesn't stand up in court, so evidence was always crucial. When no evidence was discovered, the facts simply converged into theories, which made it easy for a defense attorney to create reasonable doubt.

His notes had curled edges and a few coffee stains, but it was the content that mattered to Detective Healy. He spread out his notes and ordered them by the names of those he had interviewed. He picked up a paper with Michael Poong's name. He had written, "NOTE to file: When I spoke to Michael Poong (sales manager for Inhaber-Taft), I told him that Debbie Kaminski (sales rep for Inhaber-Taft) had told me that he coached the sales reps to promote the highest dose of MELAVOX as safe and appropriate for long term use. He adamantly denied this. He stated he would never instruct his sales reps to tell a physician anything about a product that is outside of the FDA approved indications. It's a classic case of 'he said/she said.' I doubled back and asked a couple of the sales reps about what Debbie Kaminski alleged, and they concurred (on condition of anonymity) that what Debbie had told me was true. This information validates Dr. Friedman's rationale for the doses he prescribed.

At one point, he had considered Dr. Schaeffer as a possible suspect. He read from his notes: "The DNA samples proved that Lee had sex with

Edgar Schaeffer on the day she went missing. The absence of trauma indicates the sex was consensual. During my interview with Dr. Schaeffer, he was forthright about his affair with Lee. I am convinced it was nothing more than a casual affair for both Lee Young and Dr. Schaeffer. There was nothing to suggest that Lee pressured Dr. Schaeffer to leave his wife in order to marry her. No evidence of blackmail and no evidence to support Dr. Schaeffer as a suspect."

Initially, the prime suspect was Dr. Friedman. Detective Healy had written, "The affair was the only motive for Dr. Friedman to kill his wife. After a thorough investigation, I believe that Dr. Friedman had no prior knowledge of the affair."

One miscellaneous item caught his attention: What happened to Lee's wedding and engagement rings? He noted that a vengeful husband usually removes the rings if he finds out about an affair. Detective Healy remembered Dr. Friedman asking about the rings. He had neglected to inform him that the Wilmington Police Department received a call from a pawnshop in Woodstown, New Jersey. One of the teenagers who found Lee's body had apparently removed the rings and tried to sell them to a pawnshop in the same county.

Detective Healy read the information obtained from his deputy. "My deputy, Mike Devine, watched Dr. Friedman's house for a full two weeks and observed no suspicious activities. Dr. Friedman simply went to work and came home again. His behavior and demeanor were consistent with that of a man mourning the loss of his wife."

Detective Healy had completed his analysis of the facts, and he was satisfied by a gut feeling that he had left no stone unturned. He dropped his pen onto the desktop and leaned back into his chair. He shook his head and thought, "It's enough to make you afraid to take prescription medicine."

Donald opened the refrigerator and took out some cheese and olives. He nibbled at the cheese while he selected a bottle of wine. The telephone rang just after he put the bottle onto the kitchen island.

"Dr. Friedman, it's Detective Healy."

Dr. Friedman felt the cheese reflux into his throat. He forced himself to swallow and said, "Hello detective."

"I'm ready to conclude the investigation and I wondered if I could stop by for a few minutes."

"Sure. When?"

"Is this a good time for you?"

"Ah . . ." Dr. Friedman looked down at his bare feet and partially opened robe. "Can you give me about twenty minutes? I was just in the middle of another phone call about a patient."

"Sure. Let's make it 1:00 then."

"Alright, 1:00 is perfect."

"My apologies for interrupting you, Dr. Friedman."

"Not at all. I'll see you soon."

Dr. Friedman raced up the stairs and shed his robe onto the bedroom floor. Next he flung open the shower door and turned on the spigots. At the first sight of steam, he stepped in.

He showered, shaved and dressed. His feelings vacillated between an ego driven feeling of invincibility and waves of panic.

As it neared 1:00, he stood at the ready . . . waiting . . . and then the doorbell rang.

"Detective Healy . . . hello . . . come in."

"Thanks for making some time for me today Dr. Friedman."

"Of course." He led him into the next room. "Have a seat Detective."

"Thanks."

"Can I get you something to drink?"

"No. No thank you."

Dr. Friedman said forlornly, "I haven't eaten anything again today." Then he worried the detective might notice a lingering aroma of herbs and sausage from his earlier meal so he said, "I made myself breakfast but I wound up tossing it out."

Detective Healy gave him a consoling grin and then got right to the point, "As I've told you before, there are standard procedures that I must follow in an investigation. And this case was a complicated one."

Dr. Friedman stiffened and then self-consciously tried to relax his posture.

The detective continued, "The DNA samples were reviewed and, as suspected, the semen was matched to Dr. Edgar Schaeffer."

Dr. Friedman cast his eyes downward to appear upset. He said nothing.

"I met with Dr. Schaeffer and he admitted to having an affair with Lee."

Dr. Friedman let out an exasperated sigh and said, "Bastard."

"But he said Lee had no intention of leaving you and . . . I'm sorry to put it this way but, apparently they both just saw it as a casual affair and nothing more. There was no emotional involvement."

Dr. Friedman laughed a little and said sardonically, "Well, I'm happy to know they were just having fun and weren't in love with each other."

Detective Healy quietly uttered, "touché."

There was silence between them for a moment and Dr. Friedman had a feeling the detective was finally on his side. But to his chagrin, Detective Healy said, "You may recall that, in the eleventh hour of the investigation, one of our CSI investigators was concerned that he didn't find any weeds in the tracking on the bottom of Lee's running shoes."

"Of course I remember. Did you discover anything further?"

The detective had to lie; oddly enough, to save his credibility. He straightened his posture and said, "I caught up with the investigator late in the day on Friday. In fact, I apologize. I should have called you about this on Friday night but my girls were in a play at school and we took them out for ice cream afterwards. I guess it was after 9:30 when I got home and I thought it could wait until Saturday. But, as it turned out, yesterday was an unusually hectic day. He sighed and then added, "The bottom line is that the investigator and I decided it was not a valid concern. You see, Lee's body was discovered close to the road, indicating she was only in the field long enough to stumble to a fall. As I told you before, her shoes were scuffed up in a manner consistent with the direction of her fall."

Dr. Friedman put his hand over his mouth and closed his eyes for a few seconds. He was elated, but he said, "It's difficult to hear this as you can imagine detective."

"Of course it is."

"But I think it makes sense now, based on your description of where she was found."

Detective Healy said, "I wanted to tell you in person that I've concluded our investigation. Dr. Pagoshi's autopsy results will serve as a legal record of the cause of death. Off the record Dr. Friedman, it looks like you have a lawsuit on your hands."

Dr. Friedman made a grimace and raised his eyebrows at the same time. "Maybe so," he said.

Detective Healy stood up and reached to shake Dr. Friedman's hand. He said, "I'm sorry for your loss Dr. Friedman. Good luck to you."

They shook hands and Dr. Friedman said, "Thanks detective."

This time Detective Healy took the lead as they walked to the front door. When they reached it, he turned and said, "One more thing. It seems impossible to believe right now, but people do move on from tragedies like this one. Just give yourself some time."

"I'll do my best."

As he watched the detective back down the driveway, he noticed there was no Chevy Lumina in sight. He cautiously uttered, "Yes! It's over." He locked the door and clasped his hands together. He wondered how he could celebrate.

He went downstairs to the basement level of his house and into his sauna room. He turned on the steam and stripped off his clothes. He stepped inside onto the wooden floor. He spread out a towel on one of the benches and lay down on his back. He breathed in deeply and smelled the soothing aroma of cedar. Pellets of sweat dripped from every pore of his body. He felt as if he was purging himself of the toxic memories."

Chapter 27: Remembrance

Monday, March 21

AT 7:22 A.M. ON Monday morning, Debbie returned from walking Harry in the rain. After she wrestled him partially dry with a towel, she scooped food into his bowl and coffee beans into her coffee machine. She reached for the phone and munched cold cereal, as she checked her voicemail messages. The first message superseded all others because it was identified as "Urgent, sent Sunday, March 20." Debbie's heart skipped a beat as she choked on her cereal and spit it into the sink. She thought, "Oh God! I knew I should have checked my messages yesterday!"

It was a message from Grant Preston sent on Sunday afternoon.

"Hi everybody. I'm sending this message to Michael's team and Katie's team. We're going to have a remembrance service for my mother tomorrow — Monday morning — at 11:00 at the Brandywine Chapel in Wilmington, Delaware. You are welcome to attend but please don't feel obligated. We expect it to be a simple service for family and friends. I apologize for the late notice. Please keep us in your thoughts and prayers. Thanks."

Debbie thought, "I have to go. Fortunately I don't have a lunch today."

Sales reps had many days without scheduled appointments but few days without a scheduled lunch. Debbie sent a message to Katie to let her know that she would take time off territory to attend the remembrance service.

Michael Poong and his wife, Mitzy, were about an hour outside of Wilmington at 9:00. Mitzy's blonde hair was braced behind her ears so it wouldn't interfere with her view of the notebook computer that rested on her lap. She responded to email messages and created a few of her own.

Michael glanced over at her. He liked the way he could see the tiny bones of her hands almost poke through her milky white skin in the ebb and flow of her pumping motion on the keyboard. Her TagHeur watch and Yurman bangles peaked out from under her white shirtsleeves. Michael turned his attention back to the road and his satisfied grin shone through the windshield.

Mitzy was a financial manager for Morgan Stanley. A few days each month she worked from her home office, but most days it wasn't possible because of meetings with clients. And it was always good policy to put in face time at the office. But today, there was no question that she would attend the remembrance service for Lee Young. They had socialized together many times at Inhaber-Taft functions. Of course, it was no accident that they were drawn to each other. Mitzy and Michael always sought out the right connections to broaden their career networks. Today, their main objective was an appropriate demonstration of sorrow over the untimely death of the wife of a top writer for MELAVOX — Dr. Friedman.

It was just a couple of days before, when Michael told Mitzy about Lee.

"What a terrible shock!" she gasped and pressed three tiny fingers to her lips. "Do they know what happened? Was she attacked? Was it murder?" and then the unspeakable thought escaped her lips, "Did Dr. Friedman have anything to do with it?"

"The rumor is she had a heart attack," Michael said with detachment. He walked to the sink for a glass of water. After a few swallows, he said, "I'm sure Friedman is beside himself." A burp erupted from his throat with no warning, "Excuse me." He drank the rest of the water and then turned to Mitzy with an afterthought, "I guess it's tough for Grant too."

Michael slowed the car as they approached the tollbooth in Elkton, Maryland. As he accelerated to merge with traffic, Michael recalled his conversation with Detective Healy on Sunday morning. The questions didn't bother him. In fact, Brad had already called him and told him what to expect. It was the detective's focus on MELAVOX that troubled him and, worse, the comments Debbie Kaminski had made. Michael thought, "How dare she vilify my intentions and incriminate me with her insinuations! We should have gotten rid of her a long time ago . . . what a loser. She doesn't fit in anyway. She's an oddball. I could see that from day one . . . the last thing we need in this competitive environment is a squeaky wheel who's just waiting for her chance to blow the whistle on management! . . . Her bullshit at the district meeting was bad enough, but after this . . . she's out of here! . . . What am I waiting for? I know I can convince Katie to see it my way. I just have to come up with a scenario to make it fly with Human Resources."

Then Michael had a horrible thought that made him shudder. "What if it *was* the MELAVOX that caused Lee's heart attack?"

"Are you okay Michael?" Mitzy asked.

"I'm fine." He pushed a button and turned up the heat in the car. "I'm just a little bit chilly."

Mitzy shifted her attention back to her computer.

The sky was hopelessly gray and a spritz of cold rain drizzled incessantly. The temperature of 39 degrees was unseasonably cold for March, and wind gusts made it feel colder. Debbie made a couple of sales calls before she decided to drive over to Brandywine Chapel for the memorial service. Her glasses were covered with water beads that swam around in a dizzying kaleidoscope on her lenses. She had menstrual cramps and felt a sudden wave of nausea, before she removed her glasses and wiped them with a tissue. She thought about the service. "I hope it doesn't turn out to be a circus with the reps trying to outdo each other with feigned despair."

Dr. Friedman dusted the top of his head the way balding men do, when he entered the vestibule of the chapel. He saw Jilly transporting purple orchids, in white porcelain pots, to the front of the altar. She held one in each hand, which meant she had to make several trips back and forth to the table that held about a dozen of them. Dr. Friedman picked up the last two and started to walk up the aisle. Jilly met him half way with a warm smile. She said, "They're from Dr. DiStefano. Aren't they beautiful?"

Dr. Friedman grinned. "Yes, they are."

He followed Jilly to the marble altar and admired the way she arranged the orchids. Initially, he thought the cobalt blue urn was an adornment for the altar. As he admired the gold trim around the edges, it struck him. The urn was filled with Lee's ashes! Suddenly, he was crestfallen. He reached his hands to his face and shifted his balance. Grant came out of nowhere and grabbed him. They both thought he might faint.

Donald waved him away with his hand. "I'm okay. Thanks Grant. I just need to sit down."

Grant and Jilly ushered him over to the nearest pew. But in an instant, Donald's remorse dissipated. He thought, "I wonder if her feelings for me were ever real. Maybe Edgar wasn't the first one . . . maybe Edgar was just the latest one. I'll never know."

He looked directly at the urn and thought, "Thanks to you, I'll be worth more than Edgar . . . a dozen times over . . . and then some." He turned around and was surprised to see the chapel filling up. He saw Larry Berman and Joe DiStefano sitting next to each other. Their wives sat together on Larry's right side. He worried, "I have to remind Joe that Larry doesn't know the truth. He might just think I confided in Larry."

Dr. DiStefano grinned at Donald and gave him a wink. But Donald couldn't respond in kind. He knew all eyes were on him, so he gave Joe and Larry a cursory wave and wore a hopeless grimace on his face. Then he turned and faced the front of the chapel. Fortunately it was appropriate for him to be antisocial at the moment.

The sales reps hung their raincoats on the racks in the vestibule and stashed their umbrellas in the corner in one big homogenous clump of black metal mush. They slicked back their hair and tugged at the bottoms of their sport coats to straighten out the wrinkles, as they entered the chapel. They wore navy blue and charcoal gray suits and a practiced look of empathetic grief. They reminded themselves to tone down the swagger as they made their way down the aisle. Their demure descent into the pews belied their burning desire to see and be seen. They weren't thinking about Lee while they were waiting for the service to begin. Instead they were planning their strategic maneuvers to shake hands with as many doctors as they could before it was over. And no one was going anywhere until Dr. Friedman witnessed the solemnity of their sorrow. If the family announced a reception after the service, they were all going. After that, most of them planned to go home. As expected, many physicians were in attendance. They would simply report their physician sightings as sales calls.

Grant and Jilly sat beside Dr. Friedman. Lee's parents sat quietly and respectfully in the pew in back of them. They would have felt disingenuous in the first pew. Lee had made her choice many years ago. She had slipped away from her family "as easily as a bird molts its feathers," her mother had said.

Her father thought of his wife's disturbing words when they neared the chapel. She had said, "Lee put on a new skin, as slyly as the serpent does. She hid from her roots and that is what pulled her back into the earth."

Now the minister stood by the altar and faced the mourners. With outstretched arms he looked up toward the heavens and then down. He slowly raised his head, as he brought his arms together and folded his hands in prayer. The sidebar conversations stopped and everyone shifted into a respectful silence. The minister said, "Today we remember Lee Young and the joy that she brought to us."

Donald looked down at the floor, feigning a sullen disposition. He thought, "Let's get this over with."

The minister continued, "We also hope to comfort those closest to her in this time of grief. It is often said . . ."

That was the last phrase that managed to garner the undivided attention of the alleged mourners. The pharmaceutical sales reps and their managers turned out in force. Inhaber-Taft was not the only company represented. When the word got out about a memorial service for the wife of Dr. Friedman, there was no more important place for the sales reps to be. A show of sympathy over the loss of his wife was an important building block in their relationship with him. After all, if a sales rep convinced Dr. Friedman to write for his or her product, he had the potential to write enough scripts to push a rep's numbers over the hump of planned objectives.

The minister ended his eulogy with, "Family and friends of Lee are invited to Harry's Grille for a luncheon. Thank you for coming today."

Molly giggled and whispered to Blaire, "Hey, for once, lunch is on him!"

Blaire maintained a serious expression, as she whispered to Molly, "Yeah. That'll be nice for a change."

Debbie caught Dr. Friedman's eye as he proceeded down the aisle, ahead of the crowd. He glared at her with disdain. She worried, "Why did he look at me like that? . . . Maybe I'm imagining things."

As they stood and waited their turn to proceed out of the chapel, everyone was checking each other out to see who was there and to make note of the no-shows. Debbie saw Katie MacDonaugh and she wasn't surprised. She thought, "Of course it's good business for Katie to be here. I'm sure Michael Poong is here somewhere too." Then she spotted his slight frame and their eyes met. She grinned at Michael but he looked right through her with a dead stare. She thought, "Oh God. I wonder if the detective told him what I said . . . or maybe David Clarke told Michael that I ratted him out for being drunk after the district meeting." She watched Michael's wife, Mitzy. She was talking to Dr. DiStefano's wife as they made their way down the aisle to the foyer of the chapel, where Dr. Friedman, Grant, and Jilly formed a tiny reception line.

When it was her turn, Debbie shook their hands and was relieved that this time Dr. Friedman had a serene look on his face. "Thanks for coming," he said.

Debbie said, "I'm sorry about your loss. I'll keep you in my prayers." She noticed that his eyes immediately shifted to the next person and again he said, "Thanks for coming."

Debbie walked over to the slushy pile of umbrellas and talked quietly to a few of the reps she knew. She picked up her umbrella and then walked out of the chapel. There were physicians and reps talking and laughing at the bottom of the stairs that led to the parking lot. Debbie thought, "Can't they at least wait until they get to the reception? Nobody has any respect anymore." She looked in the direction of her car and started toward it.

Just as she shut the door of her car, it started to rain heavily. She watched people launch umbrellas and dash to their cars. Keys dangled in anticipation because every moment counted. It could mean the difference between tousled, damp hair and something resembling a rat's nest. She pulled her car around and sat in a line of traffic waiting to exit the parking lot. She set the switch for her windshield wipers to a faster pace and followed the cars that headed toward Harry's Grille.

Jilly said, "I'll drive."

Grant didn't argue. He sat quietly in the passenger seat. He thought it was disturbing that the minister had handed him the urn and a plastic bag at the same time. He had said, "You might want to protect the urn with this plastic bag."

They were among the last to leave the chapel, and by the time they arrived at the restaurant, the parking lot was almost full. Jilly had to park the car quite a distance from the entrance.

Grant turned to Jilly with a forlorn expression and said, "Do we have to do this?"

"No . . . but we should." Jilly leaned over to kiss Grant and brushed her fingers against his cheek. "It'll be alright honey."

Grant shook his head in agreement but remained silent as Jilly got out of the car. He turned around to put the urn in the backseat and then started to cry. The sound of voices made him stop self-consciously, and he wiped his face. He could hear Jilly talking to someone and then realized it was his father. Jilly said, "Well, he's doing as well as can be expected Mason."

Grant grabbed for a tissue in his pocket, blew his nose, and ran his fingers through his hair. He got out of the car and looked at Mason on the other side of the car. "Hi Dad."

They met halfway around the car and embraced. Mason kept his hand on Grant's shoulder and said, "Come on. Let's go inside."

When the luncheon was over, Dr. Friedman felt exhilarated as he drove home. He thought, "The worst part is over. Now I just have to wait for Larry to do his part."

Larry Berman had taken him aside at the restaurant and said, "We just have to wait for a response from the corporate legal department of Inhaber-Taft."

Donald started to smile broadly and then caught himself. His eyes were smiling but he kept a straight face and said, "You filed?"

Larry gripped Donald's shoulder with fatherly affection. He said, "Bubby, I've got you covered. We're on our way and I'm going to win this one for you. There's no way these bastards are getting away with this!"

Donald reached out his hand and then decided to hug Larry instead. Suddenly, Donald felt a tap on his shoulder and he immediately changed his facial expression to a practiced look of grief. When he saw that it was Dr. DiStefano he said, "Hey Joe."

Dr. DiStefano gave Donald a consoling hug and said, "Donald, promise you'll let me know whatever I can do to help."

Dr. Friedman said, "Thanks Joe. I'll do that." After all, they had to keep up appearances. But Donald felt strange. He knew he could trust Dr. DiStefano with his terrible secret but he couldn't help but wonder if Larry was keeping his secret too. He never uttered a word to Larry about his guilt yet somehow, in that moment, he felt as if all three of them knew.

PART IV

The customer (physician) is always right . . .

Chapter 28: The Dog Days of Summer

Three months later, mid-June

"EXCUSE ME DR. Friedman, I have Dr. DiStefano on line two."

"Thanks Joan." As he began to walk briskly toward his office, he heard a pharmaceutical sales rep call out to him, with the same words he hears at least a dozen times each day:

"Hi Dr. Friedman. Do you have a minute?"

Dr. Friedman turned around because he didn't recognize the voice. It was a new sales rep. And she was gorgeous--young, Black, tall, with piercing green eyes and a short haircut.

Dr. Friedman was intrigued so he stopped briefly and said, "Not right now. I have to take a phone call. What company are you with?"

She smiled and reached out her hand to shake his. Dr. Friedman shook her hand. He was surprised to feel excited when he grasped the tiny hand with such smooth skin.

She said, "I'm with Stampford Pharmaceuticals and my name is Yvette."

His momentary infatuation subsided when he heard the name of the company. Stampford was one of many small pharmaceutical companies that would surely be gobbled up by one of the big players. He couldn't even think of which products they had. He asked, "What products do you sell?"

She said, "DURASOL. It's a generic Ace Inhibitor for the treatment of hypertension."

Now Dr. Friedman was really sorry he wasted a moment talking to her. He said, "Yvette, someone on my staff should have told you that we ask sales reps to catch up with our physicians in the sample room down the hall. We're too busy to be interrupted in the hallway when we're in between patients."

Yvette was apologetic, "I'm sorry Dr. Friedman. I didn't know."

He said, "It's okay. No problem." Then he continued on to his office and shut the door.

Yvette was left standing in the hallway, feeling embarrassed. She thought, "Great. The first time I call on Dr. Friedman and he's already pissed at me." She swallowed her pride and walked across the large office area to the doorway of the sample room. There was another sales rep in there talking to Dr. Bichotti. Yvette knew about the unwritten rules of professional courtesy. She was told about them when she spent a day in the field before she was hired. If another rep is talking to a physician, get out of the way. Yvette poked her head into the reception area and said to Joyce, "I'm sorry. I'm a new rep and I didn't know that I was supposed to wait for the doctors in the sample room." She motioned to the rep across the hall with Dr. Bichotti and said, "I'll go sit in the waiting room until she's done."

Joyce smiled and said, "Okay. No problem."

Yvette said, "Thanks," and opened the door to a packed waiting room. She spotted the only empty chair and quickly went over and sat down. Almost immediately, the man in the chair next to her started sneezing and coughing. She didn't want to offend him by getting up and walking away, so she remained seated. She thought, "I guess I better get used to being around sick people everyday." She put her sample bag on the floor and as she reached into her briefcase to take out her laptop computer, the man sneezed loudly and a strand of mucous landed on the arm of her suit jacket. She squinted her eyes and furrowed her brow when she saw it lying there on her sleeve. She was at a loss as to how to remove it from her jacket.

The man said, "Excuse me. I'm sorry."

Yvette said, "It's alright." She stood up nervously and noticed the restroom on the other side of the room. She thought, "Thank God." She walked into the bathroom and shut the door. She pulled out a bunch of paper towels and wet them with hot water. Then she wiped her sleeve clean and proceeded to wash her hands multiple times. She talked quietly to herself in the mirror as she dried her hands, "This day can only get better."

Dr. Friedman said, "Joe, what's up?"

"Donald, hey, what's up, buddy. Listen, I wanted to give you a heads up about this MELAVOX problem."

"What MELAVOX problem?"

It had been three months since Larry filed Dr. Friedman's lawsuit against Inhaber-Taft. Larry was having ongoing discussions with their corporate legal department and it looked as if they were moving closer to an out-of-court settlement.

Dr. DiStefano said, "I'm starting to see a correlation between the use of MELAVOX and the incidence of heart attacks and stroke."

Dr. Friedman lowered his voice, even though his door was shut and said, "Well Joe, you're a Cardiologist, so why is it a bad thing if you're seeing thromboembolic events caused by MELAVOX? If anything, this will only strengthen my case. And since when do you prescribe MELAVOX anyway?" They both knew he would only prescribe Prescott-Williams's "me too" drug, TENAVOX, which was indicated for osteoarthritis. And although he was a cardiologist, most of his patients knew he would prescribe a drug for whatever ailed them.

Dr. DiStefano said, "I don't prescribe MELAVOX. I never have. But these patients are referred to me by their family practice docs who had them on MELAVOX for osteoarthritis and pain. Then they throw a stroke or an MI and land in the hospital. The family docs are consulting me and starting to ask if I think there's a connection to MELAVOX. The other day, Steve Roberts reminded me about the METAPO study to back up his assertion that it's the MELAVOX that caused heart attacks in two of his patients. I've been holding out on reporting the adverse events to Inhaber-Taft because . . ."

Donald finished the sentence for him, ". . . because Inhaber-Taft will have to turn the information over to the FDA. Shit!"

"You got it Donald! Then the FDA will demand a new warning label for MELAVOX. And once that hits the media, patients are going to start claiming that any adverse reaction was the fault of the drug."

Dr. Friedman said, "Then a couple of savvy lawyers will start advertising a class action lawsuit."

"That's why I wanted to give you a heads up. I know you're trying to settle your lawsuit out of court. We both know you'll never get as much money if you're forced into a class action suit. But listen, my ass is on the line. I have to report this stuff to Inhaber-Taft. And these MI's and strokes are increasing exponentially because so many docs are writing scripts for the max dose of MELAVOX."

"You're right Joe. I don't want to be involved in a class action lawsuit. I'll get peanuts if that happens."

"You're goddamn right. The only players who make real money in a class action suit are the lawyers." Then he lowered his voice and whispered into the phone, "Hey, did you get rid of your Inhaber stock yet?"

"Yeah. I called my broker a few months ago and dumped the stock. I figured they couldn't come after me for insider trading because it was only natural that I would want to sell my stock in a company whose drug killed my wife."

"Good. It's good you got rid of it right away because I have a feeling the FDA is going to wind up taking MELAVOX off the market."

Dr. Friedman asked, "Hey, what are you doing about TENAVOX then?" Prescott-Williams had launched their COX II Inhibitor at the beginning of May.

Dr. DiStefano said confidently, "I've been prescribing it since it hit the market." But he knew what Dr. Friedman was alluding to, so he added, "It's not going to be a problem because it doesn't inhibit COX II to the extent that MELAVOX does, so it's not going to cause people to stroke out." He whispered into the phone again, "Between you and me, MELAVOX is a goddamn effective pain reliever — probably the best non-narcotic out there. TENAVOX doesn't provide the same level of pain relief, but you know I'm a Prescott-Williams guy."

Dr. Friedman laughed and said, "You don't have to remind anybody about that Joe. Listen, thanks for heads up. I'm going to call Larry right now and tell him to get this thing settled."

"Cool."

Dr. Friedman asked, "Is it possible for you to hold off for a couple more days before you report your findings to Inhaber-Taft?"

"Donald, you know the FDA wants us to report adverse events as they occur. But I'll wait another week if you need it."

"Alright, let me call Larry. Thanks again Joe."

"Sure."

Dr. Friedman immediately called Larry Berman.

"Larry, it's Donald. We have a problem . . ."

Larry knew from previous product liability cases that physicians were expected to report adverse events to the pharmaceutical company who, in turn, compiled the data and reported to the FDA. There were always side effects, but it was important to watch for alarming trends in frequency or severity.

Larry asked, "Did Joe report the adverse events to Inhaber-Taft?"

"Not yet. He said he wanted to give me a heads up first. But he can only wait another week at most, otherwise his ass is in hot water."

"Alright. Relax bubby. Believe it or not, this is a good thing."

"A good thing? How?"

"We'll spin this to our advantage because Inhaber-Taft's corporate counsel is already moving closer to a number we'll be happy with. But it's time to play hard ball. I'll contact their lawyers today and threaten to go to the news media to tell them that MELAVOX caused Lee's fatal heart attack. If they think they had a problem with the METAPO Study, how do they think the public will react when they find out that a drug, which is advertised on television multiple times a day, caused the death of a physician's wife! I'll push them for an immediate settlement. And I'm sure we'll get it because their lawyers are smart enough to know they'll be staring down the muzzle of a class action lawsuit. But worse, their stock will plummet, and the news about their blockbuster drug will have people running to their doctors asking them to change their medication."

"You're beautiful Larry."

"I know. Let me make some calls and I'll get back to you."

"Good. Thanks."

Yvette looked at her watch. Almost half an hour had gone by since she returned to her seat in the waiting room. Two other pharmaceutical sales reps had entered the office and then left again when they saw her sitting there. They could tell by her good looks and the way she was dressed that she was a pharma sales rep. They would wait in the parking lot until they saw her leave. Then, it was their turn.

Yvette closed her laptop after she reported the one sales call she had made before calling on this group. She was silently practicing her product detail when a nurse opened the door that led to the exam rooms. She looked at a patient chart and said, "Mr. Menendez?" The man next to Yvette stood up and walked toward the nurse.

"Hi Mr. Menendez. Follow me please." Yvette was relieved. She sat back in the chair and relaxed for a minute, when the door opened again suddenly. This time it was the other sales rep who was finally leaving the sample room. She looked at Yvette and smiled coyly and then left. Yvette was used to women giving her the cold shoulder. Her mother told her it was because she was a beautiful, Black woman and they were intimidated by her. Yvette reminded herself of this often, and even believed it once in a while.

She stood up and gathered her sample bag, briefcase, sample signature pad, and detail pieces. She walked over to the reception desk and gave Joyce an inquisitive look. Joyce motioned that it was OK for her to go back. Yvette busied herself with perusing the sample bins while she waited for a physician. She didn't see a bin for DURASOL. She wondered, "Should I ask Joyce if I can make a new sample bin for my product? Maybe I better wait until I talk to some of the physicians and hopefully I'll convince one of them to sign for samples." She leaned against the counter and slouched her posture, while she waited. She heard someone coming down the hall. It was a woman's voice. She stood up straight and took a calming breath.

"Hi," she said anxiously as soon as the woman entered the sample room. It was a medical assistant in blue scrubs. She looked at Yvette and said in a nonplussed fashion, "Hi."

Yvette said, "My name is Yvette Moman. I'm with Stampford Pharmaceuticals. Are you a nurse?"

The medical assistant said, "No. I'm not a nurse but I might as well be one. That's what we tell everybody anyway. But the truth is, they don't want to hire nurses because they cost too much. So they hire medical assistants and call us nurses in front of the patients. In the meantime we get paid half the salary a nurse would get, but at least it's a job right?"

Yvette smiled.

"Oh and my name is Ayisha." As she reached into the refrigerator to take out a vaccine vial, Yvette noticed that Ayisha had a large tattoo of a snake on her forearm.

Yvette said, "It's nice to meet you Ayisha."

Ayisha uncapped a syringe and inserted it into the vial. She withdrew the contents and tapped at the syringe with her middle finger and then left the room. Ayisha doubled back and said to Yvette, "One of the doctors should be in here soon."

Yvette smiled. She was happy that Ayisha gave her a show of support. "Thanks Ayisha." She straightened her jacket and her posture and stood at the ready and waited.

Debbie enjoyed the respite of cool air conditioning in her car. Earlier that morning, she made her usual half dozen trips to her trunk, with cardboard boxes filled with product samples, and then back down the basement steps for more. So far she had made three sales calls and was intermittently sweating outside and cooling off inside.

She felt apprehensive as she drove to the Wilmington office of Better Health Physicians. She had followed Dr. Friedman's instructions to lay low for a while at their offices. Katie MacDonaugh had agreed that by now Joan had enough time to cool down after the incident that left Debbie and Joan at odds with one another. Initially, Debbie was relieved that Katie was nonplussed by the whole thing, and she easily moved forward. But lately, Debbie noticed that Katie was not as bubbly and friendly when they worked together. She thought Katie was sometimes abrupt and even aloof with her, but she didn't know why.

During her exile from the offices of Better Health Physicians, Harrison Johnson called on them each week to ensure they had enough samples at both locations. Then one day, out of the blue, Debbie heard that Harrison Johnson was fired! There were rumors about the cause but it remained a mystery. Debbie couldn't get in touch with him because he had to return his company-owned cell phone and he was no longer allowed access to the voicemail system or company email. She discovered his home phone number was unlisted. If he had committed some egregious behavior, everyone would know about it, but it was the vague nature of the cause of his termination that made everybody nervous, especially Debbie. She recalled her last conversation with him.

Harrison had said, "Joan is constantly leaving me voicemail messages asking me for more samples at the Wilmington office — even if I just left them the day before. I know they see a lot of patients and use a lot of samples but it's weird. I mean, she leaves me messages every single day. And after you told me about what they did to you, I can't help thinking that it's Dr. Friedman behind it. He's always busting my balls. He's always ribbing me about getting me fired. I feel like him and Joan are trying to set me up or something."

Debbie had an eerie feeling that Harrison might be right. She had said to him, "You know, one time Dr. Friedman said to me that he was going to get rid of you first and then me."

"Why?" Harrison asked with an earnest despair in his voice.

Debbie hesitated a moment. She decided to tell him. "I hate to say it, but Dr. Friedman has made comments to me that were very prejudiced."

Harrison laughed and said, "You noticed that too?"

Debbie felt like a weight had been lifted because she could finally talk to someone about it — someone who would believe her. She said, "Harrison, he's not just prejudiced toward Black people. He has said terrible things to me about German people. He knows I'm not German, but he says it to hurt me in an indirect way because he knows that my ex-husband was German and my current boyfriend is German."

Harrison asked, "Why does he want to hurt you?"

"Who knows? For the same bizarre reason that he wants to make your life miserable . . . which is to say, he doesn't have a reason. He doesn't need a reason."

Harrison said, "Right. He's just a ball buster because he can be. He's a sick son of a bitch."

"Yeah. That's the sad truth."

Harrison had said, "I'll just keep my head low and make sure I keep them happy, although that's getting harder to do."

"All we can do is try Harrison."

Debbie pulled into the busy parking lot of Better Health Physicians. She was listening to NPR on her car radio. It was the top of the 11:00 a.m. hour and time for the news update, beginning with the weather report. She parked her car and stopped for a minute to listen.

" . . . and more record high temperatures for the second day in a row. It's expected to reach a high of 98 degrees by late this afternoon. The current temperature is 92 degrees with lots of sunshine. The American Heart Association is reminding the elderly and anyone with a history of cardiac disease to limit outdoor activities. Those who suffer from asthma and allergies are alerted to poor air quality and, as always, keep your pets cool and out of your vehicles. It only takes about 15 minutes for your dog's body temperature to increase to life threatening levels when they are left in a hot car, regardless of whether the car is in the shade or the sun. Depending upon your dog's age and general health, your dog could suffer a heat stroke or malignant hyperthermia."

As she got out of the car, Debbie said out loud, "Ninety two degrees! Phwew. It feels hotter than that."

She was wearing an A-line dress with no sleeves. It was one of her favorites — a pale yellow color, accented with a string of pearls. She glanced at the van parked on the other side of her car. It was an old van with chrome around the windows and she was temporarily blinded by the bright sun that bounced off the chrome. She squinted and looked away toward the cars on the other side of the lot. The macadam was recently resealed, and it was already so hot that she could see iridescent steam rise above the smooth, blacktop surface. She bent down and reached into the backseat of her car to get her sample bag. She dropped some papers onto the ground and grumbled, "Shit!" She dusted the dirt from the papers and gathered her belongings together.

As she shut her car door, she thought she heard a yelp from the direction of the van. She looked over and saw a big brown Labrador Retriever panting in the window. He looked at her with sad eyes and yelped again. He was panting heavily and now his tongue drooled on the window that was cracked open just about two inches. All of the other windows were shut except the one he looked out of. Debbie was horrified. "Oh my God! He'll die in there from heat stroke by the time they finish waiting in the doctor's office."

She hurried toward the office. She saw a patient signing in at the reception desk as she entered, so she remained near the door to be courteous. The air conditioning blasted extremely cold air throughout the room and she immediately felt her sweat evaporate. She almost felt guilty about her relief from the heat when she remembered the big dog in the hot van outside. She glanced around the full waiting room and asked, "Does anybody here own the van in the parking lot with a dog in it?"

No one said anything. A couple of people looked at each other or shifted in their seats.

Debbie directed her attention to a man who made eye contact with her. She said to him, "I just heard on the radio that it takes only about fifteen minutes for a dog to suffer heat stroke."

A woman with a raspy smoker's voice said defensively, "It's my van, and my dog is fine in there."

Debbie looked in the direction of the voice and saw a woman in her forties who looked haggard from the heat and from life. She was sitting next to a teenage girl, who must have been her daughter. They both glared at Debbie. Neither one of them made an attempt to head for the door to take care of their dog.

Debbie was careful to be diplomatic in her tone, rather than accusatory. She said, "It's probably a good idea to open up the windows and let the dog get some air."

The woman snapped back, "He *does* have air. I left a window open."

Debbie said, "Yeah. I saw that, but it's opened just a crack and your dog could suffer heat stroke by the time you're finished here."

The woman straightened her posture and swept back the hair on her neck. She wore an expression like she was itching for a fight and said, "How dare you tell me how to take care of my dog. I take that dog wherever I go."

Debbie was shocked by the woman's ignorant, stubborn attitude. She shook her head and realized there was nothing more she could do.

The woman and her daughter whispered to each other. The young girl started to get up. But her mother drew her arm across her daughter's chest and motioned for her to sit back down.

Debbie saw that the patient at the reception desk had finished, so she walked up to the window. "Hi Joyce," she said with a smile, but her heart was beating wildly. She was already nervous about how Joyce and Joan and the rest of the staff would react to her. Now she compounded her troubles by getting a patient angry at her.

Joyce smiled and acted as if she had just seen Debbie the day before. She said, "Hi Debbie. You can go back."

Debbie smiled. She was so relieved that Joyce was friendly. She decided to follow her cue and pretended that no time had lapsed since her last visit. "Thanks Joyce."

She opened the door and immediately turned right into the sample room. She was surprised to see a rep there. She said, "Oh, I'm sorry. Joyce said it was alright for me to go back."

Yvette smiled and said, "Oh, it's OK. I'm new and it's my first time here." Debbie was happy the rep seemed genuinely nice.

"My name is Yvette Moman. I'm with Stampford Pharmaceuticals."

Debbie set her briefcase down on the floor and reached out to Yvette with a smile. "I'm Debbie Kaminski with Inhaber-Taft."

Joyce walked into the sample room. She looked at Yvette and said, "I'm sorry. I forgot you were still here."

Yvette said, "It's OK."

Debbie said, "I'll go back to the waiting room until you're done. It was nice to meet you Yvette. Good luck."

"Nice to meet you too. Thanks."

Joyce opened the door to the waiting room and held it for Debbie. She said, "I'm sorry about the confusion."

"No problem. I don't mind having a seat in the air conditioning on a day like this."

Joyce asked, "Is it really that bad now?"

"Yeah. They just said on the radio that it's already 92 degrees and it's going up to a record high of 98."

"Wow. I'm glad we have a rep bringing lunch today so I don't have to go outside."

Debbie sat down and thought, "Great. My first day back at this office in months and what else could go wrong."

Then she noticed that the woman who owned the van had an empty chair next to her. She thought, "Good. Maybe she let her daughter go outside to open up the windows for their dog." She didn't dare say another word to the woman. But she was curious. She thought, "I'm probably going to have to wait here a while. I could pretend that I forgot something and quickly go out to my car to see if they took care of the dog."

She got up and walked out into the searing heat. She looked to her left and saw the teenage girl across the parking lot with the dog from the van on a leash. Debbie grinned and thought, "Thank God. I think I may have saved that dog's life! I guess she had to save face and not do anything about it until I left the room."

Debbie didn't even bother to go to her car. She just turned around and went back into the office and returned to her seat in the waiting room. This time she noticed the woman was gone. She must have been called back to an exam room.

Within minutes, the door opened and Yvette walked into the waiting room. She caught Debbie's eye right away and smiled.

"It's all yours."

"Thanks."

Debbie checked the sample bins to see what they needed. As usual, the bin for MELAVOX was empty. She thought, "Wow. These offices go through that stuff like water."

Suddenly, she heard a voice yelling, "Who do you think you are!"

Debbie's heart pounded in her chest. She recognized the voice. She turned around and, sure enough, it was Joan.

Debbie didn't even feel her mouth drop open, until she started to speak. She stammered nervously and said, "Katie . . . you know her . . . she's my manager . . . anyway, Katie said it was OK for me to call on your practice again." Fortunately, her confidence grew and she regained her composure as she spoke.

But Joan's face was contorted with contempt and she glared at Debbie for a moment before she said, "That's not what I'm talking about!"

Debbie was beside herself. She said, "I don't understand," although she had an inkling that it had something to do with the patient and her dog.

Joan admonished her, "After everything that happened the last time you were here, you have the nerve to come into this office today and berate our patients!"

Now Debbie knew that Joan was referring to her conversation with the woman about her dog. She swallowed hard and thought it was wise to assume a calm demeanor in the hope that Joan would follow suit. Finally, she said calmly, "I just made a comment about the heat and that it was dangerous to have a dog in the car in this heat."

Joan didn't respond. Debbie thought it was a good sign. "Maybe she realized she overreacted."

But Joan said, "That's not what our patient told me. She said you yelled at her and accused her of trying to kill her dog!"

Debbie protested, "No. I didn't say that . . . I . . ."

Joan interrupted her and said, "Our patient said that you told her you were going to call Animal Welfare and report her."

Now Debbie was overwhelmed. She felt a lump in her throat and her eyes started to fill up. She knew she was in a no-win situation. Like Harrison, she was being set up. The only way out was to maintain her composure. She swallowed back tears and took a calming breath. She said, "Joan, I would never say something like that to one of your patients." As the words came out of her mouth, it was an eerie reminder of what Joan had done to her the last time she was there. But she desperately continued, "Joan, please believe me. I did not say that."

It was no use. Joan was unmoved. Once again, it was her word against Joan's — only this time, she had a feeling Joan would be the winner.

Joan seemed to relish her power. She made a crooked half smile and said, "Debbie, we've had problems with you before, and it seems that you're always causing trouble and then lying about it."

"Joan, that's not true."

Joan said glibly, "I'm afraid I have to ask you to leave the office."

Debbie said nothing. As bad as this moment was, she had an intuition that things would get much worse when she tried to explain it to Katie McDonaugh. Again, she thought of Harrison, and she knew Dr. Friedman would back up Joan this time. She thought, "And then it will be my word against hers *and* Dr. Friedman's."

As she walked past Joan to leave in quiet defeat, Joan said, "I'll talk to Dr. Friedman about this, and I'm sure he'll be contacting your manager."

Debbie's heart jumped into her throat. She started to speak, "But I . . ." She stopped herself because she knew if another word came out, she would burst into tears.

She walked out of the office, only this time the heat felt good because she was shivering. When she approached her car, she slowly lifted her eyes to the van across from her. Now, all of the windows were open and the dog's eyes met hers. He was panting but he looked healthy. Debbie grinned at him, as tears rolled down her face.

She pulled out of the parking lot and thought, "I guess I better call Katie and tell her what happened. It's better to be proactive. Who knows, maybe she'll even believe me. She seems to have a good intuition about people. After all, she said it was apparent that Joan has it in for me for some reason. God only knows why . . . Oh who am I kidding? It's not just Joan, it's Dr. Friedman too . . . they'll get rid of me just like Harrison . . . just like Dr. Friedman said he would."

Katie was initially abrupt in her tone. "What happened now?" was her first response.

Debbie immediately felt defeated. Katie was taking the *other* side before she even heard what happened. But she calmly continued to provide Katie with the details.

She thought she had gained an ally when Katie concluded with, "It sounds like Joan has some serious problems — with drinking and with you. Let me give Dr. Friedman a call and get a read on his reaction. In the meantime, go home and relax."

Debbie had a mixed reaction but she decided to be positive and cling to the notion that Katie might be on her side. "Okay. I'll head home now. I think I need a cup of tea . . . or maybe a glass of wine." She laughed a little and Katie did too.

Then Katie added, "But I'm afraid I have to ask you to stay off territory until this is resolved."

Debbie was stunned. She wasn't expecting this. She thought, "Oh my God. It sounds like she'll decide whether or not I *am* to blame, based on Dr. Friedman's reaction. I knew it!"

Katie broke the silence, "Debbie, are you still there?"

Debbie spoke timidly, "Is this thing going to get more . . . complicated?"

"I don't know Debbie. But as your manager, I have to follow the policies and procedures set forth by the Human Resources Department. I should tell you that this may include disciplinary action. And while we're sorting it all out, it's normal procedure for an employee to be instructed to stay home for a few days in the interim."

Debbie started to cry and Katie heard her sniffle. She said, "Debbie, I'm sure that our fact finding efforts will support your innocence. If you haven't done anything wrong, then you have nothing to worry about."

She wished she could believe it, but she knew her innocence would have little to do with the outcome. She thought, "Michael Poong . . . oh God . . . wait until he hears about this. He hates me already. He's been waiting for an opportunity to get rid of me."

Katie said, "Alright, let me give HR a call and then I'll call Dr. Friedman."

Debbie felt numb. She could only manage to say, "OK."

As she drove home, Debbie worried, "Mark will think I'm such a loser if I get disciplinary action. Who would have thought it was possible . . . *me* . . . getting disciplinary action."

She recalled many years before, when she worked as a secretary in the Labor Relations Department of Human Resources. She constantly typed up Written Warnings. They were issued to union employees for their unacceptable behavior — everything from excessive absence, to foul language used with a supervisor, to fist fights with coworkers.

She thought, "I used to smirk and think, 'what a bunch of losers — adults getting disciplined at work. No wonder so many kids are messed up.' Now here I am . . . a professional pharmaceutical sales woman . . . getting disciplined. I didn't even know that non-union employees could be disciplined."

At home, she made herself a cup of tea, in spite of the heat. Her mother had always made her tea when she was upset. When she finally sat down in a chair in the living room, she looked across the room at the navy blue shoes she had just taken off. They were comfortable, but the leather was wrinkled around the instep. The slight heels were scratched up and worn from pounding the pavement. Debbie felt a wave of melancholy as she swallowed her tea.

Chapter 29: Playing Into Their Hands

Same day

DR. FRIEDMAN HAPPENED to be in his office when his phone rang.

"Are you sitting down Bubby?" Larry asked.

Donald smiled. From Larry's tone, he knew it was good news, but he wanted to keep his cool. He didn't sit down. Instead, he continued to sift through the mail on his desk and said in a playfully whiney tone, "What . . . what . . ."

"We've got a settlement."

"And? . . ."

"Twenty-two million my friend."

Now Donald sat down. It was more than he had expected. He laughed a little and rubbed his forehead in disbelief. "Larry, you son of a bitch! When do we celebrate?"

"I'm already in my car. So the question is, where do we celebrate?"

"How about Toscana? The bartender makes a great martini."

"I'm on my way," Larry said.

Donald laughed and said, "No wait, wait. I'm at the office!"

"So leave."

Donald laughed again. He felt giddy he was so happy. "Give me an hour to tie things up here."

"Alright. One hour Donald."

"Larry, I owe you big time."

"I know you do. To the tune of fifteen percent to be exact. And Donald . . ."

"What?"

"I usually get twenty percent."

Donald laughed. "I know. I appreciate the discount. Now let me get out of here."

"Go. Bye."

Donald hung up the phone and clapped his hands together. He thought, "It's over. It's finally over . . . all of it. Thank you Lee. I'm twenty-two million dollars richer thanks to you. And thanks to my brilliant plan!"

His phone rang again. He thought it might be Larry calling back, but it wasn't.

"Dr. Friedman, it's Katie McDonaugh."

He already knew this was about Debbie Kaminiski. "Hey Katie, how are you?"

"Not so good today. I'm afraid we've had another altercation between Joan and Debbie Kaminski."

Dr. Friedman said, "It's much more serious than that. Apparently Debbie Kaminski harassed one of our patients." He looked around the room for a minute and thought, "I need new office furniture." He was feeling haughty and powerful. He said, "Let's cut to the chase Katie. Debbie Kaminski has managed to alienate my office manager and now she is harassing my patients. I think you know that my group accounts for a very large percentage of your business in this area."

Katie said respectfully, "Of course I know that."

He continued, "And Debbie and all the other reps know this, and yet Debbie continues to conduct herself in an unprofessional manner when she interacts with my staff. At this point, I see no reason why we should continue to do business with Debbie Kaminski. She has to go."

"I see."

He wanted to make sure that Inhaber-Taft didn't just transfer Debbie to another territory. He wanted her gone. He felt as if he had nothing to lose at this point. It was over. He didn't need Debbie at arm's length as he did when he feared that she might piece something together about Lee.

Katie was taken aback. She anticipated that Dr. Friedman would give her a hard time and rake her over the coals about her rep, but she didn't think he would go this far.

He said, "Katie, I'm in the middle of something and I can't spend any more time on this. You have my recommendation."

Katie said, "I understand how you feel about it but . . ."

He cut her off and said, "Katie, right now my perception is that your batting average isn't very good. First Harrison and now Debbie. Talk to Michael Poong. He seems to be doing better at hiring professional reps."

Katie was not only insulted but alarmed by his derogatory comments about her judgment. She didn't dare offend him and make matters worse. She said, "Alright Dr. Friedman. I'll call Michael right now and we'll get together with Human Resources."

"OK, good."

"I'll work quickly to remove Debbie and find a replacement."

"Fine. I have to go."

Katie expected a show of gratitude for her ability to turn on a dime and make a decision based on his wishes. His terse manner made her uneasy. She wanted Dr. Friedman to like her. She said, "I apologize for the disruption to your office staff and your patients." There was silence. Then Katie was shocked to realize that he had already hung up. She caught herself sitting there with her mouth open. She swallowed hard and then punched Michael's number into her cell phone.

"Hey Katie, what's up?"

"I'm afraid I have some bad news." Katie told Michael about the events of the day.

Michael had a big grin on his face during most of the story. He thought, "Perfect. She played right into our hands. Now I have nothing to worry about because she's lost her credibility. Nobody will listen to a whistleblower after she's been fired by the corporation. Timing is everything."

Michael asked, "Did you talk to HR?"

"Actually, I didn't tell Dr. Friedman, but I called HR before I talked to him."

"What did they say?"

"Bill Houck advised me that in a 'he said/she said' case, it's up to the discretion of the manager based upon the employee's past performance. He said I should talk to Dr. Friedman and assess his reaction, which should weigh heavily upon my decision."

Michael said, "Well now you know what Dr. Friedman wants you to do. Call Bill back and tell him that our top writing physician for MELAVOX wants Debbie fired. Did you run it by David Clarke yet?"

"No. I guess I'll call him before I call Bill Houck back."

"I have a better idea. Let me set up a three way conference call and we'll both chat with David Clarke at the same time."

Katie resented it, but she knew she had to defer to Michael. She said, "Good idea. Call me as soon as you get David on the line."

"I will."

Within five minutes, Katie's cell phone rang and Michael had all three of them on a conference call. David Clarke easily agreed that Debbie should be terminated after he heard the details. After all, he had his own baggage to hide and he still resented Debbie's assumption that she had an 'in' with him because they had worked together many years before. He remembered his conversation with her at the district meeting and her opinions about Michael's drunkenness. And he remembered the envelope full of TOXYCONTIN that dropped to the ground. Although she didn't know what was inside, it unnerved him when she handled the envelope as she picked it up. She just had a way of being in the wrong place at the wrong time. And David Clarke knew it was never a good idea to have a potential whistleblower on his team.

David said, "It was inexcusable behavior, and it's in our best interest to concur with Dr. Friedman's wishes. He accounts for a large percentage of our region's business. Go ahead and call Bill Houck and have her terminated effective this Friday."

Katie felt badly for Debbie, but she didn't hesitate to proceed with whatever David Clarke wanted her to do. She said, "Alright I'll call Bill Houck. It looks like we have an open position to fill."

Michael was excited. He said, "Hey, let me call Dr. Friedman and ask him if he knows anyone that he'd like to recommend for the opening. That way we're making it abundantly clear that we will continue to defer to his wishes."

"Sounds good to me." Katie said. She was envious of Michael's relationship with Dr. Friedman. There were many physicians in her district with whom she shared friendly relationships, but Michael's popularity with both physicians and upper management, was impossible to compete with.

"I'll call you back after I talk to Friedman," Michael said.

"Thanks Michael. And thank you David."

David said, "No problem. Have a good one, and get this position filled ASAP. We have to meet our sales objectives."

Michael said, "We will."

Dr. Friedman was enveloped by a blanket of heat when he walked out of his office building. He thought, "Wow. It *is* hot as hell out here today!" He behaved like an actor escaping the paparazzi whenever he left his office through the back exit. He had to focus on the goal of getting to his car before a patient or a sales rep spotted him and pounced on him for his time and attention. He quickly got into his car and drove away.

On his way to Toscana, Michael Poong called him on his cell.

"Hey Michael, what's up?"

Michael said, "Katie called me about her conversation with you regarding another incident with Debbie Kaminski. I'm with you one hundred percent. Katie is talking to Human Resources as we speak, and Debbie will be terminated by the end of the week."

"Perfect."

"Is there anyone you have in mind for the open position?"

"I can't think of anyone at the moment, but let me think about it."

Michael was quite familiar with Dr. Friedman's concise manner of speaking and he mirrored it back to him. "Good. I'll wait to hear from you."

"Bye Michael."

Dr. Friedman thought, "I'm impressed. They certainly didn't waste any time in complying with my request." Suddenly he remembered the new rep. He laughed and said out loud, "That's it! Perfect. I'll suggest that gorgeous Black rep that came into the office today. What was her name? Babette? . . . no . . . Yvette . . . from some no name, little shit company . . . Stampford . . .Stampford Pharmaceuticals." He laughed again and thought, "This is too beautiful. How can so much good happen in one day? If Harrison Johnson ever tries to claim that I was a party to racial discrimination, I can refute it by pointing out that I championed the hiring of Yvette."

He hit the redial key on his phone. "Michael, it's Dr. Friedman."

"Hey, Dr. Friedman, what's up?"

"There's a new rep with Stampford Pharmaceuticals. She was just at the office today. Her name is Yvette but I don't remember her last name. She was poised and professional, and well versed in her product knowledge. And she's gorgeous."

Michael laughed. "She sounds great. You said her name is Yvette with Stampford?"

"Yeah."

"OK. Consider it done. I'll find out her last name and get in touch with her to schedule an interview."

Dr. Friedman said, "Do me a favor."

"Name it."

"Tell HR at Inhaber-Taft, and also Yvette, that I recommended her."

"I will do that Dr. Friedman."

"Good. Thanks Michael. I have to go."

Dr. Friedman parked his car at Toscana. He thought, "One more call before I go in."

"Joe, hi it's Donald."

"Hey Donald, any news?"

Dr. Friedman laughed and said, "I can finally afford to buy a house like yours!"

"You settled? How much?"

"Twenty two million."

"What! Holy shit!"

They both laughed and then Dr. DiStefano said, "Now you need to refer more patients to me so I can try to catch up with you."

"OK you've got it. At our next staff meeting I'll remind the docs in our group to send you all their referrals."

Dr. DiStefano said, "Hey, now I have to report these adverse events to Inhaber-Taft. This is going to fuck them over big time. Pharma investors will sell their Inhaber stock and buy Prescott-Williams instead. My Prescott stock will soar."

Dr. Friedman said, "So tell me about these adverse events. Do you really think the heart attacks and strokes were caused by MELAVOX?"

"Definitely. But off the record, it's not a dangerous drug. I remember when it first came out, everybody was writing for the lowest dose. But when patients complain about pain, who wants to get the phone calls? So you write for the max dose. And then you have a sales manager like Michael Poong, who has his reps telling docs to write for the max dose, long term, because he wants to make a gigantic bonus . . ."

Dr. Friedman mused, "Michael Poong . . . man that guy's a whore."

Dr. DiStefano said emphatically, "Michael is a huge whore! But hey, his strategy worked to your advantage."

"Yeah. I'd say so — an advantage to the tune of twenty two million dollars."

They both laughed. Dr. Friedman said, "Hey listen, I have to go."

"Sure. Sure. Me too."

"I owe you big time Joe."

"Ah, come on. What are friends for, right?"

"Thanks."

Dr. DiStefano said, "I'll catch you later. I have to make a call to Inhaber-Taft about some adverse events."

Dr. Friedman smiled. "Yeah. Now would be a good time to make that call. Bye Joe."

He walked into the bar room of Toscana and immediately spotted Larry. When he looked up from his empty glass, Larry gave him a big smile. They clasped hands and then hugged briefly. Larry patted Donald on the back and said, "*Mazel Tov.*"

"Thanks Larry. Let's have a drink."

Chapter 30: Pounding the Pavement

Three months later, September 5

THERE WAS ALWAYS an eerie quiet at the Newark branch of the State Unemployment Office. Each week Debbie was required to drop off a form she filled out with information about the jobs she had applied for during the previous week. This provided the State with evidence of due diligence. In return, she received a weekly unemployment compensation check. The amount was less than her base salary at Inhaber-Taft, and it was calculated using a formula that she didn't care to understand.

As she walked toward the drop-off box, she initially straightened her posture and tried to look confident. But she could feel her shoulders slump again. "What a loser I've turned out to be," she told herself. She worried that a pharmaceutical sales rep might drive by and see her. It just so happened that this satellite facility of the Unemployment Department was located in an office complex that housed several physicians' offices.

She felt empty and diminished and, as the weeks passed, she was sliding into depression. She wallowed in self-pity as more letters, emails, and faxes went unanswered by potential employers. Worst of all, now she was hearing her *own* voice taunting her after job interviews, "You're too old to be hired as a pharmaceutical sales rep."

Often, she made matters worse by dredging up memories of the day she was terminated.

After Katie McDonaugh uttered those fateful words, ". . . we have reached a decision to terminate your employment with Inhaber-Taft," she began to cry. She felt pathetic when she looked at their indifferent expressions, which oddly helped her to pull herself together.

They had met in the lobby of the Christiana Hilton. Debbie wiped away tears as the three of them headed toward the parking lot. It was standard procedure for Katie, and the HR person, to follow Debbie home after their meeting. Katie had to conduct an inventory of the samples of Inhaber-Taft products, which Debbie stored in her basement.

After about a half hour in the basement, Katie had also counted every sales give-away item, such as pens and notepads. She said, "We'll have a UPS truck pick up your remaining samples and promotional items tomorrow."

They returned to Debbie's living room, where she had her home office set up. Katie removed the laptop computer and printer from her desk. They were property of Inhaber-Taft. Debbie was embarrassed by the dust that surrounded the bare patch where her printer used to sit.

The Human Resources Specialist was busy chatting on her cell phone, while Katie checked the drawers of Debbie's desk for any Inhaber-Taft items. Oddly, Debbie felt compelled to be pleasant, even though she felt violated and upset, especially when the HR person started to laugh on the phone in the same room. "Maybe it's a personal call, but how can she laugh at a time like this?" Debbie thought. She must have read Debbie's mind because she opened the door onto Debbie's small patio and continued her conversation outside.

When Katie finished going through Debbie's desk, she stood up and reached out to shake her hand. She said, "You'll be alright." Maybe it was that moment of maternal tenderness that caused Debbie to well up with tears again. She felt a big lump in her throat and she couldn't speak.

Then Katie asked, "Do you have your car keys? . . . Oh, and your cell phone."

The tender moment vanished. Debbie thought, "Of course she doesn't care about me. She just fired me for God's sake!" She sniffled and rubbed her nose. "Oh sure. Let me get them for you." It was surreal. She responded as if Katie had asked her for a soda or a cup of coffee.

Meanwhile, the Human Resources Specialist opened the screen door from her yard and walked through her house toward the front door. She gave Debbie a patronizing grin and said, "Good luck."

Debbie grinned but said nothing. Then she turned to Katie and gave her the car keys and her phone. They shook hands for the last time. This time Debbie didn't well up with tears. She wanted to appear capable of accepting her fate. She looked at Katie and said, "Thanks for everything."

Katie said, "Thank *you* Debbie."

She stood in her doorway and watched Katie drive away in her company car. The Human Resources Specialist was already laughing on her cell phone again, as she drove away in Katie's car. And that was it. In a moment, there was no Ford Taurus wagon parked in front of her house. She watched the trees sway in the breeze for a minute and then shut the door.

Debbie dreaded telling her family that she was fired. It was humiliating because it was something that just didn't happen in her family. Everyone worked hard and got promoted. But deep down, Debbie knew she could count on them.

"How could you let that happen?" her sister shouted into the phone. Debbie was stunned. She thought for sure her sister would be empathetic and see the injustice of the situation. But the call ended with both of them angry at each other.

Fortunately, her parents were more understanding. Or at least she thought they were — until the whole family was at a cousin's wedding several weeks later. Everyone was enjoying the cocktail hour before dinner. Debbie's father was midway through his second martini when her uncle walked up to him, as he stood flanked by Debbie and her sister on either side. The conversation had begun to make Debbie uncomfortable when it meandered into the career accomplishments of their respective children. Debbie's father concluded with, "All of my children are successful." Then he tipped a glance at Debbie and grinned and said, "Well, except Debbie." Her uncle and sister laughed because they knew her father loved to tease. Debbie was embarrassed but she forced herself to laugh a little to prove she could take the kidding. Sure enough, her father uttered his infamous line, "Oh, you know I'm only kidding." After a few minutes, she slipped away and walked up to the bar to order a martini.

Debbie *was* impressed by Mark's reaction. When he arrived at her house that night he said, "Hey sweetie. I thought maybe you weren't home because I didn't see your car."

Debbie burst into tears and he knew the worst had happened. They were both nervous that morning. Mark had agreed it was odd that Katie said she was bringing Susan Lange from the Human Resources Department with her.

After Debbie told him everything, Mark said, "You always have me to take care of you. Don't worry. You'll find a better job easily with all of your sales awards and experience."

"I hope you're right."

"Why don't we get outside in the fresh air and take Harry for a walk?"

After a while, Debbie said, "You know Mark, it's weird, but after twenty three years with Inhaber-Taft, I feel like it's a relationship breakup. It's really sad." She started to cry and Mark hugged her.

"Don't ever feel bad about yourself Deb. It's completely unjustified that you were fired." Mark hesitated and then added, "You know, you could sue them."

Debbie looked at Mark and said, "I have to admit the thought crossed my mind. But unfortunately Mark, it's my word against Dr. Friedman's. If Inhaber-Taft believes him, I'm sure the courts will too. And even if they did take the time to sort things out and really dig for the truth, the lawsuit could be tied up in court for as long as Inhaber-Taft wanted to drag it out. In the meantime, it would cost me all of my savings in legal fees. In the end, they would probably decide in favor of the *good* doctor and the *ethical* pharmaceutical company, while I'm driven into financial ruin in the process."

"I hate to admit it, but you're probably right. It's better just to move on." Mark tightened Debbie's hand and they were both silent for a while. They watched Harry as he walked in front of them. "Have you noticed that Harry seems to favor his left hip now and then?"

"Yeah, I have noticed that. Well, he's going to be nine years old this year."

Mark spoke tentatively, "You know, I've been thinking it might be a good idea to get a playmate for Harry."

Debbie made a half smile. "Really?" They both stooped down to pet Harry. Mark rested his body weight on the backs of his heels. One of the street lamps along the pavement stood right beside Mark. A couple of mosquitoes were drawn to the light and started to buzz around his head. He flung his arm around to brush them away and lost his balance and fell sideways. They both laughed and Harry licked Mark's face as he struggled to get up.

"Thanks buddy." He rubbed his snout and said, "Hey, how would you like a playmate to keep you company during the day?"

Debbie laughed and said, "Well, actually, he has me around during the day now."

"Hey, that's it! Now is the perfect time to get a puppy because you'll be around to housebreak him and stop him from chewing up the furniture."

"Good point. What kind of dog did you have in mind?"

"A customer of mine has a Jack Russell Terrier. He's a cute little bugger and he's quite a character."

"Really? Did I ever tell you my friend Rose Heinrich breeds Jack Russell Terriers?

"No. I don't remember hearing that."

"Yeah, she loves them. She said she'd never have any other breed of dog. She convinced her husband to enter them in agility contests — you know the ones they have at steeplechases and county fairs."

Mark said, "Hey, don't you remember a while ago your brother showed us a video of his friend's Jack Russell Terriers in an agility contest?"

"That's right! Oh my God, it was hilarious. They're so hyperactive. And they're tough little dogs too. Remember when they crashed into an obstacle on the agility course and they would just bounce right back and keep going?"

"Yeah, they're really intelligent dogs too, which means they should be easy to train.

"And I think it's a good idea to get a different breed. I mean, if we got another Lab it would feel awkward — as if we were trying to replace Harry."

"I think getting a puppy now would be a fun distraction for you and it would help us both later on, when that day comes." They hugged each other and the crickets seemed audible for the first time.

Debbie wiped her eyes and said, "It's been a long day."

"Yeah, it has. Let's go home."

Debbie had been on nine interviews for pharmaceutical sales jobs. The interviews went well, but each time she received a rejection letter. She knew it was almost impossible to prove age discrimination in the hiring process. "But what else could it be?" she wondered. She had received awards for exceeding sales volume and market share objectives. She had consistently good work performance reviews — year after year. And one year she even won the prestigious Vice President's Club award.

Each day she searched for opportunities on the Internet and in the local newspapers. She sent out an average of ten to twelve letters per day. Over time, she saw a pattern of a 5% response rate for her efforts. This included rejection letters. Most employers or recruiting agencies didn't even bother to respond. She considered changing her service dates for Inhaber-Taft because it revealed her age.

"Something's gotta give," she thought, "or else there's something else going on. There has to be an explanation."

Then one Saturday afternoon, she went to Janssen's Market in Greenville, where they held a farmer's market outside each week. After buying some tomatoes and corn, she went into the store to browse. She was meandering down the cereal aisle when she saw Dr. DiStefano. She immediately felt nervous and uncomfortable because it was the first physician she had bumped into since she was fired. She swallowed hard and summoned her courage. Finally she reminded herself that Dr. DiStefano was a bizarre person who had the dubious ability to normalize everything. This enabled him to put people at ease, but the flip side was that he expected, in return, a very blase reaction to his own inappropriate behavior.

"Hi Dr. DiStefano," Debbie said with a genuine smile.

"Hey Debbie! How are you?" As usual, he invaded her personal space and got very close to her face. He said with excessive drama, "I heard you had a nervous breakdown." Then he raised his eyebrows up and down, and his eyes were wildly excited.

Debbie kept her cool and laughed a little. "What are you talking about?"

He whispered in her face, "Rumor has it, you had a nervous breakdown in Dr. Friedman's office and Inhaber axed you because of it."

Debbie didn't know whether to be angry or cry. She was becoming so insecure that the later choice won out. She felt her eyes start to fill up. When Dr. DiStefano saw this, he quickly said, "Oh Deb, don't worry about it. Everybody has a bad moment now and then. I'm sure it's only half the story that's been getting around. Don't let it bother you." His attention deficit disorder kicked in, as he looked away from her. "Hey Deb, I've gotta run." He touched her arm. "Call me if you can't find anything. There's plenty of work at my office."

Debbie felt strangely comforted by his offer of work. But by the time she got into her car, she saw things more clearly and said out loud, "What an asshole! He blurts out, in the middle of the grocery store, that he heard I had a nervous breakdown! If anybody has a mental problem, it's him! God . . . he is just so slimy and contemptible."

She backed out of the parking space and headed home. "And who the hell created this story about me having a nervous breakdown? . . . who am I kidding? . . . of course it was Dr. Friedman! Jesus! No wonder nobody is hiring me. I might as well forget trying to find a job in the pharmaceutical industry . . . or anything to do with healthcare, if it's in the state of Delaware!"

Ironically, once Debbie heard Dr. DiStefano's version of the cause of her termination, it became clear to her for the first time that she really had been treated unfairly. Initially, she was so shaken up by events that unraveled so quickly, her insecurity got the best of her. Katie had cited the dire causes of her termination — the two incidents with Joan in Dr. Friedman's office. Debbie had said, "But Katie, you agreed that I had done nothing wrong in the first incident. I was actually trying to impress Dr. Friedman's group by showing up at the eleventh hour with the samples they needed. And in this recent incident, all I did was make a comment to a patient about a dog. And again Joan lied about what I said." But Debbie could see that her mind was made up. The meeting's purpose was not to discuss the events, but to carry out a decision Katie had already made.

Tragically, if anyone had concurred with Debbie's opinion when she contradicted Michael Poong's sales strategy for MELAVOX, they may have saved the product and, most importantly, they would have saved people's lives. Ironically, a few months after her termination, the sales numbers for

MELAVOX had begun to decline. More and more sales managers were seeing their team's MELAVOX sales trends flat-lining and then dropping. It became obvious they would never reach the much higher objectives for the new year. And then word spread about Michael Poong's success and the strategy he was using. His name was mentioned again and again as the Vice President of Sales lauded his team's performance. Michael had the only district team in the nation who had exceeded planned objectives. The other sales managers began to implement Michael's sales strategy of promoting the max dose for long-term therapy.

As a result, the adverse event reports for MELAVOX were increasing. More patients were having heart attacks and strokes after long term therapy with the max dose. Inhaber-Taft was dutifully turning over the information to the FDA.

The FDA took strong action. They issued a warning letter to Inhaber-Taft's executive management to have the sales force inform physicians of the adverse event reports and remind them of the appropriate dosage approved by the FDA. Additionally, the FDA sent out mailings to physicians with the same information, and even specialists were warned to strictly adhere to the prescribing information.

Soon, both sales volume and market share for MELAVOX were dropping. The sales graphs now depicted a consistent downward trend--even for Michael Poong's team. Michael could see it was time to save himself. He began to tell his reps to "remind your physicians that the max dose of MELAVOX is indicated for **acute** pain and only as *short term* therapy--five to ten days." It was as if his previous strategy never existed. He never admitted he was wrong; he never even acknowledged that he was changing the promotional strategy.

The truth was, Michael was running scared. Rumors were circulating that adverse events, including death, were mounting so quickly that Inhaber-Taft's executive management was considering pulling the drug from the market. Michael knew if that happened, the next step in order for the corporation to save face, would be to look for a scapegoat — someone at the middle management level who would take the fall.

In the interim, doctors were switching to the Prescott-Williams drug, TENAVOX, which was in the same therapeutic class but much less potent than MELAVOX. The stock price for Inhaber-Taft was dropping, while Prescott-Williams enjoyed an increase.

Chapter 31: The Steeplechase

Friday, September 18

IT WAS THE third week in September, a few days before the official start of autumn. For the past few days and nights it had rained so heavily that Debbie wore rubber boots when she took the dogs for a walk. There were deep curbside puddles and many of the single homes in the development had their front lawns submerged into little wading ponds. Flowers were uprooted from their gardens and mulch and woodchips littered the pavement. Each time she returned home, her clothes were soaked and she had to dry Harry and Mortimer with a towel.

Their Jack Russell Terrier was almost five months old. They had driven to Rose Heinrich's home in Maryland and picked him out of a litter of puppies. He had a cute little, white piglet tail, and it was always erect. Rose said it was his antenna for mischief. He was a white, shorthaired "Jack" with an auburn face and ears. He had a muscular physique. The hair was sparse enough on his broad chest to reveal his pink skin with brown flecking. Mark called it a marble belly.

Debbie picked the name for their new puppy. She decided it should be a British name because the breed had originated in England. One day she burst out laughing when she thought of the name, Mortimer. It was perfectly formal and proper, yet quite a contrast for a little puppy with a wildly energetic disposition. Mark laughed too when he heard the name. Most of the time, they called him Morty.

Harry was becoming mellow with age but he seemed to enjoy it when Morty coaxed him into competing for a tennis ball in the yard. In the afternoon, they both loved to stretch out in the sun by the sliding glass door. At night, Morty nuzzled his snout into the warmth of Harry's belly. They were quite a pair and everyone commented on how cute they looked. Debbie smiled as she watched the two of them prancing in front of her. Harry walked behind Morty, who always lunged ahead of the pack. There were times when Debbie was certain that her right arm would be pulled out of the socket when Morty saw something that excited him, whether it was another dog or a group of children, or a piece of trash blowing in the wind. Sometimes Morty would grab a toy that a child had dropped in the grass. Debbie would try to take it out of his mouth, but he would growl playfully and hold it in a tight grip. One time she laughed out loud when she noticed that Morty had apparently picked up a small rubber dinosaur from somebody's yard. The dinosaur's legs stuck out from one side of his mouth, and the dinosaur's head and neck popped out from the other side.

Debbie sipped her coffee and then opened the louvered doors of her bedroom closet. She looked at all the simple, classy dresses that she used to wear to work. She missed wearing them, but now she had a reason to pick one out. "Which one should I wear?" She put her coffee cup down on her bureau and reached up to the shelves above her dresses where she kept her hatboxes. She pulled all four of them down onto her bedroom floor. She sat on the floor and carefully inspected each hat. They weren't overdone. They had just the right touch of adornments to accompany the style of the hat. She was trying to decide what to wear to the Point-to-Point steeplechase on Sunday. It was held every year on the third Sunday in September at Winterthur Museum and Gardens. It was an old-fashioned, grand affair; attended by the "who's who" of Delaware, as well as an even greater number of "wannabe's."

Once Debbie decided on a hat, she knew exactly which dress to wear with it. She began to put the other hatboxes away, when her mood changed suddenly. She thought, "What am I doing? How can I go to the Point-to-Point where I'll probably see a bunch of sales reps and doctors? They'll ask me what I'm doing now . . . and what if somebody brings up the rumored nervous breakdown?" She walked over to her bed and sat down. After a few minutes of self-pity, she opted for the company of television. She looked at the clock as she reached for the remote. She thought, "Oh good, it's almost time for Oprah. Maybe I'll just watch a few minutes of the show, while I put the rest of my outfit together for Sunday."

She was proud of herself for deciding not to wimp out by staying home from the big event. She thought, "I have to get out there and stop being afraid to see and be seen."

The audience was clapping as Oprah entered the stage and smiled. When she stood center stage, she waved in a way that said, "Stop gushing." Suddenly a news broadcaster's voice interrupted the show, as the screen simultaneously switched to an anchorman sitting at a news desk. The anchorman said, "We interrupt this broadcast to inform you that Inhaber-Taft has voluntarily pulled its drug MELAVOX from pharmacy shelves due to a startling increase in cardiac events. It is alleged that several patient deaths may have been caused by the medication."

Debbie's eyes widened, and she stood perfectly still. She couldn't believe what she was hearing. Finally, she swallowed hard and said, "Oh my God!" The first person she thought of was Michael Poong . . . and then Dr. Friedman.

Two days later, on Sunday morning, Debbie went to church at 7:30 a.m. She went home and made bacon, eggs and pancakes. That was their big treat on the weekends when they were at her place. As they finished eating, Harry and Morty were sitting by the table. Mark said, "OK guys." He leaned over and gave them each a piece of bacon.

"Ouch!" Mark and Debbie laughed. "You're supposed to stop at my fingers Morty!"

They carried the dishes over to the sink. "I'll do them," Mark said.

"No, I'll do them."

"Deb, go get your shower and start to get ready. I'll do the dishes."

"Alright, if you insist." Debbie kissed him and then ran upstairs smiling. She was excited to go to the Point-to-Point, and they agreed to bring Harry and Mortimer with them.

Within thirty minutes, Debbie was ready and stood in front of the mirror admiring herself in a plain, lilac dress with a hat of the exact same shade. It wasn't a big, floppy hat, nor was it a tiny pillbox hat. The brim was about two inches wide and it framed her face, which had a healthy color from the late summer sun. She wore a short string of pearls that rested on her collarbone and a tiny, silver pin, shaped like a rose.

By 9:45, the car was packed with their picnic cooler and blanket. Harry laid on the backseat and Morty panted excitedly. Mark looked handsome in his khaki pants and a white polo shirt.

By 10:00 they were nearing Greenville shopping center, which was about two and a half miles from the entrance to Winterthur. Traffic slowed to a crawl because there were so many cars entering the grounds. Mark and Debbie had general admission tickets, which meant they had to park on the lower grounds with most of the other attendees. Ticket holders wore wristbands in a color that indicated where they were permitted to park. Cars were filled with young singles, older couples, or families with children and their dogs.

As they finally pulled into the parking area, Debbie watched as people carried chairs, blankets, picnic baskets and coolers, filled with beer, wine or champagne. Men wore shorts and t-shirts, or khaki pants and polo shirts. Some wore golf pants in bright yellow, pink, green, or navy blue with alligators, palm trees, or frogs on them. They wore designer sunglasses and watches; sneakers, docksides, and loafers. Some older men were dressed like country gents in their seersucker suits and ties. The renaissance men wore panama jack hats and their white shirts hung defiantly outside of their shorts.

The women wore every variety of dress--from revealing tank tops and shorts to dresses with hats, pearls, diamonds, and white gloves. Some wore sandals or sneakers, while others wore spiked heels that were better suited for posing than walking.

For a much higher fee, the well-to-do crowd could drive their vintage cars onto a section of the grounds near the big, white tents. They set up elaborate tailgate parties around their cars. The food and beverages were not the tailgate fare of football games. French and Mediterranean cuisine, and an array of complicated hors d'oeuvres were served on china, with cloth napkins and engraved silverware. Crystal wine and champagne glasses sparkled in the sunlight, atop white tablecloths. A centerpiece of fresh flowers was an important touch for those who participated in the competition for the best tailgate party. The judges were formidable and included local politicians, chefs, and restaurateurs including George Perrier, the renowned chef and owner of Le Bec Fin and Brasserie Perrier in Philadelphia. The categories included best gourmet meal, most original tailgate theme and best presentation. Corporations, banking institutions, investment firms, and pharmaceutical companies rented tents to entertain clients in style. They had buffet stations and open bars. Some of them had live music that included R&B, jazz, and big band sounds. They had to keep the volume to a respectable level so they did not interfere with the dubious purpose of the event, which was of course, the horse races.

By the time they parked Mark's car, Mortimer was wearing out the upholstery in the backseat as he bounced from window to window. As Debbie turned around to put the leashes on the dogs, she nudged her hat against the roof of the car. She looked into the rearview mirror to straighten her hat. She began to feel anxious again. What would she tell the sales reps and physicians when they asked, "So what have you been up to?" She worried, "What will I say? 'Oh, I'm currently caught up in the mind bending cycle of applying for jobs, going to interviews, getting rejected, and collecting unemployment.'"

Mark sensed her nervousness by her silence, and the look on her face. He said, "You look beautiful Deb. Just relax and enjoy the day. When people ask what you're up to, you can say you're enjoying a break from the working world. They won't know what to say next, because they'll secretly wish they could do the same."

Debbie smiled. "Thanks Mark."

"Come on guys. Let's get this car unloaded." Mark took Harry's leash and Debbie took Morty's.

"Can you hold them both for a minute while I get the picnic basket and blankets out of the trunk?"

"Sure."

"Wow. This basket is heavy. What do you have in here?"

Debbie said, "Cheese, crackers, champagne, strawberries. You know. The usual stuff we eat on Sunday afternoon." They both laughed.

"Did you bring something for the dogs?"

"I brought dog food and bowls but I think they'll be more interested in sharing our food."

"Hey Deb, can you take Morty and the blankets, and I'll take Harry and the basket."

They walked across the grounds and up the steep hill that led to the vintage cars and tailgate parties.

Debbie said, "Thank goodness it finally stopped raining. I almost forgot what a sunny day looked like." The event was held rain or shine. Debbie's shoes were already muddy around the edges. The temperature was not yet warm enough to dry out the sopping wet grounds left behind by the heavy rains over the past week.

Morty tugged on Debbie's arm and steered her toward one of the tailgate parties. He smelled food and friendly people.

"Oh, he's so cute! I have two Jack Russell Terriers at home. They have the run of the house but they love to chase the cats and mice in our barn." Debbie smiled at the charming older woman. She was wearing a floral skirt and a white linen blouse with a string of pearls, but her hands were rough like a woman who spent more time outdoors with her horses than she did inside with manicures and pampering. That was the kind of woman Debbie liked. It was the kind of woman she wanted to be, if she ever had enough money to buy a barn and horses.

Harry wagged his tail wildly as he and Mark approached Debbie and the older woman. She petted Harry and said, "Hey, you're a handsome one."

Debbie said, "He's our dignified gentleman and Mortimer is our crazy kid."

"Well, enjoy them." The woman turned toward a man who handed her a glass of wine.

Mark said, "Let's find a spot."

After the hill crested, the grounds sloped gently downward toward fences that enclosed the makeshift racetrack. There were already lots of people sitting on blankets and chairs, or chasing after kids and dogs.

"There's an open space." Mark pointed to the right.

"Looks good to me."

They spread out their blanket and settled into their spot. Debbie took out two bowls and filled them with water for the dogs. "Are you ready to pop the champagne?"

"Sure why not." Mark said.

She took out two glasses and popped a strawberry into each one. She twisted off the wire around the bottle and gently released the cork until it popped.

"Good job, Deb."

"Thanks."

Mark said, "I'll make the toast . . . To new adventures."

"I'll drink to that."

About a half hour later, the Jack Russell Terrier agility races started. Debbie and Mark had agreed not to get Morty involved in the races after Rose Heinrich informed them that competitive training made the dogs even more hyperactive than their baseline.

The dog races were hilarious to watch. Debbie laughed so hard she said, "Mark, I have to go to the bathroom." She handed him both leashes.

"Take your time. You should walk around and socialize a little bit."

She thought, "He knows I'm dreading running into people, so why would I walk around and ask for trouble?" But she said, "I'm sure I'll see some people I know while I wait in line for the outdoor potties."

She was right. She was only standing in line for a couple of minutes when she heard a familiar voice. "Debbie, hey how are ya?" It was Molly, one of the Inhaber-Taft sales reps, with her friend Amanda, a sales rep for Prescott-Williams.

Debbie was a little buzzed from the champagne so she smiled with ease and said, "I'm doing great. How are you?"

Molly looked serious and said very dramatically, "Well you know about MELAVOX right?"

"Yeah, I was totally shocked."

Molly said, "So was everybody else. I mean, we knew about some adverse events, and there were rumors, but nobody thought that Inhaber-Taft would pull MELAVOX off the market. We're all just devastated. The stock price dropped ten points by the end of the day yesterday and we're even worried about layoffs."

Debbie said, "I'm sorry to hear that, but you know, most of the adverse events wouldn't have happened if the drug was promoted and prescribed according to the product circular."

Molly grimaced and looked around her, as if she worried they were being spied on. She finally said in a stage whisper, "I know what you mean."

Debbie asked Amanda, "How is your drug doing?"

"TENAVOX?"

"Yeah. I mean, it's in the same therapeutic class as MELAVOX, so are the doctors comfortable writing for it?"

Molly jumped in and answered for her. "Oh, you know the docs all love Prescott-Williams. I think they'd prescribe horseshit if it was made by Prescott-Williams." They all laughed.

Molly said, "Hey, did you hear Blaire is pregnant?"

"No. That's great. Tell her I said congratulations."

The lines for the potties were alternately short and long, as women bounced from one line to the next. Molly started to walk over to the next line a few feet away and quickly turned to Debbie and said, "Stop by to see us today. We're in the Prescott-Williams tent. They have great food and wine. A lot of the docs are there too. You should come by. We miss you."

Debbie smiled. "Okay. I'll stop by. I miss you too," she lied.

When she returned to their blanket, Mark was standing and talking to some guy that she didn't recognize. The dogs' leashes were tethered to Mark's arm.

"Hey guys!" Debbie said, as she approached Mark.

"Hey there you are — finally," Mark said.

"Sorry. But you know the lines are always a mile long." She would tell Mark later about running into Molly and Amanda.

"Debbie, this is Pete. He's another computer geek like me."

"Hi Pete. It's nice to meet you." Debbie shook his hand.

Suddenly, Morty yelped. "I think you guys are ready for a walk." But as soon as Debbie said the word "walk," Morty got so excited that he managed to yank his leash from Mark's arm and he started to run.

"Hey, come back here!" Debbie and Mark chased after Mortimer, while Harry ran alongside Mark on his leash.

Debbie was worried until she caught sight of Mortimer up ahead by the tailgate parties. He was bouncing through the crowds of well dressed people. He must have smelled the filet mignon on one of the tables because he started to pull at the tablecloth. A moment later, plates, glasses, and food went flying into the air! Mark stopped and bent over laughing. It looked like a scene from a British farce. Suddenly, out of nowhere, Debbie saw a man in a white hat and a seersucker suit stroll in front of her. She stopped and composed herself momentarily, "Hi Mr. Buckley."

He looked at her with aloof disdain, as if to say, "How dare you approach me!"

It was William F. Buckley.

Debbie wasn't surprised or disturbed by his reaction to her. After all, they were running around like nuts and she really couldn't expect him to mix with her kind. She saw Mortimer ascending a hill in the distance toward massively tall trees. Mark and Harry were in hot pursuit behind her.

"Mortimer stop!" she yelled and continued to run after him. By now she was kicking up mud and her dress was splattered. She could see Mortimer's little body bounce over the hill and, for a moment, she lost sight of him.

The crowds in the big, white tents had caught a glimpse of the farcical scene. Most of them paused only for a curious moment to check out the disruption to their conversations. Some people laughed until their children joined in the chase. Apparently, they thought it was another entertainment or game that had started without them.

Dr. DiStefano and Dr. Friedman were among the doctors enjoying the festivities in the Prescott-Williams tent. Suddenly, Dr. DiStefano's mouth dropped open when he caught sight of the dog, the woman and, by now, a crowd of children and some adults, heading for the place where he had buried those running shoes so many months ago. He thought, "No. There's no way. Not after all this time."

Dr. Friedman saw Dr. DiStefano's pained expression and turned to look in the same direction. He asked, "What's going on over there?" Neither one of them could see who the woman was from this vantage point.

"I don't know." Dr. DiStefano said and then tried to divert Donald's attention. "Do you want another?" He raised his glass insinuating that he was going to the bar for another glass of wine.

"Sure. I'll get it," Dr. Friedman said.

"No. No. I'll get it."

"You got the last one."

"OK." Dr. DiStefano watched Dr. Friedman walk toward the bar, where he was immediately stopped by a couple of sales reps, and they started to chat.

Dr. DiStefano felt his insides churning up. "Shit! Donald thinks I buried the shoes under the new fountain. I didn't tell him I decided to bury the shoes by the trees instead." Again he looked in the direction of Donald to be sure he was preoccupied. Then he discreetly slipped out of the tent and walked quickly toward the hill where the dog, the woman, and now some of the crowd were running. He lost sight of them after they crested the hilltop. He began to jog and was soon pushing his way through the group.

Debbie spotted Mortimer digging furiously in the mud, as if he had found buried treasure. Apparently the construction workers had left some trash behind and the smell of decaying garbage had caught Morty's attention. He easily unearthed a banana peal and some sandwich wrappers, but he continued to dig for something more interesting.

Mark and Harry finally caught up with them, and Mark just stood there laughing. After Debbie caught her breath, she started to laugh, but she didn't want the little guy to get away again. She figured she could grab his muddy, little body while he was still distracted by his digging.

As she picked him up, he held his newfound treasure tightly in his mouth. He growled playfully as Debbie tried to tug at it. She heard children laughing and someone approached her from behind and tugged on her arm. She thought it was Mark. She turned around with a smile and was surprised. "Dr. DiStefano!"

"Debbie Kaminski!" Dr. DiStefano forced a smile to his face, but she watched his expression change as he looked at the shoe dangling from Mortimer's mouth. He pulled at the shoe, and Morty growled.

Debbie was confused but she said, "Let it go buddy." As she rubbed his belly, Morty let the running shoe slip from his grip.

Dr. DiStefano bent over and picked up both of the shoes. He looked at them for a solemn moment and then turned his gaze toward Debbie. She thought he looked as if he had just lost his best friend. He was pale as a ghost and his mouth was open. She asked, "What's wrong?"

Suddenly, she was seized by a disturbing sensation of déjà vu. She spoke the words slowly, "It's just . . . a pair of . . . running shoes."

ACKNOWLEDGEMENTS

Thank you to the readers of this book. Thank you to the doctors and nurses who have not become jaded. Thank you to ancillary care providers, families and friends who care for the sick in the still of the night. Thank you to the scientists who continually research better ways to relieve pain and suffering. Thank you to all those who know it is intelligent to be emotional. Thank you to Patricia Spear and all those who paved the road for the rest of us. God bless the women who sweep their porches and wreath their homes with hope, even when there is havoc surrounding them. Never give up. You will get there . . . even if there . . . is here.

Thank you to my brothers Bob and Steve for always making me laugh and for being an inspiration. Thank you to my parents for your love and for giving me faith. Thank you to my husband Claus for the adventures and for suggesting that I get back to writing my book. Thank you to Aunt Connie for your good advice. Thank you Amanda, Bobby Jr., Alexis, Steven Jr., Andrew and Evan for your sparkling joy of life! Thank you Rose, Fish (James Joseph Patrick), Mary, Elisabeth, Marykay, Helen, Bill and Debbie. Thank you to my sister, Linda, for opening my eyes to the fragile artist in her soul . . . she lives in all of us. Thank you Nellie for the burning spirit that brings forth the courage to speak up when others are silent. It is a blessing and a curse.

Thank you to Reggie, Bebe and all of our beloved pets who patiently wait for us. God bless animal lovers and protectors. And to all those people and animals who think they are alone . . . let's bring them inside.

Thank you to Helen R. Carson for the front cover photograph. See more of her work at http://helen-carson.fineartamerica.com

Thank you to Deb Hartmann for the painting on the back cover.

Thank you to Juice Photography for the author photograph.

www.ingramcontent.com/pod-product-compliance
Lightning Source LLC
Chambersburg PA
CBHW080821250626
47160CB00008B/2816